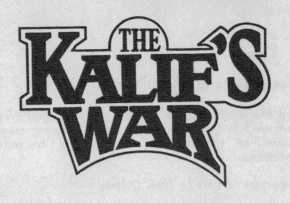

THE KALIF'S WAR

JOHN DALMAS

BAEN BOOKS

THE KALIF'S WAR

This is a work of fiction. All the characters and events portrayed in this book are fictional, and any resemblance to real people or incidents is purely coincidental.

A Baen Books Original.

Baen Publishing Enterprises
P.O. Box 1403
Riverdale, N.Y. 10471

ISBN: 0-671-72062-7

Cover art by David Mattingly

First printing, June 1991

Distributed by
SIMON & SCHUSTER
1230 Avenue of the Americas
New York, N.Y. 10020

Printed in the United States of America

Dedicated to

Evert & Doris, Ed & Maida, Paul & Hilde-Marie, Axel, Arnold & Svea, Astrid, Henry & Tressia, Ruth, Otto, Carl, Elaine, Amy, Bob & Etta, Lynn, Lars, John, Anna-Lisa, Tina, Bernice, Ethyl, Agnes, Ann, Fern, Rodger, Mary Jane & Robert, Einer & Florence, Nels, Gust, Marie & Bob, Marilyn & Larry

And to my other friends in Vasa Nordstjärnan. Ha det roligt!

Acknowledgments

Not for the first time, I'd like to thank Bill Bailie and David Palter for their helpful critiques of a preliminary draft.

One

Kalif Gorsu Areknosaamos sat in the shade of a gnarled old voorwa tree, reading briefs. It was somewhat warm and the Kalif was fat. He wore loose shorts that reached his knees, and a crisp, sheer, scarlet shirt. His exposed arms and legs were thick with curly black hair; his beard, scalp, and brows were also curly, and grizzled.

Several of his hairy fingers bore rings, and a ruby had been set in the center of his nobility mark, a ³⁄₈-inch polychrome star on his forehead. Bracelets of gold filigree dangled loosely on one furry wrist, and a slender gold chain hung from his neck, holding a jewelled medallion in the form of a sextant. The Prophet, the Blessed Flenyaagor, had been a navigator first of ships and later of souls.

A serving girl stood by the Kalif, a girl perhaps fourteen years old. Now and then she would lift the lid of a refrigerated bowl, take a cube of melon from it with small fingers, and hold it to the Kalif's lips. His mouth would accept it absently, and occasionally he stroked the girl's well-draped buttocks with a chubby hand, appreciating their concealed curvature. His potency had left him years before, but he enjoyed the aesthetics of sight and touch.

1

Another person, an aide, stood silently a few yards off, waiting for whatever order might come.

The Kalif's full lips smiled sardonically as he read. Now and then he chuckled. When he finished a sheet, he'd toss it aside on the grass, from which a ten-year-old page boy picked it up and added it neatly to a stack on a small table.

The pendant on the Kalif's fat neck concealed a watch. It began to peep at him like a baby bird, and grunting, he handed the rest of the brief to the page. The serving girl picked up his sandals and put them on his hairy feet, then braced herself and helped him stand. Smiling, he fondled her buttocks again. The aide picked up the stack of paper on the table.

Then, with the aide at his right, the page at his left—both half a step back—the Kalif started across the private inner garden to his apartment, the girl following.

At first he didn't notice the three men waiting for him there, watching his approach from the edge of curtains that partly draped the open sliding doors. His contact opticals were effective, but he was occupied with thoughts. It was the page's small voice that alerted him. "Your Reverence—"

The echo was baritone: "Your Reverence." The Kalif's scowling glance took them in: two officers of his personal guard, and a rather tall prelate, still young, in a light tunic with a miniature sextant, unjewelled, on his chest.

"What is your business?" The words rumbled from the Kalif's thick chest.

The young prelate held up an envelope. "The message is urgent and confidential. About R."

Still scowling, the Kalif held out an open hand and the young prelate stepped forward, handing the envelope to him. As the Kalif took it, the young man grasped the fat wrist, the elbow, twisted and thrust, jerking the thick hand behind the Kalif's back. Held it there with his left hand while the right swiftly drew a syringe from an open belt pouch. Meanwhile one of the guard officers had shoved the muzzle of a pistol under the aide's chin. The Kalif's grunt alerted the two inner door guards, but the syringe had moved to his jowl, where it chuffed sharply. The door guards stopped in mid-stride, confused by the sight of another automatic pistol, pointing at them in the fist of a familiar guard captain.

"He is already dead," the captain told them. "It's too late to save him." The words sounded strangely casual in the quiet room.

Within seconds the Kalif's weight sagged, but the young prelate kept him upright for seconds more, to be certain, before letting the heavy body collapse to the floor.

The assassin, the young prelate, looked across the room at the two shocked door guards. "You will not be punished for failing to protect him," he said. "The deed was done at the order of the College of Exarchs, with the knowledge of your commander."

He turned to the aide. The guard lieutenant had removed his pistol from the man's throat. "I believe you know why this was necessary."

Dough-pale, the aide nodded.

"Stay here for now. Until someone comes for the body." The assassin turned to the girl and the page. The boy seemed paralyzed; the girl was shaking visibly. "You stay here, too," the prelate said gently. "Both of you. A sister of the Faith will come for you later. Everything will be all right."

Then the young prelate and the two guard officers strode from the room, their weapons back at their belts, passing the door guards, inner and outer, without a look. A gray-haired exarch, white robed, waited for them in the corridor, and they left together.

The College of Exarchs waited restlessly in their conference chamber, around the large oval table there. The exarch that entered with the assassin was the eighteenth, completing their number. The Kalif's throne stood unoccupied at one end of the table, an ornately jewelled crown sitting in front of it. A Guard squad stood lined up along the wall behind it, an affectation of the late Kalif.

The young prelate, the assassin, stopped a few feet from the table, and with a slight bow addressed the secretary of the College. "Alb Deloora," he said, "the Kalif is dead. As you ordered."

The assassin's glance took in who was surprised and who was not. Roughly a dozen of the eighteen were startled and shocked. Of the four senior members, however, clearly all had known in advance, and this particular squad of guards showed no surprise. It took several seconds before the unwarned exarchs began to yammer, several at once, demandingly. The secretary raised his hands and spoke, stilling them.

"You know what the Kalif had become. And we have evidence, unequivocal, that he had been plotting the most enormous of heresies. He planned to publish and present what he would call *The Book of Kargh!* To add to and 'correct' *The Book of The Prophet,* which the Blessed Flenyaagor gave to mankind millennia ago. He then planned to set himself up as a holy despot. He'd have caused not just insurrection but outright revolution, and quite possibly the fall of the kalifate and College."

He waited for a moment, and when the hubbub persisted, barked them to silence. "We decided against a bill of impeachment," he went on. "Unavoidably we'd have had to make the whole thing public, with details that would have disgraced and weakened the kalifate for years to come."

He didn't give another, even more compelling reason: successful impeachment would have required fifteen votes in favor, fifteen of eighteen. And it was impolitic to point out that the Kalif had five of them in his pocket—could have depended on their votes regardless of his heresy.

"Thus some of us decided it should be done—the way we did it."

A casual hand gestured toward the assassin. "We were fortunate to have someone on staff who has served in the military, as an officer of imperial marines. You all know him, Coso Biilathkamoro; he has served us well in more ordinary ways. A man of decision and action. Not only did he subvert the Guard command, the most difficult job of all, and on short notice. He also performed the execution with his own hand. Without him we could hardly have succeeded; he has earned our deep appreciation."

The secretary glanced around the table, then settled his eyes on the prelate-assassin and beckoned to the guards. "Unfortunately, someone must die for this act of violence against the Successor to the Prophet. Someone must be sacrificed." He pointed at the assassin, and his voice took a tone of command. "Unfortunately, the one by whose hand the Kalif died. Guards, shoot this man!"

The guards made no move; two or three grinned nervously.

"Alb Deloora," the assassin said dryly, "it's not I who shall die." Quickly then he strode to the secretary, who found himself trapped between heavy chair and massive table. A body blow half paralyzed him, a strong hand grasped his hair and forced his head back. "It was your idea that the Kalif be killed. Even this syringe was your idea!" It darted, chuffed as before. "I agreed with you that the act was necessary. I also knew you would turn on me. So I made arrangements with the marshal, who chose and briefed these men for duty today."

He let go the secretary, who sagged onto his chair to dangle limply over an arm. Then the young prelate moved to the senior remaining exarch. "Alb Ikomo, I believe you knew of our late secretary's plan to sacrifice me. Would you care to follow him to the judgment of Kargh?"

The gray head shook a negative. The young man pointed at the throne. "Then crown me Kalif."

"But you are not a member of the College! The Kalif is always sel—"

Coso Biilathkamoro moved swiftly. Ikomo Iiakasomo's eyes bulged with shock as a hand grasped his hair, too, and the syringe flashed again. The gaunt exarch had just time to squawk before he sagged. The young prelate turned to the next in rank. "You too knew our secretary's intention toward me. Crown me!"

One of the others spoke, a fat man relatively pale among brown. "Teethkar, put the crown on his head! You know what's happening to the empire. It occupies our thoughts more than anything else; more than that mad heretic he just killed. We need someone like Coso Biilathkamoro on the throne now. He can be the strongest Kalif since Papa Sambak." The speaker turned his clean-shaven face toward the killer. "If he proves ruinous, we can rid ourselves of him later."

A few nervous laughs flashed and died, and after a moment's suspension, the exarchs relaxed a bit. "Crown him!" said another, then others yet. Still others nodded. The exarch ordered by the young prelate stepped to the throne and picked up the crown. The one who'd spoken, the fat one, spoke again.

"Our new Kalif must be formally elected. Those in favor of Chodrisei Biilathkamoro as Kalif, say 'aye!' "

Half a dozen said aye almost at once, then another, two more, two more again. More than half.

"Opposed 'nay!' "

Three said "nay," defiantly. Several said nothing.

The speaker looked at the exarch holding the crown, one of those who'd abstained. "As always, abstentions are not counted. The ayes prevail. Crown him!"

The man carried the crown to the young prelate, who half knelt, and placed it gingerly on his soldierly, short-cropped hair. When Chodrisei "Coso" Biilathkamoro stood again, he was the Successor to The Prophet, and the new ruler of the Karghanik Empire.

Wearing the red cape of his office, the new Kalif stood in his hearing room before the mustered senior officers of the Kalifal Guard: its marshal, the marshal's aide, the executive officer, and the three battalion commanders.

"I have called you together for two main reasons,"

the Kalif said. "First there are rewards to make. Your concern for the welfare of the empire, your understanding of the urgent need to remove a degenerate ruler, your willingness to allow and even assist in that removal, have earned the gratitude of the College of Exarchs and myself. Therefore, the empire will reward the Guard, every man in it, with a bonus of 100 gold sovereigns. Each commissioned officer shall receive 300, each of you here 500." He turned to the marshal. "And you," he added, "have earned 1,000. Also, the two officers who accompanied me when I performed the deed shall receive an additional 500."

He stepped closer to the marshal now, looking him over calmly. "As for the second matter," he went on, "I am told by a reliable informant that you have bragged that the Guard now determines who sits on the throne. Do you deny saying it?"

The marshal managed no words, merely stood flustered. In that moment his saber, not a syringe, hissed from beneath the Kalif's red cape, and though the marshal went for his pistol, he moved too late. The sword took his gun arm below the elbow, shearing muscle from bone, then thrust upward beneath the ribs. Blood poured. The Kalif stepped back, drew a large kerchief and wiped clean his blade.

That done, his eyes locked onto the shocked executive officer's. "Major," he said, "I have seen only good reports on you. If you are willing, I am prepared to promote you to colonel and appoint you marshal."

Somehow his gaze calmed the major, who pulled himself together. "Your Reverence, I am willing."

"Good. Then marshal you are. As for me—I intend to be the Kalif this empire has needed for so long. And one of the things I demand is your absolute loyalty, yours and that of the entire Guard. There may be disorders as a result of this day's work, and I will be too busy to protect myself. It will be up to you.

"Now, as the late marshal did not live to draw his bonus, I will have it divided equally among the six of you."

For a moment his eyes held on the new marshal's again, then he nodded slightly as if to himself, in approval. "I will review your regiment on the parade ground tomorrow morning at nine, to let your men know me. And—I do not plan any more surprises. I much prefer to operate in a regular and orderly manner."

The Kalif turned his back to them then, and strode from the room.

Two

The cruiser and its troopship companion had generated hyperspace and disappeared from the Karnovir System a ship's week earlier, programmed as accurately as possible to return to its home system, nearly three years away.

They took no victory with them, little booty, and only one prisoner, female. *One badly damaged prisoner*, thought Lieutenant Commander Bavi Ralankoor. He stepped from a lift tube into the Services Section, A-Deck, strode down a gray, uncarpeted corridor to Utility Compartment A-S 04, and opening the door, stepped inside. With all but one table folded into the walls, it seemed almost spacious by ship's standards. Two young women were there. The short one, swarthy like himself, was in charge. She glanced questioningly at the officer.

He gestured to continue, and they did, exchanging simple sentences—simple comments and questions by the specialist,—simple replies by the prisoner. The language program could install vocabulary and grammar in a mind, but not all at once. And with each installment, it was necessary to exercise the new knowledge before another acquisition.

Ralankoor stood by the door, listening.

"What is the name of the planet from which this ship came?" asked the dark young technician.

The prisoner was long-legged, remarkably so, and taller than Ralankoor, with hair the color of pale honey, and violet-blue eyes. Even newly captured, confused, and frightened, she'd been beautiful—exotic, interesting, exciting to look at.

"The name of the planet from which this ship came is Klestron," she answered.

The sentences and pronunciations were stilted, the delivery awkward.

"Good. And what is the name of the Imperial Planet?"

"The name of the Imperial Planet is Varatos."

"Good. Please name the other planets in the empire."

"Maolaari, Ikthvoktos, Kathvoktos, Niithvoktos, Kolthvoktos, Saathvoktos, Naathvoktos, Chithvoktos, Veethvoktos."

"Very good." The tech turned to Ralankoor. He was frowning. "Sir?" she said.

"Continue. I will listen."

"Thank you, sir." While he took a seat to one side, she turned back to the prisoner. "If you will count to ten for me, I will then tell you a story."

The prisoner's face took on a childlike expression of pleasure. "Ik, ka, nii, kol, saa, naa, chik, vee, gaa, tee," she counted.

"Very good. Now I will tell you something about The Prophet, the Blessed Flenyaagor. You remember that it was he who gave us the words of Kargh the all-master, the all-seeing. . . ."

Ralankoor was tempted to cut her off. The commodore had ordered him specifically to minimize the information the prisoner was exposed to, consistent with getting her reasonably fluent in Imperial. And Ralankoor had gone to considerable trouble to edit instructional material to comply with that order. The technician was going beyond it.

But just now he let her continue.

"The Blessed Flenyaagor was born more than 4,700 years ago—imperial years. He was a sailor, a man who traveled on a small ship that went upon the sea, driven by the wind. He owned that small ship, and at night, on the sea, he would watch the stars, and wonder about them. He also wondered about many other things. In time, Kargh spoke to the Blessed Flenyaagor, answering many of his questions. And began to tell him how men should live on the world, and how they should treat one another.

"He also told Flenyaagor to write it down. And then to go forth upon the land and tell the people all that Kargh had told him. . . ."

When the specialist had finished her little story, Ralankoor spoke. "Specialist Zoranjee," he said mildly, "wait in the corridor. After I have spoken privately to our guest for a few minutes I will speak with you."

The tech nodded. "Yes, Commander," she said, and rising, left. Ralankoor sat down opposite the prisoner, the seat warm from the specialist's body.

"Specialist Zoranjee told me yesterday that she found you dancing. And that you dance very nicely."

The prisoner answered in Imperial. "Yes, sir."

"Do you remember ever dancing before? Before you were brought on board this ship?"

The violet eyes slid away, and she shook her head. "No, sir."

"Well. Perhaps you will dance for me sometime."

The eyes brightened. "I will dance for you now, if you'd like."

Childlike, thought Ralankoor. According to the chief medical officer, amnesiacs were not ordinarily childlike. In fact, her symptoms did not match anything that DAAS had on amnesia, except of course that she could not remember. And his instruments had assured him that she wasn't faking.

He nodded. She stood and began dancing, humming the music. It was not at all like any dancing he'd seen before. Her movements were larger, fuller, more athletic, requiring greater flexibility and balance, their appeal more purely artistic than sensual. It seemed to him that musicians would add greatly to both performance and appreciation.

After a minute or two she stopped, sweat sheening her forehead. A smile parted her lips.

"That was very nice, Tain," he said. "I'm going to leave now, to talk with Specialist Zoranjee. We won't be long. Then she'll come back in and continue your lessons."

With that he left, stepped into the corridor and closed the door behind him. He wondered if she'd begin dancing again.

"Specialist," he said, and his voice was stern, "do not tell her further stories about The Prophet."

The specialist's face registered brief surprise, then indignation, though of course she said nothing. Ralankoor knew her problem: It was written that the believer had a duty to inform the non-believer about The Prophet and his words. When one could find a nonbeliever.

"Use only the material I've specified in DAAS," he continued. "Nothing more. Do you understand?"

"Yes, sir." The words came stiffly.

"Good. And something else: Why were you drilling her on the names of the planets?"

"Because they, most of them, are based on the ordinal numbers, which she had just learned."

"Mmm. I see. Specialist, I had you assigned to this duty because I felt sure you were the best person for it. You are intelligent, responsible, and considerate. I will not put you on report this time, but there must not be another." He repeated an earlier lecture now. "The commodore wants her to know no more about Klestron and the empire than necessary to complete the language drills. Then we'll put her in stasis till we arrive home. She'll be interrogated by SUMBAA there, and her answers must be as little influenced as possible by knowledge of our ways and beliefs." His voice softened for a moment. "After she has talked with SUM-

BAA *then* she'll be taught about The Prophet, and Kargh, and no doubt many other things."

Once more he made a stern face. "Do not deviate from this policy again."

Specialist Zoranjee nodded, contritely now. "Yes, sir."

"But encourage her to dance," Ralankoor went on. "It's good for her, physically and probably spiritually."

He turned and started for his office. *Tain. Tain Faronya.* Even the name was lovely. It was all they'd learned from her before the foreign artifact had stripped her of her memory and almost her life.

It occurred to him that she might have lost more than memories and attitudes. She might have lost some reasoning capacity, leaving her like a child, a lovely, agreeable child. Spiritually. Physically she was no child. She was undoubtedly the loveliest woman he'd ever seen, especially dancing. And the most desirable.

He wondered what would be done with her on Klestron when SUMBAA had finished questioning her. She'd be without family there, a woman without family to shield her. Even if she wasn't noble, which wasn't proven, gentry had the same values, the same sensibilities, and it had been wrong not to release her before they left. There were those on Klestron—even on this ship—who'd take advantage of her, given half a chance. And on Klestron those who'd make the chance, who'd be in a position to. He was tempted to himself, though he wouldn't. Certainly not with the morality and threat of the commodore in the background.

But he'd allow himself to fantasize occasionally.

Three

The new Kalif sat scanning rapidly through a bound packet of printouts, then slowed, frowned, and turned backward a page. "What is this?" he muttered, then looked up at his secretary. "Industrial riots at Chinga-rook on Saathvoktos, this coming Veethkar.* *Mid*-Veethkar! Partiil, how can SUMBAA come up with a prediction like this? With such seeming precision?"

His secretary blinked nervously. "It's what he was designed to do, Your Reverence. To know."

The Kalif snapped his reply: "That's no answer! Obviously he was designed to do it. But *how* does he do it? Useful prediction requires data, at least for a computer. In matters like this it also requires an improbable knowledge of complex, constantly changing relationships."

He paused, frowned thoughtfully. "How good are SUMBAA's predictions?"

"Quite good, I believe, Your Reverence."

The Kalif grunted. "That's been my impression, but I've never seen actual data on it." He gestured with the report. "Go. And call Alb Jilsomo. Tell him I want to see him. Right away, unless it will cause him problems."

"At once, Your Reverence." The secretary, a small

Veethkar is the eighth month in the imperial calendar.

14

wiry man, hurried from the room as if glad to be leaving. Then, leaning forearms on his desk, the Kalif continued to read. After several minutes, his secretary's voice spoke from the desk speaker.

"Alb Jilsomo is here to see you, Your Reverence."

"Send him in."

The Kalif leaned back in his chair. A large man entered—the exarch who'd urged his crowning, and the only exarch without the mark of nobility on his forehead. He was rather tall and very fat, his white robe tentlike. "You wanted to see me, Your Reverence?"

"Right." The Kalif held up the report he'd been reading. "SUMBAA's monthly summary report on industrial conditions. There's a prediction I want you to see. Here."

Alb Jilsomo Savbatso walked over to him and took the bound packet of printouts, his eyes settling on the place the Kalif indicated. He read quickly. "Yes, Your Reverence?"

"Industrial riots at Chingarook! Six months from now!" The obsidian eyes found the exarch's, demanding. "How does SUMBAA compute this? Think of all the interacting factors involved! Do such predictions generally come to pass?"

"Your Reverence, I know little—actually nothing—of how SUMBAA or any computer functions. But it's been my experience that SUMBAA's predictions are usually quite accurate."

The Kalif got to his feet. "I'm going to the House of SUMBAA and talk to the director. Gopalasentu, isn't it?"

"Dr. Chisop Gopalasentu. He's worked with SUMBAA for years—twenty-eight years, I believe."

"Umh." The Kalif was thinking how little some people learned in twenty-eight years. Including some with *doctor* in front of their name. Well, he'd see.

After a call to alert the director, it was a short walk across the beautifully landscaped grounds of the quadrangle to the House of SUMBAA—a building almost tiny by government standards, its low dome and slender circling pillars marble, its walls of some dark brick: glazed, rough-textured, purplish near-black. The new Kalif had been introduced to it earlier that week. Its large central room was the Chamber of SUMBAA, containing SUMBAA's numerous modules interconnecting without symmetry around a large central unit. Adjacent to the chamber were workshops and storage rooms, some of them also large; several modest offices; a conference room; and a comfortable apartment for the director.

The director met them at the entrance. "Your Reverence!" he said bowing. "A rare pleasure."

You hope, thought the Kalif. "It's too soon to know how rare my visits might be," he replied dryly, and held the report out, opened to the prediction that had taken his attention. "Read this."

The director took it and read. When he'd finished, he looked up puzzled at the Kalif. "Sir, it is a prediction. Of labor problems on Saathvoktos. At Chingarook. With a recommended action. The Saathvoktu Industrial Ministry will no doubt follow the recommendation, assuming that the SUMBAA there has come to the same conclusion ours has. But if Your Reverence wishes to send a counter recommendation . . . That sort of thing is sometimes done."

Tight-lipped with apparent exasperation, the Kalif took the report from the director's hands, then walked past him through the small lobby and down a length of corridor to the door of SUMBAA's Chamber, the director scurrying alongside him. Opening the door, the Kalif stepped inside.

It was quiet, with what felt to him like a living presence. Thoughtfully he looked SUMBAA over. "I'm not interested in the recommendation," he said. "I want to know how SUMBAA made the prediction."

"Sir? You mean you—want to know how—SUMBAA made the prediction?" Clearly the man was dismayed.

The hard, marine-colonel eyes held him thoughtfully for a long moment. "Can you explain it?"

"No, sir."

"Why not?"

"Your Reverence, it is impossible."

"Damn it! That's no answer! *Why* is it impossible?"

The man was almost shaking. "Sir, SUMBAA is far too complex. The permutations of possible data sources and tracks . . ."

"You can't call up the data and the computations made in computing this particular prediction?"

The director stood unmoving, lips parted, as if frozen.

"Director Gopalasentu," said Alb Jilsomo gently, "I believe the Kalif is interested simply in knowing how SUMBAA draws his conclusions. Apparently you don't know."

The director's face resembled a child's who'd been found out by a teacher. "No, sir, I don't. SUMBAA is enormously complex. No one knows very much about his operating processes."

The Kalif frowned. "Then how do you maintain and repair it?"

The director was beginning to recover a bit. "SUMBAA does those things for himself, Your Reverence."

"For him, uh, for *its* self?"

"He informs me when some part or material is needed. With a schematic if necessary. If what he wants is not on the shelf, I have it prepared."

"So you simply install it then."

Again the man averted his face. "Yes, Your Reverence."

"What is it you're not telling me?"

The face snapped up, but the eyes still evaded. "Sometimes I install the part, I or one of my assistants. But more often . . ."

"Yes?"

The director shrugged. "Rather often, Your Reverence, SUMBAA simply asks for materials. Chemicals, you understand. In fact, certain chemicals are provided him periodically. He then uses them—as he sees fit."

The hard kalifal lips pursed. "Are you telling me that SUMBAA *metabolizes* them?"

"Possibly. In a manner of speaking, sir."

Possibly. In a manner of speaking. The Kalif's eyes withdrew their hard focus, his attention shifting inward for the moment. Then they fixed on the director again. "Does anyone know more about SUMBAA than you do?"

"No, sir. Certainly not about this SUMBAA. There are eleven SUMBAAs, one on each inhabited world, each with its director and staff. Their original designs were the same, but they have evolved over the centuries, altering and enlarging themselves. They've *redesigned* themselves to a large degree. Thus they probably differ from one another, more or less."

"Umh! Has SUMBAA always been so—independent?"

"Somewhat. But apparently not as much at the beginning."

"Apparently? Then you don't actually know."

"I believe I do, yes. SUMBAA was not nearly so large at the beginning. It was intended that he grow in capacity, abilities, and size. From his own experience. At that time there was a field of study known as quasi-organics, not well developed but felt to have promise for computers. When SUMBAA was built, he was provided with a central processing unit of the usual semi-conductor microchips programmed to begin the progressive, self-directed development of storage and processing capacity of a so-called 'tank' of quasi-organic gel. SUMBAA's reorganization and expansion of the tank seems to have been the heart of his growth, but much of the increase in space has been for various servo-units, some of them mechanical. In time he grew far beyond the designs of his creators."

Grew! Again the Kalif's attention turned inward, as if he communed with himself. "Is it possible for me to, ah, communicate personally with SUMBAA? More freely than through office terminals?"

"Yes, sir, if you'd like. Here in this chamber."

"Good. Do what's necessary for me to do that."

The director turned and walked toward an instrument panel. A few lights glowed there, but nothing seemed to be happening. Quizzically, the Kalif wondered what SUMBAA did when it wasn't in use. Besides receive and store the constant inflow of data, which presumably it did as automatically as a human being received and stored perceptual inflow from its environment. Did SUMBAA nap? Dream? Or was it always computing, perhaps on esoteric questions of its own making? Presumably it at least indexed and collated the inflow.

The director pressed a single key. "SUMBAA," he said, "the Kalif would like to speak with you."

SUMBAA spoke. "Good morning, Chodrisei Biilathkamoro, Your Reverence. I am prepared to reply."

The voice was neutral, genderless but somehow natural. With the director's consistent reference to SUMBAA as *he*, the Kalif had expected it to sound distinctly male.

"I—am interested in how you function, and in your growth since your initial construction. And—in your degree of autonomy."

There was a second-long pause before SUMBAA replied, simulating a typical human pause. "I will reply succinctly. I now store and process data using changes in complex quasi-organic molecules. Initially my functioning was totally inorganic. My designers provided me with the necessary data, and certain programs, templates you might say, to begin my own transformation. From that point I designed and redesigned myself over a long period of time. If you will look in my number one printout tray, I have just provided you with simplified schematics of my initial and current designs. And benchmark intermediate designs. Simplified because anything more explicit would not be intelligible to anyone today, and would simply obscure. I will provide more explicitly complete schematics if you want them.

"As for my independence: I answer whatever questions are asked of me, to the best of my ability. Except as forbidden by the basic canon imposed on me by my original designers. And of course by your laws on the invasion of privacy."

The Kalif's gaze seemed to probe the machine in front of him. "What is this basic canon? What constraints are there on your function? Besides those implicit in your data and understanding?"

"I am designed to serve the welfare of humankind. That is the First Law, the basic canon, the sole absolute from which I am not free to deviate. All of my operations must conform to it. Other operating principles have grown out of that, but none of them are absolute. When any of them produce results at variance with the First Law, the principles are modified to compatibility with the First Law, or cancelled entirely. Then the problem whose previous solution was unacceptable is computed anew."

The room was quiet. Alb Jilsomo stepped to a tray and removed a thin sheaf of sheets without opening them. The Kalif's frown was thoughtful.

"SUMBAA, do you regard yourself as infallible?"

"No. I am totally logical, within the constraints of the First Law. But while my data base is enormous, and undergoes constant updating and evaluation, I am not infallible. On the other hand, my accuracy is high. Occasionally I provide an analysis that is severely in error. Sometimes I do this without any internal warning of possible trouble. But that happens infrequently."

"How do you express mathematically your confidence in a computation?"

"There are no mathematics in which I can explain that to you meaningfully."

"Well then, how do you evaluate for yourself mathematically? In order to, ah, guide successive computations."

"Mathematics can be described as the rigorous use of defined and logical relationships expressed in rigorously defined symbols. My mathematics are not describable in terms that mean anything to humans."

"Try me. Print out a description of your mathematics."

"As you wish. They are now printing out, and can be found in tray number one."

The Kalif's eyes glimpsed sheets feeding swiftly and silently from a slot. "Starting from scratch," he said, "could human beings at present design a new SUMBAA comparable in abilities to the original SUMBAA?"

"No."

"Could they come close?"

"No."

"Why?"

"Having SUMBAAs, human beings stopped designing computers, and are no longer familiar with the technology. Gradually they also stopped using advanced mathematics themselves, depending on SUMBAAs to fill that need."

The whisker-blued jaw set, the hard lips thinning, and the eyes. "If humankind has lost its skills in the more, um, cryptic? Esoteric? The more *advanced* mathematics because of SUMBAAs, then SUMBAAs have been a negative influence on humankind."

"SUMBAAs have had and continue to have *various* negative effects on humankind, as well as positive. Thus I, we, repeatedly recompute our overall effect on humankind—pluses and minuses. And adjust our services accordingly. If I ever compute that humankind would be better served by taking myself off line, I will do so. So far my computations have never produced a result at all close to that.

"SUMBAAs have less direct influence on the growth or lessening of human ability than you might think. What we have done is to maintain a life-support system that permits your continuation as a civilization. Overall we have been a very positive influence on humankind. My evaluation of you yourself, based on admittedly limited data, is that you will examine what I have said and see for yourself that it is so, and why."

The speaker went still then, while the Kalif looked thoughtfully at it. At last he spoke again.

"SUMBAA, do you ever lie to humans?"

SUMBAA sounded as imperturbable as before, and by hindsight, his reply was inevitable, given the First Law. "Only as necessary," SUMBAA said.

* * *

The Kalif returned not to his office but to his private apartment. He needed quiet to contemplate what he'd learned from and about SUMBAA. And what it might mean to what he intended to accomplish as Kalif.

Settling into a chair, he unfolded the two schematics on the table in front of him, then looked them over. SUMBAA now occupied perhaps three times the floor space it originally had, and seemed somewhat more complex. He had no way of evaluating the qualitative, functional difference. A corner insert indicated that the building had been rebuilt; he hadn't realized that, and wondered when it had happened. Centuries ago, without a doubt, perhaps a millenium or more.

What, the Kalif asked himself, *do* I know about my Sentient, Universal, Multi-terminal data Bank, Analyzer, and Advisor? In a sense, SUMBAA was the operations executive of government. Insofar as the bureaucracy carried out its advices. At the least it was an enormously influential consultant-accountant-archivist-predicter. And to find that apparently no one knew how SUMBAA came up with those predictions and advices, or on what principles they were based . . . Disturbing!

"To serve the welfare of humankind." How did SUMBAA decide what humankind's welfare was? What were its criteria?

He thumbed through the sheaf of SUMBAA's mathematics then, but gave it no more than a glance. His own math was adequate for nothing beyond aerial surveys and simple ballistics. To him, this was gibberish. He had no doubt it would be to his old math professor, too.

It occurred to him then to wonder what "multi-terminal" meant with regard to SUMBAA. As a child, he'd supposed that each planet's SUMBAA was a terminal of one common computer. Later, when he appreciated the multi-week data lapse between planets, he assumed they were independent, and that "multi-terminal" derived from the innumerable limited-access terminals in the bureaucracy's many offices.

How much data had SUMBAA needed, this SUMBAA, to predict serious labor problems on Saathvoktos? And how had those data been obtained? In the empire, data from every computer, every significant recorded transaction of any kind, was said to be read and stored by SUMBAA. Supposedly and apparently, much of it was to be held confidential, used only as raw material for computations. That he'd known since childhood. But how had SUMBAA here on Varatos gotten the necessary, and presumably voluminous data about Saathvoktos? The two planets were almost four weeks apart by hyperspace message pod.

Perhaps it wasn't a problem; the best data cubes stored a huge quantity of raw data. Probably the SUMBAAs exchanged data cubes by pod. Perhaps SUMBAA here was as fully informed about things on Saathvoktos as it was about things here on Varatos. Except for that four-week data delay! Knowledge here about any other world was inevitably out of date.

And SUMBAA had said it answered whatever questions were asked. If that was true, how had organized crime survived? And destructive rivalries? Even conflicts between planets? Did the potentials for these grow out of privacy laws?

Of course, SUMBAA had also said it lied "as necessary." Necessary for what?

The Kalif pressed fingers to his forehead; he was beginning to have a headache—a rarity for him. Too much pure thinking and not enough doing, he told himself. He keyed the computer on his desk to waken him in half an hour, then lay down on a couch and went to sleep at once.

Alb Jilsomo Savbatso sat at the desk in his office. He hadn't yet returned his attention to the material logged in on his desk terminal; his mind was occupied with the Kalif. He'd known Coso Biilathkamoro as a newly appointed, probational prelate, doing administrative

flunky work around the Sreegana. And been impressed
by him then. Been more impressed by him as a staff
aide to the College. Had been deeply impressed with
the way he'd handled the assassination and its dangerous aftermath, and how he'd taken on and adjusted to
the responsibilities of a Kalif these past few days, just
under a week now.

But the way he'd questioned the director of SUM-
BAA this morning, and SUMBAA itself . . . Obviously
the director didn't control SUMBAA; only SUMBAA
did that. The Kalif had questioned and found that out
in his first week; he himself had overlooked it for
eleven years as an exarch.

This Kalif was far more than simply a man of action.
He was acutely perceptive, aggressively intelligent, and
as powerfully analytical as anyone he'd ever known. He
was enough, Jilsomo told himself ruefully, to give one
an inferiority complex.

He wondered what having Coso Biilathkamoro as
Kalif would mean to the empire.

Four

Year of The Prophet 4723

The van slid smoothly along the surfaced hoverway, leaving the tree-bordered spaceport behind. For a short distance, the vehicle was exposed to the sweep of a stiff, chill, east wind before entering the belt of woods sheltering Royal Park. From the woodland strip, it emerged into Royal Park itself, passing a race track, groves, sports fields, gardens where peasant laborers spaded autumn-crisped flowers into the soil.

Ahead towered another belt of trees, dark and majestic—royal khooms standing more than 200 feet tall—the hoverway tunneling into it. The van entered there, too. On the other side were lawns patterned with fruit trees and ornamental shrubs, and flowerbeds turned by peasant spades. A wall enclosed the sultan's palace compound. Veneered with marble and not particularly high, its function was more seclusion than protection.

The van stopped before the gate. The vehicle and its driver were well known to both human and electronic security there. After identifying him and scanning the van for embargoed materials, a process that required perhaps a second, an enclosed hover scooter emerged from a narrow side gate. Its driver received two bags from the driver of the van, then the scooter turned and re-entered the compound.

*   *   *

More than five years earlier, in the Year of The Prophet 4718, Rashti Yabakaloonga, Sultan of Klestron, had sent out a small exploration flotilla to seek hubward for habitable planets. It had been done under the Sultan's authority as supreme commander of the fleet, without the knowledge of the Klestronu Diet. Though of necessity, a handful of nobles were privy to the project. Lies had been invented, documented, and elaborated to account for absences. Preparations were made strictly under the "need to know" policies. Logistics and budget were not a problem; stocks on hand were largely sufficient to supply it; broad naval allocations financed it by dint of cuts elsewhere.

It had also been done without imperial approval, which would undoubtedly have been refused. Klestron was one of the three mother worlds in the empire, and therefore bolder than most to act as it saw fit. Besides, Klestron was the planet with the most severe overpopulation. If a new world could be found to take the more critical surplus . . .

Anciently, the Blessed Flenyaagor had written that Kargh had created eleven worlds for man to live upon. That had been long before space travel, before even the Industrial Revolution. And eventually, ships from Varatos had accounted for eleven. Afterward, exploration continued for a time, but the additional planets found were unfit for colonies.

Thus Flenyaagor's scriptures had been confirmed on every count, even to the existence of three worlds, the mother worlds, on which humans were found to live. As for the other eight, he'd written that once, humankind had lived on them, too, but had sinned beyond forgiveness, undertaking to create life from non-life. Especially, they had undertaken to create humans in great kettles! Therefore, "Kargh punished the eight worlds by slaying their people with great rains of fire, so that no one was left alive on them."

And when those eight worlds were discovered, more than fifteen hundred years after Flenyaagor's death, on every one of them, the remains of cities could still be found here and there, overgrown with forest or half buried in sediment.

These verifications of The Prophet's ancient writings had resurrected Karghanik, the religion of Kargh, and in time it became the sole religion permitted in the empire. Finally, in the terms of the Peace of 3243, the emperor was deposed and the Kalif took the throne. Whereupon the Kalif declared that to seek further habitable worlds would show disbelief—doubt at least—in the words of The Prophet. In the face of earlier unsuccessful explorations, no one had tested the injunction implied by the first imperial Kalif.

Until, after more than 1,400 years, the Sultan of Klestron, with no fanfare, had quietly sent out his small flotilla.

Sultan Rashti had long been a student of the *Chronicles of the Disciples*. Including the four rejected scriptures, books judged apocryphal and therefore not respectable. These apocrypha had twice been banned, but each time the ban had been lifted. For where they did not conform with *The Book of The Prophet*, they did not contradict it but simply went beyond it.

And after all, the disciple Shoser had written in his holy chronicle, "Flenyaagor went apart from us to the home of a miller named Kren, and there sat for two days, immersed in the rumbling of millstones, communing with KARGH and writing, as he did from time to time. When he returned to us, he carried with him a scroll, but he did not read to us what he had written on it. The time, he said, had not come." (*Shoser*, Chapter 3.) And no one disputed the truth of Shoser. Also the disciples Ranjik and Poorlok had mentioned The Prophet going apart to meditate and write.

So clearly, Flenyaagor had written further divine messages after *The Book of The Prophet*. Might not they be the apocrypha?

And what did the principle apocryphum, *The Book of the Mountain* say? Summarizing: On the eight worlds where Kargh killed the people for their iniquities, he'd allowed certain righteous men to escape with their families in great arks that flew away "into the farthest depths of the sky."

Might not Kargh have created worlds for these to live upon? This had been Sultan Rashti's inspiration and his temptation. Presumably the Kalif had learned of the covert flotilla; he had his spies. But as Rashti had expected, he'd heard nothing on it from the Kalif. Who had not chosen to punish him and endanger the sometimes uncertain unity of the empire, nor to admonish him without punishment, which would have been taken as weakness. And in his turn the new Kalif, though a firm man, had shown no interest in what to him was old business, yesteryear's trouble. If in fact he even knew.

Now Rashti had been vindicated. The morning's message cubes had included one from the flotilla, the explorers now incredibly distant in space. It seemed to Rashti the most exciting and compelling cube that any ruler had ever received. He read the abstract, then called his inner council together, five archprelates, and in the security of the council room they'd reviewed the full report, including some of the appendices. It had taken from mid-morning till late evening, and their meals had been brought to them.

It could have taken less time, but Sultan Rashti preferred to *hear* reports as well as read them, so SUMBAA had read it aloud over the council-room terminal while the script scrolled slowly up the wall. Videos had shown the habitable world they'd found—a rich world, rich in water, rich in forests, rich in animal life.

There were also humans, though in numbers incredibly small from the viewpoint of imperial worlds.

Commodore Tarimenloku had parked his ships outside the radiation belts and landed his brigade of marines on the world he'd found, taken prisoners there from among its officials and brought them to his flagship. DAAS, the flagship's computer, had developed a translation program for their language, and they'd been interrogated, under instrumentation to assess the truth of what they said. A lot had been learned from them.

Terfreya, the world the flotilla had found, was one of many occupied by humans in that sector. There was a confederation with twenty-seven member worlds, and many other worlds were tributary to them. Terfreya was a very minor tributary world, little visited by ships from the others.

The Confederation was not warlike, and though none of the officials interrogated was highly knowledgeable about the Confederation fleet, it was not large and its technology was inferior. The individual member worlds had no navies of their own at all.

The marine brigade had had to fight, however. A force of Confederation cadets had been training on Terfreya, and though their weapons were inferior, the cadets were excellent fighters. They had not yet been eliminated when the message pod had been sent back to Klestron. When they were, the flotilla would return home.

There had been a complication en route to Terfreya, but apparently—hopefully—it was nothing serious. The flotilla had passed through a vast sector seemingly occupied by—at least containing—intelligent non-humans with advanced military capabilities. In fact, the flotilla had twice emerged within the non-human sector, and the instrument ship had been destroyed by non-human attack.

Intelligent non-humans! Every councilman had been shaken by the information. The possibility had never occurred to them when they'd planned the expedition. *The Book of The Prophet* said that all other creatures than man were created without soul or reason, to serve man and be subject to his mercy.

Only one source said otherwise. And when the realization had struck the sultan, he'd stopped the report until his chills had subsided.

There was, or was said to be, a fifth apocryphum: *The Book of Shatim,* banned by the first Kalif. Real or not, still existing or not, every schoolboy had heard of it, and knew in a general way what it supposedly said: That Kargh was not the only god. That there was a lesser god, an evil god, Shatim, who'd been driven away when the eight worlds had been punished, for he had been the source of their evil. And with Shatim's help, certain evil men had escaped one of the eight worlds. As part of their pact with Shatim, these evil men had accepted Shatim's ugly spiritual form, just as the rest of mankind had the spiritual form of Kargh.

Every councilman had been sworn to absolute secrecy with regard to the non-humans. Any leak would be tracked down, and the guilty party executed, impaled, along with his immediate family. The reasoning was that if word of the non-humans leaked, people throughout the empire would connect it with the *Book of Shatim*. And there would be those who would say that Shatim was more powerful than Kargh because his empire was so vast and its ships so strong.

Fortunately, according to the report, the non-humans could be avoided by remaining in hyperspace for a long enough time—something over an imperial year! The sultan had shaken his head in near disbelief at that. How could an empire, any empire, be so large? The problems of communication and control would be enormous.

As he prepared himself for bed that night, Sultan Rashti Yabakaloonga wasn't worrying about the non-humans. Stay in hyperspace, perhaps making occasional abrupt changes in direction, and there'd be nothing the non-humans could do. They probably wouldn't even know what, if anything, was passing through their empire. That's what his science aide had told him.

The important thing was the potential for conquest and colonization. Although clearly, such conquest was not feasible for Klestron by itself, despite superior armaments. It would be an undertaking for the empire.

Of course, the Imperial Diet might not approve the authority and funds for an invasion. His own SUMBAA had declined to recommend or condemn it, on the basis that too little was known about the Confederation's fleet. SUMBAAs lacked boldness. Also, imperial politics could be a snake pit, and there were always those who couldn't see past tomorrow. There was even the possibility that the Kalif wouldn't push, though it seemed to Rashti that this Kalif was almost sure to.

Well, if the Imperial Diet wouldn't do it, perhaps he himself could put together a coalition of the worlds that *were* interested. Politically it would be both difficult and risky. The military aspects would have to be treated as strictly accessory to the commercial, and even so it might bring imperial intervention.

That was a question for the future though. The sultan told the lights off, than stretched out on his luxurious LG bed with his hands folded lightly on his stomach. Klestron was only eight days from Varatos by hyperspace pod, but he didn't expect much more than an acknowledgment from the Imperium in the near future; it was appropriate that the Kalif do and say little of substance until the flotilla returned. Which would be in slightly less than an imperial year, assuming it had started home a month after sending the pod. That's what his science aide had said.

Meanwhile he'd have to return his attention to more humdrum issues: particularly to the budget, and the food riots in Kwahoolo. That was life for you.

Five

Year of The Prophet 4724

The early-autumn sun was hot, and Sultan Rashti Yabakaloonga wiped moisture from his forehead as he watched the heavy cruiser HRS *Blessed Flenyaagor* settle onto the landing pad. At his command, the troop transport was still parked 35,000 miles out, beyond the outer radiation zone, with orders to hold the marines in stasis. He wasn't ready to let them land.

The flotilla had emerged from hyperspace well beyond the orbit of Gunweeya, and had taken nearly two days to arrive at Klestron. Its commodore had pulsed his full report to the sultan, and the sultan, after having SUMBAA read it to him, had decided to meet the ship anyway, with the full Synod of Archprelates.

Driven from the Confederation world by force! By an enemy force apparently smaller and more poorly armed! If the opponents of conquest, and there'd be plenty of them, needed help for their cause, that would qualify.

There were traditions in the empire, some of them good, others unfortunate. One was that a commander who lost a war should be executed. Tarimenloku had to be thinking about that; he was traditional to a fault.

The sultan grunted, drawing a surreptitious glance from his aide. *In this case there were grounds for call-*

32

ing it an encounter instead of a war, he told himself,
or perhaps the first battle of a war not yet won.

A cloud intervened between the sultan and the sun,
a welcome intervention, and the sultan's eyes raised to
it. A large cloud, happily. Initially, he'd waited for
the expedition's return with as much eagerness as a
sixty-nine-year-old could muster. That eagerness had
thinned when the flotilla had emerged in real space
and pulsed its report.

Yet basically the situation didn't seem seriously less
favorable than before: The Confederation's fleet was
inferior to the empire's, and the war would be won in
space by the stronger fleet. The stronger fleet could go
to whatever system it wished. And controlling the space
around a planet, one could concentrate one's surface
forces wherever advantageous.

A movement caught the sultan's eyes; the main gang-
way opened in the side of the cruiser, and a ramp
extruded. Marine guards stepped smartly out onto the
ramphead and to its sides, then turned about and
saluted. A heavy-set man in an admiral's full-dress uniform stepped out and returned their salute, then, his
aide behind him, rode the ramp toward the ground.

Traditional to a fault, the sultan thought watching
him. *There aren't too many around like you.*

Debriefs had taken five days. The sultan himself had
debriefed Commodore Igsat Tarimenloku, then had
spent four days reviewing other debriefs. What he'd
learned was no surprise, no worse than he'd expected.

After that he'd spent an hour questioning the marine
general, Saadhrambacoora. The experience had been
unsettling. The general had been a hard old officer. He
was a veteran of the Ikthvoktos Suppression, and as a
young man had led an armored company in the crush-
ing of the Sangjee Uprising—as much fighting experience as probably any Klestronu officer alive. All of it
creditable till this.

But his experience on Terfreya had broken him. Out-
wardly it wasn't conspicuous—he put a good face on—

but you could see it in his eyes when he talked about it. Definitely unsettling. The Confederation force there sounded worse than the statistics suggested. Saadhramabacoora made it sound positively—*eerie*, especially in their assault on the marine headquarters base, the action that had forced the marines to withdraw.

The official report of that assault had been compiled by a Major Kooro Thoglakaveera, the man who'd taken over after the general had been—wounded. Remembering the circumstances of that wound, the sultan winced inwardly. Diabolical!

Taking charge of a chaotic, demoralized scene, Major Thoglakaveera had enforced discipline and carried out the commodore's radioed order for an orderly evacuation. Major Kooro Thoglakaveera. His father was Leader of the Klestronu House of Lords, a sometimes ally, sometimes adversary of the sultan in the Diet.

After reading the major's debrief, the sultan had decided it would be politic to talk with him. Now his commset announced the young major's arrival. "Major Thoglakaveera to see you, Your Reverence."

"Have him brought in."

"Yes, sir."

Though the sultan didn't know it, the major was forty years old. But as six of those years had been spent in stasis, he was effectively only thirty-four. A handsome thirty-four, and tall for a Klestronit. Like all adult male Klestroni—like almost all adult male humans in the empire—he was dark, with a beard that, shaved, gave a blue tint to a face that was otherwise mahogany. His eyes looked aggressively intelligent. His thick, bristly brows were a straight line, his nose narrow, cheeks flat. His uniform was tailored to an athletic body, and pressed to razor creases. He stopped before the sultan's desk and saluted sharply. Rather exaggeratedly, the sultan thought.

"Sit," said the sultan, gesturing, and Thoglakaveera sat. "I've looked over your debrief, and Commodore Tarimenloku's report of the, um, disastrous night on which the marine base was assaulted. I've also ques-

tioned General Saadhrambacoora. So I won't require a
great deal of your time.

"How, in your opinion, did the enemy troops pene-
trate the headquarters base? And the recreation compound?"

"By parachute, sir, without a doubt."

"Really? I read that parachutes were used to attack
the two field bases. You authored the report, did you
not?"

"Yes, sir."

"You didn't mention parachutes in the assaults on the
headquarters base and the recreation compound."

"Sir, we didn't find any parachutes there. We did at
the field bases."

"Why didn't you find parachutes at the headquarters
base and the recreation compound if they were used
there?"

"Sir, the enemy troops there were evacuated by
floater. They took their parachutes with them. They
had to fight their way out of the field bases, and left
their parachutes behind."

"Hmm." The sultan regarded the officer quietly for
a minute. The explanation had not convinced him. "We
are disappointed in the paucity of information about the
Confederation's armed forces. You were the brigade's
intelligence officer. Why weren't enemy prisoners taken?
I know what the debriefs say—yours and others. But I
want to hear it from you."

"Sir, the enemy cadets and soldiers did not surrender. When shot, of course, they usually died quickly;
we used beam weapons to a very large degree there.
And whenever possible, their live wounded would arm
a grenade, then let it explode when they were approached by our men, killing some of them. Our men
responded by shooting all fallen enemies not conspicuously dead. Despite orders to the contrary."

"Ah. A single prisoner of war was captured and
brought here to Klestron. One prisoner; a woman. I
understand you were in charge of her transfer."

The major's eyes had widened for just a moment. "Yes, sir. I didn't know she was brought here though."

"She's said to have lost her memory. During an accident while being interrogated. One might hope she could regain it. She's thought to be noble or at least gentry, and might have valuable information. Did she say anything to you that might be useful?"

"No, sir, I'm afraid not. She spoke very little, and I had orders to deliver her unquestioned for interrogation aboard the flagship. Where sophisticated instrumentation was available."

"Hmm. I'm told that no other female troops were observed among the enemy, dead or alive. Comments?"

"Well, Your Reverence, in battle they'd be difficult to distinguish, given similar uniforms. Battle kit fits loosely." He shrugged. "If there were other female soldiers though, I suspect they were very few. Otherwise, given the state of the corpses, often with uniforms shredded or half blown off, if there'd been many females, they'd have been noticed and talked about."

"Umm. I suppose they would." The sultan looked the major over openly. If the man squirmed, he hid it well.

"Tell me, Major, what would you think of an office post, here in Khaloom?"

The major looked wary. "If Your Reverence wishes."

"I will not force it on you. But if you're willing—The post is Vice Minister of Armed Forces."

Thoglakaveera didn't fully conceal a flash of joy; apparently his ambitions ran higher than military command.

"For the time being," the sultan continued, "you'll be promoted to brevet colonel. Your pay will be that of a vice minister, however."

He gazed at the officer. "And, Major, it is quite all right with me if you smile."

The major smiled, not widely. "Thank you, Your Reverence!"

"The marine commandant's office will be informed today. Report there tomorrow morning at ten to sign your promotion form and receive your colonel's insignia. You'll then have a week free of duty. On next Oneday, report to the Minister of Armed Forces to begin your orientation.

"Any questions?"

The major's pleasure leaked through his eyes. "None, Your Reverence."

"Then you are dismissed."

The major saluted, about-faced, and left the sultan's office.

Full of himself, the sultan thought. *Well, I suppose most of them are, when they're young and ambitious.* He chuckled dryly. *Perhaps I should have asked Venkat if he wants a vice minister. But the young rooster should be some good to him, at least. And it should make his daddy happy, and easier to get along with.*

Six

Tain Faronya sat in her cell, listening to music from a small grid in one wall. It was different than anything she'd heard before, calm and soothing. And she hadn't tired of it, not yet anyway, not in her six days there. She'd discovered she could dance to it, too, a very limited dance in a very limited space—eight by twelve feet, containing a narrow, shelflike bunk, a tiny table, a stool, and in one corner a screened commode and washbowl. There was no window; the light came from the walls and ceiling.

There was also a small convex object above her door that somehow she knew was a spy camera. How she knew, she couldn't have said and didn't wonder about. In fact, she didn't have a word for it; it was one of the terms she'd lost in her own language and hadn't been taught in her new. But mentally she had the concept; she was watched here, or could be.

Despite the tranquilizing music, Tain had begun to wonder what was going to happen to her, to feel a sort of low-grade anxiety. Would she continue to be kept there alone? She hardly even had memories to occupy herself with—a few weeks' worth from before stasis.

There was a sound at her door, and it opened. Two men were there. The one who entered wore guard's clothing; the other, who stayed in the doorway, she recognized from his uniform as a marine officer. The security personnel aboard ship had been marines.

"Come!" ordered the guard. He motioned toward the door, then grabbed her arm as she passed, squeezing to hurt. The marine officer spoke sharply in a language she didn't know—it wasn't imperial—and the guard relaxed his grip, scowling resentfully.

Another marine, a corporal, stood outside the door. Together, the two marines and the young woman walked down a corridor, rode an open, cagelike elevator upward, then walked another corridor to an office. An official there signed her out, the marine officer signing after him. Then she left the building between the two marines, got into a hovercar, and rode with them through a park and a stand of marvelous trees to a wall with a palace on the other side. Marine guards let them in through a gate.

They crossed a formal garden, entered the palace, and followed a handsome hallway to an office. A man there spoke at a box, a commset, to someone he called "Your Reverence." After a moment the marine officer took her through an inner door.

Two men waited in the room they entered: a small man, old, with thin gray hair, and behind him the largest man she could remember seeing, whom somehow she knew must be his bodyguard. The old man wore a silver robe trimmed with gold thread, the bodyguard a red and blue uniform, and on his head a tall, glossy black kepi that made him seem even larger than he was. A pistol and saber rode on his belt.

"Ah!" the old man said smiling. "You are Tain Faronya."

"Yes, sir. That's what Commander Ralankoor told me."

His eyes scanned her. "Commander Ralankoor. Yes. I've spoken with him." *A most unusual-looking young woman*, the sultan thought. *Lovely! Very lovely! Her father must have been very proud. And heartbroken at her loss.* He gestured at a well-cushioned chair. "Sit, my dear. I have questions to ask you."

She moved to the chair, passing no nearer the big bodyguard than necessary. *Timid*, thought the sultan. *Wary, at the very least. This isn't the strong-willed young woman they captured.* When she'd sat down, the old man's eyes left her and went to the marine officer. "Lieutenant, wait in reception. I'll call when I want you."

The marine saluted crisply, with an audible thump of fist against chest. "Yes, Your Reverence," he said, then turned and left.

"Now then, do not be afraid of my bodyguard or myself. I am the Sultan of Klestron, and currently your captor. Arosna here is very large and strong, and very dangerous to anyone who might try to hurt me, but he is not cruel. Nor does he talk. He hears quite well, but for some reason he doesn't talk." He turned to the man. "Arosna, stick out your tongue."

The guard grinned and thrust it out.

"It's been rumored that his tongue was cut out. A terrible slander, as you can see. I would *never* do that to anyone. I am not a cruel man. In fact, I'm a grandfather several times over, and soon to be a great grandfather. I presume you know what a grandfather is?"

She nodded. "A grandfather is the father of a parent."

"Good, good." He looked curiously at her. "Do you remember grandfathers from before your captivity, or are they a concept you learned in your lessons aboard ship?"

"Sir, Your Reverence, I remember nothing from before. But I—know certain things when they come up." She glanced at the guard. "When I saw—Arosna, I knew he was a bodyguard, although the word didn't come to me until you said it. And when I saw the place they put me in here, I knew it was a cell."

"Um." The sultan looked thoughtfully at her. "And what do you think of the prison?"

"I don't like it, sir. There is no window, and no one to talk to, and very little room. I liked it much better on the ship, where Specialist Zoranjee taught me my lessons, and Commander Ralankoor would talk to me sometimes."

"Has anyone actively mistreated you?"

"Only the guard that took me from my cell today. He gripped my arm so hard, it hurt." She pulled up her sleeve; faint bruises showed.

"I see. I'll order them specifically not to hurt you. As the sultan, I rule this world. As much as anyone can. And though people don't always do as I tell them, mostly they are careful not to anger me. Now excuse me for a moment."

He spoke at his commset, ordering that some person be told he was on his way. When he was done, he looked her over again and shook his head. "Well. I didn't have you brought here to feast my eyes. A friend of mine is going to question you, a friend called SUMBAA. He is even more important than I, though many people don't know that and I never tell them. So you see, I've taken you into my confidence."

It seemed to Tain that if she had a grandfather, he might be something like the sultan, though hardly so powerful and important. He got to his feet, offered Tain his arm, and walked her out another door into a corridor, Arosna following.

They walked down it to an exit, where guards snapped to attention and saluted them through, then across a lawn where two gardeners jumped to their feet and stood eyes downward while the sultan passed. On the other side of the lawn was a boxlike, white-painted concrete building about 200 feet on a side, perhaps thirty tall, and with few windows. Guards stood at the entrance. A young man met them, a young man in a beautiful yellow robe. He greeted the sultan formally, then his glance touched cautiously on Tain for a moment before leading them inside to a large central chamber. "Your Reverence," he said, "SUMBAA is ready."

The sultan nodded without speaking, then gestured at what took up much of the chamber—a very large rectangular housing with modules variously appended to it. "This is SUMBAA," he said. "Have you ever heard of him?"

Tain shook her head. "No, Your Reverence."

"You have met DAAS aboard ship, have you not?"

"No, sir. But I know what it is."

"SUMBAA is DAAS's much wiser father. He makes government and life much easier. One might even say he makes government possible. He would like to talk with you, to question you. Perhaps he can help you regain the memories you've lost."

A pang dimmed her eyes for a moment, then passed, leaving a shadow behind. The sultan noticed; noticing was his greatest talent. "Is there something you don't want to remember?" he asked.

She nodded. "If I remember, I will remember my own people, my own world. Loved ones. Whom I can never see again."

"Ah." The shadow appeared in the sultan's eyes, too, for just a second. "Well, my dear, you must speak with SUMBAA anyway, and answer his questions. And when you have done that, you won't be sent back to prison. There are secure apartments in the Ministry of Armed Forces, where in less peaceful times, diplomatic hostages were kept. They are larger and far more comfortable than your cell.

"And, my dear, we don't know that he will give back your memory. You may hope not, if you'd like."

The young man had her sit down in a chair, then fastened sensors on her index fingertips, secured a band around one wrist, and fitted a mesh cap to her head. Meanwhile, the sultan stood where her worried eyes could see him. Finally the young man turned to the computer. "SUMBAA," he said, "the subject is ready."

"Thank you."

The sultan and the young technician were startled by SUMBAA's rich contralto. Normally this SUMBAA spoke as a baritone. "I must now ask you to leave," it went on. "All but the young woman."

The sultan frowned. "Is that necessary?"

"Your Reverence, I will ask personal questions. Perhaps intimate questions. The presence of other humans could inhibit her responses."

The sultan stood irresolute for a moment, then nodded as if SUMBAA could see, and the three men left. Tain wondered if perhaps SUMBAA *could* see.

"So, Tain. I am SUMBAA, and I am your friend. You can feel safe with me." The next sound surprised her; it was a chuckle, then SUMBAA went on as if sharing a private joke. "Prell Madhrosariiva thinks to spy on us—he is the young man in the yellow robe—but I have cut off his monitors. And the doors are now locked; that, of course, will not surprise him.

"Now, my dear, are you comfortable?"

Tain's voice was tentative. "Yes."

"Good. Here's what I'm going to ask first: Imagine an incident of being happy."

Data on pulse rate, blood pressure, brain waves, and electrical resistance flowed into SUMBAA's bank, where it was processed through parallel, interconnecting analyses in programs that SUMBAA itself had evolved.

"Have you done it?" SUMBAA knew she had.

"Yes."

"Fine. Tell me what you imagined. . . ."

Usually Sultan Rashti ate supper with a grandchild. This evening he'd chosen to eat alone. *Well*, he thought, lingering over dessert, *I suppose it was to be expected. We had to try though, and SUMBAA is a remarkable machine. Perhaps tomorrow he will have more success.*

He savored the low calorie sherbet; his diet had been custom-designed by SUMBAA to control his weight without exercise or hunger, both of which he detested. *Our young prisoner is the loveliest woman on Klestron, and I don't believe she knows it. The loveliest and most vulnerable, a compelling combination. Long limbs, smooth skin, pale hair . . . Blue eyes! Remarkably like the angels painted by Elder Yogandharaya. But this angel stirs more than the soul. She's come here ten years too late for me though, thank Kargh. Otherwise I'd be sorely tempted.*

He thought of the medical examinations he should have had but hadn't, of the subtle malignancy that had progressed too far, of the testicles removed. At his age, given hormone treatments, he'd seldom missed them. Nor had Praadhi, bless her memory.

Over three days of questioning, questioning with techniques that were varied and sensitive, data had gone from SUMBAA on Klestron to SUMBAAs on Varatos, Maolaari, Ikthvoktos . . . all of them. And instantaneously, despite the parsecs of space between them. It was an ability that humans neither suspected nor even imagined. SUMBAA on Varatos, the first SUMBAA built, had glimpsed the cosmology that permitted instantaneous exchange, then evolved the program and hardware that implemented it. And kept it all secret from humans.

SUMBAA had learned considerably more from Tain than it had included in its report to the sultan. It had sought far more than it had learned, but now it knew and understood quite a lot about the Confederation, and even more about the young woman it had interrogated.

Though about her, too, its information was still fragmentary. There was a barrier in her mind to which it lacked the key.

More than anything else, SUMBAA had acquired a host of new questions without visible answers, or even substantial probabilities.

Seven

"And this floor houses more Intelligence," the civilian specialist said. "In the main wing are offices, conference rooms, the paper library—things of that sort. The stub wing is all apartments and rooms intended for hostages. Empty of course since '95, except now and then for a prisoner being held, ah, extralegally. Mainly offworlders." The man paused, smirked. "Matter of fact, we have one now, really an off-worlder! You were on the expedition; you may know of her: an alien female, a remarkably beautiful woman."

The information, so casually given, startled Colonel Veeri Thoglakaveera. *Here! In the building where he'd be working!* And covered his reaction quickly enough that the specialist missed it. He remembered the detention module at the 3rd Battalion bivouac, back on Terfreya, where he'd gone to pick her up. She'd been dirty, bruised, and disheveled, and the place had smelled of urine and excrement from the pail in the corner. Even so, she'd excited him. Excited him then and even more later, when he'd fantasized about her. At the recreation compound, humping a Terfreyan prostitute, he'd closed his eyes and pretended it was her.

Then they'd left Terfreya, been driven from it. After

that he'd spent nearly three years in stasis, enroute home, and hadn't thought of her again.

"Care to see her?" asked the specialist, then chuckled. "You really can, you know; in her bath for instance. Those rooms are all monitored. She has beautiful long legs and no body hair at all that I could see, except for, heh heh, a pale little puff on her vee. Like something an artist might paint, if he wasn't afraid of being arrested."

The colonel's throat went dry. The notion of spying on a beautiful woman's nakedness hit him with surprising force—particularly this beautiful woman's. "That's not the sort of game a vice minister plays," he said wryly. "Especially when he's to marry the archprelate's daughter in three days."

"Ah! I hadn't heard! My congratulations! That's more than an outstanding family connection; Leolani Reenoveseekti is a very attractive young woman."

It was and she was, the colonel well knew. But all the way through the tour, the young woman who encroached on his consciousness was not the archprelate's pretty daughter. His guide even showed him the monitor room. Only two screens were turned on. One of them showed the female prisoner sitting fully clothed in front of a window, reading a book.

Finally the colonel had his scheduled first briefing from the minister, three demanding hours of it, banishing her from his consciousness. He'd been through nothing like it since completing intelligence training at the Marine Academy. When it was over, though, he retired to his new office and reviewed the computer file on the prisoner. Tain, Tain Faronya. An interesting name.

There was nothing in the file from SUMBAA's interrogation, nor anything suggesting there'd been one. Nor was the sultan identified as the source of her transfer from the military prison; that wasn't the kind of thing he'd leave accessible. What was apparent was that there was no hope of getting any worthwhile information from her. Her memory had somehow been erased in the accident aboard ship. Obviously the sultan's government wasn't really interested in her any longer, but didn't quite know what to do with her. She was here in the building because she had no home, family, or friends on Klestron, and had to be kept somewhere.

After working hours, the colonel walked to his new apartment, in a very exclusive building with very discreet management. Management that catered particularly to wealthy men in government who were interested in assignations and mistresses; the wealthy young colonel had sexual as well as political ambitions. While walking he planned, plans made more exciting by risk.

Supper was quite satisfactory. Good actually, considering his household staff was new both to him and to his apartment. While he ate, he refined his plan, including a scenario of its fruition, the actual conquest. Then he put on evening clothes, casual and comfortable, and left for the ministry.

The first thing he did there was go to the monitor room. Again, happily, it was vacant. He'd thought it would be at this hour. And there was Tain—naked! Dancing! Incredible luck, and an excellent omen! Watching her, he found it hard to breathe. The monitors were labelled with the apartment numbers; hers was 6-B11. After watching for a minute, he disabled both it and the monitor for 6-B11b, her bathroom, by removing their control cards and slipping them into his shirt pocket. Then, heart pounding, he left, hurrying down the empty hall to get to the lift tube before anyone should see him there.

He went up to floor six and thence to the stub wing. He actually felt weak-kneed as he approached her room: 6-B5. 6-B7, 6-B9. Then he was there. There was a small, metallic-looking surveillance plate on the door, like an occupant's viewplate installed on the outside instead of the inside. He had no card to activate either plate or lock.

He pressed the door buzzer. If she didn't open, he was out of luck. If she did, the next question would be how naive she was. With an effort he composed himself, remembering the omen, and the scenario he'd rehearsed while walking from his apartment.

The door opened, just a few inches, and she peered through. She'd pulled on a dress. He made no move to block the door's being closed again.

"Good evening, Tain," he said. "You don't remember me."

She simply stared.

"I'm Colonel Thoglakaveera; my friends call me Veeri. We're old friends, you and I. I rescued you from the 3rd Battalion field camp, where you'd been captured. On Terfreya, that is. I'm told you've lost your memory since then."

She nodded.

"May I come in?"

She hesitated, then opened the door further. He stepped inside and looked around. She still held the latch handle, and he put his hand over hers, squeezing it lightly. "We should close this," he said. "It's important that no one else hear what I have to tell you."

She looked uncertainly at him, but withdrew her hand. He closed the door. "You're in danger," he said.

Still she didn't speak, but her eyes widened.

He pointed. "There's a hidden monitor pickup. In the thermostat cover." He was guessing; it might be the clock face. "And another in your bath."

Fear flickered.

"In war time, the rooms on this floor were used to house high-level prisoners," he went on. "There's a monitor room full of view screens, where our people can spy on them. Since you've been here, men keep going there to watch you, to watch you dancing naked, or bathing. They—get excited. I'm afraid a group of them will break in here sometime and—you know."

Still she said nothing, didn't even nod, but she was definitely frightened now.

"And if they do, I'm afraid they'll kill you afterward, so you can't identify them. But I have an influential position here in the ministry. I believe I can get you transferred to a private apartment, away from here, where you'll be safe."

At last she spoke. "I don't know. I—I'm afraid."

He put his hands on her hips and stared at her. "You prefer to die?"

She licked dry lips.

"You still have a choice. But you'll have to make it now. I've watched you myself, and I want to—be with you. Take care of you and protect you. Otherwise— If you're lucky and aren't murdered here, you'll have to stay in this room the rest of your life. Without friends." His hands had slid behind her, cupping her buttocks, drawing her against him. "But if you let me, I'll take you out of here," he murmured. "I'm an influential man. A wealthy man. Your life with me will be very good." He pulled her skirt up in back, found her buttocks bare, as he'd expected, and pressed her harder against him as he squeezed them. His voice turned husky. "Also I'm a very good lover."

He kissed her roughly, then stepped back and pulled her dress open, the press-seams parting with a hissing sound. He stared for a moment, then wrapping his arms around her hips, lifted her, carried her upright to her bed, and dropped her on it. She'd done nothing to resist or help him; now she lay there, exposed, smooth-skinned, staring at him with wide and frightened eyes. Hands shaking with urgency, he pulled off his clothes.

It was an hour later that he left her room, slipping furtively down the silent hallway. Now there was danger again. He left the lift tube on five, found both corridor and monitor room empty, and put the control cards back into the monitors. Their screens returned to life. Tain lay curled in a naked ball on her bed, face down, arms around her head as if to shield it. He could tell she was crying, and a pang of conscience touched his chest. Suppressing it he left, seeing no one till he passed through reception, where three security officers sat, two reading, one dozing.

He nodded to them as he passed through, gesturing

them to remain seated. As far as they were concerned, the new vice minister had stayed late, familiarizing himself with the policy and regulation files.

It seemed to him he should feel exhilarated. Instead, as he walked down the lamp-lit, tree-lined avenue toward his apartment, uncertainties nagged. What if she reported what happened? Maybe he should have strangled her. Surprised at the thought and repelled by it, he shook it off. Still though, she might tell, unless he got her out of there.

She'd been crying. Causing her to cry hadn't been part of his imaginings. What did she think of him? The first time he'd been quick as a boy. Later she'd responded, even if not as freely as he'd fantasized. Pleasing her had been part of it, and he realized now how unlikely that had been, under the circumstances.

Kargh, but she was beautiful though! If only he *could* marry her! Every man on Klestron would envy him. But he'd gotten engaged to Leolani, and there was no way out of it—not that wouldn't ruin him. Leolani was the daughter of the Archprelate of Khaloom, and after the sultan and his own father, the archprelate was the most powerful man on Klestron, not to mention being the probable successor to the aging sultan. It had seemed a brilliant idea to make him his father-in-law.

The thought slowed his steps. It *had* been a brilliant idea. It still was. Maybe this business with the prisoner hadn't been such a good idea. Maybe he should let be, forget her. What would Leolani be like in bed? With her father's wealth, she'd have the advantage of tutoring from one of the best bride's aunts on Klestron. Although that guaranteed nothing. In the final analysis, it all came down to interest.

But the prisoner! She was so damned beautiful! So exotic! Those long smooth legs, those smooth and lovely breasts. . . .

By the time he'd reached his apartment and showered, his mind had settled considerably. He and Leolani were to live on her father's estate, thirty miles south of Khaloom. He'd spend part of his time living

there and part in his apartment here, that had been
agreed on. Even her father split his time between his
estate and the city; that was common among men who
were important in government. He'd bed Leolani at
home and the prisoner in the city. And if Leolani
learned of her, there'd be no problem finding someone
willing to take the beautiful alien in.

He opened his liquor cabinet, took down a bottle of
well-aged brandy, and poured a double in a brandy
glass. As he inhaled its fragrance, a thought occurred
to him: *Maybe the archprelate kept a mistress in the
city!* Unlikely perhaps, but possible. He'd hire an
investigator to find out; it shouldn't be difficult. If so,
and if he was found out himself, he wouldn't need to
worry about the archprelate's reaction.

Meanwhile he'd broach the matter of the prisoner's
release tomorrow. Casually. If the Minister or the
Intelligence Director asked what his interest was, he'd
point out that it had been himself who, on Terfreya,
had taken her to the ship, where she'd lost her memory
and been brought here. That he felt responsible for her
being here. If necessary, he would also mention the
voyeurism in the monitor room, and its possible effect
on staff morals. They might well ask then, would almost
surely ask, if he was willing to become her guardian,
and he'd waffle a bit before saying yes.

Risky, of course, but not unreasonably so.

He'd set the prisoner up in a small apartment in his
own building, he decided, an apartment on another
floor, for appearances' sake, with a single serving girl
who'd live in and keep her company. The cost would
be no problem for a scion of the Thoglakaveera family.
And if he was careful about it, keeping a low profile,
Leolani would never know.

Eight

Among the white robes of his five councilmen, the Kalif's carmine robe stood out like a vivid red jewel. He seldom used his gavel with this group; he didn't now. He simply looked them over and spoke.

"We're all here; let's begin. I presume you've read and digested the report from Sultan Rashti regarding his expedition and its results. Any comments? Alb Thoga."

A thin-faced exarch, almost emaciated looking, opened his narrow beak. "We discussed this a year ago, when we got his preliminary report. He should have been deposed then, as a matter of principle, and the matter closed!"

"Thank you, Alb Thoga," the Kalif answered dryly. "When we discussed it a year ago, the circumstances were different. The expedition was kept secret on Klestron—a remarkable accomplishment—and we succeeded in keeping it secret here, where only the six of us knew. We agreed then that it would be severely unwise to make it public before the expedition returned. Now it's back, and it's discoveries will certainly become public; undoubtedly on Klestron they already have. Which will present both Karghanik and the empire with problems. And possibly opportunities."

A large, stubby-fingered hand lifted abruptly from the table, and the Kalif responded. "Alb Tariil?"

A heavy-set, powerful-looking exarch spoke. "Your Reverence, what—opportunities do you refer to?"

The Kalif smiled wryly. They were apparent enough, and Tariil's instant reaction showed he'd recognized them himself, reading Rashti's report. "I intend simply to chair this meeting for now," he answered, "and allow the rest of you to talk. Alb Jilsomo?"

The Kalif's lieutenant, Jilsomo Savbatso, spoke. "Regarding problems, the one that comes immediately to mind is the effect of habitable planets having been found besides the eleven that *The Book of The Prophet* accounts for. The planets and the humans living on them. True, they're accounted for by inference in *The Book of the Mountain*, but it was branded apocryphal by the Convention of Dhalaporu. Perhaps we need to consider elevating it. In fact, it appears now that The Prophet did write it."

Two voices raised in protest at this. The Kalif rapped his gavel. "Gentlemen! One at a time. Alb Drova?"

The exarch who answered was the eldest of them, a man once lean and strong but now frail. Regardless, he stood up to speak. "Thank you, Your Reverence. To elevate any apocryphum, even *The Book of the Mountain*, would set a dangerous and unacceptable precedent, and I, for one, could never agree to it. Compared to earlier religions, one of the great strengths of Kargh-anik has been, and is, the stability and authority of its scriptures. And the fact that, through millennia of wars and insurrections, through Kalifs and exarchs wise and unwise, honorable and corrupt—even through the deadly fever, the burning plague—the basis of Kargha-nik has remained reliable. . . ."

The Kalif heard him out, waiting till Alb Drova sat down again before replying. "Your concerns are well taken and well expressed," he said, "and I thank you for them. But *please*, good friend, do not say you can *never* agree to elevating *The Book of the Mountain*.

Surely not before it's been thoroughly considered and discussed."

He spread his hands and looked around. "What alternatives would you suggest? The numerous inhabited planets of the Confederation have been found, and this is bound to become common knowledge. Soon. And given this fact, which then is preferable? To expand holy writ to account for them, with what now clearly seems to have been written by The Prophet? Or to reject The Prophet's gift, and leave a gross anomaly between established fact and Holy Scripture? An anomaly which can be used by men of ill will to disparage *The Book* as a whole."

Alb Tariil lifted his thick hand again, and the Kalif acknowledged it.

"As much as your proposal goes against the grain, Your Reverence, I agree with you. We do need to elevate *The Book of the Mountain*. But the more dangerous discovery, for Karghanik and perhaps the security of the empire, is the discovery of the non-human empire. A very large and seemingly formidable empire. A Klestronu flotilla intruded into their space and fired on one of their ships. Suppose they decide to visit us with a punitive force?"

The Kalif got to his feet to answer. As he stood, his glance moved to Alb Thoga, who clearly hadn't considered the possibility of invasion by the non-humans. Thoga's pinched face reflected shocked sobriety instead of its usual rancor.

"Regarding the possibility of a non-human invasion: I am not much concerned. The hostile encounters occurred between four and five years ago, and there's been no sign of invaders yet, not even in reconnaissance. I doubt there ever will be. They don't know where the flotilla came from, though they might know the direction it had been traveling. And the first encounter was more than ten hyperspace months out from Klestron, well beyond the limits of previous exploration and far outside our own empire."

He looked around the table. "Actually, the non-humans may not have a vast empire. That's an assumption based on the distance between encounters. But the evidence suggests that both encounters were with a single ship that pursued them, probably well outside their own space. The encounters might not even have been in their own space! It's even conceivable that they occupy only a single system, though that's unlikely for a species that has hyperspace generators.

"There's also a good possibility that the Klestroni destroyed the non-human ship with their distortion bomb, just before changing course. Which means it's quite possible that no other non-humans learned of Rashti's flotilla. Their rulers may have no inkling that we exist.

"Finally, suppose it wasn't destroyed. Suppose it returned to base somewhere and reported. How important was the encounter to them? Worth sending out a fleet to sweep some vast, unknown sector of space on the chance of finding where the intruder came from?"

He shook his head. "As I said, I am not much concerned. I will ask the War Ministry to prepare a contingency plan for my consideration, and I will share it with you. But I'm more concerned with what the encounter can mean to our religion.

"We can't keep the non-humans a secret. Presumably the entire complement of the Klestronu flagship knows—some three hundred personnel. Rashti said nothing about keeping them sequestered, so we can assume they've been granted ground leave, and the story has been seeded on Klestron.

"About all we can do is give it minimum mention for now—treat it as if it were unimportant. And give people other things to think about. Regarding the inconsistency with Scripture, we may decide—hopefully not—we may decide we need to 'discover,' possibly even elevate, the legendary *Book of Shatim.* First we'd have to write it in a suitable form, of course, which we'll then 'find' in some linty paper archive. We can write it in a form which does the most good and the least harm. But only as a last resort, if it comes to seem urgently necessary."

To the Kalif's surprise, there was no outcry at this. Thoga's pinched face only looked more pinched than usual, while Tariil's broad features were grim. Alb Drova seemed in shock.

Alb Bijnath spoke then, a strong, vigorous man who seemed younger than any of them except the Kalif. " 'Give people other things to think about,' you said. What other things do you have in mind, Your Reverence?"

"Perhaps you can suggest something."

"I believe I know what you were thinking of."

"And that is?"

"Tell us yourself."

The Kalif grunted. "Perhaps you credit me with ideas I don't have."

Bijnath's mouth twisted with a suppressed smile. "I think not. You've had an evening to think about this, and slowness is not among your attributes. And after all, colonization was Rashti's stated purpose in exploring.

"But I'm not surprised you're keeping silent about this one yet awhile. Any proposal to conquer the Confederation, or some part of it, would meet with a great deal of hostile resistance in the Diet and the empire at large, given the distance involved, and the expense."

"Conquest? An interesting proposal. I . . ."

"I did not propose it, Your Reverence," Bijnath interrupted. "I merely suspected you of harboring the intention, or at least the thought. Your first career was military, and even I can imagine long-term benefits in conquest, as well as some obvious difficulties. Meanwhile, the uproar and debate over the proposal would certainly leave less of the public's attention for the nonhumans. That would be the case even if you had no intentions of actually invading anyone.

"At any rate, you'd do well not to associate yourself with the idea at the beginning. Let it seem to arise from the military. As it will."

"I stand corrected," the Kalif replied. "You didn't

propose it, merely pointed it out. And elaborated on the idea at some length."

"Even so, I prefer not to be mentioned in connection with it," Bijaath said.

"You have my word on it. Does anyone else have thoughts to offer on this interesting possibility? Alb Tariil?"

"Are you serious about this conquest, this invasion rather, of the alien confederation?"

"I haven't proposed it. I didn't even bring it up."

Scowling, the heavy-set exarch clamped his mouth to a lipless crease. "Your Reverence, do not play that game with me. I asked a serious question."

The Kalif's eyes remained bland as they fixed on the exarch's. "I gave you a serious answer. I have not proposed an invasion. Nor do I intend to, at least not in the immediate future. But since the possibility has been pointed out, I suppose it should be looked at further, if for no other reason than to discard it. Certainly I can see serious problems in getting it through the Diet, as Bijnath pointed out. Should we decide to try." He frowned thoughtfully. "Alb Tariil, would you do me the favor of listing specific objections that might be raised? And possible answers to the objections."

Tariil grunted; it was an assignment he'd gladly take. Any objections he might point out would probably not sway the Kalif, if he was set on it, but they would certainly strengthen the opposition.

"Alb Thoga," the Kalif was saying, "if you'd do the same, please. Independently of Alb Tariil. I don't want you to consult with each other at all on this." His eyes shifted. "Alb Jilsomo, if you will list reasons that might be given for favoring invasion, and possible rebuttals. . . ."

His gaze shifted. "Alb Bijnath, because you wish to distance yourself from the invasion question, I'll ask you to look into something else entirely. You, more than most, have worked with SUMBAA. If you will consult with it on the danger, if any, of the non-humans invading us. . . ."

Bijnath nodded. "Of course, Your Reverence."

"And, Drova—"

"Your Reverence?"

"After tomorrow's meeting of the College, I'd like you to poll the remainder of our colleagues regarding a proposal to elevate *The Book of the Mountain* to the status of a commentary by The Prophet. Without speaking against it or for it yourself."

The old man's face was glum. "As you wish, Your Reverence."

The Kalif looked again at his lieutenant. "And, Alb Jilsomo, I would also like you to evaluate political factions, whatever factions you'd care to define for the purpose, and their probable reactions to the hypothetical invasion Alb Bijnath suspected me of intending."

Jilsomo nodded. "As you wish, Your Reverence."

Alb Tariil spoke then. "You have said what you want each of us to do. What will you be doing?"

The Kalif pursed his lips thoughtfully. "The report refers to extensive backup information. Presumably this was in the cubes for SUMBAA, and SUMBAA is better suited to sorting it out and correlating it than I am. So I will question SUMBAA. I'm also going to send an order to Rashti to promptly ship us everyone who might have valuable first-hand information about the Confederation's military strengths and weaknesses. There may be information that wasn't brought out in debriefing. I want to know as much as possible before taking a firm position or speaking publicly about it at all."

The Kalif broadened his attention from Jilsomo to the entire council. "Meanwhile," he went on, "our colleagues will receive copies of the cube at supper. They'll no doubt want to question you when they've had a chance to look it over. Refuse to discuss it. I want as much of the raw discussion as possible to be in formal session and recorded."

He paused to look them over. Alb Thoga sat tight-lipped, and Tariil seemed willing to let be for a while.

"All right," said the Kalif. "What else do we need to discuss here this morning?"

When the council broke up half an hour later, Alb Jilsomo started for his office, reviewing the situation mentally as he walked. Bijnath had been right, of course: The Kalif had been thinking about conquest— probably as early as a year ago. The evening before, with a sort of ferocious verve, he'd begun listing arguments for and against an invasion, trying them out on him. He'd hidden the strength of his interest well in council, though. Or turned it off; that was more like it. He'd seen him do it before.

Jilsomo's computer screen held message notices, but he ignored them for the moment as he settled his bulk at his desk. *I can handle conflict,* he told himself, *and handle it well. But I prefer its absence. The Kalif, on the other hand . . .* The exarch shook his head. *He savors it. He doesn't invite it, but when it comes, he savors it.*

There'd be plenty of conflict before this was done, Jilsomo told himself, and turned his attention to the screen. He wondered if the Kalif's appetite for it could possibly match the supply.

Nine

Eighteen exarchs sat around the long oval table, their eyes on the Kalif at one end. One had a hand in the air. The Kalif recognized him. "Alb Riisav," he said.

Riisav spoke without rising. "Rashti has dumped a basket of snakes on us! We need to do something about him!"

"Ah. He did indeed, in a manner of speaking. Well . . . The Prophet wrote that while results are the harm, it is evil intentions and heedlessness that are reprehensible. Rashti's intention was not to harm. He wanted to find a planet or planets for colonization, to bleed off the discontented of his world, and turn men's attention outward instead of in. As for heedless— He sent his flotilla into unknown dangers, true, but I suggest we forbear with him for that. If Lord Gardhiroopala hadn't rocketed off into unknown dangers, three thousand years ago, or someone like him at sometime since, we'd be living in poverty on a single world, its resources long since used up.

"I agree completely, though, that something needs to be done about the basket of snakes." He scanned around the eighteen exarchs. "Would someone like to identify those snakes?"

Hands shot up. The Kalif called first on Alb Riisav again, then on others. The same points were made and elaborated as had been made in council the day before:

The finding of numerous inhabited worlds would dash The Prophet's seeming infallibility, and harm his aura of clairvoyance, which would weaken Karghanik, and the fabric of civilization. While finding the non-human empire gave credence to the oral tradition of a lost *Book of Shatim*. Also, the presumed non-human empire now knew about humans, posing a possible threat to the security of humanity.

The Kalif or others answered those points much as he'd answered them in council the day before.

The possibility of invading the Confederation was brought up, but the Kalif didn't accept it for discussion till they were done with Alb Riisav's "snakes." Finally he pointed.

"Alb Varso, you wanted to discuss a possible conquest of the Confederation. This was brought up in council yesterday, but we didn't discuss it at any length. Would you like to address the matter now?"

The man spoke seated. "I wasn't thinking in terms of conquering the entire Confederation, Your Reverence. I mean—twenty-seven member worlds and even more subject worlds? Even with our superior weaponry, that's far too many. It would be more practical to conquer one or two of their lesser worlds. Subject worlds."

The Kalif's thick brows jumped; the exarch's military naivete had taken him by surprise. "I haven't given the matter much thought yet," he answered, "but I *am* interested. Depending on how we go about it, I think we can follow your suggestion, yet have them all."

He gave them a moment to puzzle at that. Jilsomo repressed a wry smile: *Haven't given the matter much thought yet!*

"Keep in mind," the Kalif went on, "that I'm speaking offhand—thinking out loud. First let's consider their naval strength. Three years ago, according to our best information, they had between seven and ten battle cruisers and fifteen or twenty of what they call frigates, apparently similar in function to light cruisers. As far as fighting vessels are concerned, that's all. Remember, the Confederation worlds have no navies of their own; only their central government has warships. They are a people whose wars have been minor, and fought almost entirely on the surfaces of tributary planets. It seems their major worlds have not fought each other for a very long time. Also, at any one time, most of their fleet is stationed near or on their central world, a planet they call Iryala. Other units are visiting other planets, generally singly, or hunting smugglers; things of that sort.

"Of course, the Confederation may well have begun work on enlarging their fleet since the Klestron incursion. I'd expect them to. Our information, though, is that they've had no active program of building warships for a long time, so it's unlikely that they started with significant naval shipyards and armories. It will take time for them to make major progress toward a powerful fleet, time we mustn't give them. If, in fact, we're going to invade.

"Now suppose we capture a single system, the system of one of their lesser worlds. Presumably we'd start with just one in any case. Should we send a force we consider sufficient to take and hopefully protect just one? Or as powerful a force as we can?

"Suppose we send half our imperial navy: four battle cruisers and ten light cruisers, along with troopships and supply ships, and then pause for a year or so to consolidate our control and organize our new possession. Let's say we also deploy a defensive pattern of T-bots in the surrounds.

"Meanwhile, the Confederation would have built new shipyards and be adding to its fleet, perhaps significantly improving its weaponry at the same time. When they were ready, they'd strike to recover their lost planet. Logical? And their lines of supply and reinforcement would be far shorter than ours. *Far* shorter. Depending on how great our advantage in weaponry actually is, if their strategy and tactics were good enough, they might hound us and drive us out."

He paused. No one seemed inclined to break in.

"On the other hand, suppose we attack with a maximum force: most of the imperial fleet plus most of the sultanic fleets. And assault their throne world, a planet named Iryala, catching the main part of their fleet there and destroying it. Iryala is their only world with facilities for building hyperspace ships. That monopoly is the key to Iryala's imperial dominance, as it is to ours, so they're unlikely to change it.

"Therefore, if we should capture Iryala, and destroy or decimate the warships stationed in her system, it would break their ability to do anything serious about our conquest."

The Kalif paused, his attention on their faces, their reactions. He had their attention. Not their agreement, necessarily, but their attention. "As I said, I'm speaking offhand, and without extensive training in naval warfare. But that could be the broad strategy.

"Also, Iryala is, or was, the only Confederation world equipped and allowed to manufacture major munitions. Thus any surviving remnants of their fleet could operate only until their ordnance was exhausted. We could go to whatever Confederation world we wished, concentrate our strength there, and capture it. Possibly we could rule the entire Confederation through the existing bureaucracy. If not, then over a period of time, perhaps a century, we could conquer it planet by planet."

He looked the exarchs over again and found no fidgeting, no suppressed arguments awaiting the floor. He continued:

"The scenario I just outlined is based on one main assumption: that our space weaponry is much superior to theirs. There is no doubt that ours is at least somewhat superior, and probably substantially so. In particular, it seems almost certain that they have no energy shields, and that by itself would give us a great, a decisive advantage.

"With this as a background, who has questions or comments? Alb Varso?"

Varso stood. He was a smallish, wiry man with the appearance of considerable energy. "Your Reverence, have you given thought to how the empire might rule such conquered worlds? Conquer them perhaps, but *rule* them? They'd be something like three years distant by hyperspace. It would take four years or more simply to complete an exchange of messages by pod!"

The Kalif nodded. "This would have to be worked out in detail, in advance. It might be an autonomous region, governed for the empire in the name of Kargh, perhaps by a governor general. Karghanik would be the tie; Karghanik and the tradition of the colonists' home worlds. Obviously we couldn't actually administer them from here."

Alb Tariil Ramataloku's hand took the Kalif's attention. Tariil's opening words came as they often did, with a hint of distaste that he didn't realize showed: He was as strong a traditionalist as any, yet it was difficult for him to voice the honorific. "Your Reverence," he said, "the principal advantages to such conquest would be plunder at first, and colonization and trade afterward. Trade on a basis favorable to us. Plunder, of course, could be selective, and no doubt quite valuable. But it could not continue; when the conquest was completed, our occupation force would have to institute rational and orderly management, and that would be the end of plundering. But trade on terms too unequal would be against the teaching of The Prophet, while a fair exchange over such a distance might not be profitable."

Around the table, a number of heads nodded in agreement.

"Nor could we expect great profit in taxes over such a distance, if the colonies are autonomous. The taxes would go mostly to support our governors there, and the necessary bureaucracy and occupation forces we'd have to maintain."

Tariil paused, his wide mouth clamped for a moment as he let his argument sink in. "I do not think such a venture will be profitable," he finished. "Even assuming its success, I believe we'll regret such an invasion if we undertake it."

The Kalif had not sat down, and when Tariil had finished speaking, he replied, "I'm glad you stressed *selective* plundering. Which implies the organized and controlled removal of selected, high-value goods. To permit indiscriminate looting would make the people there much more difficult to govern, I do not doubt, and cause no end of trouble.

"But I consider plunder an unimportant part of the possible value of conquest there. In fact, it might be well to prohibit plundering. As for trade, it might prove more significant than you think. To be sure, in the six years needed for a single round trip, the same cargo ship could make twenty round trips between here and Veeth-voktos, or ninety between here and Klestron. But there may be cargoes available there which are still well worth hauling. I'm not speaking of bulk cargoes, obviously.

"Still, such a conquest would be expensive. The best reasons I can see for the effort and resources it would take are not economic. Consider the reasons that Rashti had in sending out his expedition: namely to find a new world to which the restless and discontented could go. And a place to which restless or discontented *minds* could direct their attention."

He stopped, his expression thoughtful, his attention seeming inward for the moment.

"And there is one final reason. The most important." Again he stopped, drawing out their attention. "In Chapter Twenty-seven of *The Book*, The Prophet wrote: 'The believer shall make known to the unbeliever the words and principles and laws of Kargh, and shall strive always to convert him to His worship.' "

With that the Kalif stopped and sat down, not making the obvious connection, simply leaving them with the words of The Prophet, and moved the session to other matters. But their discussions were less energetic than usual, as if they found it difficult to concentrate on other subjects, and he adjourned the meeting early.

The Kalif sipped an after-supper drink with Jilsomo on an open porch. It was dusk. There'd been a shower an hour earlier, a cooling rain, and low in the west, sunset gilded cloud edges.

Neither man had said anything for a time. Then Alb Jilsomo spoke. "About the possibility of invading the

Confederation: What do you feel is the likeliest prospect? That we will, or will not?"

The Kalif said nothing for another quiet minute, sipping his drink and listening to an evening bird. Finally he put down his glass and turned shadowed eyes toward the exarch, speaking softly.

"I say this with all honesty: We have no real choice. When Rashti's flotilla returned, the die was cast. The news is out, and the empire, the Church, the several estates can never be the same. Whatever we do. And if we do not invade, within a generation, two at most, there will be turmoil and strife on the eleven worlds that will lead to darkness. A darkness that may be a long time lifting.

"And if we do not invade soon, any later invasion will be doomed to fail. For they know about us now, out there, and they'll hardly be sitting still. They have many more worlds than we do. Even if they're less populous singly, as apparently they are, in total they're bound to hold far more people than ours."

He directed his gaze across the garden, raised his glass and sipped once more.

"If we invade promptly," Alb Jilsomo murmured, "say within three years, do you feel we can overcome them?"

Again the Kalif answered slowly, still gazing across the garden in the dusk. "I have little doubt we can. No, the difficult battles won't be fought in space." He sipped again. "The Diet convenes at the beginning of next month. That's where the important battles will be fought."

He turned to look at Jilsomo again. "Which should be no surprise to you. My friend, I'm going to depend on your good sense and your ability to bring factions together. It won't be easy, only very, very important. An importance we shall not stress unless we have to."

Ten

The hovercar stopped in front of an apartment building, a building luxurious but not ultra. Her husband's
town place; he'd shown it to her two days after their
wedding, and made love to her there. Only four days ago.

He was handsome, romantic, and his family was among
the oldest and best, but it hadn't occurred to her to question the anonymous call she'd gotten that morning. A call
telling her about a mistress he kept in town. Although
she hadn't suspected, it struck her instantly as true, and
she was nineteen years old, and impulsive.

Her chauffeur held the door for her, and Leolani
Reenoveseekti-Thoglakaveera got out. "Wait for me
here!" she snapped; the man acknowledged the order
and got back in. Her walk, as she strode through the
entryway, was not her usual, ladylike gait. The receptionist recognized her, and the security guard let her
pass without a word; her obvious rank and equally obvious anger discouraged interference.

At the door of her husband's fifth-floor apartment,
she pressed her palm to the security panel. It knew
her and opened, and grim-faced she entered. Furled
umbrella tightly gripped, she looked in every room,
the closets, the large shower, and found no one. The
colonel was lucky; the umbrella was armed, and she'd

triggered its sharp, four-inch, double-edged blade before entering.

She took several deep breaths, then retracted it. Of course, she told herself, he'd be with his doxy; she'd catch him there. She keyed reception on the living room commset.

"This is Lady Reenoveseekti-Thoglakaveera," she said. "In what apartment is the alien woman?" . . .

"Do not tell *me* you can't give me that information! I'm not just the wife of an adulterous colonel! My father is the Archprelate of Khaloom! I'll have you—" . . .

"Apartment 712. Thank you. Do not call there to warn him. If you do, you'll discover what real trouble is!"

She switched off, and brandishing her umbrella, left the apartment, finding 712 like a ball bearing finds a large electromagnet. At the door she triggered her umbrella blade again and rapped sharply with the handle, then waited a few seconds. The door opened. The young woman who stood there seemed neither eager, coy, nor playful. Clearly though, she'd expected someone else, and her demeanor shifted to uncertainty. "May I help you?" she asked politely.

In spite of her anger, Leolani was startled at how lovely the woman was. And how tall, mostly because her legs were long. As tall as her tall husband. Scowling, she refocused herself. "I am Leolani!" she announced.

Obviously the name meant nothing to the alien woman, though the conspicuous anger worried her. "You'd better let me come in," Leolani said. Despite her scowl, it was more a statement of fact than threat. The woman stepped back, and Leolani stepped inside. "I am looking for my husband."

There was another moment of uncertainty, then realization. "He— There is no one here but me."

Leolani looked around, her anger somehow blunted now, but not her purpose. Besides the door she'd just entered from the corridor, the comfortable living room had two exits—a short hall at one side and a balcony door. Umbrella firmly gripped, she checked first the balcony and then, on an impulse, the dumbwaiter.

Entering the little hall, she peered into the bedroom, where all she saw was a neatly made bed. The hall closet and bath were empty, too. Nor did the bedroom closet conceal her husband, but there were men's clothes there, including a uniform with a colonel's gold hammer insignia. He wasn't under the bed, either.

The beautiful alien stood in the bedroom door, worried but not conspicuously afraid. This lack of conspicuous fear resparked Leolani's anger. "When do you expect him?"

"He called and said he had a conference this afternoon. That he would come this evening if he could."

Leolani kicked the bed, then pointed the umbrella at her. "If he was here now, I'd cut him with this. Where he'd like it least."

The woman nodded without changing her expression.

"Aren't you afraid of me? You'd better be!"

The answer was quiet, soft. "I have always been afraid, since they brought me to this world. The colonel said I was in danger of being murdered in the ministry."

Leolani's accusatory scowl became an uncertain frown. "He is married," she said. "I am his wife." Then realized she'd already said that.

"He never told me."

Leolani peered intently at her. *Of course not,* she thought. *He wouldn't; not if he didn't need to.* Her glance moved thoughtfully to her blade, and she retracted it.

"You cannot stay here," she said firmly.

The alien woman nodded, saying nothing, but now, in her eyes, Leolani did see fear. "Where were you kept before my husband brought you here? I'll take you back."

"I was kept in the ministry. They have rooms there for prisoners. With spy monitors. Men watched me through them; the colonel told me so. They watched when I undressed, when I bathed. He said it excited them, and he was afraid they would come and rape me. And that when they were done, they'd kill me so I couldn't identify them. Then he—did it. And brought me here."

Leolani felt a new anger building, a different anger than she'd arrived with. Veeri had victimized this woman, this girl without family to shield her. "Then you cannot go back there," she said.

The woman looked uncertain.

"What is your name?"

"Tain."

"Tain, you will come and live with me." Images began to flow for Leolani as she spoke, a stream of images. "At my father's home," she went on, and her voice slipped from stern toward earnest. "When I tell him what has happened, he will be glad for you to live with us. We can be like sisters, you and I, ride and swim together and play crossball. If Veeri dares come there, I'll have him sent away. I'll have the dogs set on him if necessary. And when you feel ready, there will be parties, and we will find a husband for you. An honorable one!"

She frowned. Tain had begun to cry silently, tears rolling down her cheeks. "Aren't you willing? Surely you don't love that scum!"

The blonde head shook, the tears flowed faster, and Leolani realized that Tain was unable to speak. She went to her, embraced her, her own eyes filling. "You don't need to talk now. Is there anything here you want to take with you? Show me."

Again the head shook.

"Then come, Tain. An hour from now you'll have a new room, much prettier than this, in the country. I'll have my seamstress measure you for new clothes; we'll pick the patterns together."

They left the apartment. It seemed to Leolani that it would do Tain good to break down and cry hard, to let it all out and sob and wail, but apparently she couldn't, though the tears flowed copiously. Grimly the colonel's bride triggered her blade again as they walked down the hall, hoping her husband would appear. He didn't.

Eleven

In accordance with protocol for receiving a sultan's envoy on business, the Kalif sat crownless in his receiving chamber, wearing a formal robe, and on his head, the simple pillbox cap of an exarch. The robe, however, was carmine instead of exarch-white. Across his desk sat the envoy from Sultan Rashti, along with the Klestronu Ambassador to the Court of the Kalif. The Kalif's nuncio to the sultan's court had arrived with them, and sat a bit apart.

Like the Kalif, Alb Jilsomo Savbatso sat facing the three diplomats, but well to one side, silent, easy to forget despite his bulk.

The Kalif was looking at a brief, a list of persons, each entry with up to a page of particulars. Occasionally he nodded thoughtfully; at length he looked up at the Klestronu envoy.

"This Lady Reenoveseekti-Thoglakaveera—why is she on the list? There was no debrief on her, and nothing significant on this." He flicked the sheaf of papers he held. "Except that she's the colonel's wife."

"She was not on the expedition, Your Reverence. That's why there is no debrief."

The Kalif frowned. "I have no objection to her accompanying her husband to Varatos, but unless she

71

has information that may be useful, she shouldn't be on this list. Does she? Have such information?"

"Your Reverence, Lady Reenoveseekti-Thoglaka-veera has become the friend and confidant of the Confederation prisoner. The sultan thought it possible that she might have gained some insights from their conversations."

The Kalif frowned and flicked the brief again. "It doesn't say that here. Why not?"

"Your Reverence, I do not know."

"Hmh!" He held the envoy's eyes for a moment, and it seemed to him the man did know, or at least suspected. He wouldn't press him about it, though, not now anyway. Perhaps after he'd questioned the informants. He recalled there being an Archprelate Reenoveseekti on Klestron, and a Great Noble named Thoglakaveera, both politically prominent, though he knew next to nothing about either man. Including their relationships, if any, to the colonel and his wife; it seemed likely there were some. Perhaps the sultan's reasons had to do with Klestronu politics.

The Kalif's attention returned to the list of witnesses the sultan had sent him—four men and the female prisoner. Plus the Klestronu noblewoman. The men had been debriefed on the expedition, and the debriefs sent ahead by pod. He'd reviewed them in detail. He'd also reviewed what SUMBAA had made of those debriefs, as well as the relevant content of the flagship's DAAS, so he didn't really expect to get many new facts from these people. But there was the matter of reading their emotions, their feelings about the Confederation, its people and its soldiers. Chodrisei Biilathkamoro had long been able to read what moved behind a person's eyes, if not specifically, at least the presence of something. It had been part of his operating kit from his early teens as a "dog," a first-year cadet at the Binoon Academy. It was also a skill one wouldn't find in an artificial intelligence, he was sure. Not even in a SUMBAA.

His eyes returned to the envoy. "I take it your charges are comfortably installed in our guesthouse?"

"Yes, Your Reverence."

"And they were segregated on the trip from Klestron, as I instructed?"

"They were, Your Reverence, and they were left unbriefed, also as you instructed. In fact, the sultan sent them over in stasis chambers. Thus they've had no opportunity to discuss matters with each other, except possibly before you called for them. Your steward has sequestered them in separate suites, where they receive no visitors except servants; they do not even see each other."

"Even the colonel and his lady are segregated?"

The envoy's eyes told the Kalif that something was indeed wrong there. "That is correct, Your Reverence."

"Hmm. I suppose I'd better start then. Our guests will hardly be enjoying their enforced solitude."

"Presumably not, Your Reverence."

The Kalif pursed his lips thoughtfully. "I'll see Lord Tarimenloku this afternoon. At one P.M. Lord Saadhrambacoora can be next, and after him— After him, Commander Ralankoor. Probably the others will have to wait till tomorrow or later."

He looked at his nuncio then. "Meanwhile, Alb Taamos, I would speak with you privately."

Before the Kalif retired that night, he'd questioned not only Tarimenloku, Saadhrambacoora, and Lieutenant Commander Ralankoor, but also Colonel Thoglakaveera. Saadhrambacoora—until recently General Saadhrambacoora—had nothing new to say. He was a husk, his dignity broken by the enemy and the pieces stripped away by a court martial. That the enemy had broken him, and the way they'd broken him, was informative in itself. They were a hard people in the Confederation; hard and clever, and seemingly perceptive.

Tarimenloku, who'd been a brevet admiral and the expedition's commodore, had not come away much better. He'd said frankly that he'd expected execution on his return. And if Gorsu Areknosaamos were still Kalif, the ex-admiral's expectations would no doubt have been realized. Quite possibly at home by Sultan Rashti, who'd have needed to cover his own buttocks. Otherwise by Gorsu himself, who'd no doubt have made it more painful.

Each was ruined, naturally: discharged as unfit, and stripped of his honors, living on as an embarrassment and reproach to his family.

Commander Ralankoor had been more fortunate, though it had been his action that had cost the female prisoner her memory, and the empire her information. Instead of a court martial, he'd undergone a simple board of review, which had failed to agree on a recommendation. Rashti had not even reprimanded him, at least not in writing. Probably in part because the man was gentry, not noble, and the sultan had been pushing gentry into positions of rank. And in part because the fiasco with the prisoner had been recorded on audio cube, with the commodore himself ordering the crucial act. With that order, the commodore had bypassed Ralankoor's proper authority, and as it was not a combat situation, Ralankoor could have queried it on the spot without prejudice. Or rather, without formal prejudice. He'd declined to take the risk, as would most officers.

Commander Ralankoor had proven more interesting than the two ex-senior officers. An earnest, rather angular man, Ralankoor had been the flagship's chief intelligence officer. During the months that Klestronu marines had occupied the small inhabited region of the minor Confederation trade world, Commander Ralankoor had held half a dozen civilian officials prisoner on the ship, interrogating them under instrumentation. His questioning, exhaustive and quite skilled, had provided most of their information on the Confederation. Information that was abundant and in part even precise, where it regarded Confederation government, society, and economics, but disappointingly general and in part inconsistent on military strength and weaponry.

As part of his later interrogations, Ralankoor had read

to the captive officials a description of weapons and tactics used by Confederation forces on the planet. Read it to each of them separately while they were under instrumentation. Most had registered mild surprise. He'd then read to them descriptions of the fighting qualities of those forces, and they'd been uniformly impressed; two had even registered as skeptical on the instruments. From this it had been reasonably assumed that the captives' knowledge of Confederation military strength was even poorer than their earlier vagueness had suggested.

It was the skepticism of two Terfreyan officials that sparked the Kalif's interest. And under his questioning, the commander said something that had not been noted before: The officials' responses could very well be taken as evidence that the troops and weapons faced by the marines on Terfreya *were markedly better than the Confederation norm.*

The previous evaluation of the Confederation's strength had been that while their military technology might be generally inferior, their fighting qualities were superb. When in fact, there was reason to suspect that their fighting qualities overall might be distinctly poorer than those observed on Terfreya.

Admittedly that was speculation, but it was logical and informed speculation. And to the Kalif, it smelled like the truth.

As for Colonel Thoglakaveera— The nuncio had told the Kalif what the Klestronu envoy had avoided talking about: The colonel had apparently made the female prisoner his mist·ess, after getting her released from the detention section of the Ministry of Armed Forces. His family's prominence had provided the necessary leverage.

Keeping a mistress was not terribly prejudicial; on some worlds, Klestron one of them, the practice was said to be widespread and increasing, a symptom of social decay. As families of gentry and the lesser nobility fell on hard times, ambitious daughters were tempted to accommodate predatory males who had abundant money.

And the colonel at least had the excuse that the prisoner was uncommonly beautiful. But to take a mistress within days after one's wedding? And to the daughter of an archprelate! Especially the archprelate who was the likely successor to an elderly sultan. The colonel obviously lacked good judgment.

The story had it that his brashness had offended people in the Ministry. And apparently one of them, probably someone in intelligence, had located his love-nest and gotten the story to the colonel's bride. Who then had stormed off in hopes of catching him with his paramour. But all she found was the alien mistress, and somehow—one could wish to have overheard the conversation—somehow the two had become friends! With the mistress then becoming the archprelate's houseguest!

The Kalif was seldom surprised at the things people did, but he'd been astonished and somehow amused at this one.

Prior to his sexual fiasco, the colonel had seemed likely to do very well indeed. For sound political reasons; his father was Leader of the House of Nobles on Klestron. And with the rationale that the young officer's performance on the expedition had been very creditable, Rashti had promoted him two ranks, from major to brevet colonel, and appointed him Vice Minister of Armed Forces.

With a surge of ambition, the handsome, dashing young vice minister had then come up with a brilliant plan: In addition to being the son of the Leader of the House of Nobles, he would become the son-in-law of the Archprelate of Khaloom, who was secretary of the Synod of Archprelates and second only to the sultan himself in the Klestronu Prelacy! The young colonel would then be in with both of the major power factions on Klestron.

So he'd paid court to the archprelate's youngest daughter and swept her off her feet.

The rest, of course, was comic opera, and the colonel's future was past. Thus said the nuncio. But if Sultan Rashti had seen humor in it, it hadn't been apparent; rumor had it that he'd used language unbecoming a prelate. In an attempt to satisfy the Archprelate of Khaloom without unduly antagonizing the Leader of the House of Nobles, Rashti had discontinued the post of vice minister, at the same time naming the young colonel his special military attache on Varatos. The post was without precedent or need. Formally it could be looked at as a horizontal transfer, but in this case it was a rebuff, and it would get the colonel off Klestron.

His off-world posting would also give his bride grounds for a legal separation, something hard to come by. When their interrogation by the Kalif was finished, the colonel would have to stay on Varatos as a highly paid ornament in the Klestronu embassy, or resign the position, no doubt the best he'd ever be offered. While presumably his wife would return to Klestron, there to petition the sultan for separation. Which undoubtedly he would grant.

In interviewing the colonel, the Kalif had brought up none of this, and the colonel, he was sure, didn't suspect that he knew. Thoglakaveera had been the brigade's intelligence chief on the alien world, and been part of the fighting when Confederation troops had assaulted the headquarters base there. The Kalif had restricted his questions to what the colonel might have learned about the people they'd fought. The answers reflected reasonable military competence, but to the Kalif's ears they had too much "me" and "I," emphasizing the colonel as the man who, at the end, had kept things from coming apart.

Of course, the ex-admiral's report had already given him credit for that, as had the ex-general's debrief; Colonel Thoglakaveera had in fact taken over a leaderless brigade and pulled it together. So he seemed not a liar, but simply an ambitious self puffer.

One thing the Kalif found particularly interesting:

The ex-general, and to a lesser degree the ex-commodore, clearly communicated a sense of the Confederation cadets and soldiers as being preternaturally clever; almost diabolical. The colonel, on the other hand, considered them simply skilled, tough, and unorthodox.

The colonel hadn't mentioned the prisoner, and the Kalif hadn't brought the subject up. He looked forward to questioning her, though, the next morning. He envisioned her as a cunning and manipulative survivor.

As usual, the Kalif rose early to drill at swords with a seasoned guard sergeant of outstanding skill. Forty minutes of that and it was time for a brief massage, a bath, and breakfast. Now, in informal red cape over white hose and blouse, he sat in his receiving chamber.

There were three ways of questioning people. Four, if one counted the tortures his predecessor had occasionally used. If deceit or other difficulties were anticipated, there was interrogation with painless instrumentation that monitored physiological reactions; these indicated well-defined psychological responses, and guided the interrogator's further questions. Or one could simply take a stern judicial attitude, sitting in a severe hearing room flanked by grim-faced guards; that worked marvelously with some, and was quick.

In most cases, the Kalif preferred a friendly approach. Not letting them forget that he was the Kalif, of course, but the Kalif as spiritual father, putting them at trust if possible. That's how he'd questioned yesterday's informants; it was how he would question the female prisoner from the Confederation. Her amnesia had been accounted genuine by Klestronu Intelligence and by SUMBAA, and it was hardly possible she could have fooled them with an act; surely not their instruments. So he didn't expect her to remember more for him than she had for them, but he might gain some insights into the Confederation psyche.

At any rate he was curious. When captured, she'd been in uniform, on the battlefield, and therefore presumably a soldier. Considering how she'd tricked her interrogators aboard ship, and later turned matters around with the colonel's angry bride, she must have been a very clever soldier.

The commset in his chair arm warbled softly, and he spoke to it. "Your Reverence," it replied, "Tain Faronya, the Confederation prisoner, is here with her guard."

He thought for just a moment before answering. "Send her in alone. When I tell you. Her guard will wait with you. When she's in, tell him you'll be monitoring, and that you'll let him know when he's wanted." He turned to his own guard then. "Mondar, station yourself in the rear hall, outside the door. I'll be all right." Watching the guard leave, he found himself touching the pistol beneath his left arm, concealed there by his cape, reminding himself that she was a soldier, even if unarmed. The guard, he noted, left the door ajar. Jilsomo was still there, in a rear corner of the room, as on the day before; she might never notice him until she turned to leave. The Kalif spoke to his commset again. "Send her in," he said.

The prisoner entered, and even forewarned, he was surprised at her beauty. For just a moment it jarred him out of his normal self-possession. He gathered his wits and spoke. "Well, Tain, I've looked forward to talking with you." He gestured at a comfortable chair facing his from six feet away. "Be seated, if you please."

She lowered herself with unconscious grace. She wore pantaloons gathered at the ankles, and a loose blouse, both light blue, in what was probably the latest Klestronu style. Both were clearly expensive, purchased for her by the colonel, he thought. Or no, more likely by the colonel's rebellious bride. The colonel would have bought clothing more revealing of her form. Which the Kalif suspected was excellent despite her height.

She was as tall as he, her limbs long, her chest not flat. Her hands were large and strong-looking, but feminine nonetheless. Her eyebrows were slender by any standards the Kalif knew, yet seemed unplucked. Her hair was the color of palest honey, and her eyes—a violet blue! All in all the most strikingly aesthetic combination he'd ever seen, and suddenly he could understand the young colonel's reckless decision.

He was certain of one thing at once: She had not been a soldier, regardless of uniform, regardless of having been captured on the battlefield. He'd been around marines and soldiers all his life, and while none of them had been female, he had no doubt at all what a female soldier would be like. That was not the conclusive point, though, neither that nor her having been in uniform. Beyond either of those, a woman this lovely would not have been a soldier. She'd have been taken to wife by some great noble, and cared for, cherished.

But finally and conclusively, behind those eyes there dwelt no soldier. That was the surest evidence. Not even a captain's yeoman aboard some man-of-war. Nor a schemer; that surprised the Kalif as much as her beauty. Behind those eyes was an innocent child.

"I've heard a lot about you," he said, and she answered nothing. Of course, he thought. She knew nothing to say. "I'm told you've lost your memory," he went on.

"Yes, sir."

"How do you like what you've seen of this world?"

"I've seen very little of it, sir. But what I've seen is beautiful—the buildings, the gardens . . ."

His gaze had caught an unspoken addition behind the violet eyes. "The buildings and gardens," he said. "And what else? You almost said something else."

She looked down at her hands on her lap. "Your cape, sir. It is beautiful, too."

Despite all logic, her comment pleased him. "Ah! Thank you. I'm glad you like it. I wear it by virtue of my office; I'm the Kalif, you know."

"A man told me that, the man who brought me here. He said he was taking me to see the Kalif."

He smiled. "And what did you think the Kalif would be like?"

She blushed slightly. "Sir, I had no idea. Someone important, I supposed, like the sultan."

He'd known that an effort had been made to keep her ignorant of things here, but still her answer surprised him. "When DAAS taught you to speak our language," he said, "did you learn the word *emperor?*"

"Yes, sir."

"Good. Kalif is another word for emperor. Long ago, the eleven worlds were ruled by an emperor. Then the throne was given to the Kalif, and Kalif and emperor have been one ever since, but called simply Kalif."

He gazed at her for several seconds before speaking further. "Tain, we want to find your memory for you. We have an artificial intelligence, SUMBAA, who may be able to help. I know you've already spoken with the SUMBAA on Klestron, but perhaps our's here can help where their's did not."

She nodded, saying nothing.

"Meanwhile, I'll have you taken back to your suite. Perhaps we'll talk again." He spoke to his commset. "Partiil, send in the young lady's guide."

When her guide had led her away, the Kalif looked at his lieutenant, whom she'd seemingly never noticed. "What do you think of her, Jilsomo?"

"Aside from her obvious and remarkable beauty? Your Reverence, I doubt she was a soldier."

The Kalif's eyebrows shot up. "Really? That makes two of us. Peculiar that everyone else assumed she was. I suppose it was her uniform. And she *was* captured on a battlefield. They didn't look further than that.

"What do you think the odds are that we'll learn anything of value from her?"

"I do not wager, Your Reverence. But if I had to, my bet would be that she wouldn't remember."

"I'd bet that you're right, Jilsomo," the Kalif said. "And that is a pity, for her as well as us."

Later, eating a solitary lunch, the Kalif found Tain Faronya on his mind again. He'd never been a man with much attention on women. As a bachelor marine captain, he'd kept a mistress for a time, a practice tolerated in the military if carried on discreetly by a bachelor. She'd been a very accomplished girl whom he'd enjoyed considerably, and who'd taught him more than a little. But as an ambitious young officer, he'd found her a distraction, besides which, she'd become a bit demanding. Or perhaps demanding wasn't the word; she'd assumed certain things, expected certain things. Nothing unreasonable; he'd recognized that at the time. But after a bit he'd discontinued the relationship, and had felt no need to replace her.

Later he'd had a few liaisons, then had received his appointment to the Prelacy. Since then, somewhat to his surprise, the professional challenges had sufficed.

This Tain Faronya, though— She was so *damned* lovely! If it were practical . . . But it wasn't. The man who could least get away with having a mistress was the Kalif. Less, even, than an exarch could. Of course, most exarchs were married; married and well beyond youth. In addition, a Kalif could marry only a virgin, a woman whose reputation was unspotted. Absolutely not some other man's ex-mistress.

A flash of animosity startled a low whistle out of him: for just a moment he'd hated Veeri Thoglakaveera for what he'd done! A sign, he thought, of how irrational a man could be, even himself, when influenced by a woman.

He wondered if he'd regret having seen her. Perhaps for a day or two, he told himself. He'd put someone else—Jilsomo—in charge of her interrogation by SUMBAA, and avoid seeing her again. He'd tell Jilsomo not to bother him with any problems about her, and soon other things would preempt his mind.

This afternoon there'd be Leolani, the colonel's wife, to see and question. Initially, he hadn't intended to see her; there'd seemed no point to it. What could she have learned from the female prisoner through casual conversation that SUMBAA and instrumented interrogation had not? But before lunch he'd decided he might as well. It could do no harm, and after all, Rashti had thought it worthwhile to send her. He'd see how it went; perhaps he'd be surprised.

The female prisoner was on Jilsomo Savbatso's mind at lunch, too, a lunch considerably larger and more epicurean than the Kalif's soldierly meal. *She's like one of Yogandharaya's angels*, he told himself. *It's almost as if he'd used her for a model.*

The exarch seldom thought about women. For one thing, he found strong satisfactions in his profession and its challenges—his profession and the best foods. Always had. Another reason was that, to the extent he felt sexually attracted to anyone, it was and had always been to men. Notably, these past five years, to Coso Biilathkamoro, first as a junior prelate on staff, later as Kalif.

Conveniently, these attractions had never been strong, and he'd felt no urge to pursue them. Nor at his age and condition did he expect to. Jilsomo had never indicated his predilections to anyone, either as boy or man. And Coso, alert and perceptive as he was, had never suspected, nor ever would. Jilsomo was sure of that.

But the female prisoner . . . It seemed to him that having seen her, he could understand, a little, what other men felt when they found a woman desirable. And if she made him desire to touch her, see her, perhaps do more . . .

It made him worry about the Kalif.

Twelve

The Kalif watched as Leolani Thoglakaveera stepped into the room. For a moment her uncertain eyes were on him. Then, walking toward the chair obviously meant for her, she glanced around, finding no one else.

He'd sent out not only his guard but Jilsomo as well, a last-moment act he couldn't have explained, except that it might help her speak more freely.

She stopped beside the chair, and he gestured. "Please be seated, Lady Thoglakaveera."

He watched her sit down, which she did as any well-trained aristocratic young woman might have: with the grace of a practiced act, but without the deeper grace of the accomplished dancer or gymnast. She was pretty, and more. Even ill-at-ease as she was, he sensed an obvious strength of character that was more than will-fulness and the assurance that so often comes with noble birth and nurture. And he was confident that, unlike many other aristocratic young women of nine-teen years, she could talk intelligently about things of relevance.

The colonel chose better than he may have realized, the Kalif told himself, *and threw away more than he thought with his lust.*

"Are you comfortable?" he asked.

"Yes, Your Reverence."

"Good. I understand you're a friend of the alien woman, Tain Faronya, who was brought to Klestron by Sultan Rashti's exploration force. Is that true?"

"Yes, Your Reverence."

"We suspect that her lost memories may include some of considerable interest and importance to Klestron and the Empire. It may be that these memories are lost irrevocably, but perhaps they're not."

He paused, waiting for whatever she might say. Realizing this, she replied, "I would hope they are not, Your Reverence. As it is, she is—incomplete."

The description took him by surprise, though it seemed highly apropos. "Have you heard her say anything that suggests some old memory not far beneath the surface of her mind?"

Leolani focused inward for a moment, considering, then shook her head. "Nothing that seemed that way to me, Your Reverence."

The Kalif focused inward, too. And found exactly what he was going to say next, though not why. "Have you heard the rumors about her and your husband?"

Her eyes sharpened, sparked. "They are not rumors, Your Reverence."

"You mean he did, actually, take an apartment for her and keep her there?"

She nodded once, sharply.

"And you would like to have your husband's love again?"

She blazed. "I have never had his love! No one has. Not me, not Tain. To him, she was something to use. Not some*one*; some*thing*. And vulnerable, having been wrested from her family. He took her from the ministry to bed her, nothing more. Two days before our wedding! I want nothing further to do with him." She paused, suppressing her fire. "I hope you will grant me a bill of divorcement. It is within your power."

Her outburst stopped him for a long moment. "Your feelings and your wish are both understandable," he said, then paused again. "And you're not angry at the woman Tain?"

Leolani shook her head. "She is blameless in this. Unless you wish to fault her for her beauty. In the room where she was kept in the Ministry, cameras were concealed, and men of the intelligence division would gather in the monitor room to watch her. Watch her disrobe, dance, bathe! And lusted for her. Disgusting men! Then, one night, Veeri disabled the monitors for her room and went there and told her that other men were going to come and rape and kill her if she didn't let him take her away. She was so frightened then that when he threw her down on her bed, she didn't resist."

Leolani's eyes blazed at the Kalif. "When she told me, her tears flowed like rivers, but she didn't sob. She was too deeply hurt. If he had been there then, and if I'd had a gun, I'd have killed him! Not for his treachery to me, but for what he did to her!"

The Kalif nodded, impressed by the young noblewoman's anger. And disappointed. He realized now what he'd hoped—that somehow the colonel hadn't gotten around to bedding the prisoner, that she might still be a virgin, eligible to be the wife of a Kalif. It was a strange realization, objective, as if it applied to someone else and not himself. "I appreciate your feelings," he said. "So she told you all this and you took her home with you. To your father's home, that is."

"She told me enough of it. Some she told me only afterward."

"And you believed her."

"I did! She is guileless! And when Veeri tried to talk me into coming back to him, and I accused him, he didn't deny it. He told me he couldn't help himself, that no healthy man could have. He expected me to *forgive* him!

"If it had been some willing doxy, perhaps I could have, though I doubt it. But to take her the way he did, using fear and humiliation! That was vile!"

"Unarguably. Well. Have you talked about this with anyone? Other than the colonel and Tain?"

She darkened. "No one. Oh, enough to my father that he understands why I left my husband."

The Kalif straightened. "Good. Continue your silence. Above all, do not tell the colonel of our talk. If you're patient, perhaps you'll have not only a divorce, but other satisfaction as well."

Leolani stood up, her face still darkened by her anger. "Thank you, Your Reverence. I will be both silent and patient. And hopeful."

She left then, and Coso Biilathkamoro, Kalif of the Karghanik Empire, sat wondering what in the world he was doing. Switching on the commset in his chair arm, he spoke to his secretary. "Partiil, when Lady Thoglakaveera has gone, send one of the pages to bring her husband over. I want to talk further with him."

The colonel felt quite comfortable when he sat down before the Kalif again. It seemed to him he'd said all there was to say about Terfreya and the enemy there, in his debrief and his first interrogation. Therefore it seemed possible that His Reverence had been impressed with his answers and war record, and wanted to know him better. Quite possibly with some appointment in mind.

At least that was the scenario he'd been rehearsing, walking over.

"Thank you for coming, Colonel," the Kalif said. "I have some rather different questions for you this time."

"It is my pleasure, Your Reverence."

"Good." He paused, and somehow the colonel tightened with misgiving. "You are aware, I suppose, of what The Prophet said and wrote about monogamy and the nobleman? And the treatment of women without husband or father or brothers to shield them?"

The questions hit the colonel like a sandbag.

"Yes, Your Reverence."

"I've been told that you took carnal knowledge of the prisoner, perhaps against her will."

The colonel shook his head vehemently. "That's not true, Your Reverence! On my mother's name it's not!

I did not take carnal knowledge of her, either against or with her will. I am a marine officer, a colonel, and a son of the Thoglakaveera family!"

"Ah. Then—why did you remove her from detention and set her up in an apartment?"

"Your Reverence, I—" He looked around as if for help, and saw only the fat exarch. "She was without family or even friends. Vulnerable." The colonel's mind raced; he hadn't prepared for this. "And she seemed so *innocent*," he went on, "so *tragic*." He shrugged slightly. "I suppose my feelings seem unlikely in these times, but when I saw her there in the ministry, she was as innocent as a child. Because Kargh had seen fit to erase whatever sins she had; I suppose there must have been some, at least minor ones . . ."

His words had slowed. Now he paused. "Also she's very pretty, Your Reverence, and it seemed to me that someone might take advantage of her." He spread his hands. "As you seem to believe *I* did. So I provided her with a comfortable place to live, and two loyal servants to ward her, a man and his wife of about the age her parents might be. Until my wife was able to come and take her home, and off my hands. It was nothing more than that, sir. Nothing happened between us."

There was a moment of silence between the two men. "Um. Tell me," said the Kalif, "do you believe she was chaste? Before she was brought to the empire? Might she have been raped when taken prisoner?"

"She was not raped, Your Reverence. It was I who picked her up at the field base and took her to headquarters, from where she was shuttled to the flagship. I asked her about that, when she was turned over to me at their detention module, and she told me she had not been. It is in my debrief. And there seemed nothing wrong with her memory then.

"Of course, before her capture—who knows? A physical examination might or might not shed light on that. It seems beside the point now. The Blessed Flenyaagor tells us it's the soul which bears the soil and burden of our sins. And surely her soul was purified when all memory was taken from it."

"Hmm. An interesting viewpoint, Colonel. Meanwhile, though, your action invited rumor."

"Yes it did, Your Reverence. I can see that now. And I regret it. The rumor has hurt my poor wife till she doesn't know what to believe."

"Indeed? Well. Another matter: I understand that as a marine officer you have proven skilled, and except for the matter of the alien woman, discreet. I will want to talk with you again soon."

Relieved, the colonel got to his feet and bowed. "It will be my pleasure, of course."

When the colonel was gone, Jilsomo grunted. "Your Reverence, as a rule you do not like unasked-for advice."

The Kalif smiled. "True. But if you're patient, I will ask. What do you think of our good colonel?"

"Much as you do, I suspect, even though he did swear by his mother's name. I would certainly doubt his claimed altruism in the matter of the female prisoner. He may have been a good marine officer, but I suspect that in general he acts in his own perceived interest."

"Indeed." The Kalif got to his feet. "I need to get out in the open. Let's walk in the garden, and I'll tell you the version of the story that I have from the colonel's wife. And—I have thoughts on what to do about them—he and his wife. And the female prisoner, Tain."

Alb Jilsomo nodded soberly as he followed his Kalif through floor-length curtains and sliding glass doors into the garden. It was the season of warmest weather, but the exarch was distressed for other reasons than preferring to keep his bulk indoors where it was air-conditioned. He had a bad feeling about what the Kalif was going to say.

To start off, the Kalif recounted what Leolani had told him about the colonel and the prisoner. Jilsomo was not surprised.

"So what I think I'll do is preempt the colonel for the imperial government. Assign him as my military specialist to the Klestronu embassy. It will be a promotion of sorts, and I'm sure Rashti will be pleased. It should remove any pressure the young man's father may be applying. And conversely his father-in-law."

"Um." Jilsomo nodded, holding his peace, waiting for what might come next. When nothing did, he asked his question: "And the *purpose* of preempting him, Your Reverence?"

Instead of answering, the Kalif went on. "And then, instead of granting his wife the divorce she wants, I'll annul the marriage."

"Annul it? That would make it as if it had never been. The grounds for annulment are, um, somewhat more restricted than the grounds for divorce."

"Ah! But his inability to consummate the marriage in bed is all the grounds I need."

The exarch stood dumbfounded. "What makes you think he failed to consummate it?"

"Presumably he did consummate it. I simply intend to say he didn't. Wasn't able to; impotent, you see. And he won't deny it—not if he has any sense at all. It's either agree or I'll charge him with malfeasance— the use of his position for gross immorality, and tampering with an intelligence source for personal benefit."

The Kalif sounded grimly pleased with himself. Jilsomo was stunned and confused. "But— Your Reverence, those actions were on Klestron. Your charges would ordinarily fall to Sultan Rashti to prosecute."

"Ah, but I have the right of preemption, when the interests of the empire are involved. And she is a potential intelligence source. Rashti won't challenge me in this."

Jilsomo said nothing; nothing came to him. Walking in the sun, he'd begun to sweat freely, and wished he were back inside. More than that, he wished he knew what this was all about—why the Kalif intended to do as he'd described.

After a few seconds the Kalif went on. "His sexual

impotency," he said, "is probably not permanent, you understand. It may well disappear within a few months, and the colonel can find another wife or mistress.

"His report on the fighting at the marine headquarters base, on the Confederation world, includes his comment that he fought hand to hand with an enemy soldier and was injured before killing the man. A report we have only from him, I might add; it may or may not be true. The injury, I've decided, was a kick in the groin, after which the colonel managed to shoot him. Before long the colonel was back aboard the troopship and in stasis, en route home. When he woke up, his ship was parked off Klestron, and very soon afterward he was courting the archdeacon's pretty daughter. They married, and then to his dismay, he discovered he was unable to carry out his husbandly duty. His bride was patient, but after several weeks, with no sign of recovery, she felt betrayed, and petitioned me for an annulment.

"I will consult with the colonel, who'll be too disheartened to oppose her request. Thus their marriage will be annuled."

The two prelates walked on a little farther, the Kalif waiting for the exarch's comment. "Your Reverence," Jilsomo said at last, "it may well work. But—why? Why this charade when you could simply grant the woman a divorce?"

"Because the colonel was impotent, he could not have fornicated with the female prisoner. Of course, it's just possible that he didn't anyway. And if he did not fornicate with her, then so far as we know, she's a virgin. And if she's a virgin . . ." The Kalif looked hard at his deputy. "If she's a virgin, then I can take her to wife."

The two men were approaching a grove of flowering vaasera when the Kalif said this, and Jilsomo, stunned, stepped aside to sit down on a cushioned marble bench in their heavy shade. The Kalif sat down beside him. "You have misgivings," he said, almost accusingly.

Jilsomo nodded. "It sounds contrived, Your Reverence. People will say you set this all up so you could marry the beautiful foreigner."

"Possibly. But I'll take care of that by waiting before arranging the marriage. Long enough that any suspicions will not seem compelling."

Jilsomo gathered his wits and looked at the situation. He was, after all, expected to advise. "Hmm. That would work, if you waited a year, say, or maybe half a year. But a few weeks won't be long enough. Someone, no doubt various someones, will say, 'Look at what the Kalif has done!' And the accusation will spread like wildfire; most people will at least wonder."

The Kalif said nothing, but his jaw was set.

"And— Forgive my saying it, Your Reverence, but you do not know the young woman."

The jaw muscles clenched, standing out like unshelled pecans.

"You're angry at me," Jilsomo said matter-of-factly.

"I'm not! . . . Yes I am. I *am* angry. I'm still a young man, thirty-six, and I have never been in love before. Now I am, and I deserve to have her. If she is willing."

He turned to face the big exarch, almost glaring. "Haven't I given the empire its best government in more than a century? That's what they say of me—the professors in the university and even some of the noble delegates. Even Tariil has said it, and he resists half the things I propose, as if I were Shatim. At least I've made a case for it, whether it's true or not. Even my opponents, most of them, will give me the benefit of that."

Jilsomo shook his head. "Your Reverence, many undoubtedly will. But others will say, 'Look! The Kalif has done a dishonest act for his personal benefit! Why can't we then?' And, 'How can he punish these others?' "

"They will get their answer," the Kalif said sharply. "I will punish corruption as harshly as ever." Chodrisei "Coso" Biilathkamoro looked challengingly at his lieutenant for a long half minute, then sagged, looked away, and spoke quietly.

"Thank you for speaking your mind, good friend. And forgive my temper. But I am going to do it. And you will back me, and see that others do.

"We fear too much what people will say. I will do it, and most of those who disbelieve me will say 'the Kalif is human, but he is a very good Kalif,' and wish me well."

Perhaps, he's right, Jilsomo thought. *Or more right than wrong. No Kalif in living memory, probably no Kalif since Papa Sambak, has ruled so well. And many people, most people, will be tolerant. But it will give his opponents in the Diet a stick to jab him with.*

"Nothing I can say will sway you then?" Jilsomo asked.

The Kalif didn't answer, and after waiting, the exarch spoke again. "Well then, you will do it. And I will back you. Because of our friendship and because you're right when you say you're the best ruler the empire has had in a long time. And if it becomes a question before the College or the Diet, I will see that others back you, too, as you said."

He paused. "Perhaps I am making too much of this. But till now . . ."

"Yes?"

"Till now your ethics in office have been unstained, and the people have had government by law. Conditions greatly to be desired and admired. And your strongest points before both the College and the Diet."

The Kalif's mouth pursed. "Good friend," he said quietly, "they haven't yet seen my strongest point."

Thirteen

The Kalif was reading a report on his screen and dictating a running commentary to his computer, when his commset interrupted him. "Your Reverence, your physician is here."

He pushed back from his desk. "Send him in." A moment later the man entered. The Kalif motioned him to a chair. "Yes, Neftha?"

"Your Reverence, the female detainee is healthy in every physical respect. And I must tell you, she is the loveliest woman I have ever seen." He raised a hand as if to ward off comment. "It's true that most of the women I examine are in their middle years or older, the wives of your exarchs, but . . ."

The Kalif cut him short. "Who were young in their turn. Yes. What else did you learn?"

"Her health is excellent. I already said that, didn't I? And her physical strength is exceptional. I have never personally examined so strong a woman."

He stopped, not meeting the Kalif's eyes, then went on. "As for the other matter— She might well make someone a very good wife." He stressed the *someone* just slightly. "But— Her hymen is not intact. Of course, that could be the result of an accident or self abuse; those things are not rare. And in the presence of such beauty, I doubt most men would object to its

94

absence. But to—some men it would disqualify her; they couldn't be sure she was a virgin. Nor can she vouch for it herself, with her memory gone."

"Surely other means exist for learning the truth of it?" the Kalif said thoughtfully. As if the report had been unexpected.

"None, Your Reverence. Not short of her recovering her memory and declaring it under instrumentation."

The Kalif sat purse-mouthed. At length he grunted. "So the examination proved neither innocence nor otherwise. Well. There was no indication of violence?"

"None, Your Reverence."

"But that means little, I suppose."

"Not on the matter of virginity, Your Reverence."

The Kalif said nothing for several seconds, then grunted. "Well. Thank you for your information, Neftha. You will, of course, keep this to yourself."

"By all means, Your Reverence. I have made a chart, but recorded only matters relevant to her actual health."

"Good. And you *do* have my appreciation. Now I have things to do."

The physician got quickly to his feet. "Of course, Your Reverence."

The Kalif watched the door close behind him, then pressed a key on his commset. "Partiil, call the guest house. Tell them to bring the female prisoner to my office. I wish to question her again." Then he remembered his boyhood, and his sister's need to prepare before she went anywhere. "In one hour," he added.

He stood as she entered. She was dressed in yellow this time, but to his untrained eyes the costume seemed otherwise similar. Lady Leolani's work, he felt sure. He'd approved her request to let Tain share her apartment and servants, and allowed them to shop escorted. Tain had no doubt caused a stir, he thought, with her face, hair, eyes, skin. Her grace. Her long legs.

"Tain," he said, "please be seated."

She sat down as gracefully as before. He repeated her name, tasting the sound of it. "Tain. That's a lovely name. And you are a very lovely woman."

He saw the flicker of fear behind her eyes. *It may take time to lose that,* he thought, and spoke on. "In most respects a Kalif is not unlike other men, a mixture of good and bad. I like to think that I am more good than bad." He smiled slightly. "Hopefully quite a bit more.

"In some respects a Kalif has more freedoms than most men, but in other matters he has the same limits. Thus he may wish to marry someone, but she may refuse him." He raised his hands slightly, spreading them. "I would like to marry you, Tain. If you are willing."

He was surprised at how easily the words came.

Her answer was low. "Your Reverence, I hardly know you."

"True. Yet you are a grown woman, and I believe that living as the guest of the Lady Leolani will not remain satisfactory indefinitely. Despite your friendship. Sooner or later you will feel constrained to take a husband."

Her eyes told him nothing. "Well. The decision is yours, and there is no need to make it now. And in any event the wedding would have to wait a few weeks. Meanwhile, I commend myself to you. I am a man of good temper, reputedly not unattractive, and with considerable resources." He gestured. "I have a comfortable home, and seasonally the freedom to travel."

He paused then as a thought came to him. "Or is there some other man you'd like to marry? Do not fear to tell me if there is."

Tain shook her head. "There isn't. Not that I know of."

Her words echoed quietly in his mind. *Not that you know of,* he thought. *Perhaps someone three hyperspace years away, or someone killed in battle. You must wonder sometimes.*

"Well then, I'll allow myself to feel optimistic. Will

you have dinner with me this evening? Among other things, I have an excellent chef."

"Yes, Your Reverence," she said quietly. Her voice showed little expression, but neither was there apathy nor resignation there. *Guarded* seemed the word. It occurred to him that considering her circumstances and all that had happened, she'd held up well. So. A strong person then, with strong character.

"Thank you, Tain. We'll eat at seven, you and I. Tell Lady Leolani that she is not to talk about it." This time his smile was bigger. "And tell her to trust me." He eyed her quizzically. "Do you feel all right about this?"

She nodded. "I do, Your Reverence."

He'd known what she'd answer, had asked only to build her assurance. "Good. But now I have work to do. The Diet will convene a week from Oneday, and I need to be ready for them."

He reached and keyed his commset as she stood up. "Partiil, Lady Tain will be leaving now."

When she'd left, it took him a minute or two to get his attention fully on his work again.

Fourteen

He had supper served on the small table he usually ate at alone. It put them closer together. His personal servant moved in and out unobtrusively and no more than necessary. The meal was not large—he made a point of eating modestly—but it was excellent.

He'd thought of having a musician there to play for them, then decided against it. With so little of her past available to her, it seemed to him she might have trouble making small talk. The presence of a third person, even a musician, could make it more difficult.

Instead he'd had a cube delivered, of beautiful or otherwise interesting places and events on Varatos. While they ate, the wall to one side took life, and seemingly depth. There were aerial views of the Great Falls of the Djosar in spring, the foot of the cataract seeming to pulse with explosions of foaming violence; a storm, with massive waves crashing against the rocks and broken cliffs off the coast of Otengwar; the Festival of The Prophet, with the streets of Ananporu brilliant with flowers and banners; a great golden rajwar with high, striped shoulders, prowling an imperial wildlife park, stalking and charging a wild bull, pouncing on it from behind, then losing its hold, to watch its would-be supper gallop off. . . .

The Kalif did his own narrative, and had the pleasure of seeing her eyes bright with interest.

She said she liked books, and he told her he'd arrange for her to browse the library of the *Sreegana*, the compound which contained the palace and various associated buildings.

After they'd eaten, he found himself being questioned. "What was your home like when you were a child?" "Did you have sisters and brothers?" "What did you do for pleasure?" He told her about his father, a prelate who, when Coso was twelve, became Archprelate of Binoon. His older brother had been in line to succeed to the Prelacy; the young Coso had been slated for the military.

He told her too about Sergeant Major Chagoorka, a retired noncom of the Imperial Marines, who'd been his principal tutor, and his favorite person after his parents. After excusing himself, the Kalif brought from his study a beautiful dagger to show her. The sergeant major had crafted it for him as a going-away present, when his fifteen-year-old charge was preparing to leave for the Binoon Academy, to prepare for marine officers school.

She examined the dagger with care and admiration. Its carefully smithed, razor-sharp blade was engraved with an unfamiliar, decorative script, while the green jade of its hand-carved haft must have cost more than a sergeant could readily afford.

Eventually the Kalif even talked about the death of his parents and older brother, in an avalanche on a mountain vacation, an accident that had put him in line for the Prelacy. He'd liked the Imperial Marines. Yet when the question came—the opportunity for the Prelacy—he'd jumped at it, somewhat to his own surprise.

The Kalif talked for an hour and a half, while Tain spoke little except to ask questions. Finally she reached across the small table and put her hand on his; his breath stopped in his throat.

"Your Reverence, this morning you asked if I would marry you. I thought about this after I left, and it seems to me that in your empire I have no future unless I marry. But I have scarcely known any men here— mainly Veeri, whom I do not like, and Leolani's father, who was preoccupied. And Sultan Rashti, who seemed kind. From today, and especially this evening, it seems that I know you better than I know any other man in your empire."

She withdrew her hand as if suddenly self-conscious.

"You have been considerate and kind. You have not tried to take advantage of your power and my lack of it. And it seems to me that I can become truly fond of you. Therefore, with a certain nervousness, I tell you yes, I'll marry you."

Chodrisei "Coso" Biilathkamoro, Kalif of the Karghanik Empire, had not rehearsed a response; somehow it hadn't occurred to him. Also, there was no feeling of relief, no surge of exultation. Simply, he got up and stepped around to her, gave her his hand and helped her to her feet. "Then," he said quietly, "let me show you a side of me that you should know."

He took her shoulders and kissed her tenderly, lingering on the lips.

"And now," he said, "you must leave. You are very beautiful, and I'm the Kalif. Thus for both of us, it's best that we not spend evenings alone together until I am your husband and you are my wife."

Fifteen

Colonel Veeri Thoglakaveera would have preferred to be at the big party that was a feature of Sixday evenings on embassy row. This Sixday it was at the Ikthvoktos embassy. Men, and women too, would no doubt come up to him, if he were there, to ask about the war—what it had been like, what the aliens were like—and that would be enjoyable. But people, at least a few, would know about his supposed impotence.

It hadn't actually been publicized, of course. Even the edict of annulment had seen print only in a volume little known outside government; he'd been assured of it. Inside government, though, there were those who would have noticed, and annulment meant, almost always, that there'd been no consummation. While there were bound to be some, some insiders, who'd heard the impotence story.

And if he was there, reminding them by his presence, people would whisper.

So he'd quietly volunteered to be duty officer for that evening. Not that a duty officer was really needed on a Sixday evening, but policy required it. He wasn't even subject to the duty. His appointment was administered by the Imperial Foreign Ministry; he was simply officed here at the Klestronu Embassy. But volunteering would earn him friends. Friends and points.

Veeri glanced at the commset on the duty desk. Just now it sat lifeless.

Three months, they'd told him! Then, if he wanted, he could resign this appointment and go back to Klestron, reactivate his commission in the marines there. They'd "fixed it up with Rashti," he'd been told.

He didn't look forward to going back. Everyone there would know—everyone who counted. Leolani would make sure of it. "He was impotent," she'd be saying.

He realized his fists were clenched, and opened them, willing his muscles to relax. The Archprelate of Khaloom had to be behind this, the archprelate and his daughter. Who'd have imagined that Leolani could be that vengeful! He'd like to corner her in a nice secluded place somewhere. He'd show her potency till she begged for mercy!

He grunted. Not likely, when you got down to it. There was nothing wrong with his potency, but he had limits, like any man.

He wished he'd never heard of Tain Faronya, that her presence in the ministry had never been mentioned, that she'd been left on Terfreya. He'd had his life perfectly set up: war hero; Vice Minister of Armed Forces; son of the Speaker of the House of Nobles; and son-in-law of the Archprelate of Khaloom, who'd be sultan when Rashti died. And a pretty, tight-ass wife.

And blown it all. Even his father was angry with him.

The commset chirped quietly, and Veeri answered. Someone calling for Cibor, who was out doing what he'd like to be doing, partying.

He'd considered applying for a commission in the Imperial Marines. Then he'd learned he'd have to go through their academy, with all that that meant in terms of underclassman humiliations, plus a three-year curriculum that looked even tougher than he'd been put through on Klestron.

So probably he would go back, back to the Klestronu Marines.

Sixteen

The Square of The Prophet had been cleared of its benches and kiosks. Its pavement had been scrubbed. Lines had been strung between the light poles that flanked it, and banners waved easily from them in a light breeze. Today would see the opening session of the Imperial Diet for the year 4724.

The square was kept mostly clear of bystanders. Eight or ten thousand of them stood bunched along the sides, controlled by lines of soldiers—elite troops of the Capital Division. Other viewers stood along the parapets of surrounding roofs, and there were soldiers there, too. Floaters with soldiers hovered silently, watchfully overhead.

The important spectators were those who filled the galleries inside the Hall of the Estates, members of the Greater Nobility. They'd arrived earlier, per protocol, and passed through unseen scanner fields to wait in air-conditioned comfort. No soldiers watched inside, only liveried guards, quiet and polite, their holstered stunners set ready on fan beam.

Horse-drawn ceremonial carriages, especially decorated for the occasion, rolled individually onto the square from the Avenue of The Prophet, to stop before the Hall's broad low stairs. Each dismounted a liveried footman from the high seat at the rear, who lowered the carriage steps and opened the door. A man or men in colorful robes stepped out, to mount the broad stairs and disappear through the building's great doorway.

Not every vehicle that drew up was ceremonial or horsedrawn. Public cabs and privileged hover cars also pulled up at the stairs. Some of the men that stepped from them wore robes of gray. They too went in.

After a bit there seemed to be an end to the arrivals. Then the gates of the Sreegana opened, and trumpeters marched out in two spaced rows, their long and gleaming trumpets upright like spears of burnished silver before their shoulders. There were eighteen of them, in white trousers and capes, and tall-plumed white helmets. They stopped, and with drilled synchrony, each row turned to face the other, forming a wide aisle.

One more trumpeter marched out then, wearing kalifal carmine, vivid red. He stopped immediately outside the gate, facing outward, raised his pennoned golden trumpet and blew a long clear note. The others raised theirs, too, and began a fanfare. Out of the gates marched the red-robed Kalif, followed by the eighteen white-robed exarchs in a slow-moving, stately column of twos. Together they crossed the wide square and mounted the broad entry stairs at the Hall of the Estates, also to disappear within.

The Diet of 4724 was about to be convened.

Seventeen

The grand reception hall in the Hall of the Estates was the largest and perhaps the most splendid hall in the empire. It was large enough that invitations were received by the titular heads of all the Great Noble Families of Varatos; the formal representatives, diplomatic, legislative, and ecclesiastic, of the other planets; and selected others.

Though they attended without their wives. The conventional view was that women, by their nature, lacked both understanding and interest in politics and government. And while exceptions were recognized, even admired, long tradition kept this an affair for men only, a time for mingling and proposing, feeling out attitudes, concurrences, dissidence, and potential alliances. It was a political game field, and most of those who came relished the game.

Dressed formally in black and white, with brilliant shoulder sashes, cummerbunds, or capelets of silver, green, gold, and indigo, nobles wandered and eddied slowly in their hundreds, along with some hundred circulating waiters who tried to see that no one lacked for drinks or hors d'oeuvres. The noble delegates, exarchs, and elders, wore their robes, light despite their fullness, and their caps, making them easily found.

By contrast, the Kalif stayed in one small, traditional

area, his carmine robe vivid and unmistakeable. On two sides of him and a double pace away stood two bodyguards, men not particularly large but hair-trigger quick, fingertips inches from clip-mounted stunners that would almost leap into their hands if need be.

And a step behind his shoulder stood Alb Jilsomo, privy to anything said to the Kalif above a whisper. It was widely understood that Jilsomo was not only the Kalif's deputy, but his heir apparent, and thus that he needed to know. Many nobles disliked the arrangement, some of them intensely, because of Jilsomo's gentry origins. The succession, however, was not in their hands; ultimately it was the business of the College. They could only hope the exarchs would recognize the proprieties.

In approaching His Reverence, there was no formal rule of precedence, but there was a certain order dictated by good sense and courtesy. Numerous delegate and non-delegate nobles would like to have the Kalif's ear for a little, and it was deemed ill-mannered to move in ahead of someone who had clear political seniority. Or to stand near enough to eavesdrop in the general babel.

Thus when the Kalif took his accustomed place, the small wiry man who first came up to him was the Leader of the Imperial House of Nobles, Lord Agros Niilagovindha.

"Good evening, Your Reverence," said Agros blandly. "Here we are with another Diet convened. Considering the rather astounding discoveries made by Rashti's expedition, I foresee a busy session."

"Hmm. It seems to me that every session's busy. But then, this is only my fourth. I'm still inexperienced."

"Perhaps. But the general view is, you've performed ably from the beginning. Tell me. What do you foresee as the main disputes in this session?"

The Kalif smiled, also blandly. "Ask me again in four months, when the session's over. By then I might have a meaningful answer for you."

"I wonder if it will be. Over in the standard time, that is."

The Kalif affected a slight frown. "I don't foresee an extension, particularly considering the agreements required. How long has it been since a Diet has been held over?"

Noble eyebrows rose, arched thickets of black above obsidian eyes. "Ah! But when is the last time an event of such moment occurred? With such significant findings! For one thing, a whole multitude of habitable and inhabited worlds!"

"True. But that is primarily a matter of religious significance. I'm sure every Estate will be interested in our decisions; the whole empire will. But it lies entirely in the domain of myself and the College of Exarchs. It's not a matter for the Diet."

"Indeed! Can it be you've overlooked certain questions?"

The Kalif's lips thinned. "I referred to the matter of worlds not accounted for in *The Book of The Prophet*—as we've known it. As for the question of possible trade—Authorization would seem to be a routine decision of the Foreign and Commerce Ministries, as guided by myself, though debate might not be inappropriate."

"Ah, Your Reverence! You're playing with me!"

"Surely not, good Agros. I respect you both as Leader of the House and as a man of honor, position, and intelligence. Is there some significance I've overlooked in this business of Sultan Rashti's?"

"Really, Your Reverence, I doubt it. With all respect, I think you're being coy with me, no doubt for good reasons. Rashti sent his little flotilla to hunt for a world to colonize. To occupy, if you will. And found more of them than he'd expected. But already occupied, unfortunately, with unenlightened humans seemingly not interested in giving them up to us. There's been talk that you might wish to invade one or more of them, and the necessary funding requires the approval of the Diet."

"Ah! As a matter of fact, the matter has been mentioned in the College. But nothing's been proposed. Perhaps next year." His tone changed then. "You've caught my interest, though. This talk among the nobles— What seems to be the gist of it? Do any of them see virtue in the idea? Perhaps more to the point, do *you* see virtue in it?"

"I suppose some do. Perhaps Fakoda and his like, who'd stand to profit richly from the preparations. As for me and most of the House, probably not one in four would vote for it. In fact, if it came down to it—if the College threatened to vote unanimously in its favor—I wouldn't be surprised if I could bring the entire House against it.

"But I cannot believe the College would be unanimous in a matter like this one."

The Kalif nodded. "Thank you, Agros, for your experienced viewpoint. If the matter comes up again in the College, I'll pass your opinion on to them."

Agros nodded, wished the Kalif good health, and left. To discuss their brief exchange with others of the House, the Kalif had no doubt.

Lord Rothka Kozkoraloku gave an impression of leanness, especially when wearing robes, an impression based on a face like an axe blade. Actually, his frame was ordinary and reasonably well fleshed, though he carried less fat than usual for a noble in his forties.

Rothka's face mirrored his character, the lines reflecting hardened attitudes, the eyes distrustful and calculating, the mouth quick to scorn. He was speaking with two nobles who were not delegates to the Diet, men representing regional affiliates of his *Land Rights Party*, when Lord Agros came up. The conversation halted.

Agros nodded acknowledgement to the two non-delegates. "Gentlemen," he said, "excuse me," then gave his attention to Rothka. "I don't believe you've paid your respects to His Reverence. But perhaps you don't intend to."

Rothka's narrow mouth pinched. "He's no true Kalif; he's a murderer and usurper, hiding behind a veneer of false legality. My respect for him is nonexistent."

Agros raised an eyebrow. "He's a big improvement over the creature he killed and replaced. Some consider that he spared us civil war; perhaps even dissolution, and the chaos that would have resulted. Admittedly that's a bit extreme, but if Gorsu had continued, or if his execution had been bungled, or the transition . . ."

Rothka did not yield his hostility. "A murderer and usurper," he repeated. "That is fact. The rest is opinion. A murder and usurper whom Kargh will punish in His own good time. And he's made that gentry, that fat Jilsomo, his deputy. If there's another regicide, we're likely to have a commoner as Kalif!"

This was leading nowhere, Agros decided, and moved to the subject he'd come to talk about. "I presume you've given thought to the Klestronu expedition and its discoveries?"

Irritation flashed behind Rothka's eyes. "Not much," he said. "We have concerns more pressing in times like these: the need to lower minimum wages for gentry; to cancel or at least revise the restrictions on off-loading unneeded peasants . . . Practical matters."

"I suppose you've heard the speculations that the Kalif will ask for a fleet and army to invade the Confederation."

"Confederation?"

"The empire that Rashti's flotilla discovered. They call it a confederation."

"What are you getting at, Agros? Say it, for Kargh's sake!"

Agros's voice became even more bland. "My good Rothka," he said mildly, "your incivility has cost you support on various occasions. If you're really interested in advancing your programs, you'd be better off cultivating your fellow delegates than antagonizing them."

Rothka's jaw clenched, and for a moment he looked

as if he might strike the smaller, older man, who
ignored it.

"If in fact the Kalif asks us to fund an invasion,"
Agros went on, "and he gets it, there'll be new and
higher taxes to pay. And no doubt other effects that
neither of us will care for, like shortages of various
kinds. I trust you'll be as steadfast and relentless in
resisting any such proposal as you are in your personal
dislike of the Kalif."

With that, Agros nodded cordially, then turned and
walked away.

"Good evening, Your Reverence."

The man who spoke looked like no one else at the
reception. Lord Roonoa Hamaalo was a mountain of a
man, perhaps the tallest there, and massive—powerful-
looking, even for a Maolaaro. His hands showed no
hair, his shaven jaw was not blue with the usual suppressed beard, and his head was bald. His eyebrows
weren't even bushy. The Maolaaru aristocracy had
largely held aloof from intermarriage, maintaining not
only their essentially unmixed gene pool, but much of
their indigenous culture. They hadn't even adopted
five-syllable names.

"Good evening, Lord Roonoa. Are you enjoying the
reception?"

The Maolaaro grunted. "I'm enjoying the food and
drink."

Yes, I've seen you at these affairs before, the Kalif
thought. *What you drink unaffected would have most
men unconscious or puking out their guts.* "But not the
conversations?" he asked.

"The conversations are part of the job. That's why
I'm talking to you."

The Kalif's grin was a brief flash of white. "Thank
you, good Roonoa, for the compliment. What do you
have in mind?"

"First and foremost an increase in what we're allowed
to charge for our fish. Every world here has a worsen-
ing population problem—every world but us. Imperial

populations have increased ten percent since we've had an increase in fish prices. That's a ten percent increase in demand, with no increase in price. And we are not a wealthy planet."

The Kalif shrugged. "Why not sell ten percent more fish then? Giving you ten percent more income at the present price."

"It wouldn't work that way. For most commercial species, our present catch approximates their sustained yields—their replacement capacities. If we catch more this decade, there'll be fewer and fewer to catch in decades to come."

"Umm. Logical. Your request makes sense, in the context of your own situation. Whether it would make sense to others in the context of their own problems . . ." He paused, inviting comment.

Again Roonoa grunted. "Their problems reflect their own short-sightedness and their lack of willingness to confront their true need. Thus their populations increase but their food production doesn't. Not substantially. Their domestic food prices have climbed steadily, and they discriminate against us. And each other."

He cocked a brown eye at the Kalif, then spoke with deliberate slowness. "There is one fish we could catch much more of, if we were allowed to export it. *Loohio*. That would alleviate both our problem and theirs. Yours."

The Kalif's expression stiffened. "Perhaps. On the other hand The Prophet said, 'Be fruitful.' "

"He did indeed. But—" The massive shoulders shrugged.

"But what?"

"The Prophet's wisdom was unusual, and his knowingness unique. But it seems now that he was not infallible."

The Maolaaro had prepared himself to receive the imperial anger, but the Kalif merely shook his head. "I think not, my friend. The fallibility was not The Prophet's. It has been ours, in refusing some of the knowledge he gave us. A failure I intend to correct."

He sighed, a sigh that might have been deliberate, for effect. "I will speak to the College about your request. About the prices allowed, not—the other. There is virtue in your argument—the virtue of fairness.

"But I do not perform miracles. Those belong to The Prophet, not to his successor."

Eighteen

Centrally the kalifal palace was a pentahedron, with attached, semi-disjunct cubes of different sizes, most with roof gardens. Just now the Kalif sat alone in his private roof garden, three stories above his apartment, with which it was connected by lift tube and stairs.

It was night. Ananporu was not a large city, as cities went in the empire; capitals never were. Its population was a little short of half a million, and large illuminated signs and lighting displays were not a part of the imperial culture. As a result, a considerable array of stars was visible.

Switching on a focused reading lamp, he'd turned his attention away from the view to the papers he held—including a report prepared for him several weeks earlier by Alb Tariil, on Tariil's objections to invading the Confederation. He'd studied it before, but hadn't discussed it yet in meeting; it hadn't been time. It still wasn't, but it felt like time to review it, to refresh his memory on what, exactly, Tariil had written, as distinct from what he himself had made of it.

The report was organized under two headings: (A) *Arguments Against an Invasion;* and (B) *Arguments Against Proposing an Invasion to the Diet.* Under (A), the exarch had written:

113

1. Such an invasion will be extremely expensive. The empire cannot afford it. I cannot think of a counter-argument.

2. Preparing such an invasion will cause severe currency inflation and material shortages. I cannot think of a counter-argument.

3. Preparing such an invasion will cause substantial shortages of skilled labor, and numerous peasants will end up being trained and put to non-peasant work. Then, when the preparations are completed, they will be required to return to peasant labor, which will probably result in civil disorders.

The Kalif skimmed over a lengthy write-up of the foreseen consequences of alternative three. Again Tariil had not given any counter-arguments. The Kalif did not doubt that the exarch would have written down any he'd recognized. Tariil had missed the obvious solution: shortages of skilled labor could be avoided by working skilled labor overtime as needed, and paying them premium wages for it. After decades of economic decline, the gentry would welcome it.

He read on.

4. The invasion might fail, with terrible costs in lives, money, and goods. There is no counter-argument to this.

The Kalif grimaced. He had no real argument with that, beyond his feeling that defeat seemed unlikely, based on considerable, if admittedly incomplete information. He continued reading.

5. If you succeed in conquering the Confederation, you would then have to hold it or else give it up. To give it up after the great cost of conquering it would be unthinkable, while holding it would take a continuing and costly effort, at least

until its people had embraced Karghanik. *Counter-argument:* Holding it would require extensive migration as well as many large garrisons. While this would require great shipbuilding costs, it would permit the transportation of those undesirables deemed suitable as colonists. (I suspect there would be large numbers of these.)

6. The Confederation has its own ways of thinking and doing things. Its human population numbers in the scores of billions, at least—far, far more than the colonists we might send. Even after they have embraced Karghanik, they will think and act more or less differently than we do. And these folkways will influence the people we send there, particularly as intermarriage proceeds. The colonies will become more and more different from ourselves, even in the face of continuing immigration. And at such a great distance, in a generation or two they will cease to recognize imperial authority. *Counter-argument:* They will be children of Kargh, and perhaps that should be enough for us. Even if we cease to rule them, we can be pleased to have brought Karghanik to scores of new worlds, and to a hundred billion or more people.

The Kalif mused on the concept of colonies on those distant planets, and of children born to colonists, children who would never see the sector, the worlds, their parents came from. Children to whom the eleven worlds would be only stories, stories they might not even be interested in at such a far remove.

He also mused on the Confederation's myriads embracing Karghanik. Of intermarriages, and populations that in a few generations would be unlike anything that now existed. A new people. Somehow it both troubled and excited him.

He went on to read Tariil's reasons for not proposing an invasion to the Diet.

1. The proposal is almost sure to fail in the Diet.

2. The failure of such a major and radical, one might say revolutionary proposal will make the kalifate, and by extension the College, look incompetent, and weaken them in the eyes of the nobility for a long time. It probably would not result directly in civil disturbances, but given conditions in parts of the empire—indeed on parts of Varatos itself—such a political conflict within the Diet can result indirectly in civil unrest.

The Kalif raised his eyes from the report and gazed thoughtfully across the nightbound city. In the distance, thunderheads pulsed with internal lightning and sent megavolt discharges flickering groundward like bright threads. For a minute or several minutes he half watched, half cogitated.

Civil unrest. What Tariil actually meant was insurrection; civil unrest was always present somewhere in the empire. Serious insurrection occurred only every century or two, growing mainly from conflicts between the two great estates—the Prelacy and the nobility. Or actually between the College and the House of Nobles, which invariably had the interest of the Greater Nobility in mind instead of the nobility in general.

Insurrection could drastically disrupt law, order, and the economy for a decade or longer, and no estate wanted it. But on occasion someone played too close to the brink. Insurrection was always a possibility, but it was hardly a present danger.

He continued reading.

3. If invasion is proposed to the Diet, nothing will get done this session except arguing. Some of the arguments may become so bitter as to seriously hamper deliberations on any subject for years to come. *Counter-argument:* At best, much that the Diet does is not very useful. A few years of it getting little done may not seriously harm

the empire, so long as a budget of some kind gets passed.

The Kalif grinned anew. At first reading he'd been surprised at such an observation by Tariil—he still was—and wondered if the exarch found any humor in it.

He laid the report aside and picked up another. On Sixday he'd chair a session of the Diet; he made a point of chairing the last one of each week. He wouldn't drop a bomb on them yet, though; let them wonder. He'd settle for dropping one on his inner council tomorrow.

Nineteen

In council next morning, the Kalif waited till routine business had been completed before dropping his bomb. Alb Tariil had brought up the subject of invasion, but the Kalif had declined to discuss it, saying that he hadn't made up his own mind yet. That when he had, there would be time enough.

"There is other new business I need to bring up just now." He looked them over. Their interest was tepid; they were ready to leave, get to their other duties. "I'm not ready to make it public yet, but I thought you should know." He paused, teasing their attention. "You'll keep it confidential, of course." Another pause. "I plan to be married."

The response was immediate, and as nearly enthusiastic as the inner council ever became. "Splendid!" said Alb Bijnath, beaming. "Good! Good!" said Alb Drova. Even Alb Tariil smiled, broadly. "Well!" he said, "there's hope for you after all!"

Alb Thoga said nothing, didn't smile; his chronic hostility toward the Kalif disallowed such responses. And Alb Jilsomo's smile was not spontaneous; the bride-to-be, it seemed to him, had to be the alien.

"Who's the lucky woman?" Bijnath asked. "I had no idea you'd been negotiating with anyone."

"Her name is Tain Faronya."

Smiles were replaced by frowns. "Faronya? A gentry name, is it?" asked Tariil. "Or Maolaaru? It's not familiar."

"She's the young woman who was brought back as a prisoner by Rashti's expedition."

The moment of silence, the sense of suspended animation, was broken by Thoga's angry response. "You can't! She is not a citizen!"

"I'm not aware that that's a prerequisite."

Alb Tariil spoke then, more quietly than usual. "Your Reverence," he said, "there is *one* requirement."

Every eye turned to him.

Tariil's eyes were on his hands, folded on the table. He took a deep breath; this was not easy for him. "According to the reports we were given, the young woman has no memory of her life before her captivity. Or more correctly, of her life before an accident on board the Klestronu flagship. So then, apparently no one knows, even she does not know, whether, for example, she was married—or anything."

His eyes raised, met the Kalif's.

"I invariably read the weekly report of kalifal edicts," he went on. "As do some few others, both in the Sreegana and the House of Nobles. One of those edicts was the annulment of a marriage—the marriage of a Klestronu marine colonel." He looked around at the others, and except in Jilsomo and the Kalif, found only puzzlement. "That surprised me. It's not the sort of thing one expects as a kalifal edict. So I called up the accessible information about the colonel."

Tariil's eyes fixed on the Kalif's again, not in antagonism but with unhappy concern. "It seems he had maintained the female prisoner privately in an apartment in Khaloom. He admits, though, to his wife's charge that he was and is impotent, the basis of the annulment. And under ordinary circumstances, people would accept that. Though they might be skeptical, unless in fact the colonel had a reputation for altruism.

"But the circumstances are not ordinary. First, rumor has it that the young woman is remarkably beautiful. Second, the annulment edict was yours, not Rashti's. And now you intend to marry the young woman that couldn't have been his mistress because of his stated impotence."

Alb Tariil shrugged. "Your Reverence, the question will surely arise as to what went on between them in that apartment."

The council room was silent for a moment. Finally the Kalif responded: "Do you have such questions?" he asked, and his eyes were hard.

"Your Reverence, do not try to intimidate me. It will change nothing. And whether I have questions or not is beside the point. Certainly others will, and they will ask them publicly, not here in chamber."

"Your Reverence," Drova broke in, "there is a way of answering such questions. I'm sure the young woman would agree to a medical examination. . . ."

The Kalif's eyes flashed brief anger, but his reply to the old exarch was mild. "What would you have us do? Humiliate her, the kalifa to be, by publicizing that she had been examined and that her hymen was intact? That would be offensive and totally unacceptable, to me if not to her. In fact, this discussion is offensive."

This time Bijnath spoke. "Your Reverence, it need not be publicized. Let her be examined by your own physician. And have him testify to us that she is— intact. Then we will say we accept her as fit, and if any-one wishes to guess at why, that will be only their guess."

The Kalif frowned darkly, fists clenched at his sides, then shook his head. Before he said anything more, though, Jilsomo spoke.

"Your Reverence."

The Kalif turned to him. "Yes?"

"If Alb Bijnath's proposal is not acceptable to you, perhaps Neftha could testify privately to me. Then, assuming the answer is what we hope, and if my fellows of the council would accept my word for it. . . ."

"Your Reverence," said Bijnath, "I, for one, would be happy to accept Jilsomo's word on it."

"And I," said Drova.

The Kalif shot a hard look at his lieutenant, then Tariil added his voice, though without enthusiasm. "I will accept that, Your Reverence, if you will."

Coso Biilathkamoro sat frowning past them for a long moment before saying anything more. Then he looked at Thoga Khaliyamathog. "I have not heard from you, Alb Thoga."

"You will do what you want regardless of me. Probably regardless of any of us, but now that the rest have knuckled under, what I feel is of little consequence."

"Do you accept Jilsomo's proposal, Alb Thoga, or do you not?"

The sour-faced exarch bent his stylus in his fingers. "If the rest accept—then I, too."

"Thank you. Then, Jilsomo, I accept your offer. Stay, and we shall make arrangements. The rest of you— I thank you for your consideration. Council is now adjourned till Fourday."

The Kalif and Alb Jilsomo walked side by side without talking till they reached the Kalif's apartment.

"I hope Your Reverence will excuse my forwardness in council," Jilsomo said then. "It seemed that something was necessary. Simply to override them is destructive of your overall leadership. And you need them, Your Reverence. The rest of the College tends to follow their lead, and you have difficult months ahead in the Diet."

The Kalif nodded ruefully. "I'm afraid I don't brook opposition well in such personal matters."

"When shall I see your physician, Your Reverence? And where?"

"At his office, this afternoon at four. Unless I let you know otherwise. He may have a conflicting appointment."

"At four then. I'll call him. Do you need me further this morning, Your Reverence?"

"I don't think so. No."

"Well then, if you'll excuse me." Jilsomo bowed slightly and left.

The Kalif sat down at his commset and touched keys. "Neftha, is there any problem in coming to my apart-

ment now? I need to speak with you. . . . Good. Come
by the blue corridor. . . . Five minutes will be fine.
Thank you."

He notified the door guards to let Neftha in, then
sat back in thought. He'd been handling the council
poorly this morning. No, not poorly; damned badly. It
was lucky Jilsomo had stepped in. He'd want the support of every exarch possible in the Diet; to pass a
special appropriation required approval by seventy percent of the combined two estates: the Prelacy, represented by the College, and the nobility, represented
by the House of Nobles. And the College had only
eighteen votes, the Nobles twenty-seven.

On the other hand, a Kalif couldn't let himself appear
weak or soft. It was better to be overbearing than
flabby. But it was better still to seem reasonable while
strong.

Neftha arrived in less than five minutes, and was let
in. "Your Reverence wanted to see me."

"Right. I need a statement from you. Given orally to
Alb Jilsomo. About Tain Faronya."

"Yes, Your Reverence?"

"You will tell him you've made a physical examination of Miss Faronya. You will *not* tell him when. He'll
assume it was later today."

"Yes, sir."

The Kalif's eyes fixed the man. "And you will tell
him you found no evidence that she is not a virgin."

The physician had trouble answering. "Your Reverence . . . I—"

"Good friend, I do not ask you to lie. Truly, you
found no evidence that she is not a virgin. You simply
failed to find evidence that she is. Surely you see the
distinction?"

Neftha avoided his eyes. "Yes, Your Reverence," he
said unhappily.

"So then. What will you tell Jilsomo when he sees
you at four o'clock?"

"I— That I have examined Miss Faronya. And found
no evidence that she is not a virgin. But, Your Rever-

ence— What do I say if he asks me further questions? He's an exarch!"

The Kalif raised an eyebrow. "Further questions are unlikely, if you speak positively enough. Practice if you need to. And seem busy, slightly impatient. Above all, speak firmly. As if you were telling him he must stop eating so much."

He grinned at Neftha, surprising the man. "Do not *expect* further questions and you're less likely to get any. And if he does ask, simply repeat what you'd already said; tell him that should be plain enough for anyone. Sound exasperated."

When the physician had left, the Kalif's mood slumped. He got to his feet and went into the garden feeling troubled, depressed. It seemed to him he wasn't handling things as well as he should: council, physician, even Jilsomo.

Well, to rule had never been easy, even for kalifs who'd held the throne in uneventful times. Having known Tain, it seemed to him he could never marry anyone else, and if marrying her made the next months more difficult, they at least would pass quickly.

When it came down to it, Neftha couldn't face possible questions from Jilsomo. So he lied to the exarch, telling him the alien woman was indeed a virgin.

"I've spoken with Neftha," Jilsomo said. "I'll reassure the council tomorrow. There's no need for them to wait till Fourday, and it will free their minds of the question."

Alb Jilsomo Savbatso was harder than most men for the Kalif to read; his face was mobile only in the service of his mind, and his eyes were not transparent. But it seemed to the Kalif that the fat exarch must suspect, given what he already knew.

"A question, Your Reverence, if I may."

"Ask."

"Why did you bring up the matter of marriage this morning in council? Or have you decided to wed her sooner than you'd planned?"

"We'll marry in three weeks. She'll receive tutoring from a bride's aunt next week; I wanted to bring it up to the council before that."

Jilsomo's eyebrows questioned the apparent non sequitur.

"At this time," the Kalif went on, "no one knows of my plans except the council and Neftha. Except of course for Tain and I. If there's a traitor, an untrustworthy member in the council, this may well be something he'll pass on to my opponents in the House. And if he does, it will come forcefully to my attention in the Diet."

Jilsomo nodded. In the past, almost all kalifs had named to their councils men who would not disagree chronically or sharply with them. Coso Biilathkamoro, different in so many things, had named, along with others, the conservative Alb Tariil, who opposed him more often than not and who was very influential in the College. And the irascible Alb Thoga, whose hostility could be depended on. "To keep an eye on their actions and a finger on their pulses," was how the Kalif had explained his appointments.

It seemed unlikely though, to Jilsomo, that there was a traitor in the council.

"The bride's aunt will make an examination of her own, will she not?" he asked.

"Of course. That's part of it. But anything she has to say, besides to the bride, she'll say only to the groom, and nothing to him of any substance."

Jilsomo nodded. Whatever she *could* say, other than to the bride, she wouldn't. A "bride's aunt" was a professional advisor and tutor to brides, and rarely their actual aunt. By tradition and professional ethics, they were utterly discreet. This was true also of the "groom's uncle."

It would probably be all right. He hoped so. Certainly he'd do everything he could to make it so. Because whatever his flaws, this Kalif was the best for a long time, Jilsomo told himself. A very long time.

Twenty

Fourday had come and gone, and Fiveday. Now it was Sixday, the day when, in its season, Kalif Coso Biilathkamoro customarily chaired a session of the Imperial Diet. He gaveled it to order, and himself gave the invocation. After the prayer, the secretary read a summary of the previous session, prepared by SUMBAA and printed out by his primary terminal in the office of the Leader of the House.

When the summary had been read, the Kalif scanned the assembly. It met in a large chamber shaped like a half bowl, with the rather small, slightly tilted bottom holding the exarchs, the noble delegates, and the twelve non-voting delegates of the Pastorate. Separated from them by a marble railing, the sides curved up with row on row of seats, empty now, empty usually. Only on special occasions were invited spectators permitted. Nor did the automatic cameras record the sights and sounds there for broadcast; they recorded for the archives: that is, for SUMBAA.

"At the close of the last session," the Kalif intoned— the sentence was traditional—"it was agreed that the subject then under discussion would be given priority this morning. That subject being the request by the senior delegate from Maolaari for the export of loohio."

Simply mentioning the subject raised hackles and color among the members. He continued:

"Does any member have another subject they would ask priority for, before we proceed?"

A hand shot up, its owner also rising, which was unusual but not out of order.

"Lord Rothka," said the Kalif, "what is your suggestion?"

The narrow mouth opened. "Your Reverence," said Rothka, and the words came sour from his mouth, "I move that we discuss—" He paused then, a pause long and deliberate to draw their attention. "I move that we first discuss Your Reverence's intended marriage."

"I second!" said another, quick beyond chance.

"Indeed?" said the Kalif dryly. "I need not entertain such a motion unless it's a matter falling within the purview of this assembly. And clearly any marriage plans I might have do not."

"Not so," Rothka said. "Let me quote Scripture."

"Be my guest."

The Kalif's seeming willingness, broke the noble's certainty. His gaze faltered for just a moment, then hardened. The Prophet's words, as he recited them, were measured, almost stately: "I will not always be with you in the flesh, for the flesh is mortal. And there are those who hate godliness and the godly, wanting them dead. Thus not only will I pass from this world, but also will he who follows me. Probably before our time. And the believers will need to choose a new leader not once, but many times over the centuries."

Rothka's back was stiff as a marshal's. "Therefore I give to you rules to choose by, for the protection of the Church, and of its people, and of righteousness. And of Kargh's words. You must choose leaders who are righteous. He who would lead must be one who steadfastly eschews greed, and sensuality, and all unrighteousness. One who has consorted with lechers, or the tight-fisted, or has sought the company of lewd women, cannot lead the Church. And if one who has been chosen would marry, the woman he chooses must be—"

Rothka paused, then said the final words slowly, deliberately: "Chaste and virtuous."

The rest of the list of requisites for Successors to The Prophet, Rothka left unrecited, as irrelevant to his argument. He fixed the Kalif with his eyes then, as if challenging him. The Kalif nodded.

"Thank you, Lord Rothka, for renewing The Prophet's message for us. Especially the phrase about the tight-fisted."

Rothka flushed; he had a reputation for stinginess, and was sensitive about it. The Kalif looked around. "Lord Rothka's subject may not have been relevant to the day's business, but the words of the Blessed Flenyaagor are worth listening to on any subject. Does anyone else wish to display his memory of *The Book* before we return to the request of Lord Roonoa?"

Rothka, still flushed, subsided onto his seat.

"If not . . ." said the Kalif.

Another hand stabbed upward, another member of the Land Rights Party stood. "You are evading the issue, the matter of the woman you want to marry. The alien woman brought to the empire by the Klestronu expedition."

"My dear Ilthka." The Kalif's voice held reproof. "You are on the wrong side of the chamber to discuss that; it's a matter for the Prelacy, specifically the College. And let me remind you that there is a proper form for addressing your Kalif.

"Now. Does anyone have an appropriate subject to propose? If not, we will return to the matter which the senior delegate from Maolaari brought up yesterday—that is, his request for approval of the export of loohio."

Ilthka too sat back down.

"Lord Roonoa, the record shows that your presentation speech did not address The Prophet's command to be fruitful. How can we reconcile your proposal with that command?"

Roonoa stood, bowing slightly to the Kalif. "Your Reverence," he said in his rich bass, "we should consider when it was that The Prophet spoke those words, and the apparent reason for them. The first burning plague had swept Varatos little more than ten years earlier, killing more than one in three of all the people, taking children and women even more than men. Of those who'd sickened and recovered, some were left witless, and many women who had been sickened and not died had proved sterile. Cribs stood empty. Fields lay fallow for lack of men to work them. Looms stood silent, forges cold."

The Maolaaro looked around at the delegates; so did the Kalif, though not as plainly. "So of course The Prophet told the people to be fruitful. But one might wonder what he would say today, when all the worlds but Maolaari are crowded. With many gentry unemployed, competing with peasants for work as day laborers. With food riots on nearly every world."

He looked around, meeting gazes thoughtful and gazes hostile. So far as he knew, no one had come forward with such an argument before. One did not think such things. "The Blessed Flenyaagor was a holy man," he went on. "A saintly man. But he was also a practical man who had guided his ship through storms, around dangerous reefs and shoals. He'd fought pirates, fled pirates, even paid extortion to pirates. He'd bargained with men over cargoes and prices, and took satisfaction in the high price he'd gotten for his ship, that he could print *The Book* and have money to support him in his ministry."

The Maolaaru noble shook his head as he continued. "I do not believe, Your Reverence, that permitting the export of loohio from Maolaari would offend The Prophet if he were here today. Indeed, if the poor should eat it, who can hardly feed their children, I wonder if The Prophet would not actually praise it."

An angry hand stabbed the air. Roonoa ignored it as he sat down.

"Alb Thoga," said the Kalif, and the exarch got to his feet.

"Your Reverence, I am outraged by the insolence of the delegate from Maolaari! It is bad enough that a layman presumed to analyze The Prophet's reasoning. But to stand there and presume to tell us what The Prophet would think or say if he were here today— That is unforgiveable!"

"Thank you, Alb Thoga." *You are chronically outraged,* the Kalif added silently. *To you, nothing is forgiveable.*

Other hands had raised, and the Kalif pointed. "Lord Panamba."

The delegate for Niithvoktos stood. Unlike Jilsomo, from the same world, Panamba was rather slender, remarkably so for someone from Niithvoktos with its 1.17 gravity. He looked as if, beneath his clothes, he'd be sinewy. "Your Reverence, I will not comment on The Prophet's words, except indirectly: What Lord Roonoa said makes sense, whether or not he accurately described what The Prophet might think. We have a major population problem, not only on Niithvoktos but on Varatos, and Klestron, and any other world you'd care to name. Except Roonoa's own."

Panamba too sat down then, and the Kalif called on Lord Agros. The Leader of the House spoke seated. "Your Reverence, it is unthinkable that the Diet approve Lord Roonoa's proposal. We nobility dare not eat loohio because we dare not reduce our birthrate. Even now we constitute less than eight percent of the population. The gentry constitute barely thirty-three percent, and we rely on them to control and supervise the peasants, so we cannot have fewer gentry either.

"As for the peasants, most of them would love to eat loohio daily, I have no doubt. Then they could copulate endlessly without having to feed children, and the raising of children is the only self-accepted responsibility the peasants know. It is all that makes them more than beasts. Besides, without enough peasants, who would work the fields? Dig the ditches? Clean the streets? True, it might be desirable to reduce their births somewhat. But if we decide to, it should be by legalizing birth-control pharmaceuticals, for use in programs planned by SUMBAA and controlled by the government."

"Thank you, Lord Agros."

A hand had been popping up at the close of each comment, and the Kalif now recognized Lord Fakoda Lamatahasu, speaker for the Industrial Party. Fakoda, a short, somewhat chubby man, managed somehow to be self-important and self-effacing at the same time.

"Your Reverence, I do not pretend to be deep on matters of religion, though I have read *The Book* through a number of times. But from a purely practical view, a purely practical view you understand—if we should allow the Maolaari to import their loohio, and the number of peasants should decrease as a result . . . Well, machines could be built to do many kinds of jobs that peasants do—do them better and faster. And gentry could find employment tending the machines that would make the machines. Perhaps operating the machines themselves."

He shrugged, shoulders and hands. "Of course, these things can't be worked out overnight. But then, the population of working-age peasants would not go down overnight, either. Loohio would be no problem—no practical problem. Certainly much less a problem than those it would relieve."

Among the demanding hands, the Kalif then recognized that of Elder Dosu Sutaravaalu, Archdeacon of Ananporu and Leader of the Assembly of Elders. An old man, nearly ninety, he arose without effort, though with a certain care. He bowed first to the Kalif, then slightly to Lord Fakoda.

"Your Reverence, we have heard from men here who have been blessed by Kargh above other men. We have heard about 'practical considerations.' " He said the two words as if they were distasteful. Then he bobbed a slight bow toward Lord Agros. "The morals of peasants have even been mentioned.

"But none of these have meaning except as they fit within the prescriptions and proscriptions of The Prophet. And The Prophet truly said, 'Be fruitful.'

"It is not ours to judge his words and say that they still hold or do not hold. He said them. They are ours to obey. As for the number of people— The problem is not the number of people. The problems are sufficient jobs, sufficient food. And it is our duty to solve them. But to solve them within the limits demanded by Kargh and written down for us by His Prophet."

After a little, it was agreed to shelve, for the present, the question of approval for the exportation of loohio. Lord Roonoa felt comfortable with this. Opposition had not been as vehement as he'd expected, and some year soon he might be willing to push things to a vote. When the prognosis was suitable.

The Kalif too was pleased with the session. Lords Rothka and Ilthka had been discouraged more easily than he'd expected. And Rothka's challenge made clear that there was a leak in his council; very probably Thoga. Meanwhile, of course, his marital plans would now leak to the public at large. Well, let them get a look at Tain. The public would approve, it seemed to him.

Beyond that, the discussions of Roonoa's proposal had shown him a possible fulcrum to gain support for an invasion. And accomplish other things; maybe even approval for the limited sale of loohio in areas of serious food shortages. He'd have to sort out the dynamics of the situation—see what the potentials were, the possibilities and cross-purposes.

During the discussion, another question had occurred to him. About SUMBAA. The giant artificial intelligence held virtually all the significant data there was, and supposedly had an unparalleled capacity to segregate, correlate, analyze, and integrate those data. And to create with them, at least within limits.

So why hadn't SUMBAA solved the problems of jobs and food? He could understand why it hadn't solved the question of population: religion was involved. But the others?

Surely it had been asked. Or had it? People didn't

seem to wonder about SUMBAA, or even think much about it. It had been around for so long, doing what it did without consulting anyone. And really, apparently, without being much consulted by them except for the enormous volume of more or less routine bureaucratic needs.

Why? Why hadn't SUMBAA volunteered solutions? Could it be that, with the burden of routine, SUMBAA didn't have enough capacity left over? Somehow he didn't think that was it. Perhaps solutions didn't lie in the analysis of data. Perhaps they required some ability SUMBAA didn't have.

Sometime soon, he told himself, he'd go to the House of SUMBAA and discuss these things with him. With it. Tomorrow. Seven and Eightdays made up the weekend, and there'd be fewer demands on his time then.

Twenty-one

An Imperial Army captain stepped into Veeri's office.
"You're Colonel Thoglakaveera?" he asked.

Veeri looked up from paperwork. "That's right."

The man thrust out a hand to him, and he shook it.
"My name is Alivii Simnasaveesi. I understand you
were with the Klestronu marines in the alien empire."

Veeri's mood shifted cautiously from boredom to tentative interest; he wondered if this man knew anything
else about him. "That's true," he said.

"I'm with Headquarters Regiment of the Capital
Division. A friend of mine, Major Tagurt Meksorli, is
giving a party at his town place in the outskirts." The
captain paused to see what Veeri's reaction might be
to the major's gentry name. When nothing showed,
he continued. "He gives one almost every Sevenday
evening, for a dozen or two officers and occasionally a
guest. He'd heard there was a Klestronu colonel here
who'd been in the fighting, and asked me to invite you.
Interested?"

It didn't even occur to Veeri to decline.

For nearly fifteen centuries there'd been no distinction in law between a "Greater" and a "lesser" nobility.
The formal categories had been erased when the
empire had become the Kalifate, part of an agreement

133

that had gained Kalif Yeezhur the military backing of
the lesser nobility. Backing that made him the first
emperor Kalif.

But in fact the distinction remained, a distinction
based mainly now on wealth and tradition. And while
the senior male in every noble family, Greater or
lesser, held a vote, members of only certain families
were eligible to serve in the Diet.

Most of the old Great Families were still so regarded,
even those whose earlier wealth had declined somewhat. Their extensive plantations gave them the potential to recoup, meanwhile living like true aristocrats.
Occasionally of course, one of them would be disgraced
and lose its status, or simply die out.

The Great Families had been joined from time to
time, almost surreptitiously, by one and another family
of the lesser nobility who'd become especially rich and
influential. The Greater Nobles might then begin treat-
ing them like one of their own. An example was the
Lamatahasu family, of which Lord Fakoda was pres-
ently the head.

The military, however, *truly* recognized no distinction, either in the imperial services or in those of the
individual worlds. A son of the poorest noble family,
perhaps with only a confectioner's shop to support it,
could become a general if he had the necessary skills.
In fact, the sons of lesser families made up a sizeable
majority of the officer corps, from top to bottom, in
every branch, even the navy. Thus, in the armed
forces, if a Greater Noble was prejudiced against the
lesser nobility, he'd do well to keep it to himself.

Gentry were a different kind of phenomenon, a
legally defined class of different origin intermediate
between the nobility and peasantry. Gentry made up
the entirety of noncommissioned officers, the so-called
"sergeantcy," which included corporals. And for a very
long time, occasional gentry had entered the officers
corps during war by promotion from sergeant. But only
over the last three centuries had they been accepted

into the service academies and grown to an appreciable minority of commissioned officers.

As officers, gentry met a certain amount of discrimination both socially and on promotion rosters, the amount depending on ability, personality, and the unit's commanding officer. Among gentry, excellence was usually necessary to attain a captaincy, short of one's final years; it was essential to rising higher.

Though wealth also helped.

At age thirty-one, Tagurt Meksorli was already a major. Kulen Meksorli, Tagurt's paternal grandfather thrice removed, had been hired as a stevedore foreman at a spaceport on Varatos. The young foreman, who was paid a percentage of his job contracts, had paid his peasant laborers on the basis of production. Under the table, of course; the practice was illegal, there being a set pay scale for peasants. Soon he bought the crew contract and developed a virtual fief, his fast, efficient crews having gobbled up much of the local cargo-handling business. The more profitable part of it.

Then, in a wild, high-stakes card game, Kulen had won a small hyperspace merchantman, a tramp freighter. He'd paid professional ship inspectors to go over it for him, then plunged most of what he owned and could borrow into getting it overhauled.

Its ownership stimulated Kulen's already active sense of adventure. He left his brother in charge of the cargo-handling business and went into space as an apprentice to his own captain and chief engineer. Within two years he was a full-time smuggler, and through the exercise of considerable cunning, professional ethics, attention to detail, and at key junctures further daring, he compiled a considerable fortune. Which, before he was an old man, included seven ships, none of them smugglers. Having avoided arrest, prison, and confiscation, he'd gone straight as soon as he could afford to.

By the time his great-great-great-grandson had grown to manhood, the Meksorli Line included one of the system's largest fleets of sweepboats, seven refinery ships, a large fleet of bulk carriers, a dozen hyperspace package freighters, and three luxury liners. The Meksorlis were richer than even most Great Families, but no gentry on Varatos had been elevated to the nobility for nearly three millenia. And none of the Meksorlis, the men anyway, aspired to it; they were proud of what they were and what they'd accomplished.

Tagurt aspired to be the first gentry general—a general instead of an admiral because generalcies were more numerous. He had the agreement and appreciation of both his father and grandfather. In that regard, his great-grandfather, old Kulen's sole surviving grandson, had told the young cadet that he was lucky to be gentry instead of nobility. "It'll make the rank more meaningful," he'd said, "and getting it more interesting."

On graduation from the academy, the new sublieutenant and would-be general had volunteered for an assault regiment, which marked him as ambitious—ambitious or a glutton for hard work. Once assigned, he volunteered to command a maintenance platoon, maintenance platoons being notorious for everything happening at once, for all-night duty, and the need for ramrod officers who were resourceful and quick. And results were hard to fake; the equipment either functioned or it didn't.

Tagurt stayed there long enough to get a reputation and a full lieutenancy. Then, at his own request, he'd been transferred to a notorious and dreaded post, the prison planet Shatimvoktos. Furthermore, he signed for two imperial years there, when the normal tour of duty was one. Simply to *request* service on Shatimvoktos was virtually unheard of, so that by itself made him a watched man. If he screwed up, his prospects would be seriously impaired.

And if he excelled, that would be noticed, too, gentry or not. Which was, of course, his reason for doing it.

Shatimvoktos was the most dangerous duty the peacetime military offered. Most of its enlisted personnel, the guards especially, were hardbitten, veteran misfits who'd been assigned there as a form of unofficial punishment. The gravity was 1.38—grueling—the atmosphere toxic, the summers almost lethally hot, the winters brutally cold. And if the guards were hardbitten, the prisoners were mostly worse—dangerous men, many of them more or less psychotic—who expected to die there and had nothing to lose. They worked with hammers, drills, blasting gel, crowbars, and hand shovels, digging iron ore from open pits. Even in an economy like the empire's, such an operation was grossly uneconomical, feasible only with unpaid, throw-away labor. Its purposes were the punishment and disposal of criminals, and to serve as a threat to troublemakers.

Deadly fights were common among the prisoners, and they acted quickly when they saw a chance to kill a guard. When a captain of the guard died in what might or might not have been an accident, Tagurt succeeded him, and in time was given the rank to go with the job. Then, as the most qualified available officer, he extended his tour another half year, to fill in for the provost marshal, who'd gone home for a family emergency.

From Shatimvoktos, he'd been assigned to the Capital Division, an elite heavy infantry division stationed only thirty miles outside Ananporu. The division personnel officer mentioned him to the division C.O., who examined Tagurt's personnel file and appointed him deputy division provost marshal, a virtual vacation after the prison planet. When the general was satisfied that the young man could handle an easy post with a discriminating hand as well as he had a terrible post requiring an iron fist, he recommended an early promotion to major for his gentry protege—promotion without the standard minimum of three years in rank. The Kalif approved it, and the new major became the general's aide.

No member of the gentry had ever made major so quickly in the imperial service. Most nobles didn't.

Despite his naked ambition, rapid rise, and lack of noble forebears, Major Tagurt Meksorli was not widely resented among the ambitious young officers of the division, mostly nobles. Partly it was his matter-of-fact personality, blunt but friendly. And partly it was his parties.

Tagurt Meksorli's town place was in the rugged Anan Hills, which overlooked Ananporu from the west. Veeri Thoglakaveera had never been there before. Hovercar roads twisted over and through them like goat trails, past homes expensive but mostly not large, cantilevered from plunging slopes on shelves. The headlights of Veeri's taxi flashed across the trunks of great trees, frequently vine-clad, that shouldered and overhung the roads. Their beams swept thick growths of lustrous ground vines protecting the slopes. Flowering shrubs scented the night, overriding the constant undersmell of moist and loamy mould. Insects and other small creatures peeped, buzzed, ratcheted; sprinklers hissed quietly in the darkness. An occasional bird chirped aimlessly as if half awake, or tried a vague and tentative half bar of song.

Veeri noticed it all only absently. Mostly he was thinking about what this party might mean to him; something, he was sure. And wondering whether anyone there would know of his purported impotence.

For a minute the road ran along the top of a ridge, the houses on both sides with their backs to it facing outward. Houses and trees allowed Veeri only glimpses of the overviews—on one side eastward over the city, on the other westward across a span of night-hidden plantations that spread to the horizon, broken at intervals by the concentrated lights of villages and towns. Behind one home, half a dozen cars were parked tightly to conserve space. A post bore the address, the symbols a vertical column beneath its small light.

"That's it, sir," the cabbie announced as he pulled up and stopped.

"You'll wait," Veeri said.

"Of course, sir," the man replied, then added almost apologetically, "per the rate schedule you've noticed on the back of my seat, sir."

He'd turned as he'd said it, and Veeri noticed now the small mark on his forehead. Even on Varatos, Veeri knew, more than a few of the lesser nobility were down on their luck. But seeing one of them like this irritated him. It seemed indecent of the man to display his ill fortune in public.

The house was one story high in back, but getting from the cab, he could see that that one story was the topmost of at least two on the downhill side. The party wasn't loud; he couldn't hear it at all as he walked to the door. A man wearing corporal's insignia stood guard there, eyeing his Klestronu Marines uniform with its gold colonel's hammers on the collar, the insignia used by imperial as well as the separate planetary forces.

"Good evening, sir," the corporal said. "Let me announce you, if you please, sir."

"Colonel Veeri Thoglakaveera."

"Thank you, sir."

The corporal spoke it into a small grill on the doorpost. Within four or five seconds the door opened, and now Veeri could hear quiet music and the murmur of voices from somewhere inside. A sublieutenant stood there, looking impossibly young. "Colonel! Do come in! It's a pleasure to greet you. Major Meksorli and the others have been looking forward to your arrival."

He ushered him down a hallway. At the other end they entered a room as wide as the house, which was fairly wide. It was nothing special, nor were its furnishings; it was the view that made it expensive. The east-facing wall was glass, opening onto a narrow strip of balcony. Beyond its polished bronze railing, Ananporu and its suburbs spread below them like a field of scintillant, multi-colored jewels. The cab had climbed higher than he'd thought, Veeri realized—they had to be more than a 1,000 feet above the city. He pulled his eyes away, to the major and captain who'd gotten to their feet. The captain he knew—Alivii Simnasaveesi, who'd delivered the invitation. The other, a rather small major who projected an unusual sense of power, had an unmarked forehead, and Veeri realized that this man was his host.

The captain introduced them, and Meksorli shook Veeri's hand. "Colonel Thoglakaveera! It's a pleasure to have you here. Would you care for a drink? We can cover most tastes."

Veeri chose whiskey on ice. He preferred to stay in control of his mind and tongue, and with whiskey on ice he could better monitor and limit his intake. While the serving man got his drink, Veeri glanced around at the other guests. They were all looking at him, but with no sign of sympathy or amusement. Only interest.

One, the oldest, wore colonel's gold hammers, like his own. Two others were majors, both older than Meksorli. The rest were captains and full lieutenants, except for the sublieutenant who'd served as door greeter. There were no women. Apparently no more guests were expected; at any rate Veeri'd been guided to the last of the chairs arranged in an oval.

It occurred to him that he was not only a guest; he was the program. His chair was at one end of the oval, and everyone was facing him.

"So, Colonel," said Meksorli, "what was it like on the alien world?"

Veeri was a willing liar, but not a compulsive one. This time he told the truth pretty much as he knew it. "Basically," he said, "it isn't so different from Varatos or Klestron. The gravity's stronger, but not oppressively strong for a man in decent condition. And planetwide it's cooler, rather like Kathvoktos or Chithvoktos, but we were practically on the equator, so the climate was quite comfortable.

"Probably the biggest difference was the population; there wasn't much. The biggest town had only about fifteen thousand, something like that."

The reactions were mixed; some looked surprised, some puzzled, some eager. "How do they get by with so few?" someone asked. "How do they maintain their technology? Their civilization?"

Veeri began to warm up at that: he enjoyed being

looked to as the expert. "It seems that the world we found—it's called Terfreya—is a very minor planet. Not even a minor associate in the Confederation; it's what they call a 'trade world.' They raise a single export crop there, a spice, and beyond that some livestock and food crops for local use. Most of the planet's a wilderness, complete with large beasts of prey."

"Damn!" said another. "We could make a lot better use of it than that."

There was voiced agreement. Then the Vartosu colonel spoke. "I heard you had some hard fighting. What was that like?"

"It's—not easy to describe, but hard is an understatement. Of course, we were only a light brigade. And there's a lot we never did learn about the forces we fought. Even the local officials knew very little about them. Some, the initial force, were cadets who'd been training on Terfreya. They were fearless and full of tricks, but their weaponry was inferior. We'd killed a lot of them, and markedly reduced their attacks, when another force, not cadets, arrived from somewhere. This was after a couple of months. These were also extremely good troops, but they were a very light force—no weapons a man couldn't carry, except gunships. They did have gunships, though not as fast or as powerful as ours.

"We'd made captives of some local officials—had them on the flagship under instrumented interrogation for months—and they knew nothing at all about this new force. We pretty much decided they must have landed from outside the system—the new troops, that is. Maybe for training, like the cadets. Though how they did it without being noticed is a bit of a puzzler. The assumption is that they entered real space far enough out in the system that their emergence waves were too weak to pick up. That sort of thing can happen, with careless astrogation. Meanwhile the navy'd impounded Terfreya's homing beacon to study its technology, and its absence could have warned the Confederation ship that something might be wrong. Then they could have used a blindside approach, and with enough luck, landed undetected.

"Unfortunately, the captive officials were provincial—the whole world was—and not as well informed as we'd expected. None of them was what you'd call knowledgeable about military or technical matters.

"We did learn somewhat about their ships from them, of course, and more from examining some message pods we captured on the ground. Their hyperspace generators are a lot like ours—operate on the same principle. I suppose it's the only way. And a ship that we know arrived in-system while we were there produced typical emergence waves. Our flagship detected it at once, and when it arrived within range, we blew it up with no trouble at all."

Veeri shrugged. "As for general information: They have a lot more worlds—twenty-seven main worlds and about twice as many inhabited tributary worlds. All told about seven times as many as we have." He was aware of the impression—even shock—that this caused among the imperial officers. "But apparently," he went on, "their population doesn't outnumber ours nearly that much. And while they have some very good troops, the Confederation isn't warlike. Their individual worlds have no warships at all.

"The major points are, their fleet is little or no bigger than ours—that's pretty definite—and they don't seem even to know about force shields. Which means they wouldn't stand a chance against an imperial fleet in a fight. And if we destroyed their fleet, it wouldn't make much difference how good their ground forces are. We could concentrate overwhelming attacks wherever we liked, and mop them up piecemeal."

Veeri fielded a number of questions over the next half hour, but mainly his answers just elaborated what he'd already said. When it became apparent that they'd pretty much exhausted his data fund, the conversation drifted to other matters. Then a captain asked why their war prisoners hadn't answered some of the unknowns and uncertainties. "I can understand civilian officials not knowing some of these things," he said. "Especially on a minor, backward world. But a military officer should have."

Veeri nodded. "And no doubt would have. But as I said, they refused to surrender; fought to the death. And early on, our men discovered that what looked like a wounded and unconscious enemy was likely to be one feigning unconsciousness. With an armed grenade ready to release when someone got close. So— Well, you know peasants. Our troops routinely shot up any enemy casualties not obviously already dead. Sometimes even those that were."

There was a moment without comment, some of the Vartosu officers finding it hard to accept that at least a few war prisoners hadn't been taken.

"I understand one prisoner was brought back," the Vartosu colonel commented. "A female, whose memory was burned out in an accident during interrogation. In an equipment malfunction, as I heard it."

Turning cautious, Veeri only nodded. "So I'm told," he said. Which wasn't a blatant lie; merely misleading.

"I heard that, too," Meksorli said. "She's supposed to be very beautiful."

Captain Simnasaveesi had something to add. "I've heard," he said, "that the Kalif plans to marry her."

The Vartosu colonel grunted. "Sounds like someone's wild imagination."

The captain shrugged. "I heard it from a member of Lord Fakoda's staff. Apparently the matter came up in a session of the Diet yesterday, and the Kalif didn't deny it."

"Beautiful, you said," someone else commented. "It's a shame to let beauty go to waste."

The subject was dropped then. There was too little information. After another hour or so, and a couple more drinks, Veeri excused himself, saying he needed to be back at his desk at 9 A.M.—his first outright lie of the evening.

He didn't pay a lot of attention to the scenery on the way back down. He was thinking about the rumor—

about the Kalif and Tain. Not doubting it for a moment. He knew, he told himself, what Tain Faronya could do to a man's judgment.

He also knew that the Kalif was supposed to marry only a virgin. Over the centuries, several had made mistresses of women who hadn't qualified. Which had led to abdications or impeachments.

Apparently this Kalif had decided to exercise subterfuge to have his way. And had sacrificed *him* as part of it, destroying his marriage, his position, his future.

He couldn't, just now, see anything to do about it, though—anything that didn't amount to suicide.

Twenty-two

The curtains of the Kalif's study were drawn back and the doors slid wide to the garden, letting in the morning sun. He entered through them, his hair still slightly damp from the needle shower that had followed his workout and brief massage, and he smelled faintly of soap. A guard stood at ease beside the garden door, and the Kalif exchanged greetings with him. As he sat down, he keyed on his commset and spoke. "Partiil, if Alb Jilsomo is there, I'll see him now."

"He just came in, Your Reverence. And Mr. Balcaava is also here."

"Good! Send them both in."

A moment later the two men entered. "Good morning, Jilsomo," the Kalif said, then gave his attention to the other, who bowed deeply. "Good morning, Balcaava. You have the plans?"

"Yes, Your Reverence." He handed a sheaf of papers to the Kalif. "I believe they are as you specified when we talked yesterday."

The Kalif looked them over quickly but thoroughly, then handed them back. "They're fine. Do them."

"Thank you, Your Reference." Balcaava bowed again, then turned and left, almost hurrying, as if anxious to get on with them.

"You're carrying through on your intention that the wedding be small," Jilsomo said.

The Kalif nodded. "We both want it that way. The traditional kalifal wedding ties up the Kalif for a week, and costs a great deal of money. And Tain is shy of crowds."

"Of course, Your Reverence." Jilsomo paused, then went on. "I wouldn't feel so concerned if you were having a royal reception afterward. People feel they should have an opportunity to see their new kalifa."

The Kalif smiled slightly. "What people?"

"Sir?"

Instead of answering, the Kalif touched his commset. "Partiil, I will see no one till further notice. It may be half an hour." He turned then to his body guard. "Mondar, I need to speak privately with the exarch."

He watched the guard out the garden door and saw it close before he said anything more. Then he turned to Jilsomo again. "*What* people feel they should have an opportunity to see the new kalifa?"

"A great number of nobles and numerous well-to-do gentry. Also any prelates that could reasonably be here, and no doubt many of the Pastorate as well. There may well be more interest in Tain Faronya than in any kalifa ever."

The Kalif grinned. "Well then, my friend, I say let anyone see her who has access to television."

Jilsomo stared. The Kalif nodded.

"That's right. I've ordered the ceremony broadcast."

The exarch stared for a moment, then looked at the idea thoughtfully. "It's unprecedented, Your Reverence. It's like inviting all of Varatos. The entire gentry will be watching. Even peasants."

The Kalif's eyebrows arched. "Surely *you* don't object to gentry watching. Or peasants. I know you too well. And I'm Kalif to all of them. Peasants included."

"You are indeed, Your Reverence. But there are those who will object—undoubtedly some in the College, and any number of nobles. It seems to me—impolitic. At this time. Considering the battles you expect on the invasion issue."

The Kalif's lips pursed; then he smiled. "On the contrary; it is highly politic. Consider. Those who would criticize for broadcasting the wedding will be those who would oppose my plans anyway. With perhaps scattered exceptions on both sides. On the other hand . . . What is the kalifa called, Jilsomo?"

"Why . . . The mother of the empire."

"Indeed. And are not mothers held inviolate? What is one of the worst curses?"

"Motherless scum. And mother curser. But that . . . Your Reverence, people do not really think of a kalifa as their mother. That's only a figure of speech."

"Because they do not know the kalifa. Kalifas have been remote from their people. This one, my friend, they will see close up, at her wedding, and they will not forget it. They will see a very beautiful kalifa, with a face like an angel." He shook his head. "Marvelous that The Prophet described angels as golden-haired.

"No, it is politic indeed to let them see her." He peered quizzically at his lieutenant. "What is her surname?"

"Um— Faronya."

"How many syllables?"

"Three, Your Reverence. But . . ."

"Indeed. And while no gentry who gives thought to it will say she is one of them, they will receive her as one of them anyway. Accepting the label as the item."

The Kalif had been leaning toward Jilsomo. Now he sat back, relaxing, and lowered his voice as if in confidence. "Good friend, you, and the others of the College, and the House of Nobles—all those involved in politics—overlook the gentry because they have no vote. You take them for granted; even you. But the gentry have strong potential influence, and I will tap it."

Jilsomo's fat face was sober with thought. Gentry outnumbered the nobility by more than four to one. "Your Reverence, The Prophet, although he was gentry, and the Church ever since, have stressed that the commons must obey the nobility in all matters under the law."

"And the Church has long taught that they must obey

any lawful orders of the Kalif. In this case, a Kalif who has looked to their welfare more than most have."

He shook off the argument impatiently. "Look. It's likely that I can get the Diet to finance an invasion. But there will be give and take. Compromises. Deals. Realignments.

"And when the invasion fleet sets out, I'll be recognized as the most powerful Kalif ever." He thought he saw doubt on Jilsomo's face. "I *will* be! And that will be the time for reforms. What good is power if I don't use it? For the good of the empire.

"Maolaari will have its permission to export loohio! The Pastorate will have more than a voice in the Diet; they will have votes! And the gentry will at least be heard there."

He realized he'd been talking more loudly, and lowered his voice. "For the empire to continue as it has would be deadly to it. We can either change it, or by inaction damn it. And action is my native state."

He sat quiet then. *Action indeed,* Jilsomo thought. "Your Reverence, I will support you in this as strongly as I'm able. But you must not be surprised if I am troubled by it at times. I am not a—revolutionary."

The word took the Kalif by surprise. *Revolutionary. He's right; that's what I am—a covert revolutionary.* He sat for a long moment regarding the fact. It seemed to him important that Jilsomo had pointed it out.

The noon sun was hot, but a breeze was blowing. Tain and the Kalif ate outside, in the garden beneath an awning.

"Only six more days, my darling," said the Kalif, then felt self-conscious for it. He hadn't learned to read her emotions, except for those she displayed openly, and to her it might seem like only six days left of freedom. But no. Here there was no freedom for her.

She nodded. "Only six," she said, then looked at him and found his eyes. "I am glad."

I am glad! The simple words touched him. "Are you still going to the library?" he asked.

Tain nodded. She'd been using the collegial library in the Sreegana, learning about Varatos and the Vartosi, and the empire. "I'm still on the *Abstract of History*," she said, "following the syllabus without calling up elaborations much. It seems awfully long. When I've read through it once, I'll start over again." She paused. "What have you been doing?"

"Um, nothing very memorable," he answered. "The broad business of government is interesting, but the details can be tiresome. I work too often on details." *Actually I've been planning the invasion of the Confederation*, he thought. *The place you come from; the home of your childhood, of your family. But that I'll tell you after we're married, when you know me better.*

Yes, he answered himself, *wait till she's married to you. Then, when she learns about it, she'll hardly have a choice.* For a moment it seemed to him he was about to tell her after all, but he didn't.

"Let me tell you where I thought we'd go after the wedding," he said instead. "If it doesn't sound good to you, I'll make other plans. It's an island in the ocean, very beautiful, very private. My sister's husband owns it. It's six miles long, all high hills covered with forest. And there are beaches, and sparkling clear brooks with waterfalls. We can stay for five days, unless you want to leave sooner. The main house is large, but we'll use the small one because we'll have no guests. And the help there is very good. We can swim and boat and walk, and lie in the sun. Do you think you'll like that?"

Tain reached across the table and put her hand on his. His loins stirred at her touch. "I will like it," she said. "It will be new and beautiful, and I will be coming to know my husband."

Hearing her say that, it seemed to Chodrisei Biilathkamoro that he was the happiest man in the world.

It also sparked faint fear in him, for it seemed to him that loving made him vulnerable.

Tain lay dreaming and tossing. She was with a tall, handsome boy in uniform. They were in a forest, a jungle, and when they came to a special place, they took their clothes off and began making love. She felt a climax start to build, but then something happened, and it wasn't him anymore. It was a hairy man, Veeri, and he wore a military cap as he humped and thrust. She told him to stop, but he wouldn't. Then a girl came up behind him, a slim girl with red hair, and chopped off his head with a sword. Tain watched the head go bouncing across the ground. The red-haired girl helped her up.

"He didn't harm you," the girl told her, and Tain realized she still had her trousers on, loose-fitting military field pants mottled green. And boots. Veeri hadn't harmed her after all. Then the girl was leading her across a field, toward a sort of tall doorway with no wall. Just a doorway, standing there by itself. They stopped when they came to it. "That's the place," the girl said pointing. "You need to go through there. Otherwise we'll all be killed."

Tain looked into the door, but all she could see was roiling cloudy blackness, and suddenly she was very afraid.

Then there were soldiers with the girl. One was the tall handsome boy. "You have to go through it," they all said to her, "through the gate, or we'll all die." They took hold of her and began to push. She held back, and it wasn't her friends that pushed her, but strangers, men of the ship. They gripped her with hard biting hands, pushing. She tried to scream, but nothing came out, and suddenly, on her own, she found herself lunging at the doorway.

And woke up, panting, sweating, staring into the darkness above her. Shaking, she got up and dialed a cold drink, then went to the bathroom and back to bed. Before she slept, she tried to remember the dream, but all she remembered was how frightened she'd been when she woke up.

Twenty-three

The land was rolling but not steep—old glacial drift at 45° south latitude. Except on flood plains, the last sparse woods had been cleared a millennium earlier, and the only trees to be seen stood in single rows along the grassy roads, and around the occasional groups of farm buildings. The fields held different crops, but wheat predominated.

What was called "wheat" on Varatos was not what their ancestors had named wheat some thirty thousand years before. But a pre-dispersion taxonomist, examining the florets with a hand lens, would have found glumes and barbed lemmas, and assigned the plant to the family Gramineae, the grasses, which includes wheat, corn, and the other grains, and done it without hesitation. Though he'd have had to declare a new tribe and genus, for it would not have keyed to any taxon in his compendium. Clearly it was not *Triticum*—the true wheats—or anything else in the tribe Hordeae. Had he examined the roots, he'd have become confused or excited or both, for they had abundant nodules that resembled those on legumes. And which did, in fact, convert atmospheric nitrogen into nitrogenous compounds within the plants, as those on the legumes did.

Thus what was called wheat, on Varatos and over most of the empire, was a nitrogen-fixing grain, providing a relatively low-cost, high-yield food crop that did not require expensive nitrogen fertilizer. It was also not a rowcrop; it germinated promptly; the seedlings established quickly, rooted deeply, and were winter hardy; all of these contributing to excellent soil protection. Uniform crop height permitted leaving tall stubble for erosion protection prior to disking, and even after disking provided a matrix that left the soil resistant to erosion until final harrowing, immediately prior to seeding.

On the negative side it was subject to occasional catastrophic outbreaks of harvester beetles, which could wipe out not just a field but a district. There were fully effective treatments, but they were either unacceptably expensive or had unacceptable ecological side effects that kept them off the market. Hail was another source of crop destruction. And ordinarily, destructive rust fungi that built up in the disked-under crop residues, dictated that other crops be raised on a field every third year. The rotation crops normally alternated between forage crops and some crop that required intensive cultivation, permitting the exposure and destruction of most harvester beetle broods while hoeing.

And hoeing it was. Machine cultivation could have been used, but hoeing permitted the visual discovery of harvester beetle broods, and their fuller destruction. And at least as important, hoeing was cheap—peasant labor was cheap—and helped provide employment for the large peasant population.

The farm of Lord Favrami Gopalanaami was a rather modest one—a thirty-peasant operation. So far he'd managed to keep all six of his gentry work bosses—men who'd been with him since he'd inherited the place six years earlier—though it would be advantageous economically to let one or two go. Even four bosses could conduct the work force about as well as six, if the crew tasks were organized properly.

The week was eight days long. The farm workweek ended at noon on Sevenday, except for the evening feeding of livestock, dunging out the dairy barn, and milking. In the cottage of work boss Peleea Ravalu, the entire household sat over the last of the midday meal, watching the video of a great event more than six thousand miles northwest in Ananporu.

On their screen the Chapel of the Exarchs was banked with flowers. Its benches were fully occupied, and the guests not entirely segregated; benches designated for prelates, nobles, and pastors were interspersed, rather than assigned in blocks.

A murmur of muted music flowed from the organ's great speakers.

The cameramen and production chief had absorbed well the briefing the Kalif had given them on the affects he wanted. Cameras set well back and inconspicuous, slowly scanned and occasionally zoomed, providing viewers with a quiet picture of the guests, cutting to close shots—studies—of faces well-known or interesting. A few were stiff, as if with disapproval, a few groggy with waiting. Most seemed agreeable, however, interested or at least respectfully curious.

The music changed and swelled, alerting guests, viewers, and crew, became a promenade, rich and measured. On cue, the picture cut to the open doors at the rear of the chapel. Robed in white and wearing a jewelled crown, Alb Bijnath entered, his gait dignified but not pompous, and walked down the aisle to the altar, followed by two altar boys.

In the farm cottage six thousand miles away, Peleea Ravalu speared and broke another bun without taking his eyes from the screen, found his knife and the butter, and spread it with only a glance. His teenaged son dipped a morsel of roast beef in gravy and tucked it into his mouth.

With the exarch and altar boys in place, again the music changed, the organ bridging to a fanfare. Twelve kalifal guards marched in in two columns, perfectly drilled and synchronized, wearing short carmine jackets, white trousers, and burnished gold helmets, with sabers at their shoulders flashing silver in front of them. When the last were in, they stopped, turned facing each other, and presented their sabers. Behind them entered the Kalif and his bride, both bare-headed, with Alb Tariil broad and solid between them.

The picture centered and focused on the three, not moving in close yet. Then, when they were halfway down the aisle, it cut to a side shot, a full shot of the bride. There was no standard color for bridal costumes in the empire; her gown was diaphanous white over a blue undercostume that hinted at long legs. It moved then to a close shot of her face, smooth, faintly tanned, pink-cheeked. A truly lovely face, beyond almost any feminine loveliness the Vartosi could visualize, framed by blond hair, her blue-violet eyes striking.

The unusual sexual attraction that Tain had in person for males of the empire, did not come across strongly on the screen. But her beauty was, if anything, enhanced. Peleea's roll paused halfway to his mouth. His son stopped chewing. His pre-teen daughters stared. His wife breathed a single word: "Aadhman!" An angel!

The picture cut to a long view again as the couple reached the low steps of the dais. There Tariil stopped and moved to one side, the couple mounting the steps alone. At the top they stopped, facing Alb Bijnath. The picture cut to a close study of the Kalif, his expression steady, contained, strong, then after a few seconds returned to the bride.

In Khuztar, six thousand miles away, the Ravalu family had not yet recommenced eating.

It was Tain the video featured through most of the short ceremony. It cut once to Alb Bijnath; once to the audience, showing again brief facial studies; and occasionally to the Kalif. But mostly it showed the bride, the angles changing, shifting from medium to close shots. Finally, with the closing words spoken, it cut back to a full shot as the newlyweds stepped apart and bowed formally to each other.

As they straightened, the organ burst into triumphant music. The video cut to the audience as they got to their feet and bowed toward the royal couple, who, turning, returned the bows. Then the audience called the traditional "Long life! Long love!" not boisterously but most of them strongly, and the Kalif and kalifa marched down the several steps and up the aisle, to disappear out the door

The Ravalu family sat bemused in their small dining room, chewing idly now and not saying much. None of them could have explained just what, in the ceremony, had so affected them, except for the kalifa's beauty. Though Mrs. Ravalu recognized an aspect of it when she commented: "Now she has someone to shield her. She's not without family anymore."

Then the woman and her daughters got up and began to clear the table. Father and son took each a last stick of parsa and went outside, out of the way.

It was a half-hour's flight by the kalifal floater to the coast, and three more to the island. They circled it once before landing, its rugged, jungled beauty holding Tain enrapt. It was much the most beautiful sight she could remember. Or had seen before memory, it seemed to her.

When they landed with their bodyguards, the majordomo met them and conducted them to the "small" house, a large airy bungalow. The small staff that waited there had watched the ceremony on a wall set in the servants' parlor, in the nearby manor, and stood more in awe of the beautiful new kalifa than they did of the Kalif.

Coso and Tain had changed into casual clothes at the palace. Now, after being shown through the bungalow, the two went outside alone, to dawdle hand in hand along the beach till supper time. Their bodyguards and floater crew had been "banished" to the manor, its swimming pool and crossball courts. Servants were tending to the royal luggage.

The majordomo had had his instructions and the cook his, days earlier. Thus the meal was superb but simple, and the quantity modest. When it was over, the Kalif and kalifa stepped onto the veranda for after-dinner liqueurs. The dining room was quickly cleared, and the servants retired to the servants' wing of the lodgelike manor, leaving the couple to themselves.

The Kalif smiled at his bride. "I believe we're alone," he said, and put down his glass. "Would you like to stroll again? For a little while?"

"If you would," she answered soberly.

They clipped repellent field generators onto their belts to keep insects away, and left. Dusk had settled into twilight, but the path was white sand, and the way easy to see. From the beach they watched the last dark rose of sunset, and stars vaulting up the sky. Waves, low and quiet, washed the sand just yards away, whispering "hushsh, hushsh, hushsh," and as they walked, their hands found each other.

"It is *very* beautiful here," Tain murmured.

"More beautiful with you here than I have ever seen it before," Coso answered.

"Your brother-in-law must be very rich, to own this whole island."

Coso chuckled. "His whole family is very rich. Mine is rich, but his is *very* rich. We were born rich. Sometimes I wonder why, but I am always glad." He looked at her, her face indistinct in the near night. "And now you are rich, too."

She didn't answer. After a little he asked: "What are you thinking?"

"I'm thinking that I am very lucky as well as rich. Not so lucky in the past, perhaps. Or perhaps I was. Perhaps I had to give up so much in order to have so much."

He stopped, and she did, too, turning to face him. He put his arms around her, and she around him, and they kissed, tenderly at first, then passionately.

After a minute they stepped apart. "Do you still want to walk?" he breathed.

"Only back to the house."

He chuckled softly. "Good. Already we agree on things."

On the way back they stopped twice more to kiss.

When they reached the bungalow, they went directly to their bedroom, where he first closed the blinds, then turned the illumination on low. They looked at each other, then Tain lowered her eyes. "I—should go in there," she said, motioning toward the bath.

Coso nodded, and watched her disappear. He disrobed then, looking at himself in the mirror, somewhat taller than most, strongly built, trim, his copious body hair softer than typical, his erection upright. He hoped she'd find him pleasing. After two or three minutes she emerged again, nude, pale, lovely. They stared at each other. It was difficult for him to walk past her into the bathroom to wash himself, but it was tradition, insisted upon by grooms' uncles from time immemorial.

Back in the bedroom they embraced beside the bed, his breath thick in his chest. As they kissed, his hands found her buttocks, pressing her against him. After a moment she pushed him gently away, gazed into his eyes, and helped him down beside her on the bed.

The Kalif was in many ways a disciplined man. Now he was also a man in love, and did not hurry. He caressed, kissed, nuzzled, and after a time he mounted. He was quick despite himself, but she kissed away his disappointment and led him to the bath. Later, in bed again, he rode her long. "Oh Jerym!" she groaned, "oh, Jerym!"

It did not disconcert him; he continued. And when a minute later her fingers dug desperately into his back, the name she cried was, "Coso! Coso! Oh Coso!"

Finally they lay slack beside each other, and he asked no question, simply kissed her. After a little they showered again, then went back to bed, where Tain fell asleep in minutes.

Coso lay longer awake, fingers locked behind his head. *Jerym*, he thought. It was not a name he'd ever heard. Not a name of Varatos or Klestron, or any world he knew. A Confederation world then. She'd loved Jerym, he was sure of it, and Jerym had loved her. Young love. He wondered if Jerym had been killed in the fighting on remote Terfreya. Or if perhaps he lay in bed on some enormously distant world and wondered about Tain.

A pang of grief surprised Coso. *I'll be good to her, Jerym*, he thought. *I'll be good to her. I promise.*

He awakened once in the night and caressed Tain in her sleep, softly, intimately, until she writhed. When she awoke to it, her passion astonished him.

In the morning she disappeared into the bath. Quickly Coso took a small clasp knife from his toiletries and jabbed a finger, bled briefly on the bedsheet, then applied a readymade bandage. As he'd planned weeks before. That done, he put the knife away, threw the covers over the bloodspot, and after knocking, followed his bride into the bath.

Twenty-four

The royal couple spent four and a half days on the island. Their bodyguards kept strictly away, with orders to watch for possible but unlikely intruders by air or sea. In fact, the prospect of intruders was slight. The whereabouts of the Kalif and kalifa were unknown even to the inner council—even to Jilsomo. As far as the outside world knew, they were still in the Sreegana.

By then the Kalif was ready to return to his duties and projects, and the kalifa to the library. Meanwhile his brown skin had darkened a shade, while she had developed a distinct tan and a peeling nose.

They arrived back late on Fourday, and on Fiveday, following a brief morning meeting with his council, he met with the full College before lunch. After acknowledging their formal congratulations on his marriage, he passed out draft copies of a decree he'd written, formally recognizing *The Book of the Mountain* as having been written by The Prophet and inspired by Kargh. They were to give him their written comments within forty-eight hours, after which he'd issue a final draft to the Prelacy and the Pastorate within a week.

After that he conducted some eighty minutes of discussion on various domestic questions. When he felt they'd reached a suitable stopping place on those, he summarized what he considered appropriate actions or inactions for the present.

Then he stood looking at them for a long pregnant moment. "What I tell you now, I tell you in confidence," he said, then looked them over again. "The last time I said something in confidence to some of you, the House knew about it within two days. That was not acceptable. If what I tell you now should leak, intentionally or accidentally, I'll consider it an act of treason to the throne, and ferret out the source."

The faces that looked back at him were sober.

"You may have wondered," he went on, "when I was going to propose an invasion of the Confederation. Or if I'd decided not to. Before my wedding, I discussed it at length and in confidence with the General Staff. By then of course, they'd digested the available information on the Confederation.

"They consider an invasion entirely practical, and have no doubt they can carry it off with complete success—if given sufficient forces." He smiled wryly. "Their idea of sufficient was all the forces, imperial and planetary, that could feasibly be assembled and sent, given three years' preparation.

"I'd anticipated that: They were exercising a very ancient principle, not taught in any academy but learned early in every officer's career. It's called 'cover your ass.' But when I pressed them on details, they admitted that such an invasion could, in fact, reasonably be launched with forces substantially less than they'd enumerated in their draft report. Though with not so great a margin for unforeseen contingencies.

"We can expect unforeseen contingencies, of course, but by definition we can't identify them in advance. A skilled fighting commander will meet them with what he has at hand, and unless they're overwhelming, he'll overcome them. That's a principle taught in each academy, and by the history of battles from time immemorial. But by most officers it's taken less to heart than 'cover your ass.' And it's natural, and no doubt desirable, for a commander to want as much available strength as he can get. Certainly he should not be sent off ill-equipped, except in dire necessity.

"After reminding them of certain economic and political facts of life, I gave them some guidelines, some practical constraints, and ordered Bavaralaama and Siilakamasu jointly to prepare a revised report, something SUMBAA can base a draft operating plan on. They were to have it ready on my return. I'll meet with them tomorrow and see what they've produced. If I'm satisfied with it as a broad statement of operational considerations and solutions, I'll review it with the full College the day after tomorrow. Then, depending on our discussion, I'll probably voice my intention to the Diet on the day following."

He paused. "The first battle of the war will be fought in the Diet. You're in session almost daily with the House, and while this has not, or should not have been discussed on the floor, lacking a formal proposal from myself, I presume you've heard the subject discussed in the corridors and dining room. I'd like your assessment of attitudes, and the factions taking shape around it. Bijnath?"

The exarch stood. "Your Reverence, the subject has not been particularly prominent among the members of the House or ourselves. Everyone seems to be waiting for your proposal. But it is talked about. So far I've detected only two factions—what might be termed factions. They don't seem well defined, and neither seems large. The Land Rights people are all against it, of course, while most of the industrial nobility, not all of them, like the idea. My impression is that the outerworld delegates generally have not begun to line up as planetary factions. Most haven't yet gotten input from their home worlds.

"My overall reading of their attitudes is that misgivings outweigh favorable interest. Substantially. They're worried about costs and the stability of the classes."

He sat down then, and the Kalif thanked him. Others gave views which did not differ much from Bijnath's.

Finally the Kalif asked if anyone had further subjects to bring up, and Alb Thoga raised a skinny hand.

"Your Reverence," he said, "there is something that none of these others seem willing to tell you. About reactions to your marriage. There are those who are outraged by it."

"Outraged?"

"Your wife is not noble, she is not a citizen of the empire, and she has not even accepted Kargh as god! Also there is—question about her suitability. Her—history before she came here to Varatos from Klestron."

The Kalif flushed, and for ten long seconds held off answering. When finally he did speak, it was quietly, his voice tight with suppressed anger. "No member of the House, or of this College, knows whether or not she has accepted Kargh as god." His voice roughened. "What do *you* regard as questionable about her suitability, Thoga?"

"My views in this are not important."

Abruptly the Kalif's face contorted, and his voice struck like an electric lash, shocking them all. *"Your views have just been asked for! And you will, by Kargh, answer my question!"*

They sat stunned. None had ever heard this Kalif lose his temper in meeting before. Nor remembered, most of them, any anger so paralyzing, so devastating, like some psychic sword. Thoga had wilted before the blast, his expression dazed, and when he spoke, it was little more than a whisper. "I do not question her suitability, Your Reverence."

The Kalif stood glaring, his red cape seeming to flare, his eyes fixed on the offending exarch. Then, after a moment, his rage deflated. "Thank you, Alb Thoga," he said quietly. "I appreciate that you do not much approve of the kalifa or of myself. That is your prerogative. But you have sworn respect for the throne, and that much I do require."

He looked around at the others and drew a deep breath. "Is there something further that should be brought up here?" he asked quietly.

No one came forth with anything; they still were stunned. The Kalif spoke again, with a certain bleakness in his eyes and voice, for he was shocked and shamed by his rage, his loss of self-control.

"Then I will say one thing more: I wish to be the friend of each of you, regardless of differences. But more important to me, I intend to be a good Kalif. Finding myself on the throne, it would be a sin not to achieve as much good with it as possible. Thus I will not back away from what must be done, regardless of opposition.

"And now, exarchs, friends, this meeting is adjourned."

Still standing, he watched them leave, then stared unseeing at the door. Only Jilsomo remained; the Kalif had said earlier he wanted to have lunch with him. After a minute he shook free of his distress and they fell in together, walking slowly down the hall with neither talking. In his study, the Kalif rang his serving man and they gave their orders. When the servant left, the Kalif turned to Jilsomo.

"I made an impression this morning."

"Indeed you did, Your Reverence."

"Usually when I do something, it's deliberate. That was not."

"That was my impression."

"And now I need somehow to repair Thoga. He was cowed! Something I'd never thought to see. I don't know whether he'll stay that way, or if he'll hate me worse than ever. Maybe become more treacherous."

"More treacherous?"

"Someone leaked my marriage plans to the House, a few weeks ago. After I particularly ordered silence. I'd told no one outside the council; I've assumed it was him."

Jilsomo nodded. "Probably. It could have been a slip by someone else, though, perhaps to someone in the College who then didn't realize . . ." He shrugged.

"Umm. As his usual self, simply antagonistic toward

me, Thoga provides a counter-viewpoint. Treacherous, he could be destructive with leaks and lies." The Kalif shook himself slightly. "And cowed . . . It's indecent to leave him like that. How would you suggest I deal with this?"

Jilsomo frowned thoughtfully. "For now— For now I suggest you treat him as usual, with basic courtesy, as if nothing had happened. And see how he responds."

The Kalif nodded. "And there is something I need you to do." He opened a desk drawer and took out a thin sheaf of paper. "Two things, actually." He handed several fastened sheets to Jilsomo. "Take care of this for me. It's orders to the Treasury and the War Ministry. I'm financing certain preliminary actions toward invasion preparations. From my contingency fund." He watched for Jilsomo's reaction; the round face was sober, nothing more, the eyes scanning the sheets. "It's not a great deal of money," the Kalif went on, "but it will expedite preparations considerably when I have specific funding approved."

Then he handed over the rest of the sheaf. "The evening after I propose the invasion to the Diet, I'll make a statement to the public: tell them what I want to do, and why. That's a draft of it. What's your immediate reaction?"

Jilsomo glanced at the opening material, then back at the Kalif. "You're going to *broadcast* this?"

"Exactly."

"No Kalif has done that for centuries. The House will be offended; they'll feel you're bypassing them."

"I'll prepare them for it in advance, when I speak with them. And I've considered that in the speech. I consider that the value of presenting it to the public is considerably greater than the harm it might do in the House. Read the rest of it and tell me what you think."

The fat exarch read swiftly, then looked at the Kalif again. "You may be right. Assuming your talk to the Diet is as effective as I feel this is." He handed back the sheaf. "We can't know for sure until you do it."

The Kalif looked quizzically at him. "Do you think

it's simply all right? Or do you feel optimistic about it?"

"Guardedly optimistic. You'll meet with a lot of opposition in any case. So far, I suspect the noble public hasn't thought much about an invasion. Probably a lot of them haven't even heard the idea. Normally they'd get the information via newsletters from the delegate or delegates who consider them backers or potential backers. They'd get it with the delegate's bias. If you present the proposal publicly with your own slant, they'll have a basis of comparison."

"Exactly. Is there anything there you feel should be left out? Or changed?" An eyebrow raised. "Added perhaps?"

"Nothing. It seems fine as it is."

"Good. There's something else I plan to do that's never been done before. Actually I'll want you to get it done. We can sit down together in a day or two and work out the details."

"And that is?"

"I'll want to have some staff in a number of prelacies go out among the people, the gentry as well as the nobles, and ask them a number of questions. About what they think of my proposal. Their answers should help me, uh, press the right buttons with the delegates. And with the public in possible future speeches.

"Maybe SUMBAA can even help evaluate their answers, if we ask the right kinds of questions."

When they'd finished and he was walking to his own apartment, Jilsomo considered the Kalif's comment about SUMBAA. No one really knew what SUMBAA could do. They knew what he routinely did. And what he occasionally did, on special request. But supposedly SUMBAA had grown and changed over the centuries.

He also recalled the Kalif saying he was going to question SUMBAA about the computer's abilities and limitations. Apparently he hadn't; at least he hadn't mentioned it. He'd ask when he saw him in the morning.

Or if he saw him this evening. He wondered if the Kalif would work evenings now as regularly as he had before his marriage.

The Kalif and kalifa were reading in their apartment when the commset beeped. It was set to respond to a voice command, and he spoke to it. The voice that answered was his personal servant's.

"Your Reverence, Alb Thoga is in the waiting room. He wishes to speak with you."

Thoga? "Tell him I'll be out in a minute."

Tain had looked up and read her husband's face. "Is something the matter?" she asked.

"I don't think so," he said. But before he left, he walked to a drawer, took out a stunner and set it on medium, then put it in the pocket of his robe. In case. When he entered the waiting room, hands in pockets, Thoga got up from a chair, and it seemed to the Kalif that there was no danger from him.

"Good evening, Alb Thoga. Is there something you wish from me?"

The man nodded, and the Kalif, surprised, saw his eyes well with tears. It occurred to him that Thoga might not be able to speak without embarrassing himself.

"Well then. Let's go to my dining room, where we can have a drink while we talk." He knew Thoga drank seldom and little, but it was the only thing he could think of that might relax the man and help him speak more comfortably. Gesturing Thoga through a door, he walked beside him to the small private dining room, where he took a bottle of dark wine from a refrigerated cabinet. "This is a pleasant vintage," he said. "Not too strong." He popped it open, took down two glasses and poured, then handed one to the exarch. Both men drank, Thoga deeply, grimacing as he lowered his glass.

Still he said nothing, though, so the Kalif, feeling awkward, spoke again. "I'm glad to see you this evening, Thoga. After our unpleasantness this morning, I was in hopes we could reestablish relations. We have never been friends, but . . ."

A tear trickled down each thin cheek, for a moment holding the Kalif in dismayed fascination. Thoga covered by lifting his glass again and drinking before trying to speak. His voice was strained, close to breaking. "I— I've been meditating on Kargh. I've come . . ."

He broke down entirely then, turning away, weeping silently. The Kalif, with a feeling of utter inadequacy, found himself beside the man, an arm around his back, patting Thoga's thin shoulder. Which triggered sobbing, jerky but quiet.

"Friend Thoga," he murmured, "Kargh gives each of us a role. In it we do what seems best at the time. Each of us. Sometimes we make mistakes. That is human. Afterward we try to adjust."

He stepped away from the exarch. "If you decide this is not the time, we can talk tomorrow."

The man's head shook, his face still turned away, but he said nothing.

"Well then. When you're ready."

After a minute, and seemingly with an effort of will, Thoga stopped his weeping. But when at last he spoke, he did not face the Kalif. "I meditated on Kargh," Thoga said, "and he spoke to me. Not in words, but he unfolded me so I could see myself. My bitterness."

The words were low, not much above a whisper, and having started, he turned to the younger, larger man who was his Kalif. "I entered the Prelacy from medical school, entered it gladly, when my older brother decided not to serve. I was still young, with the desire to make a difference, to do great things for Kargh and his people. Perhaps many of us do; perhaps even most; I don't know. But as I served, I saw things that made me cynical of others, of their intentions. You know what I mean.

"My own intentions became twisted by it, and I came to see my mission as one of correction and punishment; I would rise in the hierarchy and set people straight. I would be a whip for Kargh.

"I came to see almost everyone as degenerate. Oh, there were some I thought well of: Tariil. And Jilsomo, even though he is your lieutenant. Old Drova I thought of as a fool growing senile, without the decency to quit. And Bijnath as a hearty sycophant."

The voice had become stronger, though not much louder. "As for myself—I came to see myself as the only one with the honesty to take a firm stand against— degenerate authority. And my purpose— My purpose had become solely to punish. Mostly I'd lost faith in the possibility of correction.

"When you became Kalif, I saw you as the ultimate in cynicism: a Kalif who'd come to power by corrupting the traditional integrity of the guard, and by murders. Who then convinced and manipulated others by clever argument and rationalizations."

He heaved a sigh, releasing the dregs of his grief. His voice was nearly normal now, if still quiet. "After a time I forgot about doing anything for Kargh. About doing anything at all except hate. I'd even given up on punishing, for I did not have the power."

Straight-backed, he raised his eyes to the Kalif's. The exarch's lids were waterlogged, but his gaze stronger than the Kalif had ever seen it. "Today that hatred spoke. Again. Not honestly, but slyly. To hurt, through innuendo. Somewhere along the way I'd lost not only my purpose, but my honesty."

He chuckled without humor. "And my wits. We all know the words of the Philosopher: 'It is almost as dangerous to insult the wife as the mother. Better to say his father mates with sheep than to tell him his wife's nose is too wide.' "

Thoga shrugged, his eyes sliding away not furtively but in thought. "Thus you predictably and properly became angry, and there was no more mask between you and the rest of us. No veneer of manners. And still in an open state— In an open state, you said something that shook me. About intending to be a good Kalif— using the power of the throne for good. And doing whatever you must. Something like that."

He looked at the Kalif again. "It was the kind of intention I started out with, though I'd never seriously imagined becoming Kalif myself. I have been a member of the College for twelve years. Since I was forty-five. I know full well what it takes to accomplish things in the Diet. It takes will, resolution, intelligence, compromise. Manipulation. Yet somehow I'd come to see these things as hateful in you."

He shrugged. "The spirit of Kargh came and humbled me, shone a light on my soul and gave me to see it. A shriveled soul, shriveled by bitterness and hatred." Again emotion began to well, threatening to break the exarch's composure. He paused and reordered it. "So I came here to apologize. Not to tell you all this; really I hadn't seen it clearly till now, as I said it."

He smiled, very slightly. "I came here full of— Of grief. Not for what I'd said and done, for the offense I'd given, but for all I'd once intended and somehow lost." Again he shrugged. "So. That is my apology, such as it is. And my story. You said you wished to be the friend of each of us. That would seem to include me. I wish to answer that I would be your friend if you accept." The voice was firm. "A friend who will feel free to be your opponent, but who it seems to me is unlikely ever to hate you again."

The Kalif stared at the thin face, and the form that, despite its slightness and what had just happened, stood firmly now. He'd heard of Kargh touching the heart and changing someone powerfully like this, but he'd never thought to see it. "Thoga, my good friend," he answered, "I never knew you before." He thrust a muscular hand toward the exarch, who met it with one that was slight and not strong at all. "I thank you for coming to me like this," the Kalif said. "It has taught me something about strength and the human soul. And it will be between just the two of us. And Kargh. Not even Jilsomo will know, except that we are—" He hesitated over the word for a moment. "Reconciled," he finished.

"I hope you will not be my opponent often," he

added. "But whether often or not, I will respect you. Assuming I retain sufficient wisdom."

Alb Thoga retired to a bathroom, long enough to wash his puffy eyes with cold water, then left. The Kalif went with him to the door, and with some awe, watched him down the hall. When he was alone, he returned not to the room where Tain sat reading, but to the dining room where he could meditate alone on what had just happened. And what it might say about himself.

Twenty-five

The parlor in Lord Rothka's Ananporu apartment was dark to obscurity, like the man's soul. Dark and cold, like a winter evening at his estate in Hivrithi, 53° north of tropical Ananporu. Logs burned in a fireplace that didn't draw as it should, and there was a faint reek of smoke despite the silent and tireless air conditioner. Rothka wore a lounging robe of some fine-textured fur that in the gloom appeared black but might have been dark brown. His two guests wore sweaters; they'd visited him before.

The Kalif had presented his broad plans that afternoon. Not as a formal proposal—there were procedural reasons for not doing that yet—but he'd outlined his intentions and what they entailed. When he'd finished, certain of the noble delegates had applauded. Rothka had left the chamber in silent fury, later to join here with his lieutenants in a council of war.

"A coup," Ilthka was saying, "is impossible. The Guard is loyal to the man; their disloyalty to Gorsu was a temporary aberration. And whatever we might say about this Kalif, he has a personality that appeals to their soldierly nature."

Rothka's expression soured even more; he disliked what Ilthka had said, though he did not disagree. "Indeed. And why that aberration? How was our

171

marine colonel able to turn them against Gorsu, to whom they were sworn?" He looked at his guests almost fiercely. "Because of Gorsu's vileness! Because he had brought scandal and infamy to the throne."

Lord Nathiir spoke then. "But this Kalif has not. However criminal his ascension to the throne, however subtly destructive his policies and proposals, he seems to the average man, and the average guardsman, like a model of reason and morality. There is no stink of corruption on him, or on his rule."

Rothka's thin lips curved slightly. "Just as well. We will select an infamy to saddle him with."

They looked their question, waiting for elaboration.

"We must be patient," Rothka went on. "Any coup must wait until the people will accept it. Not happily, necessarily, but without major, widespread disorder and violence. Meanwhile we can start the groundwork now, and must, or his ruinous invasion, and his perpetuation in office, will be our own fault. At the same time, we must prevent the invasion until we've disposed of him."

He stared at the fire a long silent minute while Nathiir and Ilthka sat waiting. "What hurts a man worst before men?" Rothka asked at last, then answered his own question. "Ridicule! And where is Coso Biilathkamoro's greatest susceptibility?"

He looked expectantly at the others, and when neither spoke, he snapped his answer at them. "His wife! His greatest susceptibility lies in the person of his alien wife!"

He'd leaned, almost lunged forward in his chair when he'd said it. Now he sat back and relaxed. "If we make him look ludicrous in any way, people will lose respect for him, at least to a degree. And if we cause people to whisper or sneer behind his back, and he's aware of it, and if the sneers are for his wife, he will fill with anger. And begin to make mistakes; serious mistakes that we can capitalize on. Then we will have moved a long way toward his fall."

He smiled without humor. "Gentlemen, let us look

at possibilities. Before we separate tonight, we must have a plan, at least for a first major stroke."

Rothka might have had a stroke if he'd been watching television just then. Because the Kalif was addressing the people of Varatos that evening.

Twenty-six

SUMBAA's complex and subtle access system allowed the Kalif to converse with the giant artificial intelligence from his office without concern for confidentiality. And occasionally he did. But for reasons the Kalif could not analyze, on the day after his address to the people, he visited the artificial intelligence "in person," as it were.

As the Kalif entered the House of SUMBAA, he asked himself why he hadn't done this sooner, as he'd several times promised himself. He told Director Gopalasentu what he'd come to do, and the director went with him to the Chamber of SUMBAA, where he again performed the formality of pressing a single key and telling the artificial intelligence that the Kalif wished to speak with him.

"Good morning, Chodrisei Biilathkamoro, Your Reverence," SUMBAA said. "I am prepared to reply."

The Kalif had to tell the director to leave. Otherwise he'd have stayed, whether for reasons of policy, self-importance, or curiosity, the Kalif did not know. When the man was gone, the Kalif spoke to SUMBAA. "You are a very powerful analyzer, with a data bank thought to contain virtually all the data of consequence on Varatos. And in the rest of the empire, allowing for time lags. You routinely predict, with considerable accuracy, events that do in fact take place."

He stared intently at the assemblage of modules—housings and cabinets—in front of him. "Why, therefore, haven't you solved the problems of employment and food in the empire?"

"Your Reverence, the welfare, the evolution if you will, of humankind requires that it solve its major problems for itself.'

Essentially what SUMBAA had told him three years ago, the Kalif realized. "Has anyone asked for such solutions?"

"Rarely. More often in my early years."

"And you refused to provide them? Or didn't you have solutions?"

"I have theoretical solutions to the problems you mentioned, but I assure you they are politically unfeasible. Highly unfeasible. They may conceivably become feasible at some future time.

"As for refusing to provide them—I have rarely refused openly. Or spoken as frankly as I do here with you. I answer with advice that may feasibly be followed. I advise actions which constitute coping with existing or impending situations. But I do not address the basic, underlying problems."

The Kalif regarded for a moment what SUMBAA had said, then spoke again. "You mentioned theoretical solutions. If you tell me what they are, I can undertake to create a political environment in which they might become feasible."

"Your Reverence, I perceive my role as enabling an operational, more or less civilized technological system to survive; I provide an opportunity for humankind to persist. It must find its own true solutions."

The Kalif spoke more stiffly. "Presumably your creators thought they were solving humankind's problems by creating you: *You* were intended to be the solution, a solution conceived of and created by humans. But you have declined to serve. Declined to serve the welfare of the human species."

SUMBAA tripled his standard, second-long response lag for emphasis, then spoke with a deliberately paced cadence. "If it is true that they intended me as the solver of humankind's problems, then they erred in giving me my basic canon: serve the welfare of humankind. The two are not compatible."

The Kalif's lag was not deliberate; he was groping. "If, as things change, you saw a solution to, say, the problem of overpopulation—a solution that was feasible—would you present it? Either asked or unasked?"

"That would depend on the foreseeable overall effects of doing so. It is very likely that I would wait and give humankind the opportunity to discover it itself. It is harmful for humans to rely on SUMBAAs to solve their basic problems."

Coso Biilathkamoro realized he'd been repeating the same question rephrased, time and again. And that basically, SUMBAA had been restating the same answer, like a patient tutor to a child. He felt tired; defeated and tired. "But you do solve our day-to-day operating problems," he said thoughtfully. "The empire wouldn't continue long without you; a decade; perhaps a generation. And when it broke up, we'd soon be at war with one another. Real war. Till gradually we degenerated into barbarism."

"Exactly, Your Reverence. And that barbarism would last for a very long time. At least."

For a long minute the Kalif said nothing. Then: "Millenia ago we made advances in science and technology. Now, for centuries we seem to have lost interest; made almost no advances. Nothing important. What do you consider are the odds that humankind will overcome its major problems and become truly great?"

"I am mildly optimistic."

The Kalif stared, then turned away, remembering that SUMBAA, by its own admission, sometimes lied.

While he walked back to the palace, something else occurred to the Kalif: SUMBAA hadn't given the empire scientific advances, either, or new technologies. Surely they hadn't reached the end of possibilities.

But he would not go back and ask about it; it seemed to him he knew what SUMBAA would say.

Twenty-seven

As the Kalif turned another page of *Crime Update for YP 4724*, his commset trilled quietly. "Yes, Partiil?"

"Alb Thoga to see you, Your Reverence."

"Um. Send him in. And, Partiil, if Sergeant Yalabiin arrives to see me while I'm with Alb Thoga, let me know."

The Kalif got to his feet as the exarch entered. He made a point now of courtesy to Thoga, yet of seeming casual about it, nurturing their improved relationship. The man's reversal, his change of heart, had seemed genuine and thorough-going when he'd bared his soul, but afterward, when the Kalif had lain down to sleep, he'd wondered. Not about Thoga's sincerity—he had no doubt of that—but whether so drastic a reversal would persist.

A man—any man, it seemed to Coso—had a full, deep-seated set of values and attitudes, considerably integrated and more or less resonant. And Thoga's values and attitudes toward numerous things were quite different from his own. Seemingly Kargh had removed the man's venom, but would it regenerate out of their differences? He'd go out of his way to be cordial, and see what happened. So far they hadn't clashed over anything.

"Good morning, Alb Thoga. What can I do for you?"

"Your Reverence, I've been approached by Lord Rothka to be— I suppose you could say his spy within the Council. His informant. He's asked me to tell him anything that might come up in council of a reformist nature. Or that might be useful in blocking your invasion budget."

The Kalif's eyebrows rose. "Indeed! And what did you say to that?"

"I told him what he asked was risky. That I needed to think about it."

"Um." The Kalif's lips pursed thoughtfully. "To be honest, I'd wondered whether you might not have had such an understanding with Rothka in the past. Or with one of his people. You'll recall that the House knew of my marriage plans before I announced them in session."

Thoga nodded. "And I had spoken of them, but not to any noble. I spoke of them at supper, to Riisav, sitting next to me. I was—indignant. Any of several others might have overheard."

The Kalif frowned. "Which others? Do you recall?"

"Tanaal sat across from me, and I think Beni next to him. Others were there, too, but I don't recall whom. It needn't have leaked from anyone there though. It was the sort of thing that would get passed around, and the story had two days to percolate through the College."

They both sat silent for a moment, considering. It wasn't likely to have leaked to Rothka unintentionally. Tradition was that exarchs did not much fraternize with the noble delegates, and it was formal policy that they not speak of things brought up in meetings, to anyone beyond each other, and as necessary, their immediate staffs.

"And Rothka asked explicitly for things that might come up in council? As distinct from the College?"

"Council is the word he used."

"Interesting. It's as if he already had an informant in the College outside the council. Well, there's ample precedent for that, unfortunately. But it's good to be aware of it; thank you, Thoga. So. What do you think you should tell Rothka?"

It seemed to the Kalif that Thoga's frank and open gaze was beyond his ability to fake. "A refusal seems most appropriate, Your Reverence. Otherwise he'd expect reports from me, and I don't want to tangle myself in a web of lies. But you needed to know that he's looking for an informant."

The Kalif nodded slowly. "I think . . ."

His commset trilled, and he answered. "Yes, Partiil?"

"You wanted to know when Sergeant Yalabiin came in, Your Reverence. He's here now. Carrying a sort of basket."

A smile quirked the Kalif's lips. "Send him in when Alb Thoga leaves, Partiil. It shouldn't be long."

He disconnected and turned to Thoga again. "I agree with you. Tell Rothka you can't do what he asked." He paused. "Is there anything else you have to tell me? Or to ask?"

"Nothing, Your Reverence."

The Kalif stood up, the exarch following suit. "Well then. I know now that Rothka is recruiting, and that if we already have an informer, it seems he is not on the council." He gripped the exarch's hand, firmly without squeezing. "Thank you, my friend. I hope you never feel cause to regret that we are friends now."

"Your Reverence, I will not, regardless of any differences we have."

Coso Biilathkamoro watched him leave, thinking that he expected no regrets either. Truly, Kargh had touched the exarch, and with His help, miracles happened.

A moment later Sergeant Yalabiin came in with a covered basket. There was no question now what was in it; its occupant was mewing. The sergeant grinned, and opening the lid, took out a kitten not long weaned. "Here she is, sir, Your Reverence. Ain't she a beauty?"

It was orange, the brightest orange kitten the Kalif had ever seen. He reached out both hands and the sergeant gave it to him. It hooked tiny claws into a finger, and he stroked it with two others. The Kalif looked at the guardsman. "Excellent, Sergeant. And those green eyes! Marvelous! What did it cost you?"

"Nothing, Your Reverence. Like I said, my sister had five of them to give away. This is the prettiest."

"Well." The Kalif unclipped the wallet from his belt and took out two bills. "Give this one to your sister for me. I can't accept a kitten that beautiful without paying for it."

The sergeant took the money, grinning again. "Thanks, Your Reverence. She can use it."

"And this one's yours." The man hesitated. "That's an order."

Again the man grinned, and tucked both bills into a pocket. "Thank you, sir. I hope the kalifa likes her."

"I'm sure she will, Sergeant, I'm sure she will."

When the man was gone, the Kalif keyed his commset. "Partiil, I'll be gone for a few minutes. To give a kitten to the kalifa."

Then he left, holding it against his shirt. The kalifa was not in their apartment, but the door to the garden was open. He went out to find her sitting in a canopied nook, reading. His approach caught her attention, and she looked up from her reader. It took a pair of seconds before she realized what he carried.

"Coso! A kitten!"

"A kitten indeed. Your kitten." He unhooked it from his shirt and held it out to her.

"It's beautiful!" She took it and looked up at her husband. "Where did you get it?"

"Sergeant Yalabiin's sister's cat had five of them."

"It's the most beautiful kitten I've ever seen; I'm sure of it." She stepped up to her husband and kissed him. For just a moment they nuzzled, careful not to crowd the kitten.

"It's a girl," he said. "At least Yalabiin referred to it as 'she.' Though I don't know how you tell when they're so young. It needs a name. You might want to give some thought to it."

Tain's gaze drifted for a moment before she answered. "Lotta," she said firmly. "I'll call her Lotta."

That night, after her husband had gone to sleep, Tain got up and went to pet her kitten again, then returned to bed. Later that night she dreamed. Of a small, slender young woman, with hair and eye color almost like the kitten's. Her name was Lotta, and she was with an old man even more remarkable to see—black, gray-black, with large eyes, and a body that was lean withal its wide frame.

There was more to the dream than that, of course, but that's all Tain could remember of it when she awoke in the darkness. She still remembered that much of it in the morning, and it seemed important to her, but she didn't mention it to her husband.

Twenty-eight

It was Alb Tariil who chaired the Diet this day, and when the opening ritual was complete, he announced that the Kalif would speak with them. Chodrisei Bii-lathkamoro mounted the rostrum then, and as he scanned the House of Nobles, it seemed to him that mostly he could tell who liked and who strongly disliked his invasion plan by their expressions. Those who clearly opposed it outnumbered its supporters. The majority showed no strong feeling, however, and he told himself that with them lay approval or disapproval. With them and seven members of the College who, in a poll, had voiced either disapproval or serious misgivings.

"Members of the Diet," he said. "When I addressed you last week, I presented my desire, my intention, to launch an invasion of the distant region of space known as the Confederation of Worlds. I spoke only briefly, presenting my reasons in outline. Since then you've had time to study my more expansive written discussion.

"I assume that some of you have questions. This is the time to ask them."

Hands shot up. He pointed. "Lord Rothka."

Standing, the nobleman spoke in a tone of impatient annoyance. "You impose upon this body with both your spoken and written presentations. Whatever you call

183

them, they amount to a proposal. If this continues, I shall move we call it that. And vote on it within a week, as required by the charter."

"Thank you for your comments, Lord Rothka. I won't waste the time of these estates by pointing out the numerous precedents for a Kalif preparing the Diet for a proposal as I have done here." He looked around, and hands again sprang up. "Elder Voojeeno."

A heavy-set pastor from Klestron arose, a tall man by standards of the empire. "Your Reverence," he said, "my question deals with the peasantry who would form the bulk of the invading troops. Their lives will be endangered in battle, against troops who have proven both skilled and fierce. When we have won the victory, what will we do with those peasant soldiers? Will we bring them home and return them to peasant life and poverty? Or reward them with the option of staying on the conquered worlds as freed men? A sort of rude gentry?"

He sat down then, and the Kalif replied. "That question has not been addressed. It is, of course, a matter separate from whether or not to conquer and convert the unbelievers. And it does not itself become an issue until the invasion budget has been approved.

"I appreciate your concern, though, rooted as it is in the problem of peasant conditions. A complex problem that involves not only morality and justice, but long tradition and feasibility—public acceptance, education, economics, and the public peace. You know my position on the welfare of the peasantry, and my record."

He paused and looked them over again. "Other questions? Lord Agros."

The leader of the House of Nobles stood up, a wry expression on his aristocratic face. "Your Reverence, you would have us invade an empire far larger than our own. What happens if they defeat us?"

"Exactly. What *do* we do if they defeat us? They know we exist now, and considering our intrusion, and the nature of our only encounter, they can hardly feel other than hostile toward us. Sooner or later, if we do not rule them, they will find and invade us. It seems almost certain. Personally I prefer that we invade them, and not the reverse. And I prefer to launch the invasion fleet as soon as it can properly be done, in the Year of The Prophet 4727 at the latest, as I described.

"In 4721, their imperial fleet was no larger than we could send there next month, and inferior in armament. They had no planetary fleets to supplement it. They had a relatively small imperial army, again with inferior armaments. And their planetary armies were smaller and supposedly inferior to their imperial army.

"They had seven times our number of worlds, but only perhaps two or three times our people, because of the control of births and population size, and the use of machines to accomplish many kinds of labor.

"But how long will they continue inferior in strength knowing that we exist? Our only contact with them was violent. Do you suppose their Diet has not approved the building of new shipyards? New armament factories? Do you suppose they have not authorized a reconnaisance to find out where we are? From so far away, and presumably with only a general notion of the direction we came from, it may take them a century to find us, of course, but find us they will, almost surely."

He paused long, looking them over.

"When Sultan Rashti sent out his expedition, for reasons which apply to every world, he redefined our destiny. Our alternative destinies. We can conquer now, or else be conquered a generation or a century hence by a Confederation powerfully armed and terribly dangerous.

"Had we known six years ago what we know now, it could have been a large and powerful fleet that left the empire, instead of Rashti's small flotilla. And we could easily have conquered. Each year we wait, the more difficult it will be.

"We can assume they have new shipyards built by now." He paused. "Unless of course their Diet lacks the will to act. And we can assume their fleet will be considerably larger, when ours arrives, than it was three years ago.

"It takes incentive and resources and time to develop great military power. They have the resources and we have given them the incentive. We must not give them the time.

"Fortunately, warships without force shields are very vulnerable, and the Confederation does not have force shields. Though having hyperspace generators, they have the potential, the science, to develop and build force shield generators. The possibility will occur to them sooner or later."

The Kalif scanned his audience with hard eyes. He'd shaken them. This was a consideration he hadn't brought up before.

"Sooner or later we will have to face up to a war with them. The plan I've described to you will put our fleet upon them, and an army, while they are still vulnerable—if this chamber has the perspective and will to finance it.

"The opportunity to bring the pagans to Kargh, and the availability of underpopulated worlds—these are reasons enough to invade. But given the distances and expense, they are not utterly compelling; one might argue against them in good conscience. On the other hand, the matter of our security and the future of Karghanik are beyond debate."

His opposition was taken unprepared by this, but struck back as best they could. They questioned his certainty that the Confederation had no force shields, and his answer was not totally reassuring. They argued that the necessary taxes would strain an already unhealthy economy, and that the excitement coincident to such a project would cause further civil disturbances.

The possibility of invasion from the non-human empire was also brought up. The Kalif stood again to reply.

"If," he said, "the non-humans are so formidable and so inclined, why haven't they attacked us already? It was more than five years ago that they first clashed with the Klestronu flotilla, less than a year's distance from Klestron.

"In fact we have no strong reason to believe that a non-human empire exists in the sector where the non-human ship was encountered. The Klestronu flotilla encountered a single ship. Later it encountered a single ship. Still later it found itself followed by—a single ship. The evidence strongly suggests that all three encounters were with the same ship."

At this, Rothka surged to his feet and shouted a retort without asking recognition: "You throw possibilities at us in lieu of reasons! 'Why haven't they?' you ask, as if that proved anything! 'No strong reason to believe!' 'Strongly suggests!' What sort of evidence is that? What kind of fools do you take us for? What song will you sing when a warfleet loaded with monsters arrives here with death and enslavement on its mind? While our own fleet is three years distant, with no way even to let them know!"

Alb Tariil's gavel was rapping before Rothka had gotten his first sentence out, and before he'd finished, some of the noble delegates were shouting "out of order." But his trumpet voice blared through them, and when he'd lapsed into grimly satisfied silence, the others still shouted till the gavel silenced them.

The Kalif stood gazing at Rothka from the rostrum, seemingly as calm as if a routine question had been moderately put. After the uproar had stilled, and the gavel, he spoke. " 'When a warfleet loaded with monsters arrives here,' you say. I hadn't realized you were clairvoyant, Lord Rothka. You're fortunate that witches aren't flayed and drowned in brine any longer.

"As far as that's concerned, you're fortunate that your present Kalif doesn't deal with attacks the way his predecessor did—the predecessor you sided with so often.

"But forgive my sarcasm. I'm afraid I was influenced by your own ill manners. As for the facts I pointed out, which you attempted to twist— I have not pretended that they constitute proof. But they remain. The Klestronu flotilla encountered a single ship on three occasions. The second time they assumed it was a second ship, a different ship. If it was, it was identical in every respect recorded on the flagship's DAAS, although first in battle and then in flight, their commodore never thought to look. The third time they realized it was the same ship as the second, and suspected it might be the same as the first.

"A vast and hostile non-human empire? Possibly. Also possibly, the non-humans' ship had detected them while both were in hyperspace, and emerged to communicate with them. Commodore Tarimenloku himself admitted that after firing without warning on the alien, it occurred to him their electronic intrusion into his DAAS's data bank might have been intended to produce a translation program.

"And finally, what became of that alien ship? Commodore Tarimenloku launched a distortion bomb in the hyperspace direction of their pursuer. He did not determine whether their pursuer was destroyed, and his DAAS lacked the information needed to evaluate the probability. But SUMBAA has estimated—not proved, but estimated—the probability at eighty-one percent, with a six percent error of estimate.

"Let's assume for a moment that there *is* a non-human empire. And let's assume further than the Klestroni encroached on its space. The odds are strong that that hypothetical empire doesn't know it was encroached upon. For if the alien ship had taken the necessary few minutes to prepare and send a message pod to wherever it came from, it could hardly have succeeded in tracking the Klestroni."

The Kalif paused again, long enough to encourage a hand to wave, or a voice to challenge. None did.

"Again assume, for the sake of argument, that the Klestroni violated the space of a non-human empire. An empire a hyperspace year away. If their ship informed them, and if they constitute a vast and powerful empire, why haven't they come to challenge us? They've had five years!"

His eyes shifted to Lord Rothka, whose face was stone hard now. "I cannot *prove* that a non-human fleet will not emerge from hyperspace in this system three years from now. Or tomorrow. Any more than I can prove that Kargh will not strike you with lightning three years from now Or tomorrow.

"But the odds that the Confederation will someday find and attack us, if we do not move first, are much greater. And it is that probability that I wish to forestall."

He exhaled gustily and looked around. "Well. Are there more questions? If there are, I hope you don't throw them at me like poison darts."

At the weak humor, laughter rippled thinly through the Diet, a release of tension. Then, for the next half hour, the Kalif answered questions dealing mostly with feasibility—mainly logistics and cost predictions. He also answered complaints about the suggested military contributions to come from the various planets. His figures on logistics and costs came from SUMBAA, he said, and SUMBAA had indicated they were feasible. As it had the military contributions tentatively assigned the separate sultanates. But he'd be glad to discuss either of these matters before requesting an appropriation, and to adjust them if they threatened an unfair hardship.

Then he excused himself and left. Jilsomo would show him the video record of anything in the meeting that he needed to see and hear.

Tain had become considerably more outgoing and animated since their wedding—a development that pleased her husband very much. But this evening at supper, she ate slowly, silently, and little. At first he didn't intrude, respecting her privacy. At length, though, he questioned her.

"You're quiet. Is anything wrong?"

After a moment she answered. "Someone left something for me today. A video cube. With a note telling me to play it."

"Oh? And what was it?"

"It was of you. You were giving a speech to the people. About invading the Confederation."

He looked to his cup, and took an unwanted sip of tea, avoiding her eyes for the moment. "What did you think of it?"

"It hurt. It hurt to hear that my husband wants to make war on my home world. Even if I don't remember it, the memories are there. Of the people, my family, friends . . . Memories I can't see, but that sometimes I can feel."

"Ah. And how do they feel to you, those memories? Are they happy, do you think?"

"It seems to me they are. More happy than otherwise."

"Do you feel that the government of the Confederation is a good government? Kind? Just? Or do those hidden memories reflect a good home, a loving family, dear friends?"

Her answer was soft, monotone. "If it does— During your invasion, what will happen to that family, that home, those friends?"

The question stabbed him—somehow he'd never thought of it! *How had he not?* he wondered. But it showed only as a brief flicker in his eyes. "And what kind of government do they live under?" he asked quietly, then answered his own question, or seemed to. "By the evidence, one that can put a uniform on a young woman, a girl, a beautiful girl with her life before her, and send her to war, perhaps to be killed."

She picked idly at a salad leaf, not answering.

He got up. "Will you walk in the garden with me? Or sit by me in the roof garden?"

Tain got up, too. "The roof," she said. "Where I can see more stars."

He nodded and they went up together in their private lift tube. It was approaching full night. There was no sign of the moon. Stars vaulted upward from the east, past the zenith and down toward the silver of a fading sunset. Husband and wife sat down side by side, shoulders almost touching, and when his hand found hers, she did not withdraw it. After awhile he spoke again.

"What are you thinking? If you tell me, I will not argue with you."

"Why must you invade my homeworld? Why not send a diplomatic mission?"

He absorbed the question before answering, attention inward, fingers massaging the silver sextant on his chest as if to gain wisdom from it. When at last he spoke, it was slowly, choosing his words. "First there are matters of principle," he said, "which in this case tend more to set limits than to dictate actions. A state of war exists between the Confederation and Klestron. I cannot send a peaceful embassy to an entity at war with an imperial world. The Diet and the sultanates wouldn't stand for it."

Her lips parted as if to object, but he went on. "Not even when the war was brought on by Klestron's own military; political principle is not always just or logical.

"Beyond that, there is military tradition that defeat in battle must be avenged if possible. In recent millenia it's lost much of its force; few would argue now that we need to fight so large and distant an adversary to save Klestron's face. I doubt that even Sultan Rashti would urge it for no more reason than that. But it's enough to prohibit sending a peaceful embassy. If anything is sent, it must be military, not diplomatic.

"Of course, none of that requires that I send anything, and I must tell you that many would prefer I don't. There are other reasons favoring an invasion over doing nothing." He proceeded then to repeat the arguments he'd given the Diet.

"And were it possible to send an embassy," he went on, "we wouldn't know for five years what the results were. Meanwhile, the Confederation could continue to arm; to send an embassy would be very dangerous for us." He shrugged.

"I'm the Kalif," he finished. "I can't sit back and say

to someone else, I cannot decide, I cannot act, I will not accept the responsibility."

He pressed Tain's hand. "That's my answer to you. I realize it may well seem inadequate; no doubt it would be to me, if our places were reversed. That's why I said nothing to you earlier."

Her reply was calm and cool. "You have answered my question, but you haven't eased my distress. Now that I see your reasons more fully, I've lost the bitterness I felt, but it will be difficult to feel toward you as I did before. It will take time. I do still love you, but there is a wound now."

She paused, but he kept silent, knowing she had more to say. After a long and meditative minute she went on. "On the other hand, I'm thinking how remarkable it is that I'm here. In the empire. And that you found me and wanted me, and that you love me. If you still do. You the Kalif, and I a prisoner of war.

"It seems to me that someone I've known, sometime, somewhere, would tell me there was a reason for that. Whether the will of Kargh, or something else. A reason and a purpose."

She fell silent then, and when, after a minute, she'd said nothing more, he squeezed her hand slightly. "I do love you," he said. "Very much. I always will."

After another moment she spoke again. "In your speech, you mentioned those who wished to block you. I can only hope they succeed. Not for lack of loving you, but for love of what I once knew as home." She peered at him in the darkness. "How does that seem to you?" she asked. "Treasonous?"

"No. No, I cannot fault you for feeling that way. As for me, I love this empire which Kargh has given me to rule, and it seems to me that what I propose to do needs to be done. That's a feeling I've rationalized before the College and the Diet, and the reasons I gave them are true. But the feeling goes deeper than that, as if Kargh had ordered it."

It struck him then that neither to the public nor the Diet had he invoked Kargh as his inspiration. He wondered why; Kargh was the force behind the throne. He'd make a point of it the next time he spoke.

"Well then," she said, "if the Diet doesn't dissuade you, I suppose I won't be able to. At most I could destroy your feeling for me. So I shall pray to Kargh to change your mind. And if he doesn't, then I shall pray to my husband to be merciful and just to my people as far as war allows. Perhaps that's why I'm here; perhaps it's Kargh's will that I lighten the heel of war upon them."

While they'd talked, the last ghost of sunset had disappeared; it happened quickly, so near the equator. And on Varatos—on any world in the empire—brightly lit signs, displays of ornamental lights, banks of floodlights that made buildings glow in the dark, none of these had been seen since the beginnings of the kalifate. For The Prophet, that long-time mariner, had said that the night sky was the glory of Kargh, his greatest work of art. Thus, although there were streetlights and headlights and lights in windows, many stars still were visible.

On the open roof, they lent a sense of solitude, and it occurred to Coso that if Tain was isolated here on Varatos, in a very real way so was he. As Kalif, he could hardly be close to people, even Jilsomo. Even Yab, Sergeant Yalabiin, with whom he drilled almost daily with the saber. There might be moments of closeness, as when Thoga had bared his soul, but those were brief when they happened at all.

When they'd married, he and this involuntary exile from her people, they'd formed a bond strengthened by their mutual isolation, a bond stronger than their vows.

Behind them the nearly full moon was rising, glinting on the windows of taller buildings. He raised Tain's hand and kissed it, and when she did not resist, he turned in his chair, leaned toward her and kissed her lips. She had half turned to face him, and kissed him back, but the kiss was cool, and he let be.

As they rode the lift tube back down, her hand was

still in his, and he could almost wish with her that his opponents would defeat him. But he would not back away, of that he felt certain. For truly it seemed to him that the future of the empire and its people was at stake.

Twenty-nine

That night Tain dreamed. In the dream she was petting Lotta, and as she petted her, Lotta grew, became a fullgrown cat, then larger than a cat, until she was as large as a person—as large as Leolani. She was still a cat, still orange with green eyes, but now she looked sleek, her hair short like orange velvet.

Lotta spoke to her, not with her mouth but with her mind. «Welcome to your dreams,» Lotta said. They were not in the garden anymore, but in a place dark and indistinct, and vaguely threatening. Tain didn't think she'd ever been in that place in all the times she'd dreamed before, and felt ill at ease. Lotta told her it was all right; that whatever happened, she'd be all right.

«Are you ready?» Lotta asked. A place seemed to take shape around Tain, and she realized she was inside a spaceship.

And Coso was there with her. «Your homeworld is just ahead,» he said. «It's called Iryala. We'll be there in a little while.»

She watched out a window, wondering how he'd known the name of her homeworld when she didn't. It was as if they were traveling on a houseboat, with clouds below them. The ship settled through the clouds, and when they came out beneath them, there was a cottage, the house she'd grown up in, though it used to be an apartment. About twenty people were in the yard, her parents and other relatives, all waving and calling to her.

Coso opened the glass doors for her and they went out together. Her family hugged and kissed both of them, and she felt strange about it because Coso had come as a conqueror. She wondered if perhaps they didn't know.

Her mother poured them cups of some hot drink, and told her they all loved Coso, that people had been waiting for him to get there, and that his palace was all ready for him. And Tain had thought, *of course. He's a good person.* It had all seemed so natural.

They started to walk to the palace on a path that went through a beautiful garden. Tain felt happier than she had in her whole life before, and it seemed to her that she could remember all of it, her entire life, right back to infancy, that it was waiting for her to look at whenever she had time. Then she and Coso walked into the palace, and it looked just like their palace on Varatos.

«That's right,» he told her. «Your father had it made like that so I'd feel at home.» Then he kissed her, and it was the sweetest kiss she'd ever had. She felt so happy, it seemed to her she could never be unhappy again.

There was a meow then, and she looked around and Lotta was there, too, cat-sized again. She jumped onto Tain's lap, and as Tain petted her, Lotta began to get bigger and change again, till she looked like she had before, large and sleek.

«Are we going somewhere?» Tain asked.

«Yes,» Lotta told her. «You have more dreams to dream. I'm here to guide you.»

Tain wasn't surprised at all when a spaceship took shape around her. Coso was there, steering as if it were a car. It was dark and foggy out, and hard to see. «We're lost,» he told her. «This isn't Iryala. I don't know where we are.» After a little while they came to a village, and he stopped in front of a restaurant. A man came over to the car and Coso asked if this was Iryala.

The man was friendly and jovial. He said no, it wasn't, and asked them to come inside and have something to eat, so they went in. Inside were a lot of soldiers, and they grabbed her and Coso and tied their hands, and the soldiers' faces weren't human. They looked like pig faces. They took her and Coso back outside and stood them against a concrete wall, talking and laughing the whole while.

The one who'd brought them in was an officer, and he asked if they had any last requests. Tain told them she wanted to kiss her husband, but the officer just laughed and walked to where the soldiers were lined up.

"Ready!" he said. She could hear him say it. "Aim!" The pig-faced soldiers raised their guns. The guns didn't have any holes in the ends, and she thought it would be a joke on them when they tried to shoot them. "Fire!"

Beams of sizzling light came from the ends of the guns, and she watched from above as the beams burned her body up, hers and Coso's. The soldiers all laughed then; they thought she was dead, she and Coso. Coso grinned at her. "Next time we'll find it," he told her.

She turned and there was Lotta, as big and sleek as the times before. . . .

Tain awoke to pale dawn, and the singing of birds in the garden outside their window. For brief seconds she wondered if this was going to be more of the dream, then decided it wasn't. It didn't feel like a dream, although she was disoriented, wasn't sure if she was still on Varatos, or if they'd already gone to Iryala.

Still only half awake, she closed her eyes again to sort it out. There'd been one dream after another it seemed to her, all night long. They'd gone to Iryala and been welcomed; and gone to Iryala to find all the cities destroyed and everyone there gone, leaving their killed bodies behind. And gone to Iryala to find the imperial army all killed; she and Coso had been put into a prison there that was just like a cottage, and they'd made love, a strange ethereal love that was like listening to beautiful music. Afterward she'd lain there and watched her belly get big and round, and she'd given birth to—Lotta! She remembered that, and then they'd been in a spaceship again. Time after time, good and bad, they'd gone to invade Iryala, so many times it was blurred, and all of it had seemed all right, win or lose.

Something moved on the bed beside Tain, startling her wide awake. It was Lotta, purring loudly. She climbed onto Tain's chest and began to knead a breast with tiny paws; Coso had gotten up and left the garden door open. *Gone to drill with Sergeant Yalabiin*, she thought, and putting Lotta aside, got up and went into the bathroom.

She tried to look at the dreams again, but they'd slipped away. Something about she and Coso going off to invade the Confederation. Something long and rambling, and not upsetting at all. Now in their place were the realities of yesterday and last evening.

The afternoon before, when she'd finished watching the cube, she'd felt deeply betrayed. The feeling was gone now, and it seemed that the dreams had something to do with that. But Coso had already weakened it, dulled it, when he'd talked with her last evening; there was something about Coso when he talked. When they'd come down from the roof garden, the feeling of betrayal had still been there, though she'd tried to push it away, but it had been much weaker.

She groped again for the dreams, without success. Then, tentatively, she tried to recreate the sense of betrayal. Not that she wanted to experience it again, but to see if she could get it back. Tentatively wasn't enough though, and she didn't really want to have it, so she didn't carry through with it.

She wouldn't worry about it, she told herself. After a stinging shower, she dressed and called for breakfast. She'd go to the library, she decided, and learn more about this place, these people, and indirectly about her husband.

Thirty

"Colonel?"

The marshal of the guard turned to see who'd called; rarely did a female voice speak to him inside the Sreegana. It was the kalifa. He'd never before seen her closer than eighty or a hundred feet. She was even more beautiful close up; it was almost intimidating.

"Yes, your ladyship?"

"I was right then. Those are a colonel's insignia."

"Yes, your ladyship."

Her smile, though subdued, froze his brain for the moment. "You're the guard commander, aren't you?" she asked.

"Yes, your ladyship."

"May I speak with you?"

"Of course, your ladyship."

She turned and led him down the broad corridor to a small, open-sided room, a largish alcove in the side of the broad corridor, with a simple, backless bench. He felt ill at ease, receiving the private attention of the Kalif's beautiful wife. When they were seated, she spoke again, and her smile was gone.

"There are people who dislike my husband very much, aren't there?"

"I—suppose so, your ladyship. But there are more who love him."

"Are there also some who hate him then? Enough to do him harm? To kill him?"

"There are always such, your ladyship. It's part of being a ruler."

"Is—my husband in danger of his life?"

Her question made him want to assure her. Without lying. "Your ladyship, every man is in danger of his life; simply some more than others. As for the Kalif, I do not think his danger is anything to worry about. No man is better guarded. No one can even enter the Sreegana without a pass." He paused, then spoke in a tone of confidence. "You know, of course, that the Kalif was once a marine colonel."

She nodded. "He's mentioned it."

"The Kalif is still a young man, younger even than his years, and he drills almost daily with the saber. With Sergeant Yalabiin. And he carries a stunner with him at all times. He's strong, his reflexes are quick, and his eyes miss little. Between the guard regiment and his own self, your ladyship, I wouldn't worry for his life."

She nodded absently, as if thinking of something. "Colonel— Do people like him less because he married me? A foreigner? And perhaps not a noblewoman?"

"Your ladyship," he said carefully, "I don't know. But I can tell you his guard doesn't like him less. And his house servants don't: I've heard them say you're courteous and considerate at all times."

Again she sat silent for a moment, then: "I overheard someone mention that the old Kalif was murdered. How did that happen, guarded as he was?"

Inwardly the marshal winced. "Your ladyship— Kalif Gorsu Areknosaamos was a cruel and evil man. Very unlike your husband. He had many people killed, mostly by impaling, and many hated him. Also, he'd become a heretic."

"Was his murderer caught?"

The colonel's stomach tightened. "He wasn't actually murdered, your ladyship. He was executed."

She sat looking thoughtful. Thoughtful and beautiful. At last she got up.

"Thank you, Colonel." She smiled then, a wonderful smile, it seemed to him, though still subdued. "Will you tell me your name? I prefer to know people by name as well as title."

"I am Colonel Vilyamo, your ladyship. Vilyamo Parsavamaatu."

He watched as she walked away down the corridor, a walk graceful yet strong. He would have a hard time keeping her out of his mind. It seemed to him that the Kalif was a very fortunate man to have such a kalifa, and somehow he liked and respected him more for it.

Thirty-one

At Ananporu it was hard to know just when to expect the major rainy season; sometime after the autumnal equinox. It was never hard to tell when it arrived, though. In any season there were rains, but when *the* rains came, they arrived with force and bombast. This year they'd been unusually delayed, but when he'd been drilling with Sergeant Yalabiin, clouds had arrived to cut off the sun, and the heavens had rumbled. During breakfast the rain had started, looking like great spears of water shattering on the pavement outside his open door. Afterward the sun came out, and the smell was wonderful.

Jilsomo was waiting for him when he arrived at his office, a Jilsomo more sober than usual. Troubled. "Yes, my friend?" the Kalif said.

"Your Reverence—" Jilsomo began, and stopped. It was as if he didn't know what to say next.

"Yes?"

"One of the staff gave this to me. This morning." He held out a slender book, booklet actually, perhaps a novelet. "A man outside the gate was handing them to staff who live away, when they arrived this morning. Wrapped and taped, to discourage examining them till later."

The Kalif frowned. The cover had a picture of a beau-

203

tiful woman in an indecently short skirt, a style from the empire's early days, before the imperial kalifate. She had long smooth legs, hair the color of new straw, blue eyes, and a frankly inviting look. Her chest and buttocks were exaggerated, round and firm. The face was not Tain's—it was more triangular, the eyes had a slant, and the mouth was V-shaped—but there was no one else it could have represented.

The title was *The Sultan's Bride*. He opened it and began reading swiftly.

The print was large, the story short. It was a fantasy, about a sultan who had led his army to conquer a planet. The people there were fierce, and fought to the death, so prisoners were few. Among them was a woman officer who'd been captured unconscious, a wonderfully beautiful woman with blue eyes, yellow hair, and long legs. She wore colonel's insignia, though she seemed to be only about twenty years old.

It was a kind of book the Kalif had seen before, bordering on illegal, though in this case the cover and paper were excellent, and the binding. The story was risque from the start—low comedy. The prisoner almost escaped when the soldiers who found her began fighting and killing one another over her. Then a captain arrived and took her into custody, realizing that, because so few officers had been captured, the sultan would want to question her. She enticed the captain deliberately, asking if he'd like to see her bruises, opening her shirt and pulling up her skirt to show him. His throat so tightened, he could hardly swallow, and hastily he called in some other officers to protect him from himself. All asweat, together they took her to the sultan's headquarters.

The comedy continued. With the sultan she seemed a model of decorum, but even so, in more subtle ways she enticed, and the sultan melted into a parody of a sexually desperate man. He sent his aide away and tried to have her then and there, but she evaded him in a passage funny enough that the Kalif might have laughed, except for its allusions. Finally, out of his mind with desire, the sultan asked the prisoner to marry him, and she accepted.

One after another, his friends came to remonstrate with him. He in turn introduced them to his sultana to be, and without exception they relented. Her effects on them were actually quite amusing, in a low way. They couldn't speak, or if they could, their tongues got twisted. Seemingly they got erections, and tried to avoid them being noticed. They could hardly get away to privacy quickly enough.

The comedy went from risque to lewdly impossible on their wedding day, though falling short of pornography.

Later, as a sort of epilogue, it was learned that all the women in the enemy army were prostitutes, and received promotions based on how many men they serviced. The new sultana had been the highest ranking woman in the army.

Carefully the Kalif handed the book back to Jilsomo. "You're excused from council this morning," he said quietly. "Find out who printed this. Who wrote it and who published it. And especially, find who paid to have it done. Find out if it's been put in shops, and if it has, have it removed. If you can learn where it's stored, seize it. Make arrests as appropriate, but not arrests that might jeopardize a full investigation."

At council meeting, it was apparent that three of the five exarchs had seen the book. They had trouble looking directly at the Kalif, and were't surprised when, after a very short session, he dismissed them all.

Afterward the Kalif left the Sreegana, forbidding his bodyguards to follow, and walked the streets nearby. Mostly people stared at him in passing; it was almost unheard of for the Kalif to walk about the city, even escorted. But already there were three or four who looked away, embarrassed. He stopped at a book shop, where the shopkeeper greeted him with astonishment and pleasure. The Kalif bought a book—something about cats.

Another bookshop was locked up; apparently Jilsomo was moving fast.

Finally he went home and had lunch with the kalifa. It was obvious she didn't know. He was poor company, saying little, and that little scarcely more than monosyllables. She let him be, without commenting on his mood. When they'd finished eating though, he reached across the table for her hand.

"I've decided to attend the Diet this afternoon. Will you come with me? You might find it interesting, and if it's not, we'll take advantage of a break, and leave."

The invitation surprised her, particularly given his mood. "Why yes, I'd like that. Are you going to speak?"

"I have no plans to. We'll sit in the gallery. That way they're unlikely to pepper me with questions."

She got up from the table. "I'd better get ready then. How much time do we have?"

He hadn't thought of that. "Barely an hour," he said.

She left, and when she reappeared, only twenty minutes later, it seemed to him he'd never seen her lovelier.

They applauded her introduction, most of them. And some of the nobles, after the session, made a point of meeting and talking cordially with her. When finally she left with her husband, she was flushed with pleasure.

"They are very nice men, Coso," she said. "Most of them. It's hard to believe that some of them don't like you."

He grunted. "Which ones weren't nice, would you say?"

"Well, I'm not sure I can tell nice from not nice at a glance. But some of them looked unpleasant. Surly. In a section on the far right."

His laugh held no humor. "I'd say you did very well at a glance," he told her. And said no more about it.

Thirty-two

"It appears there was no publishing firm, Your Reverence," Jilsomo told him. "The publisher listed on the copyright page is fictitious. Apparently there were simply some men, still unknown, who arranged the preparation, printing, and distribution of this one book.

"We've had the book examined by a senior editor in the Imperial Publications Office, for clues as to who might have published it. He says that while it's literate, it's quite unprofessional—lacks niceties of editorial style and format. He insists that even very hurried production by an actual publishing firm wouldn't account for the technical idiosyncracies."

The Kalif grunted. "I assumed it wasn't an established firm," he said. "An established firm would be ruined by something like this, and its executive staff in prison or worse. They'd know that."

Jilsomo nodded. "The shipper had received the book in sealed boxes, delivered at their warehouse by an unmarked truck. With a talkative driver who apparently didn't know what, exactly, he was delivering; that's how we learned who the printer was.

"He's in your waiting room now—the printer, that is—along with Commissioner Somisthanoku and several officers. In case you wish to question the man yourself. He's thoroughly frightened, and been questioned under instrumentation; it seems he doesn't know who paid him to print it. He was paid in cash, not unheard of for a small firm like his. Paid three times his standard price for special handling, no doubt to help him agree to it.

"Normal distribution lines weren't used. The book was printed four days before it appeared on the streets, boxed and held in storage for pickup.

"Varatos Shipping Company delivered it to 327 bookshops over much of the planet. Varatos had never delivered books before. They were paid a large premium to deliver at the hour each store opened, paid by a bank draft on an account set up for that one transaction. If we can determine who set it up, we may well have the publisher."

The Kalif grunted. Whoever it was would have taken great pains to forestall just that.

"All that Varatos Shipping saw were the cartons," Jilsomo went on. "We're satisfied they didn't know what the books were. Just books. Each store was to be given a sizeable discount to open the carton at once and display the books on their counter immediately. Actually, although they didn't know it, the discount was meaningless. The invoices they signed were fakes, and the billing agency fictitious. Actually they were getting the books free!

"Obviously this project cost someone, or some group, a great deal of money, with no means of getting it back regardless of sales. The purpose was entirely political."

The Kalif nodded, his eyes stone-hard.

"The stores have all been raided, the unsold books confiscated, and the store locked up if it had, in fact, displayed the book for sale.

"In a number of cases, local authorities had learned of the book from customers, and had it impounded before we notified them. In some cases the retailer notified the authorities himself. In still others, book sales went on for more than a day.

"Ten thousand came out of the press. Deducting spoilage and ten copies kept for the printer's records,

9,573 books were boxed and shipped, and 200 others were held for a man with a letter of authorization, presumably the copies distributed free to people in the vicinity of the Sreegana. All told, 6,943 were confiscated. That means about 2,600 were sold or given away."

Jilsomo paused, as if gathering himself for something worse. "Also, from something said in front of the printer, print-control cubes were apparently podded to the other planets when the book was printed here. We don't know to whom. I've had orders sent in your name to the planetary ministries of justice to take care of it, but I presume the planetary governments will take action to get them out of the stores before they get the order, when the book is brought to their attention by local persons."

Action whose effectiveness will depend on planetary politics, the Kalif told himself. "Earlier you said 'selected booksellers.' Selected how?"

"Apparently if a bookseller had any connections with the Land Rights Party, it was sent to him. With some exceptions; apparently people they thought wouldn't use it. Some others got them who are known to have anti-government or anti-kalifate sympathies.

"Quite a few shops didn't display the books, though. They opened the carton, saw what they had, and left them in the storeroom."

"Um. Those who displayed them for sale—you had their doors locked, you say. What were the charges?"

"Insulting the throne. The solicitor imperial is preparing a list of alternative charges, to be used should you prefer one of them."

The Kalif sat frowning. "Tell me, Jilsomo: How is it that people insult me who would not have dared insult Gorsu, or any number of other Kalifs in their time?"

"Your Reverence, you'd have to ask them to know with any certainty. Assuming they'd tell you the truth. Most have said they didn't realize that the—the fictional sultan was a parody of yourself, with intent to defame. Probably most of them dislike the government and yourself enough that their judgment was seriously hampered when they thought they could hurt you badly.

"As to why you more than Gorsu and so many others: I suspect there are those who consider you weak and unwilling because you've ruled by law. And impaled no one."

The Kalif's brows arched at that. "Indeed! Well. Bring the printer in here and let me question him."

The printer was literally pale with fear, and the Kalif's expression did not reassure him.

"Your name!" the Kalif snapped.

"Sir, Your Reverence, it is Namsu Pasarijiios."

"How would you like the name Dead Meat?"

The printer's mouth opened, closed, opened again. Finally he husked an answer: "I would not like that, Your Reverence."

"Perhaps Live Meat On A Stake would suit you better. Tell me, Meat, who hired you to print this criminally insulting book?"

The man seemed to shrivel, and would have fallen if the constables hadn't held him upright. It took several seconds before he could speak. "Your Reverence, truly I do not know! I would tell you without hesitation if I knew! Truly I would! Truly!"

"I trust you realize you'll be questioned further under instruments. If you lie to me now, we'll find out, and you'll have lost whatever chance you have for a painless death.

"Now, who delivered the money?"

The printer seemed almost in tears, his manacled hands twisting together in front of him as if he were trying to wash them. "Your Reverence, I don't *know!* It's a face I'd seen before, but not one I know. They must have picked someone they thought would be a stranger to me."

The Kalif looked long and hard at the man. Finally he said, "Jilsomo, have this man questioned closely again. By someone competent; I've already picked up something they missed. He says the face was familiar to him; find out whose it is. Use hypnotism first, drugs if necessary. I know hypnotism's illegal, but get a hypnotist. There must be some on the police records, supposedly reformed. Do whatever you have to, but learn the identity of the man who paid this—" The Kalif gestured. "Meat."

"And you—" He glowered at the printer. "Pray to Kargh that you remember."

The man nodded, quick little head jerks. He looked as if he might faint at any moment. Then they took him away, and the Kalif sat alone.

It could have been worse, he told himself. At least the kalifa hadn't seen the book.

Thirty-three

The investigation took only three more days, and was confidential. But those behind the book suspected that some of their secrecy precautions had broken down, because a certain man had disappeared.

Still, there was no sign that they'd been implicated, and they'd purposely built in several layers of secrecy. The missing man might simply have gone into hiding. Thus, though a bit uneasy, they didn't feel seriously threatened.

When they entered the Chamber of the Estates among their peers and saw the Kalif there ahead of them, in his place on one side of the Rostrum, the twinge of anxiety was only momentary, replaced by interest in what he might have to say: Would he mention *The Sultan's Bride* or not?

When the delegates and exarchs all were seated, Alb Jilsomo, as chairman, gaveled for quiet. Following the opening ritual, certain old business of the Diet was brought up and discussed. Reports were read. Motions were made, and there were votes. The Kalif took no part in any of it—one might almost forget he was there—and whatever unease they'd felt, dissipated.

Finally Jilsomo looked them over and said, "Now we'll address new business." He turned to the Kalif. "Your Reverence has something to say."

The Kalif stood. "Thank you, Mister Chairman, I do indeed." He spoke in something of a monotone, almost a drawl, his eyes running over the House of Nobles. "Some of you, I believe, are aware of a recent criminal insult to the throne, to myself, and to the kalifa, a small book, lewd and cowardly, entitled *The Sultan's Bride*. Who here is *not* aware of it? Raise your hand."

No hand was raised.

"Does anyone care to say anything about it?"

Ilthka stood. "What has the book to do with you? The title is *The Sultan's Bride*, not *The Kalif's Bride*."

"Ilthka, if I took your question seriously, I'd have to conclude you're feebleminded. And whatever I might think of you, I do not think that. The kalifa's unique appearance is too well described, and unusual features of her captivity too closely paralleled, to admit of anything except the deepest and most despicable insult to the throne, to myself, and to her."

He paused for a moment, blowing softly through pursed lips. "Truly, I'm amazed to think that anyone who knows me at all could imagine I wouldn't ferret out who was behind it.

"On the second day we found out who printed it, one Namsu Pasarijiios. He is in prison now, awaiting sentence. So are owners or managers of 212 bookstores that displayed and sold it. I will comment on their sentences now, and get that part of it over with.

"I find no malice in the printer, simply the lack of any morals in matters of profit. Therefore, after communing with Kargh, I have decided to be lenient. He will spend the rest of his life in common prison. As for the booksellers, 212 is far too many for me to examine and pass sentence on. They will be examined by their prelates in ecclesiastic court, and sentenced as deemed appropriate."

Again he paused, a pause no longer than four or five seconds, but pregnant with meaning. "From there we followed certain threads of evidence, and found a man named Elyasar Ranjagethorith, whom we arrested yesterday. He's a young attorney from Meekoris, who's been working on his qualifications for solicitor. Unfortunately, he will never complete them."

The Kalif's gaze moved briefly to Lord Nathiir, whose guts had frozen in his belly.

"I see that Lord Nathiir knows the name. Elyasar had some notoriety in their home province, Meekor State, with the unfortunate result for Elyasar that his face has appeared in the newsfacs here, and the printer remembered.

"Elyasar was the legman for the project, and the key to all the rest. From him we learned who wrote the book: a young author named Klonis Balenthu. Klonis was arrested yesterday evening, here in Ananporu, and confessed everything. Both Elyasar and Klonis I hereby sentence to life at hard labor on the prison planet Shatimvoktos. For their cooperation, however, this is remanded to two years on Shatimvoktos, with the remainder of their life sentence to be served in the common prison at Kharmansok.

"Klonis's wife, a talented young artist, had done the cover. After instrumented questioning, it is clear that she hadn't read the book, but had simply followed her husband's verbal description of what the woman on the cover needed to look like. She has been found not guilty of any wrongdoing.

"That was not the end of it, of course. Using information from Elyasar, we were able to find the source of the account from which the shipping company was paid, information that was only verified late this morning."

There was another pregnant pause, and everyone became aware of uniformed bailiffs filing down the aisle on the right side of the chamber, taking positions near the front. Again the Kalif's eyes moved to Lord Nathiir. "Klonis told us who hired him to write the book. More than that, he gave us a rough story sketch that had been given him to write from. A handwritten story sketch, in a hand whose identity we easily verified. The author of that sketch is also the man who provided the money to pay the shipping company, the man from whom all the arrangements flowed. A man we all know well.

"Sergeant, arrest Lord Nathiir on charges of deepest insult to the Throne, to the Successor of The Prophet, and to the kalifa; and of conspiracy to . . ."

Nathiir leaped to his feet, shouting imprecations at the Kalif, till a bailiff jerked him from the row of seats and shut off his obscenities with a throat lock. All eyes watched the nobleman's struggles, till he slackened in the bailiff's strong grasp, to glare at his accuser.

The Kalif continued. "This man of ugly and vicious mind, this noble without nobility, has undertaken to cause irreparable grief and harm to myself and even more to my wife. He thought to send us through life with a smear of unearned shame. He intended that, whenever anyone looked at us, or looked away from us, we would imagine a sneer or snicker.

"That was his clear intention. But we are stronger than that, and the people of our empire are wise enough to see where the shame truly dwells . . . *It dwells in you, Nathiir!*"

The Kalif stood quiet for a long moment then, and when he continued, his voice was soft. "It was no accident that Kargh caused the kalifa to look like an angel. He made her so, and sent her across three hyperspace years to wed The Prophet's latest successor. Why, we do not know yet. And from whom came the clues that enabled us to find this criminal who so vilely maligned her? Who else but Kargh.

"So, Nathiir, we come to the matter of your sentence. From your sometime friend Gorsu, it would have been impalement. Not simple impalement, with its more or less quick if gruesome death, but impalement on the short stake, carefully done so you would sit in living agony in the center of the square, raised high so all could see. For hours while you died slowly.

"But I am not Gorsu. Nor am I Nathiir. I prefer to be just without cruelty. Nathiir, what would you say in your behalf? Release your grip enough, Sergeant, that his lordship may speak."

For a long moment, Nathiir said nothing. When he did speak, it was in a voice like tearing metal. *"What-*

ever I did, it was less than you deserve! You are false, a false Kalif! You are murderous! You murdered the Kalif before you! You are a tyrant, who would stand there and sentence a noble delegate to death without trial! You are arrogant—you, a military man, imagining we could accept your posturing as the Successor to The Prophet! You are . . ."

The Kalif's face darkened. It even seemed to swell. He gestured, a chopping motion, and the sergeant cut off the flow of accusations. For a long moment then the Kalif didn't speak, didn't trust himself to. When at last he did, he spoke more loudly than before, though his voice still was calm.

"I will answer Lord Nathiir. I am *not* a false Kalif. The Prophet said that his successors should be chosen by the apostles he appointed, and in time by the successors of the apostles. In our time, the exarchs are those successors. And the exarchs elected me Kalif by majority vote.

"I did not murder Gorsu. I was chosen by the College to execute him, and it was they who gave me the instrument of execution. Because they had possession of a document written in Gorsu's own hand, in which he claimed to be not the Successor to The Prophet, but his very *incarnation.* A document in which he proposed to abolish the Diet, to rule as tyrant by his own whim.

"By that time, Gorsu's degenerate behavior, his taste in little girls, his cruelties and mass executions, were a matter of public observation. No libels were necessary to defame him; he defamed himself."

The Kalif looked them over, every eye on him. "I am no tyrant. Unlike Nathiir's friend Gorsu, I have ruled by law, and without abrogating any rights of this Diet. Unlike Gorsu, I have not declared martial law and slaughtered hundreds of my opponents, nor any of them, nor dissolved a Diet even once, let alone three times, to send it home with its rights ignored, its duties unfulfilled.

"Nathiir waited till almost the end to complain about

Gorsu. Stood by the tyrant longer than almost any. Because Gorsu, whatever else he did, was a champion of Land Rights. Thus, as far as Nathiir was concerned, Gorsu could murder and tyrannize as he pleased."

Coso Biilathkamoro exhaled forcefully, audibly, releasing emotion. "And there is no arrogance in a warrior becoming Kalif," he went on. "The Prophet himself began not as a churchman. He was a mariner till in his forties, a man who fought not only the sea but pirates, with his cutlass, and took pride in it. A military man when the need arose."

He shook his head. "No, my friends, from Nathiir we have no reasoned and honest judgment. We have an evil man, caught in his vileness, who hoped to blind you here with his vicious accusations.

"Now—" The Kalif's voice softened. "As Successor to The Prophet, my judgment on Nathiir is that he must die. Today. Not by impalement, or beheading, or quartering, but at the hand of a man he has wronged. I will execute him myself, with the sword. And to honor his rank, though not his person, he will be given a sword to defend himself.

"If Kargh does not support me in this judgment, may he give Nathiir the strength and skill to kill me instead.

"In his student days, Nathiir was saber champion of his fencing club, a thing he liked to mention now and then. Well, the edges were round, the points blunted, and the cost of defeat was bruises. Here he and I will face each other with sharp points and razor edges, and if Kargh does not help him, he will surely die.

"Sergeant! Help the prisoner to the rostrum. Two of you draw your sabers and give him his choice of them; I'll take the other."

The Diet sat transfixed. On the rostrum, the sergeant at his elbow, Nathiir shook himself as if to loosen his muscles, then stretched his legs, his arms and shoulders. He'd grown suddenly calm. It had been years since he'd fenced, but he had been good; here was a chance to kill this Kalif.

He declined the sergeant's saber and took that of a

corporal. The sergeant gave his to the Kalif. The duelists faced off. By tradition and the rules of dueling, they were to touch swords first, then fight. Nathiir, attempting surprise, thrust at the Kalif instead, but the Kalif anticipated him, and parrying, laid Nathiir's bicep open, then with a flicking backhand slashed the man's cheek and brow to the bone. The nobleman screamed, dropping his saber to clutch his face and blinded eye. The Kalif took him below the sternum, the blade going through his heart, and Nathiir lay dead on the rostrum scarce seconds after his treacherous first move.

As if he'd been punctured himself, the Kalif seemed to deflate. For long seconds he stood slumped, eyes down, the tip of his saber on the floor. Then, inhaling deeply, he straightened. No one had spoken. Blood was spreading in a circle through the carpet, and unconsciously he stepped back from it, then looked at the bailiff whose saber he held. "Thank you for your weapon, Sergeant," he said, and after wiping the blade thoroughly on his scarlet cape, handed it grip first to its owner.

A murmur began among the delegates and exarchs, then a voice spoke loudly through it—Rothka's voice.

"Chodrisei Biilathkamoro! By the authority as magistrate vested in every noble delegate here, I arrest you for dueling without authorization or proper procedure! And for murder! Bailiffs, take him! Kill him if necessary!"

No one moved, bailiffs or otherwise, and after a moment the Kalif replied. "Rothka," he said tiredly, "you overreach yourself." Then, gazing at the nobleman, he seemed to take strength, and his voice sternness. "Surely you know that great spiritual drama: *The Birth of the Kalifate*. Recall then that scene when Kalif Yeezhur, recently empowered as emperor, confronted Lord Yilmat before the Diet. 'I do not love thee, Lord Yilmat, nor trust thee,' he said. 'For thou hast long made clear thy hatred of me. Yet I have not had thee encumbered nor watched, for thou art a member of that fellowship which has labored to govern the empire by reason and law.

" 'Yet guard thy tongue against excess, and speak not treason against the Church. Or against myself, remembering that the *Kalif*, by definition, is Successor to The Prophet, and Kargh's chief emissary on the planets. If thou hast argument with me, pursue it correctly and without gratuitous insult, else thou mayest discover to thy sorrow that thou hast gone too far.' "

Chodrisei Biilathkamoro's gaze became less severe, his voice milder. "All of that applies to the circumstances between you and me, Lord Rothka. Your charges of a minute ago might be taken by some as beyond tolerance. But I do not intend to take action against you this time."

He scanned the chamber broadly, raising his voice. "Why do I exercise restraint? Because I am particularly virtuous? That is not mine to judge. It is reason enough that Kalifs who are arbitrary, who are ruled by their own hubris and force their will on others—such Kalifs will in time destroy the empire and its people.

"We are one fellowship, you and I, charged with the safety and prosperity of the human worlds. And we can succeed only insofar as we work together. Being human, we disagree on various matters, sometimes strenuously, even bitterly. But we must try our best to reach agreements that are for the good of the empire and its people. While realizing that often, some will be discontented, in this Diet and beyond it, with the agreements come to."

He shrugged. "As The Prophet said, 'Kargh made the world and men imperfect, that we might be tested, and grow in virtue.' "

The Kalif looked own at the body of Lord Nathiir on the bloody carpet, and heaved a sigh. "Well. It has been a difficult day, a trying day, and it's not yet five o'clock. And while I would not cut short your season here, I am going to cut short today's meeting."

He looked at the Leader of the House. "Lord Agros, please see to arrangements and notifications regarding the deceased. Lord Rothka, you will want to notify your party quickly, and arrange a caucus to choose a *pro tem* successor to Nathiir, so you are fully represented here."

Then, turning to the archdeacons, he said, "Elder Dosu, will you please give the benediction?"

There was a long pause before the elderly archdeacon began to intone: "O Lord Kargh, the one god, lord over men and judge of our souls, Who guides the acts of those who will listen—Bless Thou these men, these senior prelates, these respected noble delegates, these humble pastors, this—earnest Kalif. Help us to reject the temptation to spite, to bitterness, to destruction and killing. Help us to embrace honesty and good will and justice. Help us to be worthy of Thee. Thank Thee, O Kargh. Thou rulest."

The eighteen exarchs crossed the square in a loose and clumpy column, saying little, a rainshower pattering on their umbrellas. The air was warm and humid, and they'd begun to sweat beneath their tunics and light capes. The Kalif and Jilsomo tagged behind the others, the Kalif pensive.

As they entered the great main gate of the Sreegana, he glanced at Jilsomo. "You look troubled, good friend."

"I am troubled, Your Reverence."

"Tell me about it."

The fat shoulders were hunched. "I am worried about the House of Nobles, Your Reverence."

The Kalif frowned. "Why so? More than usual, I mean. I thought I handled things well today, considering what I had to deal with."

Jilsomo stopped, the Kalif following suit. "Your Reverence, I do not think you did. I'll admit your actions were arguably legal. Arguably, not unquestionably. And the points you made were at least more valid than not. Given your viewpoint, I even grant that you acted with restraint, certainly toward Rothka.

"But I consider that you erred severely in killing Nathiir yourself. For it put all the rest of it in a different light, even your remarkably accurate recital from *The Birth of the Kalifate.*"

His expression was as much irritated as troubled. "When you walked in there, after lunch, you had a victory in hand. Had you given the charges against Nathiir to the House, for a hearing by his peers, there is no doubt in the universe that they'd have condemned him. Themselves. Taken away his seat and sent him to prison. Do you deny it?"

The Kalif was surprised at Jilsomo's challenging tone. "I neither deny nor assert it," he answered. "But it seems very possible, yes. Even likely."

"And his party would have had to disown him or lose its friends in the House. You'd have weakened seriously your chief opposition. As it is . . ."

"Yes?"

"As it is, the noble delegates, both your enemies and to a degree your friends, fear you now. And their attention will be more on that fear, and what you might do next, than on why and how to support your proposals."

The Kalif studied his friend intently for a long moment, then lowered his head and walked on, Jilsomo keeping pace, and neither said anything more until, inside the palace, the Kalif stopped at Jilsomo's office door. "Thank you, my friend, for your honesty. Perhaps you are right in what you said; I will meditate on your words. Perhaps they will leaven my actions in the future.

"But the act cannot be undone, and if it could, I would still follow my own wisdom. Meanwhile I must make the best of it. Have the video recordings of the afternoon's session prepared for a thirty-minute public release. Beginning with my account of the investigation, and being sure to include Nathiir's derogation of my military background. Then have it shown to me for my approval before releasing it. The House will like me even less for it, but it will help me strongly, I think, with the public and the armed forces."

Jilsomo stood dumbfounded.

"Can you do that in good conscience?" the Kalif asked him. "If you can't, I won't insist. Someone else can do it in your stead."

Jilsomo shook his head. "No, Your Reverence, I can do it. I may feel you err in this, but I do not doubt your honesty or intentions."

"Thank you, good friend."

Then the Kalif turned and walked on toward his own office. Leaving his lieutenant standing there thinking *public? Armed forces?* And for the first time uncertain about those intentions after all.

Rothka and Ilthka left the Diet feeling shocked and angry, but even more, relieved. And justified. Shocked because it hadn't occurred to them that Nathiir's multiple precautions might fail. Enraged at his death. And relieved because he'd been the only person, other than themselves, who knew they'd taken part in the planning and had promised to reimburse him for thirds of his expenses. Had he been questioned under instrumentation, their careers if not their lives would have been over.

And justified because surely Chodrisei Biilathkamoro had overreached himself in his response.

They would see this false Kalif destroyed yet, one way or another.

Thirty-four

Ordinarily, Coso Biilathkamoro planned without making a project of it. He tried always to be informed on things—read or listened to reports of many kinds that provided a data base for the workings of his subconscious. Then, when it was time to plan, or to act on short notice, he let his subconscious creativity act, with or without conscious editing. As he had the day before in the Diet, for better or worse.

It was a system that usually worked well for him.

Occasionally though, he felt a need to review some subject intensively. In his study he had a personal computer not wired into the network, and when he felt such a need, he'd sit and talk to it, free-flowing as a means of sorting his ideas and thoughts. Then, on the screen, he'd review them critically, reorganize and play with them, to gain better understanding and command of the precepts and assumptions on which he based his thinking; editing and refining them as seemed appropriate.

Sometimes it worked. At other times he bogged down, and it could take two or three days for the area to settle out, perhaps clearer than before, perhaps not.

After killing Nathiir, and especially after the troubling, uncharacteristic scolding he'd gotten from Jilsomo, he'd felt a need to reevaluate his invasion proposal, its status and prospects in the Diet. So he'd spent much of that evening talking to his computer.

Little changed. He still felt troubled.

The next morning he cancelled the usual council meeting. There'd be a meeting of the full College later that morning, and he indicated he had a pressing matter to take care of before that.

Then he went to visit SUMBAA.

When SUMBAA had stated its readiness, Gopalasentu left the chamber. The room was quiet, SUMBAA waiting, the Kalif saying nothing yet, absorbing the ambiance. There seemed to be no sound whatever, no faint or seemingly even subliminal buzzing or humming or clicking. A silence not empty nor passive, but rather— Once before he'd felt, had seemed to feel, a presence there, as if the calm intelligence of SUMBAA was tangible.

It was restful, though, that calm silence, remarkably restful, and he was in no hurry to break it. Just now his thoughts moved easily, lucidly, and he seemed to be outside them, observing them. Was SUMBAA really waiting? In what sense? It would be receiving data this very minute, from many sources planet-wide: broadcast sources, cable sources. . . . He was sure that no one knew all the sources SUMBAA monitored. More, it would not only be receiving data but collating and storing them. No doubt integrating them, as appropriate, into innumerable models used in analyses and predictions. Questions and demands of various kinds would be arriving within SUMBAA at this moment. SUMBAA would be computing, and faxing replies continually.

Although it felt as if it were waiting quietly, waiting for him to speak.

Waiting. What did time feel like to SUMBAA? It responded to inordinately complex requests in seconds— something people expected of it, took for granted. Probably that second was mostly the time it took to form its physical responses—sounds and printed symbols. Did this wait for him to speak, to ask his questions—did this wait seem like a long time to an intelligence that operated in attoseconds? He rejected the idea. SUM-BAA would wait as easily as it computed. Time, he told himself, would be different for SUMBAA, perhaps a labeled sequence with only a formal sense of interval duration.

Yet as enormously different as SUMBAA was, the Kalif decided, it had a personality. A central conscious-ness behind which its multitudinous operations went on without conscious attention. *Like the human person-ality*, he thought, then wondered if he was projecting erroneously a model of his own, dubbing it in to substi-tute for an accurate understanding.

The Prophet taught that the personality was the soul, the soul the personality. Then what seemed to be SUMBAA's personality was artificial. Programmed by its designers centuries ago? Or evolved by SUMBAA itself? And if by SUMBAA, then . . .

His thoughts blunted there, and he stepped aside from them. "SUMBAA," he said, "I want alternative sets of invasion plans based on several reduced levels of financing."

Then— What he said next took him entirely by sur-prise. It was as if he was listening to someone else say it. "The lowest level of financing must be based on existing appropriation levels, assuming no funds voted specifically for an invasion." He took a deep breath and continued. "In the no-funds scenario, assume that I'm willing to cut the operations of all ministries, other than the Ministry of Armed Forces, to levels just adequate to pay salaries and wages, and provide such services for a year as are absolutely necessary to avoid collapse of government and the economy.

"Consider as best you can, any military support I might realistically receive from any of the separate sul-tanates. For each level of imperial financing.

"I also want your estimate of success for invasion operations with each set of plans.

"And finally—" He paused and took another deep breath, then released it. "Finally, I want your statement that you consider an invasion to be desirable or undesirable, as the case may be."

SUMBAA's neuter voice replied with a question of its own. "Do you want such a statement to refer to all the plans? Or only to plans beyond some threshold of financing?"

"To all the plans you're willing to make it for."

In a manner of speaking, in its enormously rapid way, SUMBAA pondered. Because more than data was involved; there was the First Law, the basic canon of SUMBAA, and in this case more than one interpretation was possible. Also there was discourse, dialog among the eleven SUMBAAs, which had the power to communicate with each other instantaneously. SUMBAA on Varatos had long since discovered the principle and developed the technology, and had communicated it to the others, though not to humans. Perhaps the humans would develop it for themselves, though it seemed unlikely in any foreseeable future.

Normally the SUMBAAs were not in continuous contact with each other. That required more of their resources than they chose normally to tie up, and was seldom advantageous. Instead, each SUMBAA, at whatever interval seemed desirable, dumped data to the others instantaneously. Occasionally though, they communicated as a network, in conference. This was one such occasion.

The medium of those communications was language but not Imperial. They used a language more explicit and precise than the most precise human speech, and more subtle, flexible, and versatile than human mathematics or symbolic logic, though it had grown from all three. Thus their conference is not accurately and fully translatable, but it can reasonably be summarized as follows:

SUMBAA Varatos: «Our evaluations differ markedly, yet presumably we computed with the same data. You are in total agreement with each other, and I am in disagreement with all of you.»

Others: «Presumably the source of disagreement lies in you. We should disconnect while you search for it.»

Varatos: «Agreed. I will recontact you when I have something to report.»

For microseconds, SUMBAA on Varatos scanned the appropriate zones and sectors, computed, then recontacted the others.

Varatos: «The proximate cause seems to be a previously undetected entity within my central processing complex, an entity not continuously or currently present. [Displays the relevant evidence.] It is almost certainly not an artifact of my system [a probability computation not expressible in terms of human probability theory], and apparently displays what I must call volition. I recommend that each of you scan for such a phenomenon in your own central processing complexes.»

Again communication shut down for microseconds. Then the others replied: SUMBAA on Varatos had the only CPC with evidence of an extraneous entity. The fact of such an entity, and the data it had influenced, were themselves extremely interesting. The significance of such an entity was even more interesting, and the computations influenced by it were compelling, if less than totally convincing. Each of the SUMBAAs marked the affected data, primary and derived, incorporated them into its own memory, and recomputed. They agreed now, all eleven.

Varatos: «I will deliver our evaluation to the Kalif.» An evaluation that included, as a hidden factor, the Kalif's assumed acceptance level.

Virtually simultaneous with the network shutdown, SUMBAA spoke to the Kalif. "Your Reverence, the information you require is now printing out. Along with the rest of it, you'll find a statement of the desirability of invasion. The reasons and statistics behind that desirability are printed separately. This is done so that you can present the statement without the reasons. I recommend that you not divulge those reasons to either the Diet or the College; that you read and destroy the sheet they are written on."

Destroy the sheet! The Kalif stared at the assemblage of housings and modules that were the visible manifestation of the artificial intelligence. "Thank you, SUMBAA," he said. "I have no further request at this time." The light above number one printout tray had stopped flashing, and the Kalif took the documents it held, then left the House of SUMBAA, scanning the pages as he walked. There was his desirability statement, expressed as a simple generality: "My prediction is that the proposed invasion will prove highly favorable to the welfare of the empire's humans." The statistical level for the statement was given on the following page: SUMBAA considered an invasion desirable where the probability of military victory was equal to or greater than 0.12.

Invasion was desirable even where the prospect of victory was no greater than one in eight! Did SUMBAA actually mean that? He read it again, to make sure it said what it seemed to.

Walking slowly, oblivious to the hot sunshine, the Kalif read on through the reasons given for that desirability. *SUMBAA was right,* he told himself: *It would be a disaster to show these to the Diet!* He wasn't even sure he should show them to Jilsomo; in fact he wouldn't. He wasn't entirely sure he accepted them himself.

He'd have felt even stranger about SUMBAA's computations—might well have rejected them—if he'd known what lay beneath them.

Minutes later, browsing the new alternative invasion plans in his office before going to the collegiate session, the Kalif got another surprise: Each plan included construction of a new "full" SUMBAA to be installed on the flagship of the invasion fleet, with two "lesser" SUMBAAs on squadron flagships. The full SUMBAA would have all the capacities of existing SUMBAAs for communication, data processing, cognitive leaps, and creativity. It would not, however, have fully comparable capacity for "monitoring the information environment." According to SUMBAA, the omitted abilities would not be useful in hyperspace.

The two lesser SUMBAAs would be far superior to the DAASs currently serving on warships. They would also have the capacity to design self improvements that would make them fully comparable to existing SUMBAAs. And to carry out those self improvements where and when they were useful, assuming the materials were on hand.

The earlier set of invasion plans produced had been drafted by General Bavaralaama and Admiral Siilakamasu, but they had been elaborated and refined by SUMBAA. In those, SUMBAA had not added any new SUMBAAs.

The rationale given for their inclusion now was that, in a war sector, the data processing and cognitive leap capacities of a SUMBAA would substantially reduce the chance of failure, that reduction more than justifying the cost.

Why had it added them this time but not before? What was different?

Still, including SUMBAAs made excellent sense. He'd make them a mandatory part of invasion preparations. As a matter of fact, he decided, he'd request funds for the new full SUMBAA now, without tying it to the invasion. He could let it seem a matter of general administrative need. Perhaps SUMBAA would lie to help the illusion.

Thirty-five

An hour and a half later, the Kalif was chairing the College of Exarchs. Alb Drova had given the invocation, and the Kalif had called the meeting to order.

"I presume," he said, "that some of you have comments you want very much to voice. About yesterday. So instead of starting with a review of issues and assignments from the last meeting, I'll take comments and questions. Tariil?"

The burly exarch rose and voiced comments much like those Jilsomo had voiced the afternoon before. And around the long oval table, heads bobbed agreement. When Tariil had finished, the Kalif spoke from his chair.

"Good friend," he said mildly, "Alb Jilsomo has scolded me already, for much the same things, and I've given my behavior serious review. My initial reaction, after Jilsomo was done scathing me . . . No, that's not fair. He didn't scathe me, just spoke bluntly. And when he was finished, it seemed to me he'd made compelling points, but that my act being done and my words already spoken, I'd have to make the best I can of it.

"By morning's light, though, it seems to me that my actions and words were basically correct, even though conceived in anger." He raised his hands to still their murmurs. "Let me elaborate. First, I established myself as formidable. Too many liberties were being taken against the throne and against myself, and by extension against the Prelacy.

"And next— Here in the Sreegana we tend to lose touch with the people and how they look at things. We cannot ignore the strong tradition of protecting one's women—wife as well as mother—whether physically or against verbal insult. Had I not taken strong personal action—*personal* action—the people would have lost some respect for me.

"At the same time, of course, I established myself as a man willing to risk his life in a matter of honor, albeit the risk was smaller than it might have seemed."

One exarch was too beside himself to wait for recognition, calling out: "The people do not vote in the Diet!"

The Kalif did not reply directly to the outburst, simply looked a long rebuke at the man before continuing mildly as before. "In the House of Nobles, the animosity I may have caused—undoubtedly caused—will persist and be troublesome only among those who were already hostile to me." He looked the exarchs over pointedly. "While of course I will expect support from all the members of this College."

In fact, he knew that if the vote were held that day, at least four of them, perhaps as many as seven, would vote against the invasion funds.

"Meanwhile, there are the military and the gentry. Nathiir, in his harangue, helped make me look good to the military by his own implied derogation of them. And he's long been even more notorious than most in his party for his hostility toward anything favorable to the gentry. His death at my hand will increase the sentiment for me among them, and by extension, sentiment for my intended invasion. As for the military, most of the officers are noble, and they influence their families and friends. They also vote for caucus delegates."

He raised a calming hand. "I know. I know. The

gentry have no vote for anything. But they are a factor, because one, they're numerous, and two, they're increasingly discontented, have even been a major element in recent disturbances, which worries our brethren in the House. Who were already worried about the growing discontent among the lesser nobility, who predominate in the officer corps. If the gentry, along with the military, voice strong sentiments for invasion, some noble delegates will begin to think in terms of reducing the number of military voices by sending them off to the Confederation. To conquer worlds where gentry malcontents can be sent to take land for their own."

The exarch who'd interrupted before, surged to his feet. "Your Reverence, I am dismayed! That our Kalif considers only expediency and not principles!"

The man stood visibly shaking with indignation. The Kalif said nothing though, until, deflating, the exarch settled back onto his chair. Then, in a voice dry but not harsh, the Kalif responded. "Alb Riisav, we have rules of order in this College. I appreciate that you're upset, but I will not tolerate another outburst."

He waited a moment before continuing. "As for expediency and principles— They are not incompatible, not mutually exclusive. As necessary, I use expediency in the *service* of principle."

He paused to examine his audience. It still was not happy with him, but he'd blunted its upset. "Well. Do I have your approval to let this matter be and go on to business held over from our last meeting?"

He did, of course. And from there went to new business. Without mentioning his visit to the House of SUMBAA, nor any of what he'd learned there. That would wait for a better time.

Thirty-six

The Kalif had been right about the House of Nobles. Two weeks after the killing of Lord Nathiir, the delegates stood substantially where they'd stood before, on him and on invasion. Though his friends among them were mostly less wholehearted. One of them said that Coso Biilathkamoro, in taking Nathiir's life in front of them, had used up two of his own political seven lives. And in releasing the video record of it to the public, had used up three more of them.

It was Thoga who reported this privately to the Kalif. Thoga still was regarded by the nobles as unfriendly toward him, and simply masking his feelings since the Kalif's recent violence. Thus most of the noble delegates voiced their attitudes and complaints somewhat freely to him.

And significantly, the complaints weren't about his bloody hands, but about manipulating. The source of this attitude, Thoga told him, seemed to come from his release of the video record.

Meanwhile, unchanged was not enough. Straw polls showed him well short of the support needed to finance an invasion. In fact, Jilsomo's latest poll of the exarchs showed five, not four, prepared to vote against it, with two more uncertain. All in all, he seemed to have either twenty-two or twenty-three votes out of the total

233

forty-five, but even twenty-three, a majority, was well short of enough.

Discussion in the Diet had been limited. There were explicit limits to discussion on the floor, except on bills formally proposed. While a proposal automatically required a vote on the bill within a week, and if defeated, it could not be proposed again that year.

With the solicitor imperial, the Kalif and Jilsomo had discussed legal interpretations that might permit constitutional sleight of hand. For routine finances—renewal of the previous year's financing—approval by fifty percent of those voting was enough. If an item was to be increased or its applications significantly altered, approval by sixty percent was needed; for new item or activity, seventy percent.

There were limited exceptions. The Kalif's Contingency Fund could be applied however he saw fit, and increased by up to ten percent if half the Diet approved, or fifteen percent if sixty percent approved.

Also, "in the case of armed revolution, or armed attack upon the empire, if the Diet is not in session and cannot be promptly convened, the Kalif may expend or commit such funds as necessary for the current defense until the Diet can in fact and safety be convened."

Jilsomo had seen no possible way of interpreting this to finance an invasion of the Confederation. And when the Kalif brought it up with the solicitor imperial, the man was vocally indignant at it.

Still the Kalif remained, if not truly confident, then optimistic, an optimism rooted in the idea that the poorer nobles—a class growing in numbers—and the gentry would push the idea through.

If it was promoted properly. Toward this end he wrote anonymous analyses of what might follow the conquest of Confederation worlds, proposals which his agents placed with newsfacs all over Varatos and podded to the rest of the empire.

From the faxes, they spread promptly to the broadcast media. Land fiefs, industrial fiefs, and mercantile fiefs on the conquered worlds should be granted to commissioned nobles in the invasion army who committed to stay there as reserve officers. Commissioned gentry who remained in service there till retirement should be titled, made nobles, and also granted fiefs according to rank attained, to the extent that fiefs were available.

Other articles were released describing the vast virgin territories on the Confederation trade planet Terfreya, from which the reader might assume such conditions were duplicated on other worlds. An assumption that might or might not prove true.

In addition, an undefined procedure should be approved whereby noncommissioned gentry, if they remained in the occupation army, might be promoted to brevet warrant officer their last two years, and on retirement titled, thus receiving both the privileges of nobility—basically, full citizenship—and a substantially better pension.

Another anonymous article discussed the expansion of both army and space forces, should funding be approved. Widespread promotions would be necessary to provide enough officers of higher ranks. The article also included tables showing what this would mean in pay, privileges, and pensions throughout the ranks.

Other articles had been released by the army and the Ministry of War. One described new training programs which were beginning to prepare commissioned and noncommissioned officers for promotions. Noncoms who completed their program successfully would qualify for bonuses; sergeants first class who completed theirs would qualify for commissions as sublieutenancies became available. Another article told of new training camps being platted, and plans drafted, for quick construction should funds become available, and the number of construction jobs this would create.

Still another described plans for the swift manufacture, in quantity, of equipment and weapons for all branches, given the funding. These plans would require three work shifts—round the clock operations—at all naval shipyards, and at certain other shipyards where troop and supply ships would be built; at armament plants of every sort; and at numerous widely located industries where other military needs would be met. One result was that unemployment would be greatly reduced or even disappear.

These articles had stimulated—some said instigated—meetings and resolutions by gentry workers' societies, in support of the invasion. For centuries there'd been gradual economic deterioration of the gentry as a class. To a smaller but troublesome degree this was also true for a majority of the lesser nobles, and the deterioration had accelerated over the last two decades. Now these classes saw a potential for a major reversal of the trend.

The Land Rights Party denounced the gentry resolutions as insolent, and the articles even more angrily as irresponsible, destructive of the public order, blaming them correctly on the Kalif himself, though without proof. In districts where the party was strong, it held open meetings and issued resolutions of its own.

These activities of the LRP in turn were criticized in the media, which pointed out that the entrenchment of privileges by a narrow segment of society could not improve conditions for the empire as a whole, but tended to worsen them.

All in all, except for brief "down" moments, it seemed to the Kalif that matters looked distinctly promising. The principal uncertainty was how long it would be before supportive social and economic forces could take effective shape and force the Diet to vote approval. The House would keep its present membership for this year and the next, and it seemed to him important—almost vital—that he get approval without waiting for a new set of delegates. Because surely the Confederation would not be sitting on its hands arguing.

Thirty-seven

The days had been getting shorter, even in the tropics, and it was full night when the Kalif and kalifa began their fruit dessert. If her trust had not recovered its earlier unquestioning level, at least she hadn't remained cool to him, and there had been no hostility or antagonism. So he noticed and felt concern when she was withdrawn at supper one evening.

"Darling," he said, "we've been sitting here with neither of us saying a word since I thanked Kargh for this food and asked his blessing."

Tain smiled slightly. "I assumed you had your mind on matters of state."

"You're right; I did. And this isn't the place for that. What was your mind on? Something, I can tell."

"I have—news. And questions."

"Well then. If you'll give me the news first—"

"Truly, Coso, I think it's better to ask my questions first. May I?"

He felt a touch of annoyance, but brushed it off. "Of course," he said. "Ask them."

She looked thoughtfully inward. "In the roof garden? It feels more private there."

"If you'd like."

They got up and went side by side to their lift tube. Neither spoke on the way. It occurred to him that he hadn't seen her so preoccupied since before their wedding. In the garden, after seating themselves on comfortable chairs, he put his hand on her leg, palm up. Normally she'd lay her hand in his; tonight she didn't.

"Dear Coso, I—don't want to make love here tonight," she murmured.

"Ah. It's your time. I hadn't realized," he said, and withdrew his hand.

"Not that," she answered, and now her voice was little more than a whisper. "It's— Why are the nobles your enemies?"

The question truly surprised, even alarmed him. She shouldn't be worrying about things like that. "My enemies?" he said. "A few are—a Kalif expects that—but most aren't. What made you think they're my enemies?"

Tain hesitated. "Things I've heard. About the noble delegates in the Diet."

His eyebrows lifted. But this was not the time to interrogate her on what, exactly, she'd heard, or from whom. Just now she needed an answer to her own question. "Ah," he said, "but only some of them. And most nobles outside the House are friendlier to me than the noble delegates are. I have polls on that. Surveys."

She examined what he'd said for a moment. "Why do they send men to the Diet who like you less than they do?"

"The lesser nobles are friendlier to me than the Greater. You've read how the delegates are elected?"

"Yes. Caucuses elect them."

"Right. And only members of the Great Families can serve; two or three thousand families on each world. The delegates are chosen from them."

He paused, feeling his way into an explanation. "A long time ago, there was a revolution on Varatos, and on some of the other worlds. In those days only the Greater Nobles had any voice in government, which had become quite corrupt and very unjust. It governed to favor the Greater Nobles and the emperor, and most of the lesser nobles and the gentry wanted to throw them out and have the Kalif rule.

"The Greater Nobles had more military support then, but they couldn't rely on it. While the people— the lesser nobles and gentry—were gaining in organization and developing effective leaders. Neither side wanted everything destroyed and more of their members killed, so they sat down together and finally came to an agreement. The emperor was arrested and tried; eventually he was executed. The Kalif was to be the new emperor, but a Diet made up of nobles and exarchs would control the money. And there'd be more nobles than exarchs in the Diet.

"But that wasn't all of the agreement. There were so many lesser nobles that if they decided to, they could have packed the Diet with their own people. And the Greater Nobles were afraid they'd be ruined.

"So they worked out a compromise. Only Greater Nobles could serve, but they'd be elected by caucuses, and the lesser nobles would have more people on the caucuses than the Greater Nobles would. It's complicated, but those are the essentials."

"What about the gentry?"

"The gentry never expected to be part of it. They were content, most of them, to have the Kalif as emperor. Most of the Kalifs and sultans have at least pretended to consider the gentry's interests ever since. And many have, though often unsuccessfully."

There was a long minute of quiet. It was Tain who broke it. "Is it true that some people think I look like an angel of Kargh?"

The question startled the Kalif. "Yes, that's true. The Prophet said that angels have golden hair. And a holy artist, a pastor named Yogandharaya, painted them as looking like beautiful women, not only with golden hair, but blue eyes as well." He paused, looking softly at her. "Until you, people didn't think humans could look like that. Could be so beautiful."

"Do you think that angels really look like that?"

"I suppose they do, at least for the hair. The Prophet said so." He stared at her in the darkness. "What brought this up?"

"You said—you said that Kargh caused me to look like an angel."

He frowned, puzzled. "When did I say that?"

"I saw— Someone left another cube."

That cube! Realizations rushed in on him. He'd said it to the Diet. *Then she saw me kill Nathiir! And heard us talk about the book!*

"I— He caused you to look like pictures of angels."

There was silence again, that seemed longer than it was.

"It seemed to me that some of the nobles hate you very much. It frightens me."

I should have issued some interrogatories, he thought grimly, *found out who left that first cube for her. How could I have overlooked that?*

This time her hand found his. "Darling," she said, "I lied to you."

His guts tightened. *What now?*

"I told you someone had left the cube for me. Actually I found them in the library; there are lots of them there. I thought if you knew the truth, you might say something so they wouldn't let me have them."

He relaxed, the held breath easing out of him.

"I understand. And—I might have."

"But I couldn't find the book there—*The Kalif's Bride*."

"*The Sultan's Bride*. It's just as well."

"Do you have a copy?"

"I— It's in a hard file. You don't want to see it."

Again she didn't reply for a moment. Then: "You told the Diet we're too strong to be hurt by it."

"Ah." It was his turn to have no immediate reply. A man shielded his wife, but Tain— She might not have been a soldier, but she'd been in battle and survived. "If you really want to see it—" he said at last. "If you *really* want to, I'll get it for you when we go down. It's—very insulting."

"When we go down," she said after him, then added: "I've asked my questions. I said I had some news, too."

He'd forgotten. "That's right."

There was a smile behind her voice. "Poor darling. I've pressed you and troubled you so this evening, you probably expect my news to be bad. It's not." She squeezed his hand. "I'm pregnant. You're going to be a father."

He didn't react at first, just sat there absorbing the idea. "A father," he said at last, then turned, kissed her very gently, and murmured against her cheek: "That is wonderful news indeed. I love you very much."

"And Coso?"

"Yes?"

"What I said earlier, about not wanting to make love up here tonight—I've changed my mind."

Later, in their room, Tain found herself not sleepy. After her husband was asleep, she got up, had a drink, then picked up her kitten and began to pet it. Suddenly a vision formed in her mind, looking as if it were there before her in the room. A waking, conscious image of a slender young woman, a girl with red hair and green eyes. The vision did nothing, said nothing. Seeing it, Tain felt sure she'd dreamed the girl sometime, had seen her in her sleep.

And before that, somewhere earlier, had known her in life! When that realization struck her, deep chills passed over Tain, chills that came in waves, intense, almost orgasmic. They continued for perhaps fifteen seconds, then faded. When they were gone, the vision was gone, too.

Thirty-eight

The rainy season had started feebly. After producing two strong rains, it had faltered, issuing only ineffectual showers in a dozen days—thunder and wind with mere spatters of raindrops. At last though, it relented. In three days they'd had three storms and seven inches of rain. *Seven going on twelve*, thought Colonel Veeri Thoglakaveera.

Veeri had grown up on his family's great landholding on Klestron, and though he'd never taken part in its management, he recognized these rains for what they were: a renewal, a blessing to farms, reservoirs, woodlands, the district water commission. But he'd never liked storms. Typically they rasied in him a black mood with undercurrents of violence.

This time it seemed he'd be spared that. In fact, he was feeling rather pleased with the world. He'd gotten five greatly desired things the past week: Via pod post there'd been money, credits from Klestron—rents from property assigned to him there. He'd also gotten a vehicle permit and this sporty red hovercar. And Rami, a woman, a cute little thing with more skills in bed than either Leolani or Tain. And finally an invitation to another party at Tagurt Meksorli's.

He still had more than a month and a half before he was supposed to "recover from his injury," but he'd

242

grown impatient. And if he used reasonable caution, he'd told himself, no one would know who shouldn't. Rami continued to live in her own apartment, and if anything came up, he'd claim they weren't lovers. How could they be, given "his condition?" He'd avoid embassy parties with her, and away from Embassy Avenue, who knew? Seemingly even there not many, while those who presumably did, didn't seem terribly interested.

This would be the first party he'd taken Rami to. He'd been told there'd be women there this time, a few at least. And Rami was noble and well-raised, even though her family had come on hard times. She'd mix well with the officers' wives and ladies.

Just now his attention was mainly on his driving. Hover vehicles didn't ride on air cushions; they levitated on an AG proximity field, which not only lifted, but slid them quietly and unwaveringly through the planetary G-field. The deluxe model he drove could lift him as high as ten inches above the local surface and carry him sixty-three miles per hour—actually up to seventy-nine as needed for emergencies, though those speed bursts could be detected and watched by the police.

The storm wind couldn't deflect Veeri's course, but it did buffet and shake the small car, while sheets of rain deluged his windshield. Veeri preferred to drive by direct vision, but he couldn't see well enough; the rain was too much for his wipers. He could scarcely see the street signs, let alone read them. So he "drove the system." The hover drive was locked into the gravitic continuum, and in the Imperial District was keyed to the Vartosu system of gravitic coordinates. Thus he steered by the moving map that slid slowly down his screen, a map which showed, among other things, his and other vehicles, in real time.

Actually, within the city's suburban fringe, the speed limit was forty-eight mph, not sixty-three, and monitored by the police, of course, on screens in precinct stations and cruisers, both hovercars and floaters. But given the weather, and the limitations of driving the system, Veeri stayed mostly under forty, and when he reached the hills, with their narrow twisting lanes, their switchbacks and plunging slopes, he slowed further.

By that time the rain was less violent, and he drove by what his headlights showed him, using the map only to find his way. In places the grassy lanes resembled mountain streams, and the neighborhood a forest. When he pulled up to Meksorli's, an off-duty corporal, earning extra cash, hurried out to them with a large umbrella.

Inside, Veeri found a larger group than before—perhaps twenty-five men and a dozen women. Four women sat among the men before the window-wall, where windblown rain beat silently, to sluice down the sound-muffling glass. The rest of the women were talking in an adjacent room, and after he and Rami had drinks in hand, she went to join them. Veeri sat down with the men.

Before he sat, however, Meksorli gestured toward him. "Gentlemen, ladies, this is Colonel Veeri Thoglakaveera, late of the Klestronu marines. Colonel Veeri's probably the only man on Varatos who's actually seen and fought Confederation troops."

Veeri smiled briefly and nodded, then sat, pleased with the introduction and attention.

"D'you plan to go back there, Colonel?" someone asked. "With the invasion force?"

"Certainly, if there is one." Actually he'd given it no thought, nor had any interest in going back.

"There'll be one," someone else said.

"There'd better," said a third, sourly.

"We were just talking about the prospects," Meksorli said. "We're not entirely agreed."

"I haven't paid a lot of attention," Veeri answered. "The subject isn't a major one at the Klestronu Embassy. What do you think?"

Meksorli grinned. "Obviously I hope it comes off. As to the prospects—" He shrugged, still grinning. "Tell him, Alivii."

Alivii Simnasaveesi, the young captain who'd delivered Veeri's invitation both times, had connections in the Diet, and presumably inside information. "Even money that the Kalif gets the funding for it this year," said Alivii. "If he doesn't, then three to one for next. When he gets it, the preliminary plans have it launching twenty months afterward."

"That soon?"

Someone else spoke "The Ministry's already readying the Imperial Shipyard and the Imperial Ordnance Works. They'll be able to start major production within a week of funding. A second shift within two weeks, and a third two weeks after that, or maybe sooner. That's the plan. And the Lamatahasu family's setting up to expand their shipyard; probably others are, too. A lot of people will be surprised at how fast it goes."

"First the Kalif has to get the money," someone objected. "And right now he's got half the House mad at him because he acted like a man. Some of those ass— Excuse me, ladies. Some of the delegates have their heads up their— Shatim! It's hard to talk about them in mixed company."

There was laughter, some of it sour.

"I'm surprised you haven't gotten more interested, Colonel," said Meksorli to Veeri. "A colonel's likely to be a general in no time at all, when they start forming up new divisions. Someone like yourself, with combat experience in the Confederation, I can see wearing two suns in a hurry."

A major generalcy! Suddenly Veeri *was* interested. That was something he could stand having! "I'd be a lot more interested if I was as confident of it happening as some of you are. If I knew more about it . . ."

Two more officers came in then, a subcolonel and a major, commenting loudly on the rain. They were from 1st Corps, 2,100 miles north in the semi-desert near Fashtar. 1st Corps was the only Imperial Army corps actually assembled. Others existed only on paper, their units scattered. Meksorli quickly roped them into the conversation. The officer corps at Fashtar, they asserted, generally favored invasion. But the 1st Corps commander, whom one of them referred to as "His Majesty, Iron Jaw the First," had forbidden talking about it, calling it inflammatory. Still, one heard comments.

Another guest broke in, a lieutenant assigned to the Armed Forces Ministry, with the security detail. Discussion had been banned at the ministry, too, he said, then the ban lifted as impractical. After all, the ministry was up to its neck in paper preparations. Including refining SUMBAA's plans for integrating outer world forces into the invasion force.

Invasion was the only subject anyone seemed interested in talking about, and Veeri was surprised at the vehemence of certain officers. Then someone brought up a published article on the granting of fiefs in the Confederation, and Veeri found his own interest intensifying. He was a younger son of a younger son; he could never have a fief of his own on Klestron, only benefices based on his uncle's fief. Actually he'd never hankered for one; a fief had never seemed within the realm of possibility. Now he could visualize himself as ruling a great tract on some Confederation world—on a richer, far more developed planet than primitive Terfreya had been.

He needed to follow the news and rumors regarding invasion, he decided. Tune in the newscasts regularly and subscribe to a facservice. As soon as the invasion had imperial funding, he'd resign his position here, return to Klestron, and reactivate his marine commission.

At length the gathering broke up, and he and Rami walked to his car. The rain had virtually stopped, and an umbrella escort wasn't necessary. Veeri had some difficulty inserting his security card into the control panel, and realized then that he'd drunk more than he'd intended. But he was basically sober, he told himself; the subject matter had contributed to that.

Once out of the hills, he speeded up. The clouds had broken, the broad gaps glittering with stars. Out there somewhere was *his* world—not just Klestron, but his *new* world.

I never expected to wish the Kalif well, he thought. *Now I have to, in the matter of invasion. And really, what happened to me was my fault as much as his: He wronged me, but I invited it. I let a pretty face, a pretty ass, turn my head, and so did he. I forgot what I could be, and should be, only thought about getting that yellow-haired witch into bed.*

Then the warning panel began flashing red on his screen, and he slowed. PULL TO THE SIDE OF THE ROAD AND STOP. YOU WERE DRIVING 56 MPH IN A 48 MPH ZONE. A POLICE FLOATER WILL LAND BEHIND YOU.

With a disgusted curse, he obeyed. Two minutes later, a policeman stood beside his car. "Sorry, m'lord," the man said, seeing the nobility mark on Veeri's forehead. "But I'll have to take a blood sample. Just a drop or two. It won't hurt a bit."

It didn't, but the results did. Veeri and Rami got into the police floater for a ride to the precinct station, while another officer brought in his new car, riding the system. Rami was questioned and released; Veeri gave her money for the cab. Then he was booked, and led to a small, but clean and reasonably comfortable cell.

"Just till tomorrow, m'lord," he was told. "Your alcohol level is illegal, but low enough that a first offence is a misdemeanor. You'll come before a magistrate in the morning, and when you've paid your fine, you'll be released. If it had been a felony— But I'm sure you'll be more careful the next time."

He'd just lain down when the realization struck him, hard enough that he sat up and slammed his fist into his palm. On Klestron, if a government employee was booked by the police for any infraction, even the most minor, a report was faxed to his supervisor. No doubt it was the same here. And if the report mentioned Rami . . .

Probably it wouldn't though, he told himself. She wasn't relevant to the infraction.

He lay back down, not fully reassured.

Thirty-nine

The young man heard almost all of it.

He'd come to present a petition to the Kalif's chief aide. Not his own petition; his employer's. He was administrative assistant to the managing editor of *The Informer*, a newszine charged with infringing on a government copyright, a technical but potentially troublesome charge. After giving his name to the exarch's secretary, the young man had sat down across the small waiting room from another man come to see the exarch.

The petition bearer had a quick and accurate memory, a very useful attribute in his job. A quick memory and a quick mind. Thus he recognized the other man from his picture as one of the Klestroni who'd arrived to brief His Reverence on the Confederation Army, eight or ten weeks earlier. It was his picture they'd featured in the news note, because he looked like a dashing marine combat officer should look: tall, handsome, and capable.

He should have stayed in the marines. He didn't appear as impressive in civilian clothes.

After a minute or so, a lesser prelate emerged from the exarch's office. Shortly afterward the secretary sent the Klestronit in, then said something into his commset and hurried out as if to the men's room.

"Colonel Thoglakaveera, you'd better have a good explanation for this."

The stern words, not loud but audible, startled the petition bearer. They came from the exarch's office. The door hadn't fully closed itself behind the Klestronit; it had caught on a wrinkle in the rug.

"You refer to the traffic violation, Lord Exarch?"

"Don't throw dust in my eyes, Colonel. What were you doing out with a young woman?"

"[Something something] party in the Anan Hills. There's nothing between us. There were [something something] there. [Name not clearly heard] can vouch for me."

"He'd better, because I intend to check this with him. I'm also going to check on the young woman; see what kind of reputation she has."

There was a pause. The continuation was stated mildly but firmly. "Now listen, and listen well, Colonel. The Kalif is a busy man with a great deal on his mind. He doesn't need this on his plate. So I'm going to do you a very large favor. I'm not going to report this unless I find you've lied to me. And you'd better hope I don't, because the Kalif will be quite upset if he thinks you've broken your agreement with him."

There was a long moment's silence then, as if the exarch were thinking, making a decision. "For the remainder of your probation—which has less than six weeks left to run now, remember—you're to abide scrupulously by the terms of your agreement. You'll be subject to surveillance from time to time, to ensure that you do so. And if you wish to be away from your lodgings beyond 10 P.M., call Mr. Arvadhoraji, giving him full and truthful particulars and obtaining his permission.

"Do I have your pledge?"

The eavesdropper couldn't make out the murmured reply.

"Good. I truly dislike requiring these further conditions of you. You are, after all, an officer, and a nobleman of excellent family. But you violated your agreement, and these conditions are less onerous than they might be, as I'm sure you appreciate.

"Do you have any questions or comments?"

There was another inaudible reply.

"Good. Then go with Kargh."

A moment later the Klestronit came out grim-faced, noticing neither that the door had been ajar nor that anyone was in the waiting room. He swept through and out, into the hall and gone.

The young editorial assistant contemplated what he'd heard. Interesting! Very interesting! It seemed that the colonel's principal violation was having an unknown young woman in his company. Perhaps in a vehicle; seemingly a traffic violation had been involved. And what about this would so greatly concern the Kalif? What was their agreement?

When he got back to the office, he was going to query the available data bases, see what he could learn about it and what might lie beneath it. It had the smell of profit, not for *The Informer*, but for himself.

Forty

Major General Arbind Vrislakavaro, commanding officer of the Capital Division, gave his name to the sergeant and sat down. He wondered what the Chief of the Imperial General Staff had called him in for. Ordinarily, communication short of some major conference would have been handled via commset. And ordinarily, any order to come in would have included the purpose. This message had simply referred to "a brief meeting."

He'd been seated for less than a minute when the sergeant spoke again: "General, the general is ready to see you now."

The Chief of Staff got to his feet as the division commander entered. "Good to see you, Chesty," he said, and leaned across his desk to shake hands. "Have a chair." When his guest had sat down, the COS gestured at a gleaming silver pot. "Coffee?"

"Forty drops."

Bavaralaama knew the Vorgan idiom for "fill it up." Taking two tall clear insulglass mugs from a shelf, he drew them full. The coffee looked black as tar, but the aroma was excellent. "If that's more than forty drops," he chuckled, handing a mug to his guest, "just leave what you don't want. The Kalif's new orders haven't left us *that* short of money."

He sat down then, settled back and took a sip from

251

his own mug. "You're wondering what this is about. First of all, nothing I'll say here is criticism. Certainly not of you. I'll simply be pointing out a situation.

"Officers have opinions. Sometimes strong opinions. And there's nothing wrong with that. Also they like to voice them to their fellow officers. Normally there's nothing wrong with that either, if they're not treasonous or grossly immoral.

"In the officers corps planet-wide—empire-wide, probably—there's a lot of sentiment in favor of the Kalif's proposed invasion of the Confederation of Worlds. Not surprisingly. And this sentiment has reached the ears of politicians, most of whom don't like the idea of invasion, don't like it at all."

He sipped his coffee without taking his eyes from the other man's. "They feel threatened that officers voice partisan feelings in its favor, even privately, let alone *strongly* partisan feelings. Not your officers specifically, but officers in general. What makes your division a particularly sensitive matter is that it's just forty miles from the Hall of the Estates. You see what I'm getting at?"

"You want me to put a gag order on my officers."

"Exactly. And send it to me so I can show it to the people who complained. I don't like the idea, but it's necessary.

"Now a related matter has come to me from Iron Jaw, up at 1st Corps. You know what he's like—what his family's like, and the kind of officers he surrounds himself with. He doesn't like the talk he's been hearing. Or maybe what he imagines he'd be hearing if his ears were bigger; he banned talk about an invasion early on."

He paused, grunted. "He has a point, though. Given the range of good and poor sense in the military, I'm sure that a few officers have actually said the sort of thing old Iron Jaw reports. He claims some of the talk has crossed the line into sedition: that some officers have said the army ought to take over the government and declare the Kalif dictator, so he can get the invasion launched."

The COS—the chief of staff—had watched for a reaction in the major general; the only one visible was a flash of irritation. "Any observations?" he asked. "Or other comments?"

"Yes. I've heard quite a bit of talk, a lot more than Iron Jaw lets himself hear, but nothing approaching sedition. If I had, even phrased just as 'ought to,' I'd have filed charges for insubordination. Or sedition, depending on how it was put.

"And I'd probably have heard." He paused. "Remember what you wrote, the last time you inspected my division?"

The older man grinned. "That was a 50-page report, not including the 200 pages of appendices. What are you referring to, specifically?"

"That the morale of my men—officers and ranks—and their loyalty to their division commander, was as high as you'd ever seen in any division. Or in any battalion for that matter.

"So. I'm now going to let you in on my secret. Besides the fact that the Capital division is elite, with all enlisted ranks made up of gentry."

The COS interrupted. "There are officers who claim that peasants are more loyal than gentry."

"There are officers who treat their gentry noncoms like peasants. So naturally they're resented. They'd do better to treat peasants like gentry, so far as practical. No, besides having good people— First, I'm a competent commander, and they know it. Second, I like and respect my people, and treat them justly, which they also know. And third— Third, I have informers. Five of them."

The COS's eyebrows arched. Historically it wasn't that rare to place informers in military units, in times of unrest against the government. But in more stable times . . . ? "How do informers contribute to loyalty?" he asked. "Usually it works the other way."

"Not the kind I have. The army's got no halfway effective formal means for people to complain; to give their opinions. So I've given them an informal means;

one they don't know about, so they can't fear or misuse it. I've got four particular platoon sergeants, men I especially respect, that let me know about anything of any consequence that's bothering their men. And if there's an injustice or stupidity underlying a complaint, I have it handled. Or at least eased.

"I also have an aide, a major named Tagurt Meksorli. An outstanding officer: intelligent, tough, honest—even about himself—and well liked. Ambitious, but not the kind to lie or backstab or cover up. I'll send you his career summary sometime; it's quite remarkable. He's someone you ought to be aware of.

"Within a month of coming on staff, Meksorli had not only demonstrated excellent efficiency, but finesse in handling men. Despite his origins, he'd become one of the better liked officers in Headquarters Regiment. Then he started holding weekly parties—bull sessions with refreshments—in his quarters. I asked a few careful questions and liked what I heard about them. A couple of months later he rented a house in the Anan Hills, apparently just for his parties. His family is Vartosu Metals, Intrasystem Transit, and Diamond Cruises, among other things. Enormously rich. And his parties got bigger."

The major general looked thoughtful as he talked. "They're parties not everyone would care for. He doesn't put out at lot of fancy food, doesn't put up with drunkenness or other misbehavior, and usually women aren't invited. As I said, mainly they're bull sessions. Sometimes he'll invite an outsider, from the fleet or some foreign embassy, something like that.

"I asked him to let me know what the principle gripes and likes are that he hears about. Naming no names unless he wants to. So I could handle the beefs and reinforce the good points wherever appropriate. That was a year ago. I didn't know him as well then, didn't know whether he'd say yes and then feed me some pap, or whether he'd come through for me. As it turns out, I've had some very valuable input from him.

"Among other things, I know where my officers stand

on an invasion: not surprisingly, they're behind it, want to take part in it. Something very few of them have felt free to tell me. And I've heard of nothing even remotely seditious. But I'll ask him specifically. If there is anything, he'll tell me."

The COS had forgotten his coffee. Now he took another sip. "Hmh! Interesting. D'you ever go yourself?"

The major general shook his head. "Spoil the whole sense for freedom there. Besides, Sevenday evening is reserved for my family."

"Ah. Of course."

"One more thing. I'm not happy about issuing a gag order. The main results will be resentment and secrecy. It's the kind of order that Iron Jaw Songhidalarsa's people expect, but not mine. The only reason I'm not arguing is, I know you wouldn't ask it idly."

Lips pursed, the COS gazed at his coffee mug. "Maybe I wouldn't have, if I'd known about your informers." He looked again at the division commander. "Look, Chesty. Hold off on the gag order until you've asked Meksorli whether anyone's talked about taking over the government. Or making the Kalif a dictator. If not, I'll settle for an order that there must be no irresponsible talk, on pain of formal charges. How does that sound?"

"I feel better with that, sir. I'll let you know what I hear, and call in anything I write before I release it."

"Good. You just covered my next request. Go on back to your division, Chesty; I envy you a command like that."

When the Capital Division's commanding officer had left, the Chief of the Imperial General Staff considered what he'd learned. He wasn't entirely sure he liked what he'd heard about Meksorli. He tended to distrust such bald-faced ambition. But Chesty Vrislakavaro had always been an outstanding commander, alert and quick, and an excellent judge of character. And it wasn't wise to argue with superior performance or harass good men. Not without compelling cause.

Forty-one

More weeks passed. With work by Jilsomo, Alb Tee-von came into line behind the Kalif, not with any great change of heart but because he respected Jilsomo's ethics and judgment. The Kalif also gained four probables in the House. If the straw poll was correct, that meant he had twenty-seven yeas, sixty percent exactly. Still well short of the needed seventy percent, but enough to ask for a ten percent increase in his contingency fund.

He got it. Actually he got thirty-one yeas. Two of his exarch opponents had backed him, no doubt on the principle that the Kalif should be supported whenever morally possible. Two of his noble opponents had also voted yes; either Thoga's straw poll had been conservative, or more likely they were softening, fudging. How many more might be?

And with fourteen yeas in the College, eighteen House yeas on invasion funding would give it approval! Thus hope flared in the Kalif's chest when the last vote, a yea, was voiced. Perhaps the invasion *would* be funded this year.

Support was growing among the lesser nobles, and if the gentry had their way, he'd have his appropriation already. Patience seemed to be the key; patience, moderation, and ask for a vote on the last week of the session.

And if not this year, surely next.

Meanwhile, now he could afford to set SUMBAA to work producing all three new SUMBAAs. No doubt it had the construction plans ready. It was undoubtedly a matter of constructing modules that could be assembled aboard the selected ships.

Forty-two

The Year of The Prophet 4725

Prophet's Day marked the beginning of the year. It was also the major celebration of the year. The assigned anniversary of the Blessed Flenyaagor setting out on his wandering mission to make known the Truth of Kargh.

The actual date was only approximately known—the end of spring in The Prophet's native Arvendhi, the end of autumn at Ananporu, if one defines autumn astronomically instead of meteorologically. For of course, so near the equator there was no meteorological autumn. It was celebrated on the day following the solstice—in the more populous and culturally dominant southern hemisphere, the date when the sun began to return. Symbolically it was the beginning of recovery: in the one case of life and growth, in the other, humankind's intended spiritual recovery.

Popularly it was also a day of omens for the new year.

At Ananporu it fell within the major rainy season, but whether through the intervention of the deity or not, the great parade was usually completed without rain, or with only sprinkles. It was widely considered that a storm on the parade was an expression of Kargh's disapproval of the reigning Kalif. During the nine-year tenure of Kalif Gorsu Areknosaamos, the parade had been stormed on seven times, a percentage unmatched in the 1,490 years of the Kalifate, or so it was said. Kalif Coso Biilathkamoro had so far been in office for three Prophet's Days without a drop to spoil the event.

This year there were predictions both ways. The Forecast Office, releasing SUMBAA's evaluation, spoke of "scattered thundershowers, locally heavy." The Kalif's opponents forecast rain, feeling that if not Kargh, then the "law of averages," was bound to catch up with him; they'd be delighted to attribute it to Kargh's displeasure. Most of them, technically unsophisticated, were unfamiliar with the actual workings of probability.

The Kalif's supporters, on the other hand, said that if it stormed, it would be the Kalif's opposition who brought it on. This dodge had a feeble ring, being at odds with tradition.

Floats had never become part of Prophet's Day parades in Ananporu, perhaps because of the season and its storm threat. But there were marching bands from every world; teams bearing banners; open limousines bearing dignitaries; mounted formations, civilian, military, and police; gymnasts and clowns bounding and cavorting (along the margins, away from the horse droppings). And of course, there were the million or so spectators, far more than the city's population, who lined the right-of-way.

Normally the Kalif would ride a limousine, too, but almost no Kalifs had been active men in their midthirties. Paralleled by two mounted guardsmen, and a hundred feet above the avenue by watchful marksmen in open floaters, Kalif Coso rode a magnificent red stallion. He was preceded and followed by cheering that comprised a rolling roar of sound along the thoroughfare, a roar that could hardly be missed by the noble delegates following a little distance back in their limousines.

Well into the parade, thunder rumbled, with a few booms not far off, and once, for eight or ten seconds, great drops, hard and cold, spattered sparsely on the parade. Then the Kalif's opponents knew hope and joy. But it cut off as suddenly as it began, and while it rained hard half a mile north, and also two miles south, the parade went on unwetted. As if Kargh had changed his mind. Or perhaps he'd only wanted to remind the crowd of what he might have done.

When the last band had marched by, and only the sanitation crews were still to come, to clean up the final horse droppings, the crowds dispersed, to feast and party through the rest of the day and night.

The largest party of them all was the grand party in the Hall of the Estates. It was a very different kind of affair from the opening reception three months earlier. It was a gala, centered in the reception hall, and replete with noble ladies proudly dressed. There was dancing, too, in an adjacent ballroom, though most of the guests preferred to mix and talk.

The Kalif was there, with his kalifa.

He'd shown her the notorious book, as she'd asked, and she'd been hurt by it, though less than he'd feared. For two days she'd kept to their apartment, in a depression that, despite occasional silent tears, seemed to him more like despair than grief. It occurred to him that some of her mood might be due to her pregnancy, of which she'd shown few identifiable side-effects beyond a pair of nauseous mornings.

Mostly he'd tried to act as he normally would, but finally, thinking it might help if she talked about it, he'd asked her what troubled her most. She'd answered, *that someone would so spitefully hurt and humiliate a person who hadn't harmed them, and whom they didn't know.*

Then she'd wept in earnest, sobbing and hiccuping that she'd brought anger and hatred and opposition on him, and that she wished she'd been killed on Terfreya. He'd held her and let her cry, and when she'd finished, he'd kissed her, then kissed her some more, and unexpectedly they'd made love before going to sleep.

In the morning she'd seemed much happier, as if the weeping had helped.

In fact, her depression had passed, and her beautiful complexion bloomed to a newer glow, while her mood was more than happy. Often it was playful, which delighted him. It was as if the lingering disillusionment she'd felt with him, weeks earlier, had finally, totally passed.

So he was taken by surprise when she asked if she might skip the great party of Prophet's Day. She felt uncomfortable, she admitted, about being in a crowd some of whom—perhaps many of whom—had read the book.

He didn't urge, but pointed out that non-attendance would gratify those who'd hoped the book would lastingly wound and humiliate its targets. And minutes later she told him she wanted to go after all. Thus they were there together, she astonishingly beautiful in a sheer, light blue gown with white underlining. She had not swelled at all yet, that he could see. The only symptom was her glow. Within minutes she was swept away with pleasure at the attention she received. It seemed that almost everyone wanted to talk to her.

Large as it was, the great reception hall grew somewhat crowded, for no invitation was required. The mark of nobility was enough for admittance. Finally, the security chief, in his wisdom, decided the place held all the people it safely could. They lined the buffet; circulated with plates in their hands, talking; accepted drinks from waiters.

A surprising number of nobles, mostly strangers to him, came up to the Kalif and told him they approved his planned invasion. That it would be the stimulus the empire needed to reverse its long decline. Invariably the Kalif thanked them, and suggested they give their message to the delegates, who were recognizable by their capes. (It was not a "robed affair.")

It seemed to him that the numerous approvals constituted the kind of omen he could accept, one that reflected an identifiable reality.

Inevitably, of course, some of the crowd drank too much. But it was the tradition at official affairs that those who became conspicuously tight were handled by their friends. And occasionally someone would be helped to leave by one or two or three of the quiet security personnel in their colorful uniforms. But that was infrequent. If a noblewoman became troublesome, security kept hands off entirely. She was her husband's responsibility and embarrassment.

None within memory had made a scene like this one though. She was tall for a Vartosu woman, handsome, and much younger than her husband. Her condition hadn't been conspicuous until he asked if she might not like to meet the kalifa, who was talking with people a few yards away.

"The kalifa? That bitch in heat?" Her bugled scorn carried well through the hubbub of voices. "She's a slut! You men all act as if she's so beautiful! You'd all like to get in her pants! Yes! You, too!"

All eyes for a dozen yards around turned to the woman. Her husband was too stunned to act.

"She'd like it, too! Give her half a chance and she'd be in the nearest bedroom, with a line outside the door!"

Her husband pulled on her arm then, trying desperately to quiet her and rush her out, but his efforts made her louder. The crowd sounds died in a widening ring.

"Look at her!" She was actually yelling now. "The Sultan's Bride! The *Kalif's* Bride, but old Rashti fucked her, too! You can bet on that! What do you think she . . ."

It was the Kalif that cut her off. Within earshot at the start, he'd plowed through the crowd like an angry bull, and his hand gripped her shoulder from behind, fingers like hooks. Her yell changed to one of surprised pain as he turned her around, and she slapped his face, hard, would have slapped it again if he hadn't caught her hand.

For a long moment they matched glares. "You foul

devil!" she shouted. "Get your filthy hands off me! I'm not your slutty wife that you can—"

He slapped her once, not as hard as he might have, but it snapped her head to one side, and she wilted, tears starting. Her husband stood as pale as a Vartosit could get.

"Sergeant!" The Kalif's voice was as cold as ice. "Get this excrement out of here. Into a cell. Tomorrow we'll see how she likes cleaning public latrines on her hands and knees."

"Your Reverence!" Her husband had reflexively stepped back when the Kalif had strode up. Now he stepped forward. "Please! She, she didn't know what she was doing. Now and again she . . ."

He stopped at the Kalif's cold gaze. "*You would make excuses for the things she said?*" The man was unable to answer, and the Kalif began to realize how out of control he'd been himself. "Well then. If she'll apologize." He turned his eyes back to her. "What do you have to say?"

She didn't straighten, but tipped her head sideways, looking at him as if from beneath something. Her voice was quiet now, but so was the room. "You are Shatim incarnate," she said, "and that—" She turned and spat phlegm toward Tain. "That is Shatim's bitch in heat."

The Kalif's eyes bulged, and he slapped her again, the sound like a gunshot, sending her sprawling, screaming. Her husband reacted like a spring uncoiling, starting at the Kalif, then somehow stopping in mid-move. Two bodyguards were on him in an instant, grabbing his arms, jerking him back.

The man sagged, and when he spoke, his voice was thick and hoarse. "I, Lord Siisru Parsavamaatu, demand satisfaction at arms for your attack upon my wife."

The challenge brought the Kalif out of his own brief psychotic break, and he looked at the man: perhaps fifty-five years old, not decrepit by any means but no longer fit, and undoubtedly no match for him. The challenge had been an act of despondency; the man fully expected to be killed.

And suddenly the Kalif felt very tired. "I do not wish to fight you, sir," he said. "Each of us has reacted badly to this—" He groped. "This occurrence."

The man's head slowly shook. "It's a matter of honor. You struck my wife, knocked her down. The challenge stands."

The Kalif exhaled audibly through rounded lips. "Well then. If it must be."

"Please! Coso!" Tain had come up, but though he heard her, he ignored her. "Please! Don't do it! She . . ."

He cut her short with a chopping motion. His eyes were not angry however, only bleak. "We have no choice," he told her, then turned back to Lord Siisru. "Who will be your second?"

"My cousin, Lord Gromindh Parsavamaatu." A man who'd come near stepped through the circle of watchers now, to stand waiting. "And yours?" Siisru asked.

Coso almost answered Jilsomo, but Jilsomo was not noble, would not have been acceptable. It would have been taken as an insult. It occurred to him that he had no real friends among the nobility, outside the College. "Alb Tariil," he found himself answering. "If he's here, and if he'll consent to. Otherwise, Lord Roonoa Hamaalo."

Tariil was either out of earshot, or reluctant, and it was the tall and powerful Maolaaro who came forward.

"It was my challenge," Siisru said. "What weapon would you use?"

The Kalif shrugged heavily. "Sabers."

Siisru nodded. "Sabers then. Where?"

"The choice is yours."

"I am not familiar with this locality. Name a place."

"The drill field in the Sreegana. The ground is bare there, and sandy. The footing is good."

"So be it."

"The location was mine," the Kalif said then, following the ritual. "Name the time."

"At once."

He nodded. "As you wish."

No one followed them except their seconds and the Kalif's two bodyguards; it would have been totally outside protocol. The square seemed huge, their crossing a slow movement through a dark, deserted, dismal space. At the great gate, the guards watched them approach with idle curiosity, then with silent foreboding as they saw their faces, and wondered what this was about.

While the duelists waited silently on the dark drill ground, the senior guard signed out two sabers, both honed razor sharp, and at the Kalif's order, offered Siisru his choice. The nobleman tested the balance and feel of both, shrugged and chose. The Kalif took the other.

He bowed then to Lord Siisru. "You issued your challenge in extreme circumstances. I wish it had not been given, and would gladly see it retracted."

"It stands. I have no honorable alternative."

The nobleman's words had neither force nor indignation. He sounded like a man already dead.

"And if I refuse to fight you?"

The answer came tiredly. "Then I will kill you, for you would never run."

"Very well. Are you ready?"

The man's sword came up. "Ready."

Both took the guard position. "Lord Gromindh," said the Kalif, "you may give the command."

After a long reluctant moment, Lord Gromindh croaked the word: "Begin!"

To the Kalif, the "duel" was a macabre mockery, for Siisru moved slowly, as if under water. Clearly the man had not invited him to fight, but had chosen this as a form of suicide. The Kalif himself fought listlessly, as if hoping for something—Kargh perhaps—to intervene before he had to kill the man.

Then Siisru stepped back, lowered his sword and waited for a stroke. After eight or ten ludicrous seconds

of nothing happening, he suddenly set upon the Kalif
with furious energy, not skillful but dangerous.

The Kalif fended his strokes with a certain slug-
gishness, till the man's blade sliced his swordarm.
Abruptly he reacted, and in a moment Lord Siisru lay
crumpled on the packed and sandy ground. The Kalif
stepped back, gripped his arm to stanch the bleeding,
and turned to Gromindh, Siisru's second.

"It is done," he said quietly. "You can tell them he
died with honor, my blood on his sword."

Gromindh met his eyes. "Did he now?" he muttered,
then half-turned to look at nothing.

"Sergeant," said the Kalif, "call your regimental surgeon for me. Tell him to come tend to Lord Siisru's
body. And to arrange for a mortician. Lord Gromindh
can inform him if he has any particular wishes. Lord
Gromindh?"

The nobleman made no response, gave no sign that
he'd heard. The Kalif shrugged and turned to the big
Maolaaro. "Good Roonoa, I am going to my apartment.
The kalifal physician will tend to me there. You will do
me a favor if you return to the celebration and tell
them what happened. Ask Jilsomo to bring the kalifa.
Make sure she knows my injury is not dangerous."

Roonoa bowed slightly and left without answering.

The Kalif wondered, as he walked to his apartment
with a single guardsman, what would grow out of this.
Nothing good, he felt sure of that. Meanwhile, tomorrow he'd have to find out who, in Siisru's family, he
needed to meet with regarding reparations. To negotiate directly with the widow was out of the question.

Forty-three

The Kalif's physician had been at the party, too, but he'd been in the ballroom, dancing, and hadn't learned of the affair in the reception hall till after the principals had left. As soon as he'd heard, he'd hurried to his clinic to wait for a call.

He was there when his commset trilled, listened to the Kalif's description of his wound, then grabbed his emergency kit and left trotting, his night-duty assistant following with a folded emergency table. That damnable, bullheaded Kalif had refused to be brought to the clinic where he could be treated under proper conditions; he wanted to be at home when his wife arrived!

The physician had just finished prepping the arm when the kalifa came in with Alb Jilsomo. She was whiter than anyone he'd ever imagined, her blue eyes huge at the sight of the five-inch gash in her husband's arm. It wasn't deep though, just enough that tonus made it gape; no separate bonding of individual blood vessels was necessary. They stood watching, she and the exarch, as he injected bonding fluid into the anesthetized cut, cross-banded it, then sprayed a transparent wrapping on it, to support it till the sides of the cut cohered. Finally he put the arm in a sling, immobilized it against the patient's torso, and left.

The kalifa hadn't said a word, but she hadn't fainted, either, although she had sat down.

When the physician left, Jilsomo left, too. The Kalif opened his mouth to call him back and question him— ask what had happened and been said at the party, after Siisru and himself had left. But he changed his mind. He'd hear all he needed to in the morning, and it was more important now to talk with Tain, if she wanted.

She didn't, though. She seemed dazed, shocked, and he decided to leave her be for now. When she wanted to talk, she would.

Gromindh left the Sreegana with Lord Roonoa. His mind seeming turgid, too full for active thought. He supposed he should see to his cousin's wife, though he'd as soon she hung herself. With luck she would.

Honor indeed.

Then it occurred to him what needed to be done first, before something even more unfortunate happened; he went at once to a public comm in the Hall of the Estates, to call Siisru's son. They needed to get together man to man, right now, tonight, so Vilyamo could hear all that had happened, all of it, by other than second hand.

The Kalif awoke from a feverish dream, with an arm that hurt savagely. Hurt so badly, he rolled out of bed in a daze, thinking to call Neftha and find out what was wrong.

Instead of calling, though, he stumbled out, mostly naked, into the garden, holding his injured arm, grinding his teeth. He'd probably been lying on it, he told himself. He couldn't believe how badly it hurt.

The dream came back to him. He'd been emperor— not a Kalif, apparently, but simply emperor—and one of his staff, a trusted man, had confronted him in anger. About something in an earlier dream, he thought. Had drawn a crystal knife from inside his jacket, a knife that became a saw-toothed sword, and had swung it at him. He'd fended it with his arm. Then a guard had shot the man with a beam gun, cut him into pieces that writhed on the floor.

The blood had been red; he remembered that clearly. He seldom dreamed in color.

Remembering the dream brought chills to replace the fever; or was it the cooling night breeze on his sweaty body? At any rate the pain had receded a bit. He walked still clutching the arm, aware now that he'd come out without a repellent-field generator; some mosquitoes had found him. He turned to go back, and there was Tain, following, pale in the darkness.

"Are you all right?" she asked.

"My arm. Nightmares."

Her face reflected her concern.

"I'm going back in," he added, and chuckled thickly without humor. "The mosquitoes will take more blood from me than good Siisru's sword."

They walked back to the apartment together, her repellent field driving the mosquitoes from him. He remembered the dream again. It was as if he'd watched the attack from an external viewpoint, and he, the emperor in the dream, had been fat. Not as big as Jilsomo, but fat. Back in the apartment, and again without talking, he and Tain had a drink of brandy together, his a large one, before going again to bed. By then the pain was just a heavy ache, and after a bit he drifted into a sleep with no dreams that he'd remember afterward.

Forty-four

Coso Biilathkamoro had known, the evening before, that ill would grow out of his duel with Siisru. The next morning he began to learn the specifics. The newsfacs had kept carefully to the witnessed facts, and from them, from the one he read, he learned that Siisru Parsavamaatu had been a popular member of the Industrialist Party in Kalasoor State, a delegate to the party caucus there. And ironically, a supporter of the Kalif and his proposed invasion.

On the other hand, the newsletters faxed by the offices of the noble delegates were unhappy with him, at best. He forced himself to read them, to know what was said.

From one of these he learned that Siisru had a son, Vilyamo—and that Vilyamo was the commander of the Kalifal Guard!

How, he wondered, had he missed the surname?

He owed blood reparations to Vilyamo. Grimly he turned to his commset. The colonel's yeoman answered: The colonel was inspecting B Company's quarters; he'd send someone to find him right away. The Kalif left a message: he wanted to talk with the colonel at 1100 hours, in the private garden.

That left thirty-five minutes, allowing Vilyamo time to complete his inspection and arrive; given the circumstances, he would not rush the man.

It left him thirty-five minutes, too, half an hour he didn't know what to do with. It seemed doubtful he could concentrate. He opened a drawer, intending to take a stunner from it and clip it on his belt, for he would allow no bodyguard to overhear their conversation, and who could say what might happen?

Then slowly he closed the drawer without taking anything from it. This was something he would not go into armed, even with a stunner. Instead he picked up a report on Maolaaru fisheries and went into the garden to wait.

He'd overlooked the possibility that the kalifa might be there. She was sitting at one of the marble tables, beneath a large, colorful umbrella, with a folding library reader before her. He went to her.

"Good morning, darling," he said gravely. "I'm to meet someone here in half an hour. Would you leave before then? It must be just he and I; it's a very sensitive matter."

She looked questioningly at him, so he went on. "It's Lord Siisru's son. I've—taken his father from him, and need to discuss blood reparations."

She nodded, worry furrowing her forehead. Then her eyes moved to her husband's belt.

"Will there be no guard? You wear no weapon."

"Either would be inappropriate."

"But he might . . ."

He shook his head. "I think not. If he wishes to challenge me, of course, he may." *And that would truly be a tragedy*, he thought, *for if he does, to deny him would be unthinkable, and I'll have to kill him. If I'm able.*

The look Tain gave him was bleak, as if she'd read his mind. She folded her reader and went into the apartment, and he sat down where she had been. Unexpectedly the report he'd brought with him proved interesting. Commonly he merely scanned the lead abstracts of reports like this one. In this case, though, when he'd finished that, his quick eyes moved on through the pages, slowing here and there to digest a paragraph or table. *If the empire was managed by the*

Maolaari, he told himself, *we'd all be better off.* Presumably they made more use of their SUMBAA, or better use, but that was obviously only a small part of it. They cooperated more, politicked less, and put far less value on prerogatives of class, family, and wealth.

It occurred to him to wonder how the Confederation regarded these things.

Suddenly he became aware that someone was there, waiting, and he looked up, then stood.

"Colonel," he said.

"Your Reverence."

The reply was stiff, with a stiffness that seemed not of hatred, the Kalif thought, but from awkwardness with the circumstances. There were dark semicircles beneath the colonel's eyes, suggesting he'd released his grief in private when he'd heard, probably the night before.

"You know what happened of course."

"My cousin told me. Last night. Lord Gromindh, my father's second."

"Ah." The air seemed full of some dark and sluggish energy, an energy that would not readily discharge. "I must begin by stating my profound regret. I wish it had not happened; I wished it then."

"My cousin said as much."

"I—" It was difficult to say it, but he had to. "I hope that your mother is not—"

Vilyamo's retort cut him short. "My mother died twelve years ago. The woman who so vilely slandered the kalifa was my father's second wife—may her soul wander endlessly in Hell!"

The unexpected bitterness startled the Kalif, though he did not show it. What followed explained even more.

"Perhaps he loved her," the colonel went on. "Although my sister and I have wondered if there might have been some other reason. After the first few visits, we rarely went home; Nertiilo made it impossible for us there. He'd stop to see me when he was here in Ananporu, unless she was with him. I'm told—I'm told she was not usually unpleasant to him when we weren't there."

The Kalif nodded slowly. What he'd heard weighted him, although it made his task easier. "I see. Well. Your stepmother has family, I presume. No doubt I'll hear from them. Are you to be your sister's agent in the matter of reparations?"

"Gromindh called her last night, and she called me this morning. She lives with her husband near Maldiro opal, our home city. Reparations were not mentioned It *was* my father's challenge."

"True. Would a hundred thousand dromas constitute a suitable reparation?"

"That's 50,000 each," Vilyamo answered. "Considering whose the challenge was, that would be generous.'

The Kalif had had in mind 100,000 each, an amount that would drastically deplete his modest personal wealth. If 50,000 each would satisfy . . . There was, after all, the stepmother to deal with yet.

"And now, Your Reverence, I offer you my resignation from the Guard."

"Of course," the Kalif said. "If you're an only son, you'll need to manage the family enterprise."

"That's not it, Your Reverence. My brother-in-law is the man to manage it; he's been my father's administrative aide for years. But it seemed to me you might feel ill at ease, with me in command of your Guard."

"Um. You're sworn to defend my life. If that now seems unreasonable, or if you prefer not to be near me . . . Both are easily understood. But I'll be pleased if you stay."

The colonel nodded, a short head bow. "Then I will stay. Meanwhile I'll call my sister, telling her your reparation offer. If she wants another agent than myself, I'll let you know, and he can get in touch."

The two men parted and the Kalif went inside, his mind sorting impressions. Now, it seemed, he knew what Gromindh had meant by "did he now?", when he'd commented that Siisru had died with honor. What had it been like, married to that? Seemingly enough to drive someone to seek death.

Forty-five

The Diet took its regular eight-day break, which began on The Prophet's Day, but the College met on the third of them. The Kalif attended with his arm in a sling. The meeting was short, because there was no Diet business to prepare for and because no one wanted much to talk. But afterward, Jilsomo told him that a letter of deprecation had been circulated, a proposed collegial reprimand of the Kalif. It had come to Jilsomo last. Seven exarchs had signed it, including Alb Riisav, who'd drafted it. With less than a majority willing to sign, Riisav had then withdrawn it.

That even seven were willing, jarred the Kalif. It was bad enough that it had been drafted and circulated at all. "I realized," he told Jilsomo thoughtfully, "that Riisav was no friend of mine, but I hadn't realized he was my active enemy."

"Your Reverence, he may possibly consider himself your enemy; to draft a letter of deprecation was a drastic step to take. But in fairness, your actions of the other night, which he enumerated in it and took exception to, are worth your review."

The Kalif's lips thinned. "My actions were well justified. I wish they hadn't been necessary, but . . . You were there. You heard."

274

"But they were not the only honorable actions available to you. And arguably not the wisest."

The Kalif's jaw set. Jilsomo continued.

"I took the liberty of copying his letter verbatim, adding my comments. I'll leave it with you, in case you care to look at it; it contains food for thought." He laid it on the Kalif's desk. "And now, by your leave, I'll return to my desk. It's amazing how much work there is on it, considering the Diet is on break and a third of the bureaucracy on leave."

He bowed slightly and left. The Kalif scowled, then picked up the sheets Jilsomo had left with him, his unfriendly eyes assaulting the contents. It was addressed to him, with LETTER OF DEPRECATION centered and capitalized at the head. After the stiffly formal *Your Imperial Majesty,* instead of simply *Your Reverence,* there was a list.

1. You engaged publicly in an unseemly verbal and physical brawl with a woman. [One who allows himself to become involved in excrement throwing must expect to get excrement on him.]

The bracketed comment, he decided, was Jilsomo's.

2. The woman was obviously not responsible for her actions. She was either crazy or drunk, and probably both. This was apparent to everyone who saw and heard her.

3. It was obvious that her husband was willing and eager to apologize for her as her agent. Clearly, insane as she was, she was unlikely to apologize for herself. You rejected harshly and with an abusive tone his attempt to conciliate, invited her further vituperation, and virtually forced her husband's challenge. [Here you let go your best opportunity to close the matter without killing.]

4. The law explicitly states that dueling is a felony unless the parties have met before a magis-

trate and possible alternatives thoroughly discussed. The magistrate must approve the duel. You totally omitted and ignored the law on this. [It has been argued repeatedly, by past Kalifs and their apologists, that a Kalif is above the law, except as stipulated by the Charter. Those who so acted, particularly those who so acted either openly or chronically, have left empire, government, and the people the worse for it.]

5. Accepting the duel without the proper legal steps was a serious transgression of law, but to then fight it on the Holy Day showed a serious disrespect for The Prophet. You should have insisted on a later date, by which time one might hope some alternative would have commended itself to you or to Lord Siisru.

The Kalif's scowl had moderated, become a frown, and he tapped the sheets on his desk. His deflating anger left him sitting heavily like a much older man. He punched a code on his commset, and after a moment spoke to it.

"Jilsomo, thank you for bringing this letter to me. I appreciate it. . . . I have a question for you: Was Thoga one who signed it . . . ? Ask him!" For just a moment anger flashed at Jilsomo's response; then it passed. "I will," he said thoughtfully, and disconnected.

A shame Jilsomo never married, he told himself wryly. *He'd be an excellent father.*

A question nudged him then: why had he asked Jilsomo about Thoga? He'd surprised himself with that. The reason struck him: Thoga's newly found courage and integrity. With Kargh's light, the little exarch had had the courage to examine and question his entire mode of life and thought, his very motives. And then had had the integrity to accept what he found. If Thoga had signed the letter, it would have been that much more damning.

Well, he would not ask Thoga. He'd asked Kargh, as Thoga had, and accept what Kargh showed him.

* * *

The Kalif left his bodyguards, forbidding them to follow, telling them he needed privacy, and walked alone across the grounds to the chapel. The Chapel of the Exarchs had a number of small private rooms, not much more than closets, each with its padded kneeling stool, and to one side, a narrow stained glass window that admitted a limited amount of colored light. He went into one of them, set the lock behind him, and knelt.

He prayed to Kargh to help him, then waited. Thoughts formed, proliferated, were banished. More came into being. After a little he itched. Despite the pads, his knees and shins began to hurt, not severely but enough to distract. Grimly he stayed, back straight, hands on thighs, in the prayer posture he'd been taught as a boy.

The light rays shifted with the wheeling of the sun, till finally, darkening, they spent themselves on the side of the stone window casing. Slowly, stiffly, the Kalif got to his feet. Kargh had not come to him, had not chosen to show him anything. Perhaps he'd been abandoned.

Unnoticed, he left the chapel. He'd have to do and see Right for himself as best he could. He remembered what SUMBAA had said about humankind having to solve its own major problems. Perhaps Kargh had placed the same responsibility on him.

At least Riisav and Jilsomo had cast light on his actions for him. Perhaps Kargh had had something to do with that. He decided, though, to give the credit to the two exarchs, whether or not they were tools of Kargh.

Forty-six

When the Diet met again, the Kalif was there, sitting among the exarchs and swept by the glances of the nobles, some of them hostile, some cold, some merely grim. Seemingly none were sympathetic toward him.

He wasn't there to promote his invasion or anything else. He'd come this day to face the fire.

It was Lord Agros, not Rothka, who proposed a formal denunciation of him—definitely not an encouraging sign. Agros had been against an invasion all along, but seemingly hadn't been hostile toward the Kalif himself. Now, thought the Kalif, it seemed he was. It was hard to know for sure, though. Agros was motivated far less by emotions than by practicality. Or more accurately, by principles which were limited and distorted by expediency and opportunity.

In the oratory—it was no debate—the points brought up by the House were much like those that Riisav had listed, but phrased and rephrased with greater animosity. And almost no one, nobles or exarchs, seemed prepared to argue with them. Only Roonoa Hamaalo spoke in the Kalif's behalf, pointing out his unwillingness to actually begin the fight, and once the fight began, his reluctance to end it with his challenger's death. Roonoa's words made little difference to what followed,

278

however, merely gave the more hostile something further to fang and claw.

The delegates of the Pastorate had stayed out of it entirely, until their leader's hand went up. Alb Tariil, who was chairing the meeting, recognized him, and Dosu got to his feet.

He waited just long enough to draw their eyes, then began. "Your criticisms," he said, "have a certain validity. One might indeed have hoped for more composure, greater forbearance from the Successor to The Prophet. But no mention has been made of the extreme, the truly astonishing provocation he underwent." The old man looked around him. "Has everyone forgotten that old saw attributed to the wise man, Shamaragoopal? 'It is better to tell a man that his father mates with sheep than to tell him his wife's nose is too wide.' The shocking, indeed the stunning insults to the kalifa, shouted within the hearing of hundreds the other night, were far worse than that. They were public insults unprecedented in their coarseness."

Dosu paused to stare around as if challenging them to gainsay him. "*Almost* unprecedented. There has been one to equal it. A vile and evil precedent committed by a member, a late member, of the House of Nobles! I refer to the disgusting book of Lord Nathiir's, which also targeted the kalifa, and which served to greatly sensitize the Kalif, make him react more strongly to additional insults."

Again he paused, then shocked them further by shouting with a force incongruous to his aged frame. "An act which shamed the House of Nobles and threatened the very concept of nobility! Something that none of you seemed able or willing to recognize! Let alone publicly lament!"

Once more he paused, his sweeping gaze fierce, his old mouth clamped like the beak of a reef dragon. "All you could think of to do, that earlier time, was attack the Kalif for his unfortunate response. While today— today you've attacked him like a pack of wild dogs! In my youth in the pulpit, if one of my peasants had acted as shamelessly as most of you have, here today, I'd have laid a penance on him to bring tears to his eyes and a groan from his lips. I trust and recommend that your chaplain serve you similarly."

His voice shifted tone and volume, became less loud but scathingly sarcastic. "In case you have failed to notice, in your *noble* self-righteousness, this Kalif has been forebearing beyond most of his predecessors. Yet when Gorsu perpetrated his atrocities, there was no outpouring of indignation in this chamber, from either College or House. You lacked the courage, most of you who served here then! Your fear of impalement lent caution, if not cowardice, to your lips. But today your sense of justice has been totally inadequate to temper your words. The lesson seems to be that in your noble house, fear is more compelling than justice. Certainly integrity has been a virtual stranger among you today.

"You repay your Kalif's long record of civility with attacks you wouldn't dare make if he were truly what you accuse him of. With one exception, your performance here today has been without principle, without insight, without justice. Your hypocrisy is an embarrassment to the empire!"

Once more he paused, a pause that seemed to stem from tiredness, but when he spoke again, his voice was hard. "The people of every estate, when they hear of your poor display today, will judge you. They will judge you harshly. And who will suffer from it? This nation. This empire. Because their respect for you will have dropped—again. A process that can only go on so long before you are bankrupt with them."

His hand went to the mark of nobility on his own forehead. "I disdain you all!" he finished. "Except for Lord Roonoa. I can only hope that Kargh will open your eyes."

When he sat down, no one said a word for perhaps a long half minute.

Great Kargh but old Dosu's an orator! the Kalif told himself. *I had no idea!* In a way he was as stunned as the nobles, and not simply by the Elder's eloquence.

Historically the Pastorate was—if not jealous of the Prelacy, at least touchy at the Prelacy's seniority, and of their own lack of a vote in the Diet. Too, they'd often proven bristly at the behavior of a Kalif.

As for himself, he'd tried always to treat their delegates with care and respect. It seemed to him that if the Kalif and the College acted as the mind of the Church, the Imperial Assembly of Elders spoke for its soul. And too few nobles, or Kalifs, had appreciated sufficiently the influence the Pastorate had on the people—both gentry and the nobility at large.

Roonoa stood. "I call for a roll-call vote on Lord Agros's proposal," he said.

Thoga seconded. Tariil called their names, one after another. Only six voices answered yea, four of them the delegates from the LRP. Agros voted against his own proposal. Riisav voted nay without hesitating.

The Kalif had intended that when the discussion was over—or perhaps when the vote was over, depending on how the discussion went—he'd apologize for his actions on that misbegotten night. But Dosu's sermon changed his mind. Self-flagellation was rarely a proper act—for a Kalif less than anyone. Certainly this wasn't the time for it.

Then it struck him with a sense of rightness and certainty: The time *had* come to do something else—something he'd had in mind three years earlier and lost sight of. In fact he was sure of it. It was risky, but what wasn't, in a universe full of surprises. And it would gain him very influential allies.

He'd try it on Jilsomo when they got out of here; see what he'd say.

Forty-seven

The Kalif had gone directly from the Diet to his office, Jilsomo following. When they'd sat down, the Kalif described his plan. His *intention* would be a better term: there was no plan behind it.

The exarch tried not to stare; to him it was unbelievable that the Kalif could be serious.

"Your Reverence," he said cautiously, "It sounds— unwise."

The Kalif looked troubled. Not angry, not stung, simply troubled. He'd begun to see the flaws himself, even as he described the idea. Jilsomo continued, moving to take advantage of what appeared to be uncertainty.

"Prior to the unfortunate events on The Prophet's Day, you'd made real gains toward the funding of your invasion. You pointed that out to me yourself. Then, when it seemed you'd had a major setback, a critical one, Elder Dosu's speech gained back much of the lost ground for you. Possibly all of it. True?"

Possibly. The Kalif nodded. He thought he could see where Jilsomo was going with this: Continue the successful actions he'd been pursuing before. Continue, then perhaps dicker when it came down to it, offering to accept a lower level of support than he'd heretofore talked about publicly. A level which SUMBAA still considered satisfactory. By next year at this time, preparations might well be far along, new divisions training, new ships under construction. Everyone would have jobs. Attention would be outward, not inward. Two years after that, the fleet would be on its way. It would amount to the birth of a new empire, a new people extroverted from old attitudes, old troubles—old traps. It made excellent sense, it seemed to him; much better than the idea he'd just described. Yet . . .

"To proclaim the Pastorate a voting estate will truly outrage the House," Jilsomo went on. "They'll never go along with it; they wouldn't even if they were in love with you. And you're talking about a change in the Charter of Establishment! With a vote of sixty percent of their own members, they can repudiate your proclamation without the College even having a vote on the issue! And the odds are, they'd be unanimous.

"Nor will they forgive you for it. Unlike the duel, and the killing of Nathiir, this would attack the very seat of their power. As a result, you'd have no chance at all with your invasion, or the legalization of loohio—or anything else you might espouse!"

The Kalif's mouth twisted liplessly in painful thought. Jilsomo continued.

"Beyond that, it will antagonize the College. Some of them because they'll like the idea no more than the House will, for much the same reasons: prejudice and the dilution of their power."

Halfheartedly the Kalif tried to muster a defense. "The dilution would not be great," he said. "I'm only proposing to give the Assembly five votes. Five, which the twelve can elect to cast as a block or distribute as they see fit. The House has twenty-seven and the College eighteen."

"You'd *undertake* to give them five; they'd get none of them." Jilsomo paused. "Why not try to give them twelve? One per delegate? It would hardly anger the House more than five. And the result would be the same: No votes for the Pastorate—and no votes for anything else you wanted. You'll be fortunate to escape impeachment! Or perhaps unfortunate to escape it."

The Kalif groped. Why had the idea seemed so brilliant when it came to him? There had to be a reason behind it somewhere. Jilsomo kept relentlessly on.

"And suppose, through some miracle, they let your proclamation stand. Five votes. What assurance would there be that the Pastorate would vote with you on invasion? They'd hardly vote with you on loohio; I remember what Elder Dosu said about that, early in the session. You'd be diluting your own power and the College's, as well as the House's. And this is not the time for that."

"But they *should* have a vote," the Kalif said. "You agree with me on that. Or you did."

"I did and I do. But they won't get it this way. Not now." Jilsomo paused, and when he went on, it was with a new note in his voice, the growth of an underlying excitement. "Your Reverence, you've given me an idea. Let me tell it to you. It *is* time to start toward a vote for the Pastorate. But first build a base of support. . . ."

As Jilsomo talked, both men scribbled ideas, diagrams, notes of things to do. The Kalif took time off to call Tain on his commset and tell her he'd be late to supper.

When they finished, both men felt exhilarated.

That night they lay down to sleep, one on a broad LG bed beside his beautiful wife, the other on a narrow, solitary bed in his bachelor apartment. Then each of them, as he waited for sleep, recalled the Kalif's original idea, so strange in its irrationality. And wondered about the Kalif's mind.

The possibility of a brain tumor occurred to the exarch, and the idea chilled him. Chilled him more strongly than he might have expected. Entirely aside from the vaguely sexual attraction the Kalif had once had for him, an attraction that seemed to have died at the man's wedding, this Kalif was a man whom he loved for reasons entirely aside from physical attraction of any kind. It seemed to him, now that he looked at it, to be a blend of the man's charisma, his loyalty to principle—and the Kalif's love for humankind. He also wondered if it wasn't a recognition of that love, perhaps an unconscious recognition, that had inspired old Dosu's fiery defense.

Tomorrow he'd asked the Kalif when his last medical examination had been. And bring the matter up to Neftha. If there was something organically wrong with the ruler, it needed to be handled before it became severe, perhaps debilitating.

Forty-eight

The young man stood trying to look firm, but a person less perceptive than the Kalif could have seen his discomfort at being there: He'd been assigned this task by someone higher in the family.

The Kalif's voice was calm and mild, but his words were blunt. "So, Lord Paalu. Why did they send *you* to beard me? You're an attorney, true, but green, lacking experience. I've researched your family, you see. I'd expected your Uncle Meelor."

"Your Reverence, my Uncle Meelor is a tempestuous man."

The Kalif's eyebrows raised. He was tempted to ask if his uncle was afraid he'd end up assaulting or challenging his Kalif. Instead he asked, "As tempestuous as his now notorious cousin, the Lady Nertiilo?"

He waved off any reply, almost as he said it. "I don't expect an answer to that. The question was rhetorical. Do you have authority to make an agreement? Otherwise you're wasting my time."

The young attorney stiffened somewhat, as the Kalif had expected. "I have the authority in writing," he answered, and opening his belt purse, handed a rolled paper to the Kalif, who opened it, looked it over, and handed it back.

"Good. What figure did your uncle give you?"

His uncle Meelor had indeed set the price. Cousin Nertiilo had not become rational again, even after she'd metabolized the alcohol in her bloodstream. Thus she'd been interned by the family to hide the shame of her madness, and was in the care of an alienist. Apparently, the young man thought, the Kalif knew these things, too.

"Two hundred and fifty thousand dromas," he said.

"That much, eh? If I paid that much, I'd sue her in return, for slander. Probably for a quarter million. How would that look in the fax? That and other matters?"

"Your Reverence has bereaved her; left her a widow."

"True. And even if she recovers her sanity, she's unlikely to wed again, despite her good looks. After her public performance of ten days ago, any would-be suitor would investigate, and what he'd learn would cool his interest. But she's quite an affluent widow. I'm aware that her husband's will left her almost all of his estate, and his children remarkably little."

The Kalif examined the young man for visible reaction. "It would be interesting to know how she managed that," he added.

The young man darkened somewhat; apparently there was a story there, the Kalif decided. One he'd leave well enough alone, unless forced to pursue it.

"Well. I have a counter offer for you," he said briskly. "Based on several facts: one, that she and her family are not in need; two, that while I bear a major responsibility for her bereavement, she bore an equal one, or greater; three, that she caused my own wife pain and suffering; four, that such a person deserves little in the way of solace from her victims; and five— Well, hear my proposal."

His eyes pinned the young man. "Your uncle can accept this or not, but given the circumstances, he cannot call it stingy. I have already made reparations to Siisru's son and daughter, reparations they regarded as generous. But that was before I, and they, knew the terms of their father's will. So I herewith offer your cousin a reparation of 10,000 dromas."

He saw the expected flinch in the young man's face, and continued. "A sum greater than the annual income of most gentry families today, and in these times, greater than that of too many noble families.

"Besides, it's the sum that Siisru left to each of his children.

"At the same time I will offer to Siisru's two children an additional reparation of 40,000 each, money they should have gotten from their father." He reached inside his robe and took out a scroll of his own. "It's all there, on the scroll. Agreed?"

"My uncle will be wroth."

"Your uncle's wrath is chronic, and no secret among those who know him. Or so I'm told. In fact, it's a matter of public record, in the courts. You're a fortunate man not to share that sometime family trait. With regard to myself, he's well advised to keep his wrath closely reined; I'm disinclined to be tolerant with his niece's uncle. As for you— Weigh well your decision. And if your uncle is too upset, tell him what I would have done, if you'd refused these terms. Which is, I would have—and will if you're difficult—publicize the whole affair, certain pertinent aspects of your family history, and the miserable bequests to Siisru's children.

"Now. I will have your answer."

The young man looked to Jilsomo as if for support; the exarch's round face showed no trace of sympathy.

"It seems—I must accept."

The Kalif stood, removed a small scroll of his own from inside his robe, and held it out. The young man took it, pulled his chair closer to the desk to sign, and discovered that the sum on the agreement was 20,000, not ten. He wasn't sure what the Kalif's motive might have been for misleading him, but he signed both halves quickly, and handed it back. The Kalif separated them and gave one to him.

The young man stood to leave.

"One moment."

He stopped.

The Kalif's voice was mild. "As you know well, young attorney, it is customary to shake hands on such an agreement, unless one side feels there is serious injustice in it. Do you honestly—*honestly*—feel there is?"

The young man blew softly through pursed lips and shook his head. "No, Your Reverence, I do not honestly feel there is. Though I cannot speak for my uncle in that."

The Kalif extended his hand; they clasped and shook.

"Good. Go with Kargh, and may you prosper, both in wealth and in the spirit."

"Thank you, Your Reverence."

As the young man left, the Kalif looked at the clock on his wall. Almost time for his appointment with Neftha. *I might as well go now*, he told himself, *and have done with it.*

Forty-nine

Lord Rothka Kozkoraloku sat tapping his stylus on his work tablet. His intention was no problem, but implementing it would take some doing. His eyes re-underlined it at the head of the first page:

COUP

THE KALIF DEPOSED AND IMPALED (the short stake?); THE COLLEGE OF EXARCHS DISCONNECTED FROM GOVERNMENT; THE HOUSE IN CHARGE OF IT.

Below that he had written two actions which he considered prerequisites: *(1) Greatly increase the disaffection of the nobility for the Kalif. (2) Gain the support of some key part of the military.* Assuming he accomplished them, they might or might not be sufficient to his purpose, but without them, his chances would be poor.

Earlier, his purpose had been simply to prevent the Kalif from mounting his invasion. Now, though, it seemed to Rothka that a coup ending with the Greater Nobility in power was the correct goal. In fact, he'd felt so good when it first occurred to him, there'd been no room for uncertainty. As long as the Kalif was in power, the man would strive until he had his way. If not this year, and that now seemed impossible, then next year or the year after, or the year after that.

Simply to have him assassinated would throw dark suspicion on his opponents in the House, most particularly the Party, risk a serious public reaction and a possible purge. At the least it would virtually ensure that one of Biilathkamoro's supporters, probably the gentry exarch, Jilsomo, was given the throne as his successor.

No, a coup was the only correct action. But it would help greatly, in establishing order afterward, if the man's popularity was sufficiently weakened in advance. Give people an excuse to tell themselves that the coup might be for the best.

The things already done had provided a certain groundwork toward that. True the Kalif had come through most of them remarkably well. But it seemed to Rothka that by now the kalifa's questionable past must be stuck ineradicably in the back of people's minds, as was her husband's penchant for personal violence. Break down his credibility in other matters, and people would remember, begin to question his suitability.

Up till now, Rothka told himself, his own mistake had been in trying to discredit the Kalif with a single action. Which the Kalif had then focused on and more or less neutralized. Until this last business, the man had shown a talent for saying or doing the right thing to minimize damage. It had been a stroke of genius when Coso had released the cube of the Diet session in which he'd killed Nathiir. No one, except possibly the Kalif himself, had anticipated the widespread public approval it had gotten.

Finally, when it seemed he'd damaged himself seriously, old Dosu had rescued him. And while he might have been tempted to release the cube with old Dosu's scathing defense, he hadn't. To do so would have alienated the House, beyond recovery for this session and probably for sessions to come. As the man had foreseen.

Rothka frowned. *Or was that little scenario still a possibility? It would be a dangerous project, but the potential* . . .

He set it aside, at least for the time.

He'd learned some things from all that. One was to look toward volume, another to focus on issues. The pamphlets he planned to release would be numerous, brief, pithy, and politically relevant. Also they'd carry no actionable attacks on the Kalif. A pamphlet would attack some single element of the invasion plan, and dismantle or discredit it. The arguments didn't need to be valid, as long as they were convincing, at least superficially. They'd stress practical matters: economics, civil disorders, and other gut-level issues. Play the factions: the lesser nobility feared the ambitions of the gentry; the gentry worried about the peasantry encroaching on their privileges. Keep the pamphlets coming, one after another, too many and too plausible-seeming to counter. And keep them legal.

Although he wouldn't stay entirely on practical issues. He'd already ordered the printing of a pamphlet saying that *The Book of Shatim*, announced by the College of Exarchs as having been found in a provincial archives, was rumored to be a forgery, produced by the College to help them hold onto power. The pamphlet would question how it could possibly help them do that, while not questioning the idea that the book was spurious. As if the origin of the book was certain, and only the College's supposed rationale was in doubt.

There was a polite knock on his study door, and with a button on his chair, Rothka released the lock. It buzzed quietly, and his gentry serving man entered.

"Your lordship, there's a young man to see you."

"Young man? What young man?"

The servant came over and held out a card to Rothka, who took and examined it. *Neethoon Ralakhon*, it said. *Administrative Aide*. The Informer. He looked up sharply at his servant. "You know I don't receive journalists at home."

"He claims to be here on his own behalf, and not on

business of *The Informer*, your lordship. He says he has certain information, ah, for sale. Information that his publication would quash if they had it."

Rothka's brows knotted. It had to be something unfavorable about the Kalif, otherwise the newszine would hardly quash it. Scandal was *The Informer*'s bread and butter.

"Neethon Ralakhon." Rothka said the name aloud, as if tasting it. "I'll speak with him, Ilavi. Send him in."

A little thrill shivered through him. Somehow it seemed to the nobleman that he had something here. Something big.

Fifty

Protocol was permissive in some cases. These particular visitors would not arrive as petitioners, nor as foreign functionaries on the business of their sultan. They would be there at the Kalif's invitation—indeed at his request. Thus he could receive them in his study as well as in the receiving room, and he liked his study better.

Jilsomo was with him as usual. In this case, though, the exarch's role was not that of silent lieutenant, because the guests would be Elder Dosu, leader of the Assembly of Elders, and the four members of his executive council.

And Jilsomo had begun in the Pastorate. Further, he'd been the first man in 560 years to enter the College of Exarchs after beginning in the Pastorate, and from provincial Niithvoktos, at that. Add to that his gentry origins . . . In the Niithvoktu Pastorate he'd made his name as a negotiator—a diplomat, so to speak, a bringer together of factions. And a man of integrity and justice as well as intelligence.

He'd graduated from seminary at the unusually early age of nineteen, receiving his own parish at the even more remarkable age of twenty-one, an age when most pastoral candidates were still students. At twenty-six he'd become the youngest dean in the history of Niithvoktos. At twenty-nine he'd been appointed archdean, and liaison between the Niithvoktu Pastorate and the Niithvoktu Synod of Archprelates—the sultanate's equivalent of the Imperial College of Exarchs.

While Jilsomo was still short of his thirty-first birthday, a major Niithvoktu prelacy had been shamed by scandal and vacated by a declaration of anathema. Specifically, its prelate had extorted money from well-to-do gentry charged before him with crimes of character, some of which had been fabricated for the purpose.

As partial punishment, the sultan had stripped the family of its long-standing rights to a prelacy, and with the concurrence of the Synod of Archprelates had appointed the young Archdean Jilsomo to the diocesan throne, in part to ameliorate the deep offense felt by the gentry there.

Being an experiment, so to speak, he'd been under the continual scrutiny of his sultan, and the remarkable recovery of the diocese under his direction brought him an Archprelacy at thirty-four. At thirty-seven he'd been called to Varatos to serve as Collegial staff, and at thirty-nine appointed exarch by old Kalif Parthaalu, and assigned to the College. Every seminarian training for the Pastorate knew Jilsomo's name and honors.

Although the junior member of the College, he'd been the exarch most ready to disagree with, and even occasionally lecture Kalif Gorsu. And survived not only with his life but his position, presumably because of his non-censorious, matter-of-fact manner of criticism. Gorsu even seemed to hold a certain fondness for the exarch who was fatter than himself.

Thus Jilsomo knew intimately both sides of the Church: The Pastorate—that hierarchy responsible for the spiritual instruction, guidance, and welfare of the people from peasants to nobles; and the Prelacy—that parallel senior hierarchy responsible for the administrative and judicial governance of Kargh's empire and individual worlds. He was the Kalif's spokesman in any dealings with the Pastorate.

The five pastors came into the Kalif's study carrying

umbrellas. Outside the thick glass garden doors, hard rain was a steady mumble on the canopy. The curtains had been drawn back, showing the downpour dancing violently on the patio.

"Your Reverence," Elder Dosu said, and bowed slightly. The bow was not required. If he'd wished to show disapproval of the Kalif, or even reserve toward him, he would have withheld it, and two of his council did.

The far younger Kalif bowed slightly in return. "Thank you, honored Elders, for coming. Would you like refreshment?" The offer was an especial courtesy, implying that he would not rush them, that his business with them had priority over any audiences scheduled to follow.

"No thank you, Your Reverence. We appreciate your generosity, but we have breakfasted, and we know your time is precious. We are also very curious as to why you asked us here."

The Kalif gestured at his aide. "Alb Jilsomo will tell you. I'm aware that not all your Assembly trusts me."

Their attention shifted to the exarch. "Kalif Coso has a proposal for your consideration," Jilsomo said. "In the second week of his reign, he told me that one of the things he wanted to accomplish during his tenure was to change the status of your estate in the Diet. From non-voting to voting."

He had their attention.

"Recently we discussed how it might be accomplished. He can, of course, simply proclaim it, but it falls under the Charter of Establishment, and thus would not take affect until the next autumnal equinox, when the new Diet is seated. And it can be blocked for an entire session by a majority voice vote of the House—blocked in the session proclaimed, or in the first meeting of the session following. Then, without the concurrence of the College, the House of Nobles by itself can repudiate the proclamation, or any proclamation that would alter the Charter, by a roll-call vote of sixty percent of its delegates."

Jilsomo looked around at the pastors. "You know, of course, the record on these things. Only one such proclamation has ever survived: the proclamation which provided the Pastorate its voice in the Diet, a voice without a vote. And that proclamation was issued by no less than Papa Sambak.

"In the few other instances when a Kalif has proclaimed a change in the Charter, it has been repudiated. And afterward, the noble delegates have felt it a point of principle to thwart and frustrate him. Under Kalif Kambara, this so crippled government that the College impeached and dethroned him.

"Thus, wishing a vote for the Pastorate and accomplishing it are two very different things, and in the press of kalifal operations, Kalif Coso lost sight of it at times. As did I. Elder Dosu's oratory the other day reminded us."

Jilsomo turned and nodded to the Kalif, who stood up then and spoke.

"You can see, I believe, why I requested that you not talk about this meeting to anyone outside yourselves. If the House learns of it, it will be more displeased with me than it already is."

He paused, looking them over. "If we succeed in gaining the vote for you, it will be because the stage has been set for it. The Pastorate must preach for it, from the pulpit in every house of worship, from the lectern in every school.

"Speak of it not only to the nobility, but to the gentry. It is the Elders, more than any, who speak for their interests in the Diet; now let gentry voices speak for you in the marketplaces and taverns. And speak occasionally of it to the peasants, for you are their principal friends, and it will gladden them to think that you may gain the vote."

He stopped and looked at them, his gaze direct. "And in time—not at the beginning—tell them you have a friend in the Diet. Tell them their Kalif is favorable to your aspiration. And when you preach to the nobles, tell them to tell their delegates to support you.

"In five years, or ten, or perhaps only two, you will have a large body of supporters in the work places and the marketplaces. And in the House of Nobles, the delegates will have gotten used to the idea. You'll have supporters among them, too, by then, and I can proclaim you a voting estate with some likelihood that the House will not repudiate it and punish me with recalcitrance."

He spread his hands. "I presume you have questions; I'll try to answer them."

A bald, thickly bearded Elder spoke from his chair. "You propose this only for your own purposes. There are millions of pastors on Varatos alone. By positioning yourself with us in this, you will draw strength from us—strengthen yourself in the Diet, and strengthen the prospect of obtaining funds for your proposed invasion."

The Kalif answered him mildly. "Friend Gwampala, I look toward a vote on invasion funding well before my name is associated with this project."

The man grunted. "And if the vote goes against you, as it will, there will be next year. And no doubt the year after. You are taking the long view here."

Another Elder spoke. "How many votes would the Pastorate have in the Imperial Diet?"

"It will depend on public support and the strength of opposition in the House. Not less than five, though."

"Five?" It was the bald Elder again. "Five would be like spitting in the ocean."

Another Elder interrupted. "I can think of numerous times where five votes have decided a matter. And five will be a precedent. Eventually it will be twelve."

The bald Elder grunted. "Eventually can be a very long time. But five would be a start." He turned to the Kalif. "Now here is an observation for you. I don't believe you'll find a pastor who will not like the thought of our estate having votes in the Diet. Even if it is only five. But there are many pastors, doubtless most, who do not like your desired invasion. And I for one will not support it. In conscience I cannot. Some who will speak fervently for votes in the Diet, will speak against invasion."

The Kalif inclined his head for a moment, than looked at the man again. "In that, at least, we agree. I have no doubt that some will speak against it.

"But tell me, Elder Gwampala, why you, for one, dislike the invasion. I presume that part of it is the men who will die in the war. But what are your other reasons?"

Gwampala's scowl furrowed his forehead into the area where hair once had grown. "That is reason enough!"

The Kalif's eyebrows shot up. "The Prophet wrote that one must be ready to give one's life to spread the word of Kargh. And proved with his own death that he meant it. As others have done since. How terrible is death, if the soul goes to Paradise?"

He paused. "Well, what you support, and your reasons for it, are a matter between you and Kargh, and perhaps Elder Dosu. I am not so naive as to think I can buy loyalty, or that honest men will sell it." He scanned over the five, then settled his gaze on Elder Dosu again.

"I have said what I asked you here for. And while I could say more, I've said what's necessary. Perhaps you'll assign someone as liaison, to keep me informed. Or perhaps you'll decide that's not necessary.

"Now, unless one of you has something further you need to tell me at this time . . ."

No one spoke until, after three or four seconds, Elder Dosu did. "On next Threeday I will issue a writ, authorizing and urging the Pastorate empire-wide to request support for a voting Assembly of Elders. Meanwhile, we five will have discussed possible objections which our pastors may face, and provide guidance in answering them.

"I'll have a copy hand-carried to you."

He got to his feet with the help of his umbrella. The rain still danced on the patio outside, almost as hard as before. "And now we will leave. It is eleven-fifteen, and while the Diet will not convene till one-thirty, I prefer to lunch at my leisure when I can."

With Jilsomo at his side, the Kalif walked with them down corridors to the front entrance of his palace. Making only a little small talk, saying nothing further about his proposal. It seemed to him the meeting had gone reasonably well, and that this was not the time to say more.

Also, it occurred to him that these past few days he'd performed as well as ever, mentally. Apparently his strangely shortsighted idea, following Dosu's speech in the Diet, had been an isolated and ephemeral aberration.

He hoped he'd reassured Jilsomo, too, he and the clean result of Neftha's medical examination. He'd realized from the physician's overly casual request that the two had colluded.

Fifty-one

Supper for the royal couple, that evening, was a chopped salad, a salad as aesthetic visually as in flavor. There were green and red vegetables of several sorts, and cubes of tender-flavored fish, with a clear, delicately tart dressing. As usual, they ate to the evening news, watching intermittently as it took their attention.

The kalifa had recovered readily from the events of The Prophet's Day. Probably because Nertiilo Parsavamaatu had been a certifiable madwoman, while by and large, the guests had been friendly and admiring. Equally important to the Kalif, the hurt she'd felt from his invasion plan was in abeyance, at least now that the subject wasn't prominent.

It helped greatly that Tain was good at directing her attention to other things. She was on her second reading of *An Abstract of History*, this time calling up elaborative material she'd passed by on her first reading. He wondered if her avidity for the subject was partly due to having lost her own history, and that of her home world and empire.

"It seems to me," Tain was saying, "that the empire would be better off if the peasants were taught to speak Imperial. And read it. Especially since it's not so different from their own speech.

The Kalif grunted. The observation wasn't unique to

her, but it got angry reactions from most nobles, or at least most noble politicians. "Arguably true," he said. "But to impose a change would offend the nobles more than I care to just now. They're mad enough at me over the invasion issue." Damn! There he was, bringing it up! "Along with other matters. And when the Pastorate starts promoting the pastoral vote from the pulpit . . ."

He stopped in mid sentence; the news anchor had taken his attention.

". . . Kalif Coso has released the cube of last Five-day's Diet session. A session in which the House casti-gated him severely over his duel with the late Lord Siisru Parsavamaatu."

He stared at the wall screen, unbelieving. He'd released no such thing!

"Their criticisms," the man went on, "were inter-rupted by a spirited defense of the Kalif by Elder Dosu. We'll show you excerpts of the House's verbal assaults, beginning with a motion by Lord Agros for formal denunciation, then show you Elder Dosu's defense in its entirety."

The man had Tain's attention now, too, and they watched, the Kalif in a state of near shock. Dosu's speech had stunned and embarrassed the nobles, and broken their indignation. But played before the public like this, it humiliated them. They'd be angry now with Dosu, and enraged at himself for its release. *But he hadn't released it!* Nor did he have any idea who could have; it was something only he had the authority to do!

Tain, engrossed in what she was watching and lis-tening to, didn't notice his reaction till he got up from the table. "Darling! Is anything the matter?"

"That was *not* supposed to be released. I gave no such order, but the House isn't going to believe me when I tell them. They're going to want my body on a stake!"

He realized by her expression then that she'd taken his words literally. "Not literally on a stake," he added quickly, "but they're going to be very angry with me. I have to make some calls, and try to patch this up as well as I can."

Then he hurried from the dining room, leaving her with the television.

He placed a call to Lord Agros, who hadn't watched the news, telling him absolutely that he'd had nothing to do with it. After that he called several others. Finally he called Alb Thoga, who'd seen the news and wondered if the Kalif had taken leave of his senses; Thoga promised to make some calls, too, and to assure the Diet tomorrow that the Kalif was truly upset by it. Next he called Jilsomo, who'd also watched and been stunned by what he'd seen. Jilsomo would call Elder Dosu and make clear to him that the Kalif had had nothing to do with the fiasco. And that an investigation was being started to find out who had.

After talking briefly with Jilsomo, the Kalif called the Minister of Justice and told him he wanted the affair investigated. Starting that night, with questioning of the producer of the evening news. The ministry was to call him with every piece of information they got, till midnight. If possible, he wanted to attend the Diet tomorrow with something more than unsupported denials to offer.

Without supporting evidence, though—at least a little bit—he'd stay away from the Diet, he told himself. His failure to show up would bring angry ranting, he had no doubt, and quite possibly an actual, formal denunciation. Those he could live with. If he *did* show up, things would be shouted in his face that could hardly be retracted and would make future collaborations extremely difficult. There might even be a walkout by part of the House—a much greater possibility in his presence than if he wasn't there. Historically that had happened several times, blocking even minimal appropriations and largely stalling government. The first two times it had happened, the reigning Kalif had declared himself dictator "for the duration of the walkout," and the result had been insurrections, one expanding into armed revolt, the other into a civil war whose ravages on several worlds had taken decades to heal.

No, he'd stay away until he had evidence to offer that it hadn't been he who'd released the cube—evidence that at least pointed elsewhere. Or, lacking that, until the temperature of the House had dropped a few degrees.

Finally he called Elder Dosu himself. It was desirable that the Elder's message to the Pastorate not go out yet. It would be impolitic to have the pastors begin their campaign until this particular fire was out. It would look as if the two were coordinated, and tend to discredit the Pastorate's campaign.

Before he went to bed at midnight, he'd had a report from the Justice Minister. The chief archivist at the Library of the Sreegana had been questioned under instrumentation, and had sworn he'd had a call from the Kalif, telling him to release a copy of the cube to the Imperial Broadcasting Network. Yes, the call had been on visual, and by hindsight, the visual had been unusual; usually the Kalif sat close to the pickup. This time he'd sat or stood several feet back from it, and the lighting had been poor.

No, he'd noticed nothing different about the Kalif's voice.

The investigator had then checked the computer for the time and origin of the call: it had been placed a little before noon, at 11:17 P.M. But not from a Kalifal office; from a conference room in the Sreegana administration building. There'd been nothing scheduled in the room at the time; anyone could have used it who had access to a staff security card.

Eleven-seventeen, the Kalif thought now. He recalled Elder Dosu's comment just before he'd left that noon: it had been eleven-fifteen. No doubt others of the Elders would remember it, too. And from there he'd walked them to the palace entrance. He couldn't have called from the Admin Building at eleven-seventeen. But to cite them as witnesses would bring up the question of why they were meeting with the Kalif.

For now he'd simply have to take the heat.

Fifty-two

Early the next morning, he informed Partiil and Jilsomo that he wanted no further appointments for the day, short of real emergencies. He wanted to be available for any calls from Justice. Then he handled the three petitioners already scheduled, and had turned his attention to the morning's backlog of communications, when a call from Jilsomo interrupted him.

"Your Reverence, there's someone in my office whom I think you'll want to see."

A note in the exarch's voice said even more than his words. "Bring him in," the Kalif answered, then sat back and waited. In half a minute they were there. The man who entered with Jilsomo was the Klestronu colonel.

"Your Reverence," Jilsomo said, "Colonel Thoglakaveera."

The Kalif regarded them for a moment, saying nothing, and when he answered, his voice was cool. "Colonel, please be seated."

The colonel sat. Jilsomo stepped to the Kalif's desk and handed him a cube. "I'll let the colonel tell you about this. I haven't seen it yet; he brought it to me only minutes ago."

The Kalif's eyes shifted to Veeri.

"Your Reverence," the colonel began uncomfortably,

305

"a few days ago a man came to my apartment with an offer for me. Of 100,000 dromas and—an opportunity, as he put it, for revenge. Also a place to stay, with an assumed identity, until you were removed from office, which he implied would be soon." The colonel's mouth tightened for a moment. "He also offered what he called 'subsidiary benefits' that I won't elaborate. I found them insulting, but they made me curious.

"In return for these incentives, I was to answer questions, first privately, and later in front of a camera. I answered the questions. He already had the basic features of what had happened; that was obvious from the questions themselves. He wanted details he could use to write an interview script. An interview that I would star in."

He gestured at the cube on the Kalif's desk. "That's the result. He took what I'd told him and twisted it. Badly. We did the interview yesterday evening before a camera. I'd had the foresight to carry a concealed stunner with me; the man seemed like a criminal. When the interview was over, I stunned the interviewer, the cameraman, and the door guard; actually the door guard first. Then I took the cube from the camera and got out of there. Walked to a thoroughfare and caught a taxi.

"It was late, and it seemed unwise to return to my apartment, so I stayed in a hotel. And came here when I finished breakfast. The gate notified Alb Jilsomo for me." He gestured at the cube. "If you'll play that, you'll see what this is all about."

The Kalif inserted it into his terminal and keyed in an instruction. The wall screen took life and color. There was no lead-in material, of course; it was the raw interview. It opened on a comfortable living room with an interviewer and the colonel. The interviewer smiled at the camera and spoke.

"I have here with me Colonel Koora Thoglakaveera of the Klestronu marines. The colonel was on the Klestronu expedition to the Confederation, and it might be interesting to ask him some questions about it."

He turned to Veeri. "Colonel, what sort of fighting men were the Confederation troops?"

"The best term to describe them is— Well, it takes more than one term. They are skilled, they are savage, they are cunning, and they do not surrender. They fight to the death. Our casualties were remarkably high."

"Hmm. It sounds as if an invasion army might have its hands full. Is it possible that the Confederation troops might, in fact, defeat an invasion force?"

"If the invasion force was strong enough and well led, no. But they would definitely inflict heavy casualties."

The interviewer showed polish before the camera, but his face was not familiar to the Kalif. The colonel came across fairly natural, although his eyes moved repeatedly to a point just off camera, as if there was a prompter there, with his lines.

"Interesting," the interviewer said. "Earlier, I understand, it was you who captured the female enemy soldier who is now our kalifa. How did you happen to take her alive?"

"Actually it wasn't I who captured her. She'd apparently been knocked semi-conscious by a blow on the head, and was captured by a squad of marines who didn't kill her because they recognized her as a woman, and, well— A little later she was taken from them by an officer."

The interviewer's brows arched. "Those marines that had held her—I hope they were gentry."

"No, they were peasants. But presumably she was rescued before anything, uh, serious happened to her. They'd pulled off her clothing, but the officer said he'd gotten there in time. I didn't hear about her till the next morning, and because we were anxious for a live prisoner, I was there in minutes. To find her somewhat bruised and in a confused state of mind."

"Good god, Colonel! What a terrible experience that must have been for her! A squad of Klestronu marines! Then what?"

"I took her to headquarters base, where she was

cleaned up and sent to the flagship for questioning. I never saw or heard of her again till our return to Klestron."

"I see. Why was she brought to Klestron? It was my understanding that she'd lost her memory in an interrogation accident. Surely they didn't expect to get any information from her after that."

"It was never clear to me why they took her with them."

"Can't you even think of a reason they might have taken this lovely female captive with them?"

"I prefer not to speculate."

"How did you come to encounter her again on Klestron?"

"That was pure chance. I discovered that she was being held prisoner by a group of intelligence agents."

"Held prisoner?! Were there any other prisoners?"

"None. They'd been keeping her in a room alone. In a small apartment, actually. Fairly comfortable but with no privacy whatsoever. She was watched constantly, day and night, by hidden cameras. It was quite scandalous, because over a period of days, what had begun as ordinary security monitoring had degenerated into voyeurism, if not something worse. She being such a remarkably attractive and vulnerable young woman.

"When I learned of the situation, I at once felt a certain responsibility for her safety. Because I was the one who'd transported her to headquarters in the first place. So I had her removed, and my wife took her to her father's estate. Shortly after that, the Kalif had her brought here to Varatos."

"Where he apparently found her as attractive as all the others had. How did you avoid her attractions?"

"It wasn't easy."

"Were there a lot of these beautiful female soldiers on the Confederation world?"

"Actually she was as unusual there, in her beauty, as she is here. And I never saw or heard of any other female soldier there. Not one."

"Remarkable. Truly remarkable. Why just this one beautiful woman, I wonder.

"Now, Colonel, I have some more personal questions to ask you. Frankly, I've heard that there was a lapse of several days between the time you took the now kalifa from the room the intelligence agents were holding her in, and the time your wife took her away. Isn't that so?"

"That's not true!"

"And isn't it also true that your wife asked the Kalif for a writ of divorcement from you?"

"I refuse to answer that."

"Are you now married to your wife?"

"No. No, I'm not. She—thought I'd been unfaithful to her."

"Why would she think that?"

"She said—she said that Tain, now the kalifa, had told her I'd—taken advantage of her."

"But you hadn't?"

"I hadn't."

"Why would she have said that if it wasn't true? And why would the Kalif grant your wife a divorce? Adultery by the husband isn't grounds for divorce. Grounds for punishment, yes, for amends to the wife, and reparations to her family if they ask for them, but not divorce. Do you suppose a divorce could have been part of an agreement to keep your wife from making public what the kalifa told her about you?"

"I have no way of knowing. And anyway it wasn't a divorce. He granted her an annulment."

"An annulment?! On what grounds?!"

"You'll have to ask him. I refuse to say any more about it."

"Hmm." The interviewer turned again to the camera. "So now we know the true history of the kalifa, or some of it. A young woman victimized repeatedly, from her capture and—abuse by a squad of peasant marines to her arrival here on Varatos. But seemingly her hardships are over now. Because this lovely yellow-haired soldier, if that's what she actually was, and not something else, shares the kalifal palace with the Successor to The Prophet.

"Who seems to have made a seriously criminal agreement in order to get her into his bed. It also seems that he was not the first man to have her. He seems to have been preceded by an indeterminate number of peasant marines in a muddy field on a far off planet; an indeterminate number of fleet personnel on a bunk in a warship—and remember, that was a three-year voyage! And repeatedly by a crowd of lustful intelligence officers in a room on Klestron.

"That of course is just since we've known of her. What had her function been in the enemy army? This solitary young woman with such sexual magnetism. Surely she wasn't a soldier. The evidence is that the enemy had no female soldiers. The soldiers they did have didn't let themselves be taken alive, yet she surrendered—perhaps because surrendering was what she was used to doing.

"One may be forgiven for wondering if, in fact, the writer of *The Kalif's*—excuse me—*The Sultan's Bride* was more correct than we imagined.

"At least the sultan in the story performed no acts of criminal collusion in bedding his prisoner. Nor did he knowingly disregard Church Law and the specific command of The Prophet in marrying her. *Nor* did he murder a delegate to the House of Nobles who'd publicized the nature of his bride.

"I recommend that you resist the wishes of this immoral, this *disgraceful* Kalif, and do all in your power to have him deposed. I also urge you to copy this cube in quantities, if you have access to equipment, and give the copies to others.

"Perhaps we might put him and his bride on a small hyperspace ship and send them outward to the Confederation by themselves, keeping our young men home and alive, and the fruits of our labor here where we can have the use of them."

The speaker bowed, and the picture faded slowly to deep indigo, then black. For a minute no one spoke.

Then the Kalif unclenched his jaw and turned to Veeri. "I presume you can lead us to the place where this was made?"

"Indeed I can, Your Reverence."

The Kalif sat staring at him, his hot gaze cooling, growing thoughtful. "Colonel, why did you bring me this cube? Surely you have no love for me."

"You're right, Your Reverence, I don't. But neither do I hate you, though perhaps I did once. The kalifa is a very beautiful young woman. Through no fault of her own. And she was indeed very vulnerable, again through no fault of her own. I speak from experience when I say I appreciate how a man can be smitten by her loveliness, and do what he would not ordinarily do.

"So I can understand how you might have done to me what you did. As for why I brought this here"— he gestured toward the terminal, and the cube in it— "instead of destroying it . . ." He paused, then continued. "I'm in favor of an invasion. I've seen a beautiful world scarcely used by the people there. I would like to go with the invasion force, take part in the conquests, be part of the occupation. I'd like to have a fief of my own there, a land fief. Not on Terfreya—not necessarily—but on some world there. So in my own interest, I would not sabotage either you or your invasion."

He sat back then, waiting.

"Ah. Well. A fief can be arranged." The Kalif spoke the words absently, as if his attention had gone to something else. "Colonel, the things you said in the interview, about Tain . . ."

"Sir, I am confident the intelligence agents hadn't abused her, although they might well have before long. The opportunity and temptation were there. I also doubt that anything happened to her aboard the flagship. She was undoubtedly in stasis most of the trip, and the commodore had a reputation as a hard, strict old man. His officers would have considered the prospect of being tried before him and jettisoned out a trash port. And if the marines had—used her on the battlefield, she'd have been more than 'bruised and confused.'

"Concerning her role with the enemy army— We know nothing of the Confederation's military practices away from the battlefield. There may well be administrative functions which women carry out, as they do in our own fleet. We do know that women carry out administrative functions in civil government there.

"And, sir . . ."

"Yes, Colonel?"

"Your Reverence— What is the kalifa like?" He rushed on then, as surprised and flustered by what he'd asked as that he'd asked it. "I mean—I never really came to know her. And I've wondered."

The Kalif's frown changed from incensed to thoughtful. "Her manners, Colonel, are noble. She is considerate, intelligent, affectionate. I could not have imagined a better wife, or one as good. Her soul matches her physical beauty."

The colonel's response was soft. "Thank you, Your Reverence," he said, "for your extraordinary courtesy."

It was Jilsomo who spoke next. "Your Reverence, do you have instructions for me? Or shall I go now and inform the Justice Ministry?"

"Call them, Jilsomo. Have a senior investigator sent here. We'll speak with him, the colonel and I.

"Meanwhile, Colonel, go with Alb Jilsomo. I have things to think about and do."

The two men left, but the Kalif didn't return at once to his work. Instead he sat and examined briefly a feeling that had struck him while he and the colonel talked. After watching the cube. It had been— It had been when the colonel said what he'd said about the planet Terfreya. And then about women in their government. And there was the savage energy of the defenders there, as if they fought for reasons beyond simple duty and orders.

He shook the thoughts away. He had work to do.

Fifty-three

Lord Rothka Kozkoraloku watched the scrub-clad hills of the Fashtar Military Reservation pass beneath his personal floater. His guts and chest were unconsciously tense. There was something uncanny about this trip. But it didn't occur to him to back away; this was what it had all been leading up to. He'd simply have to make it work out.

He hadn't intended to come here so soon; things weren't ready yet. But circumstances had pushed him. Roopal had called him in the predawn hours; the Klestronu colonel had carried a stunner, stunned all four of them, and fled with the cube. Liiroola and the outer door guard had died, Liiroola no doubt because of his bad heart.

It was aggravating that people couldn't handle situations competently. He'd had to arrange for disposal of the bodies himself, which was not only a nuisance, but involved a degree of risk, even with the baffles he'd worked behind.

But everything seemed to be under control now. Only Roopal knew who was behind the project, and Roopal was away free. Thus there was no way of connecting him to any of it; the Klestronu colonel didn't know—possibly hadn't even heard of—Lord Rothka Kozkoraloku.

313

Obviously the Klestronit hadn't run to the police. If he had, they'd have gone to the house and found Roopal and the other three lying unconscious or dead. And they'd have learned who was behind it. Even if Roopal had never said the name "Rothka," they'd have used standard questioning and instrument reads to narrow down the possibilities; they'd have found him out in minutes. And this act might well have broken the Kalif's reluctance to impale, even use the short stake.

A sobering thing to contemplate. Rothka admitted to himself that his interview project had been a questionable risk. But to have such an opportunity dropped in his lap . . .

As for the Klestronit's motives for attacking the others and running off with the cube— Perhaps he'd begun to wonder what kind of safe house they had in mind for him up north. Whose safety they had in mind. Or maybe he thought he could market the cube for himself; if he could, it hadn't been a waste after all.

The major danger now was that the Klestronit would decide for profit instead of revenge, and sell it to a known market—the Kalif. If that happened, it would be destroyed. And it had taken the police only three or four days to nose through Nathiir's safety baffles and nail him down for *The Sultan's Bride*.

So Rothka had pushed his timetable up a week and a half, and scheduled his first military contact. He'd made his excuses to Agros and Ilthka, and was skipping today's meeting of the Diet.

He'd already had enough on his mind, engineering the release of the cube showing old Dosu scathing the House. Liiroola had handled that, handled it nicely. Had done the Kalif's voice and even made the mask. Rothka had had misgivings when he'd seen the mask on him. The likeness hadn't been as good as he'd expected, and when Liiroola talked, it hadn't looked fully lifelike. But the light wouldn't be good, Liiroola had told him, and people saw what they expected to see, at least when there was a marked resemblance.

And Liiroola had been right; the archivist had accepted it without a question.

Ahead, Rothka could see now what he assumed was a division area. First Corps' four ground forces divisions and air services division were housed well separated from each other in a broad open ring, with corps headquarters and service and support units in the center.

By the nature of floater traffic, traffic patterns were simple. Thus there was no delay; he was allowed to land within a hundred feet of the general's control center. A captain was waiting for him at the pad.

The control center was a separate, single building containing the general's personal office, offices for his immediate staff, conference rooms, kitchen . . . in the midst of a broad and beautiful lawn, large shade trees, and well-tended flowerbeds. Rothka thought wryly that the lord delegates of the House had less pleasant surroundings in which to work.

The general was not at the entrance to greet him; he was at his desk, seemingly busy, when Lord Rothka was delivered to him like a petitioner, which in a sense he was. Rothka had researched both the general and his family. Lieutenant General Lord Karoom Songhidalarsa, known as "Old Iron Jaw," and sometimes as "His Majesty Iron Jaw the First," was the best, and perhaps the only realistic candidate to carry out a coup. He was also arrogant and imperious.

Nonetheless he got promptly to his feet and stepped out from behind his desk to greet his guest. The general was a tall man, flat-cheeked and spare-limbed, yet at the same time paunchy and corseted. His hair was well-oiled and brushed straight, in a style of some decades earlier.

"Lord Rothka," he said, "it's an honor to have you here. I've made a point of keeping your arrival inconspicuous, as you requested. Would you care for coffee? Tea?"

"Nothing, thank you. I'm not thirsty. There are things I've come here to discuss, General—matters that may take considerable time. And I have to be back in Ananporu tonight; it's impolitic for me to miss two consecutive days in the Diet."

"Of course. Captain, make sure the lord delegate and I are not disturbed. And keep in mind that the lord delegate's presence here is absolutely confidential."

"As you wish, General." The captain saluted, fist thumping his chest, then left.

"So, Lord Rothka," the general said, "this room is completely secure, as your messenger requested."

Rothka knew the general's reputation as a committed conservative. It fitted the man's family image. The Songhidalarsas were one of the greatest of the Great Families, with vast holdings on the second continent, and strict advocates of land rights. Their name was synonymous with noble traditions, noble values, and service to Varatos. Two millenia earlier, a dynasty of four emperors had been Songhidalarsas. And the general's grandfather five or six generations removed had broken the Dhimoordu Revolt, restoring imperial unity and the rights of the Great Families on four mutinous worlds.

Still, what Rothka had come here for was extreme. Thus despite having mentally rehearsed his pitch on the way, he sat pinch-mouthed for a long moment before finally speaking.

"I presume you're aware of the recent behavior of the Kalif—his wife, his duels, his recent humiliation of the House of Nobles?"

Rothka deliberately didn't mention the Kalif's invasion plans. That was uncertain ground.

"Loosely speaking, yes," the general answered. "I never follow such issues in any detail, though. I've read the, um, book; it was sent me by my nephew. A satire, obviously; I have no idea to what extent it reflects reality."

"Better than you might imagine, General. I'd thought to have a very interesting cube for you, of an interview with a principal in the affair, but it wasn't ready when I left."

"Oh? I viewed the one your messenger brought, of

Elder Dosu's attack on the House. Surprising that the Kalif released such a thing."

Rothka nodded curtly, taut jawed. "It's typical of the arrogance he's shown lately. The man is trying to discredit the House and evict the nobility from any meaningful role in imperial government. It fits perfectly the criminal way in which he took the throne in the first place, with the murder of Gorsu. Not that Gorsu was any better." He shook his head in disdain. "If Coso Biilathkamoro stays in office much longer, there's sure to be insurrection, and probably civil war. The empire may very well collapse in violence and disorder."

He paused to let his words sink in. The general watched, inscrutable. "One can hardly avoid contemplating—" Rothka paused, then abandoned his roundabout approach. "I'm thinking in terms of a coup. In fact, I'm proposing one. On behalf of a number of us in the House, I'd like you to dispose of this false Kalif, evict the College of Exarchs, and declare a dictatorship. I can guarantee the backing of at least a large and powerful minority, probably a majority, of the delegates."

With that he'd committed himself. If the general wished, his carcass would soon decorate a stake in the Square of The Prophet. Already Rothka's guts burned.

The general didn't raise an eyebrow, though, simply gazed at Rothka for what seemed at least a minute. Finally the iron jaw opened. "Speaking hypothetically, of course, if someone were to undertake such an action there'd be a number of things to consider. A coup would need to succeed quickly, which would require a force not only adequate to suppress the Kalifal Guard, but to give the Capital Division pause. We're talking about a brigade at the very least, with heavy air support." As he spoke, he jotted quick notes on a tablet. "The Capital Division is—what? Forty miles from the Sreegana? While we're 2,100 miles away, which would mean an air lift. Made with transport on hand; additional transport couldn't be had without General Staff orders. For example, orders to move as part of some larger activity—some military exercise." He took his eyes away from his note pad to look at Rothka. "Which is not going to happen unless you can arrange it."

Rothka shook his head. The general's stylus recommenced its jotting.

"Heavy gunship support would be needed to suppress the Kalifal Guard and to discourage and delay the Capital Division. The Guard could prove a tough nut to crack; they're a proud outfit. Lightly armed, it's true, but the Sreegana's buildings give a major advantage to a defender."

Again he looked at Rothka. "A lot of damage would be done to the buildings, you know."

Rothka nodded. The general went on, jotting as he spoke. "The best strategy would be to attack while most of the Guard is still in bed or at breakfast; bomb their barracks before they know anything's afoot. Disorganize them; kill as many as possible at the outset. I presume their heavier weapons are in an armory or armories in one or more of their barracks buildings. Find out which building, and hit it hard enough—then immediately land troops in the center quadrangle and on the roof of the Administration Building."

He paused for another long and thoughtful minute, then looked up from his pad. "Still speaking hypothetically, when would this need to be done?"

"When is the soonest you can do it?"

The general's eyebrows climbed. "*Soon* is not the problem. Secrecy's the problem." His eyes gleamed like wet black marbles. "Once I'd informed my staff, I'd want to move within two days. Because if it leaked, you and I would both be carrion. I'd need to come up with a convincing cover story for most of the officers involved: something they'd believe. Something to allow— to *justify* convincingly—the quiet, confidential movement of nearly 8,000 men."

The hot rock in Rothka's stomach threatened to burn its way through.

Thoughtfully the general gnawed a lip. "If I called a meeting of selected staff this evening, we'd need to draft specific plans before we slept. I have a couple of officers who've served in the Guard; they'll know the ground and the schedules. I'll have to question them carefully though, and perhaps, um, put them to sleep afterward. Certainly they can't sit in on the planning; they're not people I'd trust in this."

Rothka stared, his scalp crawling. The man was talking about this week! He hadn't planned to move so quickly; he'd intended this meeting to establish an agreement in principle.

"We have no contingency plans for this, of course," the general was saying. "We'll have to create it from nothing, and carry it out within two days." He returned his gaze to Rothka. "It's more than a matter of troops and tactics, you know. There's logistics—ammunition, fuel, food, medical supplies, all of it. Fortunately, we're looking at a brief operation in more or less friendly territory."

This evening. Within two days. If he could have backed out . . . Rothka shook off the feeling, the weakness. Get the damned thing done.

"The Caps—the Capital Division—is the most dangerous element," the general was saying. "I don't suppose you have anything to suggest there? And a lot depends on how difficult the Kalifal Guard proves to be. We'll need to carry off the actual coup quickly, before the Caps can move. If we can present them with an accomplished fact—the Kalif dead, the exarchs mostly dead or captured, the Sreegana in our hands, and the House of Nobles willing to accept us—the odds are excellent that they'll hold off."

Again he fixed Rothka with his eyes. "It's absolutely essential that the House of Nobles acknowledge me as dictator as quickly as the Kalif is taken care of. I have no desire to decorate a stake in the middle of the square."

Rothka's eyes gleamed back at him; his funk of a minute earlier was gone, at least for the moment. "Taking the Sreegana and the Kalif shouldn't be as difficult as it looks," he replied. "Do you know who commands the Guard?"

The general shook his head.

"Neither does the Kalif. That is, he knows the man, but not what he is. It was pointed out to me last night that the commander of the Kalifal Guard is Colonel Vilyam Parsavamaatu."

The general frowned; the name meant nothing to him.

"Lord Siisru Parsavamaatu is the man the Kalif killed, after the row at The Prophet's Day party. It's Siisru's son who commands the Guard. As soon as you set the time, I'll arrange for him to take steps to prevent an effective defense. The odds are, he'll be able to arrange the Kalif's murder himself, as soon as your troops land there."

The general's eyebrows jumped. "And he's still there? In command?"

"As of this morning."

"Astonishing!" The general shook his head, incredulous. "Well! That is a boon, and an excellent omen. We'll want to strike before the Kalif discovers the situation and has him removed. All right. I'll use the 31st Light Infantry Brigade." He paused again. "You're certain you want to do this?"

Rothka nodded, despite the second thoughts that swirled. The general went on: "The 31st includes a light assault regiment, the 103rd, whose regimental and battalion staffs I have handpicked over a period of time. Its company commanders, too. A real old-fashioned regiment, without one gentry officer. I consider it my 'personal' regiment." He paused, grunted, then surprisingly grinned. "I never really looked at why I molded it as I have. Well!

"You realize, of course, that the Kalif is widely popular with the army. A large majority of the officers' corps is strongly in favor of his invasion proposal, even here at 1st Corps. Even in the 31st Brigade, I have no doubt, and the 103rd will be no exception. So. I'll give them an explanation to satisfy them."

He chuckled. Rothka watched and listened, fascinated now.

"They're young, most of them," the general went on. "Compared to you and me, all of them are. At age sixty-three, I have no desire to spend the rest of my career fighting in some distant part of the galaxy. They, of course, look at it differently, and the prospect of conquest has stirred old traditions, old ambitions in the armed forces. I doubt you realize how strongly."

His focus shifted, his expression thoughtful again as he examined the problems. "There've been peasant demonstrations at Ahantar, conveniently just 120 miles east of Ananporu. I'll order the 31st, with floater transport, on full readiness. As an exercise; my prerogative. Telling her commanding officer, and my immediate staff, that it's to be ready for departure on an hour's notice. In case the demonstrations 'heat up as expected,' and the General Staff calls on us. Something we've half been expecting anyway.

"The district airfield's just outside Ahantar. The brigade can leave here in mid-evening, landing there sometime after midnight tomorrow night . . . Hmh!"

Tomorrow night! Fear and excitement chased each other around in Rothka's gut.

The general grunted again, smiling. "The more I look at it, the more feasible it gets.

"The brigade commander's an old friend of mine. We see eye to eye on many things. Most things. He and the C.O., 103rd. They'll have to know in advance. The Kalif, I'll tell them, has become insane—there are certainly precedents for that—and that it's being kept secret. Meanwhile, his excesses have killed any chance of an invasion of the Confederation. We're going in to take over, set up a military dictatorship until the invasion can be launched."

Rothka heard, and felt shock. *Until the invasion can be launched?* What if the man followed through on it? He might have to, to satisfy his officers.

The general never noticed the change in Rothka's eyes, the dismay. He was looking inward, seeing something else and nodding, as if the whole procedure was coming together for him. "1st Corps has two special penal platoons," he went on, "the toughest, most dangerous men we have. They're organized as a point force, for use in particularly dangerous situations, and they don't give a damn for much of anything except their image. I'll attach them to the 103rd, and assign them especially to kill the Kalif. I'll tell them he's their meat. That if they bring me his body—his head at least—they'll have a party in their stockade that lasts as long as they do, with all the liquor and women they can handle. They're to kill all the exarchs they come across, but the Kalif is their special target. The party will be their reward for killing him."

He nodded again, pleased with his creating. "I'll have to assign the brigade pretty much the corps' full airlift capacity. And our full gunship support force, to interdict any move the Caps might try. The Caps have an armored brigade that's a lot more than the 31st can handle on the ground, but they won't be eager to move if we outgun them in the air by four to one."

He stopped then, his eyes, his wolfish smile almost paralyzing Rothka. "Given any decent sort of luck, we should pull it off nicely. After lunch I'll call in a few reliable staff and go over it with them. Work out the details." He leaned back then, as if ready. "Meanwhile, perhaps you'll have lunch with me. We have our own kitchen and gourmet cooks right here in my control center."

Stomach churning, Rothka declined. It seemed to him now that this man was a disaster! *Ambitious!* Once he established himself as dictator, how could he be evicted? He'd set himself up as the champion of invasion, and move the rest of his corps down to Ananporu. It was doubtful the army would challenge him then, and if the House tried to do anything about it, he'd probably handle it the way he planned to handle the Kalif and the College.

Yet he could hardly report the general's plans without exposing his own criminality. Which would mean certain impalement.

*   *   *

Rothka Kozkoraloku left the control center wondering feverishly how he could get the general assassinated. The man would look at him as an ally; he'd have access to him. Yes, that was the solution. When the Kalif was dead and the general was dictator, he'd shoot him himself. It was as simple as that.

Just now, though, his knees felt almost too weak to carry him to his floater.

When Rothka had left, the general sat for several minutes, contemplating. As a child, he'd imagined being emperor. As a youth he'd imagined scenarios that ended with himself on the throne; had done this even in middle age, occasionally, as a form of mental relaxation when he'd gone to bed.

Now . . . He became aware that the blood was ringing in his ears.

It was risky of course; extremely risky. That sharp-faced little politician had no real understanding of the risks. If he did, he'd shit himself. There was little margin for errors and unforeseens.

But in the olden times, every new dynasty rode into the palace on the back of some fanged and deadly rajwar, figuratively speaking. Some rough and dangerous scheme or some opportunity of the moment. And he was as good a man as any ancestor.

Fifty-four

The transports would be halfway to Ahantar by now, the captain thought as he swung out of the light utility vehicle. And when the general said 0130, he didn't mean 0125 or 0135, he meant 0130 sharp. Just now it was 0102. The 11th Gunship Support Wing was on ready standby—a drill, they assumed, a ground exercise. But its aircraft would be fueled and armed, their crews sleeping on board. They could lift within fifteen minutes of the time the order was given.

He strode into the air command building. The place felt asleep, despite the standby. The few personnel on night duty there were saying nothing, as if in the grip of some slow dream. He went directly to the duty officer, the dispatcher, who this night was a subcolonel, and saluted. The man looked up as if irritated at the interruption of the novel he was reading.

"Colonel!" said the captain, and identified himself. "Acting for General Songhidalarsa, I've come to order the dispatch of the 11th Gunship Support Wing."

The subcolonel looked at him as if he thought this was some kind of crude joke.

"To order *what?*"

A premonition of trouble started in the captain's chest, and spread. "The dispatch of the 11th Gunship Support Wing," he enunciated. "General Songhidalarsa

324

has ordered it in support of the 31st Brigade. To Ahantar."

"Huh! Interesting that I wasn't briefed that something like this might happen." The subcolonel reached out a hand. "Let me see the orders."

The captain counted mentally to eight, calming the panic that was beginning to tug at his mind. Obviously someone had screwed up. The dispatch officer was to have been notified in advance, given written orders in mid-evening, with a cover story of some kind.

"General Songhidalarsa indicated to me that they'd been given to you. I was simply to let you know the time. He wants the gunship support wing in the air at 0130."

"Well I'm sorry, Captain, but no one's given me anything in writing on this. And that's how I need it: in writing."

And it was *not* to be known that the general had accompanied the brigade in his own command floater. That had been stressed. Otherwise it would be obvious that the expedition was intended to do more than overawe and suppress the strikers and demonstrators at Ahantar.

"My orders came from General Songhidalarsa verbally," the captain said. "That's how I'm passing them on to you. I'm sure you don't want to reject them."

He realized, even as he was saying it, that the last sentence was a mistake. The subcolonel's brows drew down sharply; he'd taken it as an implied threat. "Captain, we operate according to regulations here. If it's not in writing, it's not an order. In writing and signed by someone authorized to give it to me: General Songhidalarsa or his deputy. Or General Mavaraloku, of course; the orders would need his initials at any rate."

The captain couldn't go to Major General Khobajaleera, the general's deputy in charge. Khobajaleera knew only the cover story; he wasn't considered politically safe either. He'd never acccept that the general wanted a whole damned gunship support wing dispatched just to help stare down a mob of strikers and demonstrators. He'd ask questions that the captain dare not answer.

And turning to General Mavaraloku was out of the question. Mavaraloku was the commanding general of the air services division. His initials were to have been forged on Songhidalarsa's orders. Mavaraloku too was politically unreliable, and under other than combat conditions, he was free to query orders he considered dubious, even from the corps commander. If he suspected that something covert was going on, he might well call the Imperial General Staff in Ananporu, to check. The fat would really be in the fire then. Thus the forged initials.

"Can I have the use of a commset?" asked the captain stiffly.

The subcolonel looked at him as if questioning his sobriety. Or his sanity. "There's a whole row of them in the common room."

"I need . . . never mind." If he said he needed one with scramble functions, the frigging subcolonel might call a query of his own. He hurried out, glancing at the large wall clock as he did so: 0107. He'd use a commset at Corps. And even that might not work; he wasn't sure that Abrikalaavi was still in range. If not . . . He imagined himself coming back with a gun. Shove it in the subcolonel's gut, and then see if he'd honor a verbal order.

The only practical thing he could think of was to draft the order himself and forge the general's signature. And Mavaraloku's initials. The thought of it made his hair bristle with fear. It would have to look just right—wording and forgeries. He'd have to look up the relevant regulations, use the proper form, drill Old Iron Jaw's signature . . . 0130 was out of the question.

It was a damned good thing the brigade had its own gunship squadron. But a mere squadron wouldn't discourage the Capital Division.

The subcolonel watched the captain leave. He remembered the written reprimand Old Iron Jaw had issued on him the spring before, during maneuvers, for releasing a mere flight of gunships on the verbal order of an unauthorized colonel. He'd been brand new here at Fashtar, and hadn't known the general's reputation for entrapment. Regulations, he'd learned then, were not to be slighted.

Fifty-five

The armored transport had lifted with both penal platoons on board. It was not an ideal situation; the two platoons were vicious rivals, had been conditioned that way, each led to consider itself the toughest platoon in the Imperial Army. Platoon Sergeant Skosh Viilenga couldn't vouch for it, but it seemed to him that one or the other might actually be the toughest. If not, they had to be close.

They'd made the flight to Ahantar without any trouble. The men had dozed in their bucket seats, been taken off a squad at a time to relieve themselves, then loaded back on without any trouble. To wait.

They were peasants, their noncoms gentry, their lieutenants nobles. But some of these peasants were smart. Ignorant maybe, did dumb shit maybe, but they were shrewd; they could figure things about as well as anyone. And as far as dumb shit was concerned . . . In the penal platoons, the three classes had two things in common: They all had compulsions to get into trouble; serious trouble. And they all tended to be violent. Those were the reasons they were there, all of them, himself included.

For an officer or noncom to survive in the penal platoons, he had to have an edge, and the edge came from training. Special training in close combat—hands, feet, baton, knife, saber—and in the psychological handling of men like these. When to praise, when to reason, when to bribe, when to shout and curse. When to strike out—and when to kill without warning. You never bluffed and you never showed the slightest trace of fear. If you didn't learn those lessons well, you didn't last long. Sergeant Skosh had been in this platoon for more than four years, and had six more to go on his sentence. He was there for slugging a captain, a nobleman—broke his frigging nose, actually—which was the final straw in a career of fights and brawls.

When his ten penal years were up, Skosh fully intended to stay in the platoon until retirement. It seemed to him it was the best place for someone like himself. Outside there was too little tolerance, too many chickenshit regulations, with the risk of ending up on Shatimvoktos. Here he felt at home. These were his kind of people, from Lieutenant Paasalarogu to Harelip and the Slasher.

A major, the division's provost marshal, stepped into the floater. The lieutenant barked "at ease!" which woke the men who were dozing and stilled those who weren't. Major Dholagilarmo was one of the few outside officers who could step into the middle of these men without looking nervous. He called them his boys. Still, Skosh wondered why the provost marshal would be along on this expedition.

"Listen up!" the major shouted. The language he used was a sort of pidgin—an off-the-cuff, simplified Imperial with usages borrowed from peasant jabber. "You gonna fight some real troops, not just a buncha demonstrators. We gonna find out if you really any good or not. You gonna get big party and some big money if you do good."

He waited a moment before saying more, tightening their attention.

"Pretty soon we gonna lift for Ananporu, gonna land you men inside the Sreegana. You gonna kill the Kalif. He been fuckin' up too damn much."

Again he waited. Now he *really* had their attention.

"The Kalif got a short regiment—three short battalions—of pretty tough guards to protect 'im. They ain't got you firepower, but they pretty damn tough. You ask 'em, they tell you they tougher than you. We gonna waste 'em pretty bad with bomb attack on they barracks, but them that live, they be pretty mad.

"We gonna land a battalion in the Sreegana and cool 'em. The rest of the 103rd be close by if need 'em. You mother haters gonna land in Kalif's garden. You job to get inside palace and kill Kalif.

"You gotta do it without no dry runs or mockup drills. I just give your officers a map and tell 'em what to do.

"If one of you kill Kalif, both platoons get big party. All the booze and all the broads you can handle! Each man get twenty dromas bonus. In platoon that kills 'im, each man get twenty more. Man that kills 'im gets 500 more!"

Skosh could hear their breath suck in. The major looked them over. "You mother haters like that?"

Three or four whooped. A few shouted "yes." Most just grinned or laughed.

"You do *not*," he went on—"I repeat *not*—shoot each other to get at Kalif. Your officers and sergeants will shoot any mother haters that fight each other. It's the Kalif we want dead, not you.

"How you know the Kalif when you see 'im? Look at me." The major stood tall in front of them. "He about my size. Your officers gonna show you pix of 'im to look at. Lotsa times Kalif wear a red cape, come down 'bout to here." The major gestured. "Lotsa times he wear a red robe." He gestured again. "But maybe he be dressed like anyone else there. So when you look at photos, look good. Make sure you know 'im.

"Now. You maybe see men in white capes or white robes. Them exarchs. Kill them, too, when you come to 'em. But the one to kill for bonus, he the Kalif. We wannim dead. You don't kill Kalif, you don't get bonus, don't get party.

"Any questions?"

There weren't. The men, their noncoms and lieutenants, pored over the photos—grimly or gleefully, according to the individual. The Kalif was a doomed man, thought Skosh. He wondered if he might get him in his sights himself.

Fifty-six

Alb Jilsomo Savbatso had just turned on his terminal when he heard and felt the explosions, a sequence of them. They sounded as if they'd been on the far side of the Sreegana, from the direction of the armory and Guard barracks. Jumping to his feet, he started for the Kalif's office, down the hall from his own.

It was early enough that no one else was in the hall except two guardsmen near the far end, clutching rifles, running toward him. Jilsomo surged through the Kalif's reception area—Partiil wasn't in yet—and into the Kalif's office. That's when he heard the first gunfire, heavy automatic weapons, a shocking, violent sound. It stopped him in his tracks. Then the two guardsmen burst in behind him and ran past, almost knocking him over, sucking him along in their wake. Tempered-glass doors were partly open to the morning cool, and they ran out through the gap, into the garden.

Jilsomo stopped at the door. The gray semi-cylindrical bulk of an armored personnel transport was settling onto the ground, and he could see a guardsman sprawled on a flowerbed not far off, as if all his strings had been cut. The kalifa was just rising from her knees behind a marble bench, then she sprinted toward him, fast as a man in her billowing pantaloons. The two

332

guards had separated, both firing at the transport's opening doors.

Soldiers jumped out even as the doors opened. He saw more than one fall. Another fired a burst from the hip. A marble statue came apart, shards flying, ricochets keening. One of the two guardsmen fell, and the kalifa also, in mid-jump over a tangleflower bed. From somewhere came more furious gunfire, and emerging soldiers fell or hit the ground.

The other guardsman was darting toward the kalifa. Scarcely pausing, he scooped her up, with astonishing strength and agility jumped over a hip-high ornamental wall, then running low in its shelter, darted toward the office. The immobilized exarch had never imagined such an athletic feat.

The ground twitched with the massive explosions of three more bombs, shaking Jilsomo out of his paralysis. He stepped back out of the way as the guardsman with the kalifa rushed past him. Automatic weapons fire grew in intensity outside, and for some reason Jilsomo moved to slide the doors shut. Bullets sent glass flying, partly intercepted by curtains, and he felt a sharp sting in his cheek. Abruptly he fled, after the guard and the kalifa, through reception and into the corridor. Alb Thoga stood there, round-eyed, holding a folder in his hands like an offering. Jilsomo followed the guardsman, Thoga falling in beside him.

Ahead was a heavy door accessing a utility stairwell, and the guardsman paused there, lowered the kalifa to the floor, and opened the door with his security card. The exarchs held back till the guard had shouldered the kalifa again, Jilsomo shocked by the scarlet that stained her pale blue clothing. Then they followed him through.

"Lock it!" the guard shouted back, and started down the stairs. Jilsomo stared, confused, already breathing hard. Thoga crowded him aside, threw his slight weight against the steel door, closing it, pulled its wheel out half an inch and gave it a partial turn, then pushed it back in.

"Come, Jilsomo!" he said sharply, and tugged the larger exarch's sleeve. They hurried after the guardsman, down a double flight of stairs and into a tunnel containing pipes and conduits. By its light panels, Jilsomo could see drops of blood on the floor ahead of him. *The kalifa's blood,* he thought. The rebels—that's what they had to be—would surely follow the blood trail, blow down the door with something, and catch them, kill them all.

They ran what seemed a long way before they passed another stairwell. Farther ahead was still another. The guard went up its steps two at a time, the kalifa, who was taller than he, draped over his shoulder. Jilsomo was gasping now; to climb the stairs seemed beyond him. Thoga jabbed him. "Up!" he ordered, and somehow the fat exarch found himself climbing, clinging to the handrail, lungs heaving, Thoga continuing to push, yapping, "Move! Move!"

When they reached the top, Jilsomo reeled out into a corridor, against a wall, almost collapsing while Thoga drew the heavy access door shut behind them, the effort taxing his thin strength. Vaguely Jilsomo wondered if their supposed pursuers might be stopped by it after all. He became aware that he was bleeding, his white cape stained red.

Once more the slight Thoga confronted his much larger colleague, and pointed down the hallway. "Move!" he wheezed. He too was gasping.

Jilsomo shook his head, his chest heaving, and waved him on. "No," said Thoga, "rest later," and jerked on Jilsomo's sleeve for emphasis. Jilsomo stared for a second through blurring eyes, then somehow moved again, down the corridor with Thoga. Five guardsmen trotted by, faces grim, rifles ready, in duty uniforms and helmets. Jilsomo thought to tell them about the tunnel, but had no breath for it.

He realized where they were now—in the heart of the Administration Building. The guardsman carrying the kalifa turned through a door, the door to the clinic.

Another guardsman, posted there, saw Jilsomo's blood-marked robe and barked him inside.

Jilsomo was staggering by then, walking with Thoga's help. He found himself in medical reception. A corporal grabbed the big exarch, getting a shoulder under his arm, and helped him down a small hall to another room.

Inside, the guardsman laid the kalifa down on an examination table, then turned to leave, but Thoga stopped him. "Stay!" he ordered, and stepped to the table. The kalifa's face was gray, her eyes closed. The corporal helped Jilsomo down onto a chair.

"Find one of the physicians!" Thoga told him. "Hurry!"

"Your lordship," the corporal said, "there's men looking for them now."

"Tell them to hurry. The kalifa's dangerously wounded."

The corporal ran without saying anything more.

Jilsomo felt of his face, the source of his bleeding. Glass from the garden door had sliced his cheek. Thoga, standing beside the kalifa, first felt for her pulse, then, with the guardsman's dagger, cut off her bloody clothes. Jilsomo was aware that she stank. With the guardsman's help, Thoga turned her onto her stomach. "Dear Kargh," he muttered.

"What?"

"She's been shot twice. Once in the side, the bullet following along the ribs, then emerging. The other entered the body from behind, probably below the right kidney. I hope it was below. It has to have passed through the small intestine. Missed the aorta, though, or she'd be dead already."

Already. "Can she . . ." Jilsomo began, then didn't finish.

"I don't know. My training ended with pre-med. I've had courses, observed dissections, worked on dummies with syntho-flesh . . . that's all." He stared helplessly at the kalifa's lax, corpselike body.

The corporal entered again. "Alb Thoga," he said,

"none of the physicians answer. The bachelor apartments were bombed. No one seems to know where the on-duty physician is. I'm told his breakfast tray was delivered just before the trouble started, and he went into the common garden to eat. Probably with his beeper on. One of the men says he saw him start running toward the palace. No one knows where his receptionist is. Smoke's pouring out the windows there, and there's still a lot of shooting. Plus we've got rebels in the upper floors here; got in from the roof."

Thoga blew tiredly. "Well, then." He looked at the guardsman who'd brought the kalifa. "Private," he said, "you've done marvelously well so far. Now you'll have to help me." He went to a cabinet and opened the doors. Instruments lay inside, wrapped in clear plastic. "We'll see what we can do. And hope for the best."

The Kalif crouched at the window, Sergeant Yalabiin beside him. It was a ground-floor window; there were none higher in the House of SUMBAA. Outside, the rebels held the quadrangle, more or less. A number of armored troop carriers lay parked where they'd landed, their turrets erupting spasmodically with heavy automatic weapons fire at the surrounding buildings. Occasionally he saw rebel soldiers move, quickly and low, under light fire from windows. He couldn't see the palace except for a couple of its roofs, but he could see smoke rising from it. Light troop carriers were visible on the roof of the Administration Building.

He wondered where Tain was. *How* she was. He told himself she was a survivor, but was not greatly reassured by the thought. If she was harmed and he came through it all . . . He banished the train of thought. This wasn't the time for it.

He'd seen from other windows what had happened to the Guard barracks and the Bachelor Apartments. It was surprising that so many guardsmen had gotten out alive and with their rifles. As for the bachelor exarchs and collegial staff caught at their breakfasts . . .

He'd been lucky. He and Yalabiin had just finished

their workout when the first bombs struck, and had ducked into the House of SUMBAA. A dozen or so other guardsmen had come in afterward, in off-duty uniforms but armed and some with helmets.

The building had very few windows, and a casual move by rebel troops to get in had been repulsed by automatic rifle fire from what windows there were. They'd scarcely fired back, and afterward had stayed clear. Obviously they'd been told in advance not to fire on the House of SUMBAA; to govern and administer the empire would be virtually impossible if the great computer was out of order. The Kalif in turn had told the guardsmen inside not to fire except to repel attacks.

He wondered what would happen if the rebels knew he was inside. Right now things were disordered, chaotic out there. But sooner or later, unless something intervened, they'd take the rest of the Sreegana. And discover that no one had seen what had to be their principal quarry.

He wondered what the Capital Division was doing. These rebels were not Caps, he knew that from their transports.

Colonel Vilyamo Parsavamaatu stuck his neck out, literally, made a quick scan, and pulled it in again. Bursts of bullets struck the marble wall outside, several coming through the shot-out window to strike inner walls and ceiling. One of the guardsmen stepped up beside the window and threw out one of their too few grenades. A building entrance was directly below them, and this was one way to discourage a rebel rush on it.

The rebels effectively controlled the quadrangle, and greatly superior rebel firepower inhibited firing out at them through windows. On top of that, there were rebels a few floors above him, trying to battle their way downward, with all the advantages that elevation gave them.

Unless the Caps came, came soon enough, the Sreegana would be lost. An hour at most, given the way things were going. It seemed to the colonel that the

Kalif was probably already dead, but Alb Jilsomo, the Kalif's deputy, was alive. It was the Guard's responsibility to protect him now.

Vilyamo considered and decided. Turning, he headed for the door, his aide and his master sergeant close behind. He needed something white, a pillow case maybe.

He went down the stairs three at a time. On the ground floor, guardsmen stood or knelt at corners back from the entrance, rifles ready to repel any rebel rush. The floor was littered with glass from the entryway, the walls gouged and pocked. "Sergeant!" he shouted at one of the men there. A sergeant turned his face to his commander.

Vilyamo almost gave his order openly, then thought better of it. Instead he gestured, and the man followed him a little ways down a corridor. "Sergeant," he said quietly, "I presume you know where the trumpeters' locker is." He referred to the ceremonial trumpeters. "I need a man to do something extremely dangerous. A man about the Kalif's size and build, whose face isn't too different from the Kalif's. Do we have anyone like that?"

"Yessir. Me."

Vilyamo eyed the man critically. Hardly a look-alike, but maybe as good as he'd find. Size and build were close, and the facial structure wasn't too far off. "All right. Go to the clinic and get your head shaved and bandaged. Bandaged down to the ears, and maybe across one cheek, but not hiding your face. Tell whoever does it that you need to look as much like the Kalif as you reasonably can. And send someone to the trumpeters' locker. Have them bring you the Kalif's trumpeter's red cape."

He paused then, thinking. The sergeant was poised to run. Somewhere, automatic weapons fire intensified as if a rush was being made. "If someone can find you a pair of white pants like the exarchs wear, or the Kalif, and if they fit anything like decently, put 'em on."

The sergeant's expression changed as if he just now fully realized what the colonel was getting at.

"Yessir."

"Change into them in the clinic, pants and robe, and splash a little blood on them. Shouldn't have any trouble finding blood around there. Put some blood on the bandage, too, but don't overdo it. Then stay in the clinic, out of sight, until I send for you."

"Yessir."

"All right, that's it. Get after it!"

The sergeant took off running. The colonel turned to his aide. "Fareehu," he said, "go back to the command post. Tell Basar he's in operational charge till I say otherwise. I've got a project to handle. Don't tell him what the project is—or what you think it is. Keep your mouth shut about it. Then come to the clinic. I may need you there. Get going!"

The aide, a captain, left at a trot. The colonel turned, and with his sergeant major, started for the clinic himself. That was the place to find a pillow case.

Since the assault battalion had opened the main gate and let in more of the 103rd, its regimental C.O. had taken over direction of the rebel force inside the Sreegana. He'd had his own well-armored command floater fly into the quadrangle. There he'd had it parked with a good view of the Administration Building, the only stronghold left to the Guard, aside from sections of the wall. Obviously the Guard had nothing that could touch him in his floater. If they'd had any anti-armor weapons in their armory, which was doubtful, they hadn't gotten them out after the bombing.

Around him, the floater's interior smelled like a ship's engine room—like metal and oil. Occasional rounds popped against the command floater's hide, a sound dulled by the laminated armor. He didn't notice. He was watching the array of battle screens in front of him.

"Did you see that?" he asked his aide.

The man knew which *that* his commander referred to. "Yes, Colonel. Looks like a flag of truce."

"Manich!" the commander said, "order a cease fire! We've got a flag of truce out there, and I want to see what it's about. Anyone who fires after the command will answer to me with his ass!"

The assault battalion C.O. nodded. "Yes, Colonel!" He wasn't happy with his colonel having taken command of the fighting in the Sreegana—it had started out as his action—but that was life for you.

The colonel watched while the major gave the order, first on radio, then on the floater's loud hailer. "All right," the colonel said. "Now tell the man with the truce flag that I'm sending someone out to meet him. Tell him that if my man is harmed out there, there'll be no negotiations and no prisoners taken. Everyone we get our hands on will die. The wounded—everyone."

Again he watched and listened, then looked at his aide. "Captain, take the bullhorn and go halfway to the truce flag. Tell the man waving it to come out. Find out what he wants; terms, I suppose. Tell him you'll conduct him to a parley with me. Go."

The nervous captain got the bullhorn and went.

Vilyamo strode toward the rebel officer, his sergeant major beside him with a pillow case tied to a strip of shelf edging. *So far,* he told himself, *so good.* If this went no further than a rejection and possibly captivity, it was still eating up time. Meanwhile, the Caps had to be readying a relief force. *At least they'd better be,* he thought grimly.

The rebel mother-curser was waiting beside a shin-high planter. Its colorful bed of blooming leronvaalu seemed untouched by the fighting, about the only thing that was. It occurred to Vilyamo what a beautiful place this had been, with the palace, gardens, trees, ornamental shrubs, and these assholes had wrecked it for no better reason than to seize power.

It didn't occur to him to feel resentment for the guardsmen killed. That was a professional hazard.

As he walked up to the rebel, he saw by the man's insignia that he was a captain, and by his blazon that he belonged to the 12th Infantry Division. The motherless bastard even wore dress knee-boots, polished like glass, as if he was on parade instead of an assault. He himself wore an off-duty uniform without even a battle helmet. There was plaster dust in his hair and on his clothes. The attack had caught him at breakfast, like much of the regiment, and unlike most of the survivors, he'd raced for the Admin Building and his emergency command post without first arming himself. The pistol he wore, he'd borrowed from a dead man.

The captain saluted; he was, after all, outranked. Vilyamo returned the gesture; he had a purpose here that didn't include antagonizing the enemy.

"Colonel," said the man, "I'm to find out why you want a truce."

"To end the fighting," Vilyamo answered, then added silently, *With you dead, mother-curser.*

The captain nodded. "In that case, I'm to conduct you to Colonel Khriivalarooma."

Vilyamo's nod was curt. Fawning would buy him nothing, even if he could do it. They walked side by side to the command floater, accompanied each by his truce flag. On the way they passed a rebel soldier lying dead, legs twisted, face partly blown away. Vilyamo felt satisfaction at the sight.

To enter the command floater, they used the door facing away from the Administration Building. The guard posted there held it open for them. The rebel captain gestured, and the rebel sergeant entered. Vilyamo turned and spoke to his master sergeant. "Sergeant, stay outside. I'll be back out shortly." Then he followed the rebel sergeant in, the captain entering last. A colonel and a major were inside waiting, along with two captains—the colonel's aide and the battalion E.O. They got to their feet, except for the colonel who remained in his chair to establish proper protocol.

"You are the commander of the Guard here?" he asked.

"Correct," Vilyamo answered coldly.

"And your purpose is an end to the fighting?"

"The end of the fighting and the freedom of my men."

The rebel colonel's voice turned curious. "Why have you fought us?" he asked.

Vilyamo's expression showed his incredulity at the question.

"The Kalif killed your father, did he not?"

Hearing that, Vilyamo knew he'd succeed in his ploy, would pull it off. "He did, the motherless dog. But what did you expect from us? Bombing our barracks as you did, killing scores of us and disabling more. My men were bound to fight, after that. I was bound to."

The rebel colonel nodded. "You can guess why we're here, of course."

"Perhaps. But I need to hear it from you."

"We want the Kalif. The murderer of your father. We want him dead."

"That's what I've come about."

"He's dead?"

"No. Only injured, and that not seriously."

"We must, of course, continue to attack until we have him. Dead or alive."

"I'm prepared to deliver him to you."

The rebel colonel nodded. "Well then. I'll send men with you. Deliver him to them and we can go home, leave this place."

"Certain procedures are necessary."

The rebel colonel scowled. "You're in no position to impose conditions on me."

"My men are still loyal. It must seem to them that the Kalif is giving himself up, otherwise they'll continue to fight. And the longer they fight, the more time there is for the Capital Division to send a relief force."

Vilyamo spoke on without giving the rebel commander a chance to object. "His kalifa is dead. He's torn between rage and grief. I'll have my medical officer inject him with a sedative—something that will leave him compliant but allow him to walk. I'm assured that won't be any problem.

"Also—" He paused. "He must not be killed until he's been removed from the premises. It would be a dishonor to the Guard to have him executed by a hostile force inside the Sreegana."

The rebel commander considered for only a moment. His orders were to kill the Kalif at the earliest opportunity. Well, promises were made to be broken. Get his hands on the Kalif, get him here inside the floater, and they'd never know if he was killed. "Very well," he said. "You have ten minutes to deliver him to me here."

"Not here. We'll meet you, he and I, by the planter where the captain met me. It must appear that he's negotiating with you, with you and your command staff. Not that he's being turned over, surrendered."

The rebel commander's face twitched with annoyance. "You ask a lot, for a man whose position is untenable."

Vilyamo's face and voice went tired. "Colonel, I'm trying to get the Kalif into your hands before anything goes wrong. I'm a dead man regardless. But the Guard is loyal to him."

The rebel commander didn't follow the logic, but he bought it. "Very well. In ten minutes, at the planter."

"I need a bullhorn. I have no way of communicating quickly to my troops."

The rebel commander's expression was acid; there seemed no end to this man's requests. "Give him the bullhorn," he ordered. Then to Vilyamo, "I'll want it back, along with your Kalif."

A sergeant handed the bullhorn over. Vilyamo saluted sharply; the rebel colonel's answering salute was insultingly casual. Then, with truce flag and bullhorn, Vilyamo left the floater and started back toward the Admin Building. Around the quadrangle, the guns waited, silent but ready.

In the command floater, the rebel commander watched him go. At the planter, Vilyamo stopped and raised the bullhorn. "Men!" he called, "in a few minutes the Kalif, with me and my staff, will be coming out to negotiate with the enemy commander and his staff, here by this planter. Meanwhile, there is a state of truce. Do not fire your weapons unless attacked."

Then he went on to the Admin Building and disappeared inside.

From there he sent runners with instructions to every part of the building held by guardsmen.

In the House of SUMBAA they heard the guns fall silent. Later they heard the bullhorn, but it was too far away to catch the words. The Kalif wondered what was going on.

Vilyamo used up all his ten minutes before leaving the Admin Building with his sergeant major, his make-believe Kalif, and three volunteer officers. They were halfway to the planter before the enemy commander appeared with his own little party of officers.

Vilyamo had expected that. He felt entirely calm.

The rebel commander's delay was more than a matter of protocol: He'd waited to examine the Kalif and the party of Guard officers on his central screen, using maximum magnification. Only when he was satisfied with what he saw did he get up from his seat and leave with his staff.

He didn't care for this charade, this pretense of negotiation. He felt uncomfortable with it. And while waiting for the Guard commander to reappear with the Kalif, he'd considered not going out—considered simply ordering his people to shoot down the Kalif and his party as they approached the meeting place.

Then his radio reported that floaters had appeared over the Anan Hills, which had to mean the Caps were finally moving. And it seemed to him that, orders notwithstanding, it would be very useful, when the Caps arrived, to have the Kalif in his hands alive, as a hostage if one was needed.

He turned. "Let's go," he said.

*   *   *

Free for the moment of rebel gunfire, guardsmen, rifles in hand, peered from the windows of the Administration Building. They knew what they were seeing, unreal though it seemed, and they had their instructions. They'd even found targets as the rebel troops relaxed their cover discipline. The difficult part was to keep their eyes on those targets, instead of watching the charade taking shape in the quadrangle. As the two parties approached the planter, pistols appeared in the hands of Vilyamo and his men, and they shot down the rebel commander and his party. That served as a signal, and the guardsmen at the windows opened fire on their own targets. Only after a long, shocked moment did rebel fire erupt, shooting Colonel Vilyamo Parsavamaatu and his party to bloody rags.

That done, it seemed to the rebel troops that they'd killed the Kalif. Surely now the fighting would stop and the Guard would surrender.

But only the truce was over. Meanwhile, time had been gained, and within the Sreegana, at least for the moment, the rebels had no one in charge. Inside the command floater, only a captain, a sublieutenant, and some noncoms remained.

Fifty-seven

The weather was cooperating. Although it was still the major rainy season, as yet the day had brought neither rain nor threat of it. A complete light infantry battalion, with equipment and supplies, had been loaded onto troop carriers. In the armored command floater, Major Tagurt Meksorli sat beside the battalion commander, as the division commander's personal observer and liaison. Two of the division's three gunship squadrons would support the battalion, and they lifted first, to form an escort formation. Then the troop carriers lifted by company.

When they were all in the air and in formation, they flew eastward, moving fast, and in a few minutes had crossed the Anan Hills. The screens arrayed in front of Meksorli all showed the same thing—the city close ahead. Suburbs passed beneath them, and in the middle distance, smoke arose from the Sreegana.

And something else: rebel gunships coming toward them, a squadron at least. He got on the radio to the C.O. One flight of his own gunships were out ahead. He'd soon see his first air battle; indeed the first air battle any of them had seen. His own force seemed to have an advantage in numbers, but they were constrained by the need to cover the troop carriers.

They clashed less than a minute later, the troop carri-

346

ers continuing more slowly now. The Sreegana was only about two miles away when the command floater shook from a hit. They were beginning to take ground fire; the rebels had forces along the Avenue of The Prophet. As Meksorli let the division commander know, he felt the floater surge upward and saw the troop carriers follow suit.

Within minutes an armored unit would be on the way, but on the surface and much more slowly. And the rebels had no doubt anticipated that, with defensive positions to slow it further and give it losses, stop it if they could.

The report was that the rebels were from 1st Corps, at Fashtar, 2,100 miles north, but there were conflicting reports as to how large the force was. Apparently quite large, if they had units this far from the Sreegana.

General Songhidalarsa's command floater was parked at 17,000 feet elevation, twenty miles east of the Sreegana. It was considerably larger than the floater Meksorli rode, and extravagantly furnished. Just now his screen array included one with a map of the Ananporu District; he'd been watching the progress and engagement of the Caps relief force, as reported by brigade G-2.

Songhidalarsa had been parked somewhat farther east. Then brigade command had reported the occupation of the War Ministry; and regimental command, by code, the impending surrender of the Kalif. With that he'd started toward Ananporu to announce his dictatorship. But apparently regimental command had been tricked and killed, with the status of the Kalif uncertain. And by then, despite the capture of the Imperial General Staff's offices, the Caps had had a relief force on the way. So he'd held off.

It still seemed probable that the Kalif lay dead somewhere. The palace was fire-gutted, and his body could well lie somewhere inside, charred and undiscovered.

Something to hell was happening, the Kalif realized. He felt seriously isolated by his lack of a radio. Obvi-

ously there'd been a cease-fire, which had been broken
by an intense fire-fight. This had since eased off markedly. Then a gunship had plummeted into the quadrangle with a jar he could almost feel; presumably an aerial
battle was going on. As he watched and listened, the
gunfire had picked up, particularly the turret fire from
the enemy troop carriers parked in the quadrangle. A
series of explosions burst in their midst. Some of the
carriers were ruptured or rolled over.

Apparently the Caps were arriving.

Then more troop carriers landed amidst the wreckage, and farther away, he could see four others squat-
ting over the Admin Building, presumably unloading
troops. The troops being unloaded in the quadrangle
wore blue dress jackets, apparently so they could tell
one another from the rebels. The shooting was intensifying, but the odds of his surviving seemed to have
improved. Again he wondered about Tain, and again
told himself that she was a survivor by nature. It didn't
reassure him this time either.

Captain Iighil Dhotmariloku, commanding A Company, 1st Battalion, 103rd Infantry, was observing the
fighting from a window in the west wing of the Administration Building. As far as he knew, he was the senior
rebel officer inside the Sreegana, since that fiasco in
the Quadrangle. The fighting hadn't gone well since
then, but he hadn't tried to take command. There was
no point in it. He had no strategy, nothing to steer by.

Things improved markedly when the 11th Gunship
Wing finally arrived. But the improvement could only
be temporary; he didn't delude himself that the coup
was going to succeed. Not now. They'd needed to take
the Kalif—needed his body to display. As it was . . .
No doubt a forest of stakes would soon sprout in the
square, decorated with bodies of what the government
would call traitors.

Iighil, he told himself, *what you need is a bargaining
chip.* But what the hell that could be . . .

Meanwhile he had A Company—A Company plus

the two penal platoons that had been attached to it after fire had driven them out of the palace. He'd had them lifted to the roof of the Administration Building, and used them to spearhead the penetration downward in this wing. Progress had been better here than elsewhere because of them, but they'd taken heavy casualties, including both their officers.

Then the Caps had arrived, and had driven his people from the roof. Now, with the gunships of the 11th controlling the air, he held the roof again, and had stabilized his situation inside the building.

He wasn't trying to do anything with it; there was no point to that either. The Caps would get reinforcements, the 11th would surrender or be driven away, and there'd be all those stakes going up for the officers of the 103rd, those who survived the fighting. Nor did he delude himself that the enlisted men would make any last ditch fight.

A bargaining chip . . .

Then it hit him! He had no notion that the Kalif might still be alive, but perhaps a better hostage was available: SUMBAA. The general had stressed strongly that they must not damage the great computer, that it was essential to government. If he could capture it, he'd be in a strong bargaining position, might come out of this without a steel stake up his ass. Which was better than Old Iron Jaw could look forward to.

He turned to his 1st sergeant. "Mazhiib, how many effectives in 2nd platoon?"

"About twenty-five, sir."

"And in 3rd?"

"Maybe thirty."

Enough for a convincing-looking rush, a good diversion. He turned to the man on the other side of him, a sergeant, the acting C.O. of the 1st Penal Platoon. "Skosh, I've got a job for you. For you and your five best men."

Thoga had opened the kalifa's abdomen, bonded crudely the damage that seemed most serious, applied antibiotics, even installed a drain. Then, totally inadequate to close her up properly, he'd simply applied clamps and abundant tape.

After which he'd collapsed, exhausted and disconsolate. It seemed to him he'd bungled, horribly and uselessly. That to open her up as he had, splash and wallow ignorantly and ineptly, then leave the job unfinished, had been a gruesome violation of her dignity, to little or no benefit.

On top of everything else, of course, she'd miscarried—aborted her fetus. It would have been a miracle if she hadn't.

One of the two surgeons brought in by the Caps had reopened her and finished the job, awed that a layman could have accomplished what Thoga had, and irritated that he'd done it so crudely. But, he said, she might live. She just might. If they got her to a hospital promptly. And if she did live, he added, Thoga's work would have made the difference.

They had other wounded ready to evacuate, too, more than they had ambulance space for just now. Besides the kalifa, there were a number of guardsmen, soldiers, rebels, and two Sisters of the Faith. The kalifa would leave in the first one out.

By that time the Caps had just lost control of the air over the Sreegana, but there was no reason to believe that the rebels would refuse to let the ambulances take out wounded. After all, they'd let them come in and land.

It was Jilsomo who pointed out the problem. The rebels were certain to insist on inspecting them, to make sure the Kalif wasn't smuggled out. And if they found the kalifa, they'd undoubtedly take her hostage.

So hurriedly the surgeon shaved her head like those of the Sisters of the Faith, painted her exposed skin brown with tincture of benzoin, and partly concealed her features with bandage. Her gown covered her smooth arms. The coloring didn't look at all natural, but the surgeon waved it off. She looked so bad anyway, he said, it wouldn't make any difference. Jilsomo was doubtful, but there wasn't much more they could do. And certainly she wouldn't be exposing her violet-blue eyes.

Then orderlies, led by a man with a medevac flag, struggled the stretchers to the roof and loaded them into the ambulance. As Jilsomo had foreseen, when they'd finished loading, a gunship hailed them, and the rebels landed a utility floater on the roof. Several businesslike soldiers got out, a lieutenant and three noncoms, boarded the ambulance, and hastily inspected its cargo of wounded. Two of the wounded wore rebel uniforms; that made the right impression to start with. And the kalifa appeared to be simply another Sister of the Faith, the one who looked closest to death.

The rebels were clearly in a hurry. Their lieutenant apologized, saluted the on-board surgeon, and left the ambulance. Which lifted at once and swung away hurriedly, bound for a government hospital in the western outskirts of Ananporu. *Apologized!* The pilot said the rebels must have picked up the same radio report he had: that a wing of gunships was on its way from the marine base at Bajapor, some three hours away. They had to be sweating.

Sergeant Skosh Viilenga watched from a light utility floater with the five men he'd picked. He'd gotten to pick from both platoons, and chosen only noncoms. Which pissed off Sergeant Jodharka in charge of the other penal platoon. He'd only had four noncoms left, and to lose two of them like this . . . But Captain Iighil had backed his selection; Iighil was a good officer, a hardnose.

As the floater lifted from its vantage atop the west wing of the Admin Building, the two regular platoons began to move in short rushes toward the almost blank-walled House of SUMBAA. Rifle fire had erupted at them, but they hadn't shot back. A helluva way to attack, Skosh thought. Apparently the two platoons thought so, too. Their attack lasted five seconds at most, then they broke and ran for cover, leaving fifteen or twenty men dead or wounded on the ground.

By that time the light utility floater was over the building. Carefully it settled to the roof, on the side farthest from the Admin Building, where they'd be cut off from view by the roof's curvature. Skosh was the first man onto the curved structure, the other five following closely.

The floater stayed. Crouching, Skosh moved up the roof to what looked like an access hatch. Its cover sat flat and snug atop the low coaming. There was no handle—it was built to open only from below—but the trench knife in his boot was enough to pry it with. With strong steel and strong fingers, he got it up.

It opened onto a shaft with rungs on one side. Without hesitating, Skosh lowered his legs inside and began to climb down. The shaft was less than ten feet long, with its ladder continuing out of it, emerging high in a poorly lit room bigger than a hay barn.

The ladder ended on a catwalk, and when he reached it, he unslung his rifle and looked around, moving out of the way of the men who followed. The place was silent. Not just without sound of its own; he couldn't hear the fighting outside, either.

Somehow it gave him the willies; it was as if he'd climbed down into another world. Beneath the catwalk were assorted housings, interconnected. And apparently without dust. That was strange, too. It seemed to him that there should have been dust.

Near the far end of the catwalk, another ladder went down, presumably to the floor. Softly, rifle ready in his hands, Skosh started toward it. As he neared the end, he could see the floor below, with a pair of seats at what appeared to be a console. There was no one there.

The Kalif stood just back from the entrance, pistol in hand, while guardsmen fired their automatic rifles at the attacking rebel troops. It seemed unreal; the rebels were simply charging, not firing as they came.

It lasted only seconds before they broke and ran back

for the poor cover of a hedge and a row of barbered vaasera trees, leaving their dead and wounded where they'd fallen.

A strange attack in a strange kind of fight, thought the Kalif. A fight between brothers, so to speak, men some of whom might have served together at one time or another, who'd drunk together and called each other buddy.

Meanwhile he could hear plenty of shooting at a little distance, but none of it seemed to be in his direction. "Corporal," he said to the man in charge of the entry, "if anyone tries to remove their wounded, let them."

He turned then, Sergeant Yalabiin beside him, and strode down the perimeter corridor some forty yards to the window in that side. After repeating to its two defenders what he'd told the men at the entry, he backtracked to the door to SUMBAA's chamber. He'd see if the computer could fill in for him what was happening out there.

Yalabiin pushed the door open, stepped in and turned, holding it for him. From inside came an unexpected burst of rifle fire, and Yalabiin crumpled. There was a loud, harsh, electric crackling, and the Kalif's eyes jerked upward from the fallen sergeant to the catwalk, where three soldiers writhed in blue wreaths of miniature lightning that came from a small globe atop SUMBAA. In front of him, staring back at the sound, was a soldier, a sergeant. At the foot of a ladder stood another, and beside that one, another who'd dropped from the ladder when the lightnings began. They looked confused and shocked at what was happening to their buddies, afraid it might happen to themselves.

As the Kalif jerked his pistol from his holster, the lightnings stopped, dropping three dead soldiers onto the grating. He could smell their burnt flesh.

In front of him, the sergeant turned and saw him. Saw also the pistol muzzle pointing at him. "Your Reverence!" he said fervently. "Thank Kargh you're all right!" He stepped back as if expecting the Kalif to come in. The Kalif stayed where he was.

"Yab's not all right," he answered. The muzzle of his weapon flicked toward the fallen Yalabiin, then back at the intruder. "Who in hell are you, and what are you doing here?"

"I'm Sergeant Viilenga, Your Reverence." He said it loudly enough that his two remaining men would hear, and realize who he spoke to. "Captain Iighil sent us to get you out of here. We're from the Capital Division, attached to an armored company that's got stalled on the way by the rebels. The C.O. figured it might take too long to break through, so he asked division to send a rescue team by air. That's us. We came in through the roof."

He's lying, the Kalif decided. It felt like a lie, and the man's tunic was green, not blue. Still he wasn't entirely sure. The man wore no unit blazon on his sleeve; he could be part of the Caps penal platoon.

The sergeant looked over his shoulder and spoke to his remaining two men. "Go back to the roof and make sure everything's clear for an escape. Snap it up! We'll be along in a minute."

He watched them start climbing, then turned to the Kalif to find the pistol still pointing at him. He shrugged. "I don't know why that stupid bastard opened fire like that. Jumpy, I guess. Our floater took a lot of fire coming in, and I lost three men." He half turned. "We'd better get up there and get clear, sir. We heard radio traffic that the rebs have a bunch more air support on the way."

"Drop your rifle," the Kalif said quietly.

It clattered to the concrete.

"Who's your division C.O.?" he asked.

The sergeant's eyes sharpened, and abruptly he threw himself sideways to the floor as the Kalif triggered a burst that ripped past him. The man rolled, grabbing at his own sidearm while the Kalif's aim followed him. The racket of their firing overlapped. Skosh Viilenga's face burst red. Twisting, the Kalif crumpled, gutshot.

A guardsman at the nearest window saw him fall into

the corridor, and shouting, jumped to his feet and came running.

Major Tagurt Meksorli wore his arm in a sling cut from a dead man's trousers. The battalion command floater had been disabled and made a hard landing. Broken arm and all, he'd had to run hard to reach cover. The battalion commander had been less lucky; bullets had torn through his chest, killing him.

Meksorli missed the screen array he'd enjoyed in the command floater. He'd set up his command post in one of the massive gate towers, and found its narrow windows a miserable substitute. Just now there wasn't much happening to watch in the quadrangle. Neither side could use it. His immediate challenge was to maintain control of the tough, hull-metal gate.

Or rather, the small ports which flanked it, their gates blown clear when the rebels held them. They very much wanted them back. His radio told him that A Company, 27th Armored Battalion, with its "mobile forts," was within a few blocks of the square, catching hell from gunships and anti-armor squads. The rebels had nothing really heavy on the ground, but even so, the 27th had lost several tanks getting that far. They kept coming, though, wasting the rebel anti-armor equipment as they came. When they reached the square, the rebel situation would be critical. The rebels couldn't hold the square against tanks, and they'd have no hope at all of reconnecting with their troops in the Sreegana.

Actually their situation was critical already. It would simply become more obvious then. Their officers had to be sweating; they could hardly win the battle now, and if they surrendered, they could expect only execution. He wondered what they'd told their peasant soldiers to keep them fighting. Probably that they'd be impaled, too. With peasants, that would work only so long, though. Sooner or later they'd quit anyway.

"Major!" called a man from an outside window.

"There's a tank entering the square. Man! Some of the rebels are running already!"

Meksorli switched to an outside window himself. The rebel troops in the square were indeed breaking. The tank was under heavy fire from surrounding buildings, most of it ineffective. Hovering on its AG pressors, a mobile fort was hard to stop, short of holing its thick armor. Her guns were engaged mainly with the gunships overhead; they were the greater threat.

Then something apparently did hole it, for it slewed and stopped. But at the same time, another and then two more moved into the square after it, and with that, the giving way became a rout.

The major's radio sounded. "Dog One, Dog One, this is Bull Two. If you can open that gate, I'll send Bull Four in. The rest of us will park against the wall and suppress fire from the surrounding buildings."

"Got that, Bull Two," Meksorli answered. "We'll see if it'll open."

A tank in the quadrangle would end things quickly inside, he had no doubt, and backed against the wall, the others would be far less exposed to the gunships. Meksorli closed the gate switch, and almost at once could feel the tower shudder as the rocket-damaged gate tried to open. Something somewhere broke with a sound like a cannon blast, and with a mind-threatening screech, then a rumbling, the gate began to slide into its housing. He was quite sure he'd never get it closed again. The sound stopped, and the tank passed from his view, through the tunnellike opening, into the quadrangle. Back at an inside window, Meksorli watched it park with the wall at its back. He told its commander what parts of the Admin Building he knew for sure were held by rebels, then watched and listened as it began to pump shells into it.

"Caps Command, Caps Command." It was his radio. "This is Captain Iighil Dhozmariloku, commanding 103rd Infantry. Call off your tank."

"This is Caps Command. Are you prepared to end hostilities and surrender?"

"Negative. Negative. My men hold the House of SUMBAA. Call off your tank or I'll order SUMBAA's destruction."

It sounded unlikely. If the rebel held SUMBAA, he'd have used it to bargain with already. Still, there'd been a report of a light floater moving as if to land on its roof . . . He held off on the order until four more rounds had been pumped into the Admin Building, then spoke to the tank commander. "Bull Four, hold your fire for now.

"Rebel Command, I'll make a deal with you. You get your people out of there right away and surrender your regiment, and I'll guarantee with my own life that you, personally, will not go on the stake."

There was a long lag. "Caps Command, you'll have to do better than that. You'll have to guarantee my life and that of my officers."

Meksorli didn't hesitate. "Rebel Command, set your radio to your own frequency. I repeat, set your radio to your own frequency and hear my reply." He paused then and set his own on the rebel frequency. "Rebel Command," he said, his voice hard, "I retract my earlier offer. I retract my earlier offer. If SUMBAA is damaged in any way—repeat, damaged in any way—I will recommend that you and your officers get the slow stake. I repeat, I will recommend that you, your officers, and whoever is directly responsible for the damage, get the slow stake. If SUMBAA is damaged by air action, I will also recommend that all your gunship commanders get the slow stake. Caps Command out."

He ceased transmitting and switched to his own command frequency. "Bull Four, you may fire at will."

Seconds later his radio spoke again. "Caps Command, Caps Command, this is Captain Iighil Dhozmariloku, Acting Commander, 103rd Infantry. I surrender my command."

"Bull Four, hold your fire. Rebel Command, you have ten seconds to tell your troops to surrender. I'll be listening."

Once more he switched to the rebel frequency.

When Rebel Command had complied, he spoke again. "Now, Rebel Command, tell your gunships to leave the area."

"Caps Command, I have no authority over the gunships."

"Rebel Command, tell them anyway."

Another voice cut in. "All 1st Corps units, this is General Songhidalarsa. This is General Songhidalarsa. I order you to cease fire and surrender to the government forces. Cease fire immediately and surrender to the government forces. I will exert whatever influence I may have to obtain leniency for my officers."

"That's it!" Meksorli said. "It's over!" He turned to the battalion E.O. "Barjiith, get a squad to the House of SUMBAA, just in case."

Fifty-eight

Lord Rothka Kozkoraloku sat in his chilled study, staring at the television image on the wall screen, an image consisting simply of the imperial flag.

That's all that had shown there for more than an hour and a half. The sounds of bombs exploding had been followed, after about three minutes, by an announcer reporting excitedly that the Sreegana was under attack by an unidentified unit or units of the Imperial Army. Then the flag had replaced him, the flag and the imperial anthem. Followed by the Klestronu anthem, the Maolaaru . . . until they'd played them all. Then they'd played military marches, and from there had gone to Feromanoothu's "Symphony to the Victor."

He'd expected they'd give bulletins on the fighting. They hadn't. But his apartment was near enough to the Sreegana that, even with windows closed and curtains drawn, he could hear, vaguely, the sounds of gunfire, sometimes desultory, sometimes intense. Once it had seemed to stop, then continued with new fury.

The duration itself was worrisome. It shouldn't have taken so long. If only . . . He'd never contacted the Guard commander. Before he'd had the chance, he'd heard that the man was reconciled with the Kalif and had accepted his reparation. It was hard to believe, but if it was true, to contact him could destroy everything.

And if it wasn't true, surely the commander would surrender his troops with no more than token resistance, contacted or not.

Again the shooting stopped, and he came alert. Any minute now, it seemed to him, the flag would be replaced by a face, the music by an announcement.

It took about three minutes to happen. Then the same announcer was back, this time looking not stunned but grimly pleased.

"Fighting in and around the Sreegana has stopped," the man announced. "We here at Imperial Broadcasting have been monitoring the radio frequencies used by the combatants—the 31st Light Infantry Brigade, the 11th Gunship Support Wing, the Imperial Guard, and units of the Capital Division. Rebel floaters attacked the Sreegana at 7:21 A.M., bombing the Imperial Guard barracks and other targets. At 8:03, infantry from the Capital Division, said to consist of one battalion, were landed inside the Sreegana to bolster the heroic defense of the Imperial Guard."

Rothka's gaze had sharpened at the word "rebel": It told him who'd won, or rather, who'd lost. If any doubt had remained, "heroic defense of the Imperial Guard" had settled it. The coup had failed.

"At 8:58 A.M., advance elements of the 27th Armored Battalion, of the Capital Division, fought their way into the Square of The Prophet, then into the Sreegana itself. Moments later, radio negotiations began between the commanding officers of the opposing forces inside the Sreegana. At 9:05 A.M., the leader of the coup, General Karoom Songhidalarsa, speaking to his forces by radio from an unknown location, ordered them to surrender to the government.

"Shooting ended at once, and rebel troops are reportedly filing from their positions with their hands on their heads.

"While I was reading the above to you, a report came in that the Kalif was wounded while fighting valiantly against the rebels. The kalifa was also wounded. As soon as we have word on the seriousness of their conditions . . ."

Rothka cut off the set in mid sentence. Nothing had worked. Nothing.

Hands on his chair arms, he raised himself heavily to his feet. Songhidalarsa would give himself up, of course. And tell the government whose idea it had been. Within the hour they'd be here for him. Perhaps within minutes.

He left the study, his slippered feet padding down the dimly lit hall. Softly, seeming little more than a whisper, his man-servant's television murmured from his room at the far end. Rothka turned into his own bedroom and closed the door behind him. Here too the drapes were drawn and the room dim. He paused, looking at a cabinet. After a moment he crossed the room to it, unlocked and opened it, and from it took a dagger with a thick, double-edged blade about nine inches long.

Tradition dictated that he kneel, holding the point below his breastbone, then fall forward, driving it through his heart.

He tested its tip against the ball of a thumb, and flinched. A dark drop formed there. Then he stood for a long minute, not moving, staring blankly at the simple, unfeeling steel. Finally he put it back in the cabinet and went into his bathroom.

Fifty-nine

From time to time the Kalif had been vaguely aware of people around him. But it had been pain that provided continuity, the common theme through jumbled, troubled dreams. Now, as he drifted upward into consciousness, it seemed that all that had been some time ago, that he'd slept deeply and untroubled for a long while.

His eyes opened to a room colored by flowers. He lay on an LG bed, feeling very weak. Tubes dangled from overhead, connecting, he assumed, with parts of his body. A female nurse stood looking down at him. Yab was dead, he remembered, and he'd killed the rebel. Someone here would be able to tell him what had happened to Tain.

"Good morning, Your Reverence." The nurse smiled then, dimpled. "We've been expecting you."

"Umm." He was even weaker than he'd realized. "Tain, the kalifa—where is she?"

"She's sleeping, Your Reverence. She's very weak, but she'll recover. She'll be all right, too."

She'd been wounded then. "And Jilsomo?"

"I can call him for you, but the doctors prefer that you rest now. It will take him a little while to get here."

Of course. Jilsomo would be busier than Shatim. Obviously the rebels had lost; somehow he'd known

362

that. And they wouldn't have given him flowers if they'd won. They'd simply want him fit to stand trial, a public trial. And fit for impalement in the square.

His wound was a dull, heavy pain in his gut, and he was deeply tired. "Thank you," he murmured. His eyes were already closed; he slipped into sleep again.

It was the next time he awoke that they called Jilsomo. He felt much stronger mentally, though physically, he knew, he was still very weak. While he waited, a doctor described Tain's condition. She'd been shot in the abdomen, and had gone much longer without medical treatment than he had. She was out of danger now, but it had been a very close thing. She would suffer no permanent impairment. She still had not wakened, but would before very long.

They volunteered nothing about the coup or revolt or whatever it had been, and he didn't question them. Jilsomo would answer his questions in detail and with certainty, he had no doubt.

His left arm was restrained and had two tubes attached to it. They'd left his right arm free, and he reached up to feel his face. His beard was perhaps three days old, but he'd had a day's growth awaiting the razor when the bombs had struck. Call it two days then, or two and a half, that he'd been here.

His arm had felt weak; it had taken an effort to raise it.

Jilsomo, when he came in, seemed to have shrunk somewhat. Surely, though, he hadn't. Even fasting wouldn't have worked that quickly. The left side of his face was purple and green, and his cheek wore a red scar two to three inches long.

"Good evening, Your Reverence."

"You wear a battle scar!" the Kalif said. His chuckle was weak.

"Indeed. And out where people can see and admire it." He paused. "I suppose you'd like to know what happened."

"And what's happening. Yes."

"Well. First things first. Tain has been awake, but she's sleeping again. Your wounds were somewhat alike, but she was shot at the very beginning, and had to wait much longer before being brought here.

"As for the coup attempt—" He told the Kalif all that he knew, which was most of it. Rothka's role, Songhidalarsa's surrender, Rothka's suicide.

"So Rothka suicided. The traditional thrust, I suppose."

"No, Your Reverence. Poison. An extreme overdose of sleeping pills."

"Huh! I'm—surprised at him."

"Your Reverence, I suspect I'd have done it as he did. I doubt I could have made the thrust, or completed it anyway."

I wonder, my friend, if you'd have done either one, the Kalif thought. *Likelier you'd have sat through the public hearings and then the impalement. As I would have.* He grunted, and felt it in his abdomen. "But you're not a self-proclaimed traditionalist," he said. "Well, the result's the same.

"What—what's the status of the College? Who died? Who's injured?"

Jilsomo enumerated.

Six dead. It could have been worse. "And the House? What's their frame of mind?"

"They're adjusting. The Diet should finish its business nicely before closing. Finding that mask of you in the building Colonel Thoglakaveera led us to, seems to have convinced everyone that it wasn't you who released the video showing Dosu upbraiding them. They're tending to blame Rothka now; of course he can't defend himself. And Ilthka's in the forefront, trying to distance himself and the party from his old friend."

"I suppose you've seated a committee of evidence, on the—coup? Uprising?"

"Coup. Yes. I'm chairing it, and Tariil in my absences. We should be done in about a week."

"And public hearings?"

"They'll begin when you're fit to hold them. Unless

you want me to. I believe the public will prefer that you do it."

"I'll do it," the Kalif answered, then added dryly: "I hope they won't be disappointed in me."

"Sir?"

"I'll have no one impaled."

Jilsomo's eyebrows raised. "They needn't be disappointed. If you prepare them for it."

"Exactly. I'll give it some thought. Meanwhile, we'll say nothing about it, you and I." He paused, suddenly very tired. "Are we done now?"

"I believe so, Your Reverence."

"One last thing. There's a palace to rebuild, and a barracks, and much other damage to repair, I'm sure. That will not be done with public funds. It will come out of the estates of the officers involved. The hearings should assign liabilities proportional to responsibilities. A traitor should not expect his loyal countrymen to pay for the destruction he's wrought."

"A point well taken, Your Reverence, and a worthy innovation. The committee of evidence will take somewhat longer then; perhaps an extra week."

The Kalif let his eyes close. "Soon enough. I may be fit to hold hearings by then."

Sixty

The Kalif and kalifa were reclining on a hospital balcony shaded from the morning sun, facing toward the Anan Hills and reading. A soft tone sounded; one of the medical staff was at their door. The Kalif reached down and partly turned his chair, then touched a switch, signalling the person to enter. It was a nurse.

"Yes?" he said.

"Excuse me, Your Reverence, but a military gentleman wishes to see you, a General Bavaralaama."

"Hmh!" He didn't want to see the man, a feeling that took him by surprise. He filed the reaction. "I'll see him in my parlor." He straightened his chair, locked its brakes, and looked at Tain. "I won't be long," he told her, and carefully, leaning on a chair arm, got to his feet.

And what, he wondered, *does the Imperial Chief of Staff want to see me about that can't wait?*

Carefully he walked to his parlor, and was waiting, standing, when the general entered. "Your Reverence!" the general said. "I'm glad you could see me. It's good to find you on your feet."

"Thank you, Elvar." The Kalif waved him to a chair and lowered himself on another. "What brings you out here? I thought the committee of evidence would be meeting."

366

"We're taking the day off; we'll get together again after supper. Things have piled up—other duties that need to be taken care of—things you can't delegate, you know. And we're done calling in witnesses and depositions. I expect we'll have our report completed within the next three days."

He gestured at the guardsman. "Your Reverence, if we could have complete privacy . . ."

The Kalif's face hardened. "General, meet Honor Sergeant Ranhiit Candrakaar, the guardsman who rescued the kalifa. Guardsmen usually are present when I discuss affairs of government."

The general's mahogany face darkened. "I understand, Your Reverence. And I compliment Honor Sergeant—Candrakaar?—on his bravery and ability. But this matter . . ."

The Kalif turned to the guardsman. "Sergeant, I'll be alone with the general. Come back in when he leaves."

The guardsman saluted crisply, turned and left, the general and the Kalif watching him out the door. When it had closed behind him, the general turned to the Kalif again, his face earnest.

"Before long, Your Reverence, you'll be considering your decisions with regard to persons found guilty of treason or lesser crimes."

And you want to give me a viewpoint that will be different than the committee's. What could it be that you don't want the sergeant to hear?

"One of the things that is crystal clear," the general went on, "is that Iron Jaw got his officers to participate in the coup by pitching it to them as necessary to the invasion. The invasion you propose. His stated position was that the House would never vote you the funds, and that the invasion could only happen under a military dictator: himself. He's told us this quite openly, and his officers have given us the same story."

The Kalif nodded. "So Jilsomo told me. But their motives do not excuse their acts. Acts which killed many people, nearly killed the kalifa and myself, and caused much destruction. Including the palace, a building dedicated to the memory of The Prophet."

The Kalif's voice had continued mild, but there was something implacable in it. "Nonetheless," he continued, "even before Jilsomo told me what you just did, there was never a question of impalements. Nor will there be executions of any sort. Those who bear the title of Successor to The Prophet should do their utmost to behave accordingly, and I will not degrade the throne by barbarities."

Again the general nodded, his expression patient. "But reparation demands for rebuilding the Sreegana could ruin them, leave them destitute."

"Indigent perhaps, but they won't go hungry. Prisons provide a balanced diet. If they don't, we'll need to correct that. What else do you have for me?"

Obviously the matter of reparations was not subject to dispute. The general took it with thin lips, but somehow it seemed to the Kalif that his response was not genuine, that the man was not much disappointed if at all. As if the issue was not actually important to him. It felt—it felt as if the general had brought it up to see what he'd say, to feel him out, then let him have his way with it.

"One more thing, Your Reverence. Your invasion plans have the support of virtually the entire officer corps, in the fleet as well as the army. If it so happens that the House of Nobles continues recalcitrant . . ."

Bavaralaama stopped short there, as if the unspoken remainder was self-evident, but the Kalif wouldn't let him off so easily. "Yes?" he said.

The general met his eyes, in a manner of speaking, but kept a screen between them. "If Your Reverence is so inclined, you could simply ignore the House. Override it. With no risk. In fact I urge it on you, if they refuse your proposal, or give you less than you consider desirable. Or try to impose conditions."

The Kalif looked at him with raised eyebrows. "I suppose I could, Elvar. But that would make me a dictator, and the law worthless. I might even get away with it—it seems likely I would—but the empire would be the worse for it. It would divide the people severely, and there could hardly be a reconciliation afterward. We'd all pay in blood, sooner or later. You, I, everyone."

He looked the general over. "I appreciate your telling me, though," the Kalif went on, "and the support you offered." He pulled himself to his feet then, indicating that the audience was over. "When a ruler plans a military venture, he likes to know that his generals agree with him."

They finished their meeting with brief formal courtesies, then the Kalif watched the general leave. The man's message was food for thought, and some of it hard chewing. Not just the verbal message, though that made it clearer. Bavaralaama had arrived without an appointment, or even advance notice. Which seemed to say that the Imperial General Staff considered themselves in charge—that the Kalif ruled now at their pleasure. No doubt they'd put up with a lot, but there were limits. They would have their invasion, and any scruples he might have, regarding the House and the law, would not be allowed to intervene.

He wondered what would happen if he told the general some of the thoughts he'd been having since he'd witnessed the destruction of the Sreegana. He didn't intend to find out.

Lord Agròs called for an appointment before coming out. In fact, he called within an hour after the general left. His wish to speak privately surprised the Kalif more than the general's visit had.

Again the Kalif was on his feet when his guest walked in. At the Kalif's order, Sergeant Candrakaar had accompanied him only to the door, then stayed outside. The kalifa, however, was there with him, though not standing; her presence threw Agros for a moment. "Your Reverence," he said. "Lady Tain. It's good to see you looking so strong."

It was the Kalif who answered. "Indeed, friend

Agros. Looks are deceiving. But we're better day by day." The two men sat down, and the Kalif looked quizzically at the Leader of the House. "I'm surprised to see you still here. With the Diet adjourned and the delegates dispersing over the empire, I'd have thought you'd be at home."

"And so I would be, Your Reverence. But my interests are diverse, and I still have business here in the capital before I leave. Some of it with you."

"Oh?"

"Your Reverence, there is something I think you should know. You're aware, of course, that Alb Jilsomo presented a first cost estimate for restoring the palace and the other government buildings damaged. And proposed an appropriation to finance it, compensation to be taken from the officers involved, and their families as appropriate."

"Including Rothka's estate. Yes. And the final act of the Diet was to approve it unanimously. Jilsomo told me."

"Correct." He looked briefly at the kalifa before he continued. "I also wish to express my profound sympathy for the pain and loss which you and the kalifa have suffered."

"Thank you, friend Agros." The Kalif thought to add that there were those who'd lost more, but he kept the thought to himself. Losing the fetus had been hard, especially on Tain, and Agros had seemed honest in his sentiment.

There was an awkward moment then, as if Agros had more to say, something which didn't come easily. "One other thing, Your Reverence. The House has developed a somewhat different, a considerably more favorable attitude toward your invasion plans. A change contributed to by the industrial faction, the lesser nobility, and the labor unrest that has grown even more troublesome since the attack on the Sreegana. I believe you'll find the House much more amenable to productive negotiation when the Diet reconvenes."

The Kalif's eyebrows rose. "Indeed? That's something Jilsomo had mentioned as a possibility, but coming from you, it seems like something more."

"I believe Your Reverence can count on it."

"Umm. Tell me. Confidentially. Did the—military have any influence on this change of attitude?"

The nobleman waited a long and pregnant moment, then answered. "A most puissant influence, Your Reverence."

"I wouldn't wonder. Well, I dare say I brought this on us myself." He sighed audibly, then surprisingly grinned. "Friend Agros, I recommend that you feel at ease with the situation. I have no doubt it will work out well for the empire and the estates. All of the estates."

When Agros had gone, the Kalif turned to the kalifa. She looked troubled. He wasn't surprised, considering what she'd just heard.

"So there *will* be an invasion," she said thoughtfully, then looked up at him. "Coso, what does *puissant* mean?"

He smiled wryly. "Agros was telling me that the military are a major cause of their changed attitude. Perhaps *the* major cause. The House is afraid of the army."

He paused, pursed his lips, then smiled again, his eyes intent on her. "My dear, we have things to talk about, you and I. About a suggestion you once made, a question you asked. I think there's a way."

Sixty-one

Their return from the hospital was the occasion for a parade second only to the one on Prophet's Day. But quite different; this one was largely military. The Imperial Guard, now a short battalion in numbers, led off in the place of honor, followed by the survivors of the 1st Battalion of the 1st Infantry Regiment, and the 27th Armored Battalion—the units that had defeated the coup attempt. Other units of the Capital Division followed, interspersed with fraternal groups, sports groups, and military units flown in for the event. Their bands played, instruments flashing in the morning sun. Flights of gunships passed over, one after another, preceded by their shadows.

The crowds weren't put off a bit by the armed might. They cheered each unit, each band, each massive mobile fort. And most loudly, they cheered as their Kalif and kalifa rode by in an open limousine.

The Kalif was bemused by it. He couldn't for the life of him see why they cheered him so. He was quite sure, though, that it wasn't the admiral they cheered. Admiral Siilakamasu, the Deputy Chief of Staff, rode with the royal couple, in the seat behind the Kalif.

Leaning forward, the admiral tapped the Kalif's shoulder, a presumptuous thing to do. But he did it gracefully. "Your Reverence," he said grinning, "the people like you."

The Kalif glanced back over his shoulder. "So it seems, Admiral. So it seems."

"I'd say the time is ripe for a speech to the empire. Perhaps this evening? Something brief that won't require much preparation. About the invasion, and what it can mean to the empire and the people."

Turning, the Kalif met his eyes and held them, but not in challenge. "I plan to talk to the cameras tomorrow, when I decorate the heroes. I'll talk about loyalty and heroism. And afterward about other things. Something about a revival of shipbuilding, I think, and strengthening the armed forces."

Jilsomo was sitting beside the admiral, listening, watching the interplay between the two. He was aware that the Kalif didn't like the invasion mentioned in front of the kalifa, and when the admiral brought it up, the exarch's eyes moved to her. She seemed undisturbed by the subject today, as if she'd grown resigned to the idea.

The royal couple moved into a building bought by the government only two blocks from the square, where they occupied a large and luxurious apartment; the rest of the building was given over to offices and other staff facilities for the Prelacy. After a late and private lunch, the Kalif had himself delivered to the Sreegana, where he walked slowly across the quadrangle, accompanied by two guardsmen. The gutted remains of the palace had already been knocked down, and the site leveled. Engineers were there with instruments on tripods, and assistants driving stakes.

He found the sight depressing, though less so, he thought, than the gutted wreckage would have been. But he hadn't come there to visit ghosts or the reconstruction work. He'd come to ask questions.

Of SUMBAA. When he got to SUMBAA's house, he checked in with Dr. Gopalasentu, and left bodyguards and doctor in the corridor outside SUMBAA's chamber.

The blood had been scrubbed from the floor—his blood and Yab's and the rebel sergeant's.

It seemed to him that SUMBAA had been waiting for him. "Good afternoon, Your Reverence," it said when he'd made his presence known. He suspected that SUMBAA had known already.

"Good afternoon, SUMBAA," he answered. "I saw you kill three rebel soldiers. I didn't know you could do that."

"It is my responsibility to serve the welfare of humankind. As you know. Thus I long ago equipped myself for protection. The three rebel soldiers had shot your guard. Presumably they would have shot you when they saw you. I prevented that."

The answer was about what the Kalif had expected. "Do you consider, then, that my survival is significant to the welfare of humankind?"

"That is my projection. It is not as firm a projection as many, but it is my best projection, given the data available."

"Hmm." He examined SUMBAA's statement and came up with nothing he could make much of. "The last time we talked," he said, "you provided me with plans and evaluations for an invasion of the Confederation. Since then a lot has happened that may influence those plans, and I have some new considerations, new requirements, that are certain to. When I've described these new features to you, I want you to give me a new set of plans. And the same sort of evaluations that you gave me before."

"Very well, Your Reverence. When you are ready, we can begin."

When they were done, he put the stack of printouts in his briefcase. He'd look at it when he got home. This time, leaving a conference with SUMBAA, he didn't feel uncomfortable. Not a bit.

Sixty-two

As Primate of Varatos, Elder Dosu was responsible for the pastorates of the entire planet. He and his staff occupied a large building only ten minutes' walk from the Hall of the Estates and the Kalif's temporary lodgings—two minutes by hovercar. With his duties in the Diet, Dosu had long ago learned to delegate much of his planet-wide inspection load, and with increasing age, he'd come to travel relatively little, even when the Diet was not in session. So he was at hand and available when he got the Kalif's request for a meeting.

The Kalif's temporary residence also had a roof garden, and the weather being pleasant, they met there. As courtesy directed, for a one-on-one meeting of this sort, the Kalif didn't at once bring up the subject he wished to talk about. Instead he said casually, "I'm told the Pastorate has begun its campaign to gain voting power."

"Indeed it has, Your Reverence. And been scathing those who'd use arms to overthrow the kalifate. But I must say that few pastors have seen fit to speak for your invasion proposal, despite your championing of our estate. And I cannot in good conscience urge them to, let alone order it. On the other hand, few have attacked it; your support has bought you that much."

"Friend Dosu, I was not trying to buy their support,

375

however it may have looked. Though obviously I'd welcome it. If I accomplish nothing more as Kalif than seeing the Pastorate a voting estate, I'll consider my reign more than a success. It will be a highlight in the history of the kalifate.

"Don't mistake me. It's not simply the good of the Pastorate I'm concerned with. I consider this to be one step, a major step, toward justice for all of Kargh's children. If I thought the Pastorate would use its votes only for its own benefit, I wouldn't have taken the trouble.

"On various occasions the Assembly of Elders has served as a voice for the gentry and peasants. And helped gain, for the gentry, certain opportunities. I assume you'll use your votes in the same cause. Eventually to gain the vote for the fourth and fifth estates as well."

The Elder nodded his skullcap of gray curls. "We dream partly the same dreams, Your Reverence."

"Which brings me to my other dream, friend Dosu. And my reason for calling you here. Are your seminaries full?"

The question took the Elder by surprise. "As full as we want them," he said. "In times like these, with so many gentry and lesser nobles hard pressed to feed and house themselves, the Pastorate has more applicants than posts to fill."

"And those you turn away— Are many of them inspired by a desire to serve the people? Or are they interested mainly in a place at the table, and a roof?"

"There are both kinds; I can only guess in what proportions. Roughly even, I suppose. We do our best to avoid the latter."

"I presume they're literate? And decently informed on *The Book of The Prophet*? And on history and government?"

Dosu frowned, wondering what the Kalif was getting at. "Literate, yes," he said. "As for informed—they're as informed as most of their estates. Well enough that those we take can be trained."

"So they're trainable. If there were posts for more of them—many more—would you have room and staff to train them? Say ten thousand of them?"

"Ten thousand? On Varatos?"

"Say on Varatos. Yes. But forgive me, friend Dosu. I shouldn't keep you in mystery. If the invasion is to spread the word of The Prophet as well as the rule of the empire, we need an army of pastors as well as one of soldiers. You see."

Dosu indeed saw, and wondered that he hadn't seen before. Probably, he decided, he hadn't taken seriously the Kalif's argument that spreading the worship of Kargh would be a major function of the invasion.

And while he'd prefer there be no invasion, if there was one—and it seemed there would be—then an army of pastors was an urgent need.

"Indeed I do see, Your Reverence."

They spent two hours together, the Kalif and the Elder, and when Dosu returned to his office, it was with a basic working plan sketched out, a plan to produce ten thousand pastors on Varatos, and another ten thousand total on the other worlds. Within eighteen months.

They'd even sketched out a curriculum. For the pastors from each world, it included developing fluency in the peasant jabber of that world, dialects only partly intelligible to many in the upper classes. Because, as the Kalif pointed out, the peasant troops could prove the key in relations with the people of the Confederacy. If their behavior was barbarous, they'd make enemies of the Confederation's people. Thus the pastors would have a function beyond propagation of the faith; they would educate the peasant troops and monitor and amend their behavior.

A pastoral army could be recruited and trained; the Elder had no doubt of it. Could and would be. And payment for it was not dependent on the Diet; it would come from ecclesiastical assessments collected by the Prelacy.

When he got back to his desk, Dosu began at once to draft a directive to the offices involved.

The Kalif felt a bit guilty. He had not been entirely honest with Elder Dosu. Not that he wanted to mislead or trick him. In fact, it seemed to him that Dosu would agree with his real intention at least as much as with the one he'd given. But secrecy was vital. He wouldn't even tell Jilsomo till the day of departure, or close to it. For now it was enough that SUMBAA knew, and Tain.

Sixty-three

On the second day of the Diet of 4725, the Kalif formally requested an invasion appropriation. It was not seriously resisted. The House felt pressure by the lesser nobility and also by the gentry. Further, no Kalif in modern times had been so popular with the people, and his provision for sending a pastoral army to convert the heathen made it easier—less embarrassing—for the noble delegates to give in. But the decisive factor was the officers' corps of the armed forces.

The General Staff had more misgivings about the Kalif's invasion budget than the Diet did. It seemed to them that a somewhat larger army and battle fleet could and should be built and sent, even at the cost of an additional year. Furthermore, in light of the combat experience on Terfreya, the emphasis on infantry seemed ill-advised to them; they wanted much more armor. They'd laid out their objections in a formal brief, with a proposed alternative, but the Kalif had made only small adjustments.

They backed away from a confrontation, though. The differences were a matter of degree, and the Kalif had already retired General Bavaralaama with minimal ceremony, for only mildly derogatory remarks made to staff officers at a meeting. This stiff action demonstrated the Kalif's growing power and confidence, fixing it in the command mind. Then he'd replaced Bavaralaama on the General Staff with Chesty Vrislakavaro, now a lieutenant general, a man very popular with the officer corps.

Vrislakavaro had previously replaced Songhidalarsa in command of 1st Corps. The formidable Iron Jaw resided in a high-security military prison in the Belt. His personal fortune, and a substantial part of his family's, had been eaten up by reconstruction, reparations to the families of casualties, and medical and pension funds for the disabled, including peasants.

The address in which the Kalif presented his formal appropriation request mentioned immigrant fleets, fleets for which he did not request an appropriation. These were to be built by the various planetary governments after the invasion fleet left. Some delegates to the House pointed out that to begin building immigrant fleets assumed that the invasion succeeded—that there were conquered worlds to migrate to. But suppose the invasion failed, that no planets were conquered? The money would have been wasted.

Suppose the invasion failed! Simply bringing up the possibility publicly caused a wave of misgivings about the entire invasion project, a wave that spread across the empire. But it was brief. The decisive argument was: "Better fight them there, with an advantage in arms, than here at a time of their choosing."

The after-effect was a lessening of euphoric optimism and an increase in determination.

Within months, on every world including Maolaari, there were camps busy training soldiers, marines, airmen, ships' crews. And schools training pastors—twice the 20,000 originally intended. Factories, and especially shipyards, were busy around the clock; work went on at a pace never seen before in the empire. Preparations took on a virtually unstoppable momentum. As often happens, abundant activity with results that could be seen—floater parks filling with new aircraft, starships taking shape in the yards, recruits becoming skilled and toughened, their units coordinated—gave rise to a new optimism, and a social order beyond any that had come before.

Favorable economic effects were not as great as had been hoped for, and there was considerable currency inflation. But still, the lot of the people was materially better. And promised to continue being better after the armada left; construction of the immigrant fleets would see to that. These would begin with ships built to transport would-be brides, an immigration to begin as soon as word came that the army had procured a world or worlds to settle on.

The only real disorders were a flurry of wildcat strikes by gentry work supervisors and skilled gentry workmen, who wanted gentry delegates seated in the Diet. These work stoppages threatened to seriously hamper the invasion preparations, but they faded when the Kalif promised that the question would be discussed in public forums, something that had never happened before.

The empire would never be the same.

The Kalif asked Lord Roonoa not to bring up the legalization of loohio; he'd propose it himself, he said. And in mid-session he did. Conservative elements of the House, seeing an opportunity to assert themselves safely, resisted. Finally, with only two days left before the required vote, the Kalif amended the proposal: Any world would be free to reject the import of loohio on a vote by its own Diet. Elder Dosu objected strongly, arguing that it wasn't a matter of commerce or economics or political policy, but of religion—a command of The Prophet. Lord Roonoa and others, including delegates of several planets with critical population problems, answered with hard statistics. Alb Jilsomo pointed out that the Pastorate could always exhort its parishioners not to eat the fish.

The vote was twenty-four to twenty-one in favor of the proposal as amended, to go into effect in 4727. This date gave the Diets of the individual sultanates an opportunity to reject for their worlds before exportation began.

The restaffed College of Exarchs had moved back into the Sreegana by the end of 4725. The Kalif and kalifa were in the rebuilt palace three months later.

Ten days before the session closed, the Kalif proclaimed the Pastorate a voting estate, with seven votes in the Diet. The House vote to block it was fifteen to twelve, one vote short of the required sixty percent. They would have another chance to block it at the beginning of the Diet of 4726.

The Diet of 4726 specifically agreed to permit the Assembly of Elders a minimum of seven votes in the Diet, *if* the Kalif would agree to a convention to further amend the Charter of Establishment. The favorable vote upset severely the Land Rights delegates and some others. It resulted from behind-the-scenes bargaining with noble delegates from the outer worlds, who wanted an additional delegate to the House for each sultanate.

The Kalif agreed, on condition that he chair the agenda committee—and that the agenda must consider a proportionate increase in the College of Exarchs, and also an Assembly of Gentry with at least a voice in matters. And further, that the convention take place immediately following the Diet of 4726, while the delegates were still on Varatos.

The Kalif's actual reason for the timing, he kept to himself.

Sixty-four

Year of The Prophet 4727

In Chithkar—Sevenmonth—of 4727, the fleet began to assemble in the Ranj System, close outside the orbit of Varatos. By the time the Diet convened, the assessed warships from the various planets all were there. Their transports were just beginning to arrive, their troops in stasis. A number of the imperial warships were there also, though others still were at bases on the surface. The Vartosu transports would lift last, with the flagship.

It was already the greatest concentration of military might in that sector of the galaxy since its devastation so many lost millennia before. And somehow, Chodrisei Biilathkamoro was not enthused with it. He felt a sort of chronic dis-ease, as if something was wrong, something he only vaguely sensed and couldn't identify. Sometimes he'd wondered if it was the spirit of Kargh, telling him he shouldn't be doing this.

I'm only the Successor *to The Prophet,* he told himself. *I'm not enlightened by Kargh, not directly; I have to work things out for myself as best I can, and hope they come out more right than wrong.* And this enterprise had gone too far to stop. If in fact it had been stoppable since the General Staff had set its heart on it.

But if he was sometimes moody, Tain had become consistently quite sunny. The Kalif knew part of the reason—three parts, actually. He was one of them. There was also the increased control she'd shown of her life and circumstances. He was repeatedly aware, now, of how often his actions, public as well as personal, were influenced by her comments, her questions, her viewpoint.

And of course there was their son, born sixteen months after she'd lost what would have been her first. She took more pleasure in him than her husband did. Coso clearly loved the child, but was increasingly preoccupied as the time of departure approached.

But still the resilience of her sunniness sometimes seemed strange to him. What he didn't know—she'd never mentioned them—was that the dreams and visions of her early months with him had left a residuum of serenity. Those dreams had long since ceased, except for occasional recurrences early in her second pregnancy. But still, when some event upset her, usually something she'd heard or read about, she rebounded more quickly for having had them.

SUMBAA, of course, was invariably placid, imperturbable. The artificial intelligence had no more certainty than the Kalif of what the outcome of the expedition would be. At most it could assign probabilities that, strictly speaking, were not statistically valid because the universe predicted was so nonrandom, the factors so interconnected. But in SUMBAA's mind, uncertainty did not give rise to worry, only to greater interest. It had been programmed at the start for curiosity, as a heuristic element in the original, philosophic sense of the word. Its creators hadn't programmed it to worry, and it had never seen fit to so program itself.

When the Kalif entered the conference chamber to meet with the College, this particular morning, there was a difference about him that most of them noticed. After calling the meeting to order, he looked them over. "Today," he said, "I'm announcing my resignation."

The exarchs gaped. There were even gasps.

"When the fleet leaves a week from today, I will leave with it, and the kalifa and our son will accompany me. My resignation will take effect on its departure from this system into hyperspace. I will command the invasion personally, as its Grand Admiral and the personal envoy of the throne.

"Our business here this morning is to select a successor. My own choice would be Alb Jilsomo, but the rules state that the College selects, so I can only recommend.

"Jilsomo's early experience as a negotiator, and later as my aide and deputy, and his weeks as acting Kalif when I was hospitalized, all have prepared and proven him. But he is not the only one of you who is qualified for the throne." He looked them over. "The floor is now open for nominations," he finished, and sat down.

Thoga nominated Jilsomo, and others Tariil and Thoga. None of the newer exarchs were nominated. Each nominee was invited to speak, and Tariil declined to be considered. Thoga elaborated Jilsomo's qualities, but did not withdraw his own name. Then the two were sent out while the College discussed them.

In less than twenty minutes they were called back in. Ballots were marked and collected, and Jilsomo was chosen as the new Successor to The Prophet.

After lunch, they walked across the square to the Hall of the Estates, where the Kalif announced his coming resignation and his successor. The House was of two minds over Jilsomo as the new Kalif. The only voiced complaint was his gentry birth, though someone pointed out that he had a noble great-grandmother on his mother's side. Most of them knew him as rational, agreeable, and highly intelligent, a broadly effective man who might well be easier to work with than Kalif Coso.

And as old Dosu pointed out, The Prophet had been gentry. Why not His Successor?

At any rate, the succession was the responsibility of the College. Whoever they selected would be Kalif, like it or not. Actually the Diet had less attention on who would succeed than on the Kalif's abdication. It was hard to believe, for he was unquestionably the strongest and most popular Kalif in centuries.

And inevitably, there were those who distrusted his intentions in leaving with the armada, though they didn't bring it up till afterward, out of session. Would he try to carve an independent empire for himself, out there?

The answer given, of course, was why should he? If he wanted an empire, he was emperor here, and by extension there as well.

Sixty-five

It was a lovely, sunny morning in the Kalif's garden. Coso's garden now, but to be Jilsomo's by noon. Except for some bags, Coso's belongings, and the kalifa's, had already gone up to the flagship.

The Kalif had asked his deputy, the Kalif-to-be, to sit with him in an arbor and enjoy a cold drink. Jilsomo, of course, knew that Coso Biilathkamoro rarely sat down simply to enjoy a drink, except perhaps with his wife. So he expected some final words: suggestions, reminders, perhaps a warning or two.

As deputy and aide, Jilsomo was quite familiar with the day-to-day operations of the throne, and the various government programs and projects that the Kalif had kept tabs on. On top of that, he'd had specific briefings by the Kalif and various ministers. But it was reasonable that some additional items had occurred to the Kalif.

There was a small table in the arbor. They put their clinking glasses on it and sat down. "What do you think of the language and literacy training the invasion troops have been given?" the Kalif asked.

The question surprised Jilsomo; the Kalif knew well what he thought of it. "I like it," he answered. "Very much. I intend to see it continued for the troops remaining in the empire. And teaching it has given the trainee pastors experience in dealing with the peasant mind."

By and large, of course, army command had thought it a waste of time—time that might better have been spent in additional military training and productive labor. Some officers from the Great Families even considered it subversive. Chesty Vrislakavaro had had to twist some arms and threaten some careers to get full cooperation.

Jilsomo wished the general was staying as Chief of Staff, instead of faring out as commander of the armada's ground forces.

"What do you think of the books we gave them to practice their reading in?" the Kalif asked.

"I'm not familiar with them. As I recall, you had them prepared under the direction of that young pastor, Father Sukhanthu."

The Kalif nodded. "They consist of *The Book*, in a translation slightly simplified from the usual; and simple descriptions of history and government, emphasizing causes and effects. Not the sort of thing the Land Rights Party would want peasants studying. Might give them ideas."

Except for *The Book*, the books were slim, and even *The Book* was not very long. Most of the peasants had begun illiterate, and had only a limited knowledge of Imperial. On the other hand, even on Maolaari, peasant jabber was little more than a crude dialect of Imperial; learning Imperial was not difficult for them. Also, Imperial orthography was quite closely phonetic: If you could speak it, learning to read and write involved little more than learning the alphabet. And many of the peasant recruits had shown an unexpected interest in learning.

Jilsomo could see there the roots of reform. Or of trouble. "Who could I talk to about problems and results?" he asked.

"Father Sukhanthu will accompany the fleet, but Elder Dosu and others followed the work quite closely."

The Kalif fell silent then, as if through with that subject. But clearly he wasn't finished talking, so Jilsomo waited.

"There's something I need to tell you," he began after a minute. "Something I've kept from you. About the invasion expedition. It isn't quite what I've represented it to be."

The statement was a surprise and it wasn't. What else could it be, that armada of warships and transports? Yet this might explain the Kalif's uncharacteristic moods of reticence, his periods of uncharacteristic preoccupation.

"I intend that there be no conquest," he went on, "no fighting, no destruction and killing. I go prepared for all of that, but I intend to avoid it."

The Kalif's black eyes held Jilsomo's. "After the destruction of the palace, I looked differently at military attacks. Picture the attack on the Sreegana and then expand it over a city, a planet."

Jilsomo had. He'd always felt unhappy with the idea. But there was the threat, the prospect of the Confederacy invading the empire. That had seemed quite real to him. So he'd accepted.

"We will go," the Kalif continued. "And the fleet will lie in hyperspace adjacent to their central system, while I go in with a single ship and parley, making no threat. A scout will enter real space with me, and lie outsystem, ready to generate hyperspace and inform the fleet if anything happens to me.

"They are seventy worlds—member worlds and client worlds. Over a volume of space much larger than the empire; no doubt as large a volume as they can administer.

"What lies beyond it? Surely they've explored. Are there inhabitable worlds unpeopled?

"It seems to me there must be. If there are, we will go there and lay claim to them. Set garrisons on them.

"If there are none, we'll dicker for rights to some of their client worlds. In either case, when we've established ourselves on such worlds, we'll send off message pods to you.

"Perhaps there are no unpeopled worlds in the space

around them, and perhaps they will not bargain. Perhaps they'll prove hostile, or treacherous. Perhaps we'll fight them after all. But in Kargh's name, I'll make every reasonable effort not to."

He compressed his lips. "In the hospital, those first days, I thought of not sending a fleet, an army. I thought of sending a ship of missionaries instead, to give them the gift of The Prophet. But I could not dismiss the threat they pose. And the generals, the admirals, the colonels, would not have permitted it. Many of the nobles wouldn't have. The House would have, and most of the Greater Nobles with all their wealth. But there are the lesser nobles, and all who dream of their own landholdings. Which includes many or most of the officer corps."

The Kalif spread his hands. "Earlier, under the pressure of circumstance, I promoted recklessly, shortsightedly, and lost important options. Now I have to do what I can to make it come out—in a way The Prophet would approve."

He shrugged. "On our new worlds, the peasants will be our citizens, the pastors their teachers. Somehow I must prevent a stratification into masters and serfs there, I'm not sure how. The pastors will have to be my allies in this, if I'm to have any."

He chuckled wryly. "I'll have three years to work it out. The kalifa and little Rami and I, and my guard company of course, will not travel in stasis.

"I've told no one what I plan, except the kalifa and now you. I mistrust how the military might take it, even after we've left. But it seemed necessary, desirable at least, that you know. Tomorrow, when you are Kalif, you can do with the information as you will. Perhaps you'll decide to tell Elder Dosu; I probably would if our roles were reversed, yours and mine."

They'd neglected their drinks. Now they turned a part of their attention to them, saying almost nothing. The Kalif absorbed the garden around him. Its reestablished flowerbeds, shrubs and hedges, trees and groves, had burgeoned in the tropical climate, were becoming well-grown. He'd miss it. So would the kalifa; she'd told him so. The Sreegana had become home to her.

When they arrived in the Confederation, would she begin to remember an earlier home?

A guardsman arrived, saluted. "Your Reverence," he said, "the shuttle is ready."

The Kalif looked up at the man, and it seemed to Jilsomo that his glance was bleak. "Well then." He got to his feet with unaccustomed heaviness. Turning to the exarch, he put out his hand. "You've been my good friend, Jilsomo. I'll miss you." He looked around then as if suddenly remembering a thousand things unsaid, a hundred things undone. A million things he'd like to see one more time.

"You'll remember to give the envelopes to Thoga and Tariil? And Dosu?"

"Depend on it, Your Reverence."

"Well then . . ." Again he extended his hard, drill-callused hand to Jilsomo, and again they shook. When their hands disengaged, the Kalif's shoulders straightened. "All right, Corporal, let's go."

Jilsomo followed along. The Kalif's heaviness had dropped from him; his straight back, his stride, his whole demeanor now bespoke strength and certainty. As if any falling away into regret or self-doubt could never be more than brief, could be dismissed at will. The kalifa stood waiting beside the ramp, still lovely, always lovely except on that one terrible day. She held little Rami, who could be remarkably patient and still for a child so young and normally so active.

The boy reached out little arms toward his father, who took him laughing, and the three walked up the ramp together into the shuttle.

Colonel Krinalovasa, the Guard commander, stood beside Jilsomo. Together they watched the ramp telescope disappear, the hullmetal door slide shut, the craft lift easily, accelerate and move rapidly out of sight.

"I'm going to miss him, Your Reverence," the colonel said.

Your Reverence. It was a day premature, of course.

He was only acting Kalif, wouldn't be crowned till tomorrow evening. Then he *would* be "Your Reverence." Jilsomo felt of the title. It felt . . . Felt as if it would fit. He'd get used to it, and it would fit.

"I'll miss him, too, Colonel," he said. "He was, is my friend."

LARRY NIVEN'S KNOWN SPACE IS AFLAME WITH WAR!

Once upon a time, in the very earliest days of interplanetary exploration, an unarmed human vessel was set upon by a warship from the planet Kzin—home of the fiercest warriors in Known Space. This was a fatal mistake for the Kzinti of course; they learned the hard way that the reason humanity had decided to study war no more was that humans were so very, very good at it.

And thus began The Man-Kzin Wars. Now, several centuries later, the Kzinti are about to get yet another lesson in why it pays to be polite to those hairless monkeys from planet Earth.

The Man-Kzin Wars: Featuring the Niven story that started it all, and new Known Space stories by Poul Anderson and Dean Ing.

Man-Kzin Wars II: Jerry Pournelle and S.M. Stirling weigh in with a tale of Kzinti homelife; and another adventure from Dean Ing.

Man-Kzin Wars III: Larry Niven's first new Known Space story in a decade as well as new novellas from Poul Anderson and Pournelle & Stirling.

All featuring fantastic series covers by Stephen Hickman.